Zara Stoneley is the *USA Today* bestselling author of *The Wedding Date*.

She lives in a Cheshire village with her family, a lively cockapoo called Harry, and a very bossy (and slightly evil) cat called Saffron.

Zara's bestselling novels include *No One Cancels Christmas*, *The Wedding Date*, *The Holiday Swap*, *Summer with the Country Village Vet*, *Blackberry Picking at Jasmine Cottage* and the popular Tippermere series – *Stable Mates*, *Country Affairs* and *Country Rivals*.

 @ZaraStoneley
@ZaraStoneley
@zarastoneley
zarastoneley.com

Also by Zara Stoneley

Standalone Novels
Summer of Surrender
The Holiday Swap
The Wedding Date
No One Cancels Christmas
Bridesmaids
Four Christmases and a Secret

The Little Village on the Green Series
Summer with the Country Village Vet
Blackberry Picking at Jasmine Cottage

The Tippermere Series
Stable Mates
Country Affairs
Country Rivals
A Very Country Christmas

The First Date

Zara Stoneley

OneMoreChapter

One More Chapter
a division of HarperCollins*Publishers*
The News Building
1 London Bridge Street
London SE1 9GF

www.harpercollins.co.uk

This paperback edition 2020

First published in Great Britain in ebook format by
HarperCollins*Publishers* 2020

A catalogue record for this book
is available from the British Library

Ebook ISBN: 9780008363178
Paperback ISBN: 9780008363185

Set in Birka by Palimpsest Book Production Ltd, Falkirk
Stirlingshire

Printed and bound in Great Britain by
CPI Group (UK) Ltd, Croydon CR0 4YY

For my fabulous sisters – who are, simply, the best. With love.

Chapter 1

There are so many things I'd imagined might go wrong with this date (and when I say many, I do mean many) but this was not top of the list.

He has NOT TURNED UP!

This was not even *on* the list.

I thought I'd actually been quite comprehensive:

1. Don't recognise the guy because his profile picture is at least twenty years old – dating back to the time when he had hair.

2. Has a totally squeaky voice (think David Beckham on helium – sorry, David, I do totally love you, even my mum does) that is so off-putting it makes me feel judgy even though I really don't mean to be.

3. Is wearing so much aftershave it makes me gag. I hate too much aftershave; Dad used to spray it on liberally when I was a child and I'd get an eyeful if I was within 100 metres.

4. Hasn't got socks on. Sorry, the trousers, shoes and no socks thing speaks to me in all the wrong ways. And feet, you'd end up seeing bare feet at inopportune moments. Not everybody has nice feet.

5. Goes for a kiss on the cheek as I go for a handshake and it turns into a weird dance and ruins the whole thing.

6. I am unable to speak. At all. This has happened before.

7. He will hate me on sight and head off to the loo within two seconds of meeting me and never be seen again.

My list is actually longer than this, these are just the highlights.

So he's knocked point 7 right out of the ballpark.

What is wrong with me? Why is it so flaming difficult for me to find a guy?

I mean, everything is in roughly the right places and in reasonable working order. I do not turn into a blood-sucking vampire after nightfall and don't think I have any *totally* gross habits. Several minor, slightly annoying ones according to my ex, Robbie. But who hasn't?

I'm just your average girl. Enjoy my job, but sometimes hate my boss. Have an on-off relationship with the gym (more off than on if I'm honest). Have bad hair days more than good. Worry about whether my best life is escaping me, and really, really want to work out how to buy a house. Can't take a decent selfie where both eyes look the same and I don't look constipated or leery. And am quite often too exhausted in the evening to do anything but curl up with a good movie or book and something to nibble on. And before your mind takes you somewhere rude, I'm talking nuts of the ready salted (not hairy) type, or a nice bag of popcorn.

That is normal, right?

And I'm not being overambitious and setting the bar too high.

I'm not looking for a mate for life (though that would be nice), just a date. And movie star looks are optional.

For heaven's sake, I just want a date with a normal guy. One with a nice smile, regular job, sense of humour and decent table manners. One who I don't mind keeping my eyes open to snog, and who I wouldn't mind introducing to my mates. He doesn't even have to be parent-friendly. Or like small children. Or have a five-year plan.

Okay, I admit, some of that stuff was on my original list, but I'm lowering my standards. Needs must.

I check my watch again. It would also be nice if he could tell the time. Because it is so bloody obvious to everybody here: I have been stood up.

I resist the urge to bang my head on the bar, and instead launch Tinder for what has to be at least the eighty-seventh time in the last thirty minutes, just in case I've missed some kind of last-minute *'sorry but I've had an emergency'* type of message. Like I said, I'm not after the perfect guy; I can quite happily accept that something more important than a date with a girl he hasn't even met yet could have happened.

I might even forgive him totally forgetting he had a meet-up if his mum/dog/hamster/car has had some kind of gruesome catastrophe befall them.

Okay maybe not the last one, or last two, I'm not a complete pushover.

I stare at his photo. We've swapped so many messages and he seemed nice, sweet, caring, interesting. Not the type of man to stand somebody up.

Was he?

Who'd have thought you could actually find your soul mate (or at least a great date) hidden amongst all the swipe-left losers on Tinder?

I did.

I am telling you, the flick-left forefinger on my right hand had been developing a nervous twitch until two weeks ago, when it kind of froze mid-air and I had to work out how to swipe right. It doesn't come naturally – swiping right or thinking somebody might just be 'the one'.

He zoomed straight onto my 'possible' list. Well, he *was* the list.

He was, is, gorgeous. Totally. Gorgeous Gabe. And when we swapped messages he seemed as nice on the inside as the outside. Kind. Thoughtful. Funny. Self-deprecating.

Definitely a possibility.

The perfect guy to help ease me back into the dating game.

Okay, let's be honest here. He was the only guy after several weeks of swiping who seemed remotely normal. Wow, who knew so many people existed who wanted to thrust their appendages into a woman they don't know? In fact, I had no idea some of the things I was messaged about were legal, or even possible in one case, until I entered the murky world of internet dating.

So why am I here? Why did I sign up on dating apps, which we all know is more likely to be a route to a total self-esteem crash, than total satisfaction?

Because I am crap at finding a date. I cannot do what my mate, Bea, does and just stroll up to any guy she fancies and openly flirt.

Eurgh. I mean, *flirt*, with a total stranger? Okay, I admit it, I did try it once in the coffee shop up the road, when I was in the queue for a cappuccino, and finally plucked up the courage to say something to a guy who I regularly saw in there. We were kind of on nodding terms, but for the first time ever he smiled at me as he picked up his coffee and waved! I waved back and said I loved his new scarf. He gave me a funny look, then stepped past me to the woman behind and kissed her! OMG, the embarrassment. I couldn't go in there again, just in case I bumped into either of them. I now have to buy inferior coffee from a place further up the street, which is ridiculous, and more expensive, but necessary.

And then there was the guy in the pub (okay, I have tried to flirt more than once – this time it was with Bea's encouragement after three drinks, which made it worse). I mean, he could have been a mass murderer, married or thought I was a total weirdo and pretended he'd not seen or heard me. But I did it anyway. And he did. Pretend he hadn't seen me. Yup, it happened; it's never happened to Bea.

Then there was the guy Bea fixed me up with, who just wanted to talk about Bea, and after I winked at him suggestively asked if I'd seen a doctor about my nervous twitch.

So this is why I needed a different approach.

The issue here is that I've only ever dated one person. Robbie. We kissed for the first time when we were fifteen, started to see each other seriously (in a groping and proper snogging kind of way) when we were sixteen, had sex at seventeen, shared a holiday at eighteen, and it all developed from there. Until he left the country at thirty to find himself, and never came back. Thirty, I ask you? Which bits haven't you discovered by the time you're *thirty*?

I'm not sure if he's still looking, or if he just found out he was a different person than he expected. Or if he actually just found a totally different person to me who he decided he wanted to shack up with. The details aren't clear.

But shortly before he left I think we both realised that this wasn't 'it'. And we still had time to say so and get out before it was too late. So he did. And I'm a bit cross I didn't have the guts to do it first.

It took a while for us to admit it, because it's hard and scary to take the leap of faith. But we'd grown up and grown apart – matured into two individuals with different expectations and desires. His evolving man-buns (cool), tantric sex in a tepee (from the photos I could see on his Facebook page after he'd set off on his travels, but OMG what if people were listening?), green tea (yuk) and mung beans (not tried them, not going to try them), and looking after the planet.

I'm all for looking after the planet but I want a house of

my own (with proper walls and curtains) to have sex in, lots of coffee with the odd smoothie, and Deliveroo at my fingertips. Oh, and Netflix.

See? Totally incompatible. How did we never see that happening, and go our separate ways earlier?

Even though it was right that it was over, it was still sad. Like scooping out a section of my heart and watching it dissolve, leaving a small hollow that ached with nothingness. Like closing the door on a part of my growing up that I'd loved. The carefree, happy, hopeful anything-can-happen part.

I had lost a part of my naïve optimism. A part of my joy.

It had made me doubt that happy-ever-afters actually exist.

Up until now I'd ignored some of the shitty love experiences that my nearest and dearest had had to deal with; I had told myself that they were the exceptions and what I had – happiness – was totally possible if you went about it in the right way. I thought I was special, *we* were special. Admitting to myself that Robbie leaving was the right thing shot that theory totally in the foot.

There was a gaping hole in my soul (and the flat) after he reappeared briefly, all tanned, tousle-haired and sheepish, and packed the rest of his stuff into two very large rucksacks and a couple of bags for life.

That was the moment the sticking plaster was ripped off with stinging finality.

Saying goodbye was admitting we'd changed, that we weren't those optimistic kids anymore. That we had grown up and had learned tough love.

Yuk.

But once I'd wallowed briefly in self-pity, and eaten a lot of carbs, I agreed with Bea that I had womanly needs and that I needed to 'get out there'. I was going to date.

Easy eh? Not, it would seem!

So, anyway – taking a deep breath and pulling my big-girl pants up – I have now been single for eight months and nine days, and the closest I've come to scoring was when D. B. Tricket hesitated at the till after paying for his book. He comes into the bookshop *very* regularly. So regularly that I know the name on his payment card. He's quite shy and has a, shall I say, unusual taste in reading. He hesitated so long this time I was about to jokingly say 'move along' when he coughed twice and then a load of words came out in a rush. He had a couple of tickets for a gig, and did I fancy it? It was a well-cool local band, and I couldn't believe my luck! I told him to drop the tickets off any time cos I was sure Bea, my mate, would be interested.

D. B. turned bright red, stuttered that he would and crashed out of the shop forgetting to take the book he'd just bought with him.

I mean, why? Why did I say that? Why did that bit of my brain responsible for dating not click in and realise *he was asking me out*?

He has not been in the shop since, and he was actually our best customer by a long way.

Bea thought it was hilarious, then sobered up and said if I didn't get myself sorted soon and learn to read the signals, she'd take me out for a proper night on the pull. She's not a euphemism type of person – she's pretty direct and blunt, even when it comes to dates. Which is why she goes on lots, and I don't get any. But we are *so* different. The idea of a manhunt with her is bloody scary, so I knew I had to prove I was at least trying to find my inner date detector.

I don't want to hook up with somebody for a one-night stand because we're both pissed and our standards, morals and possibly good-judgement have gone AWOL for the evening. I also don't want to date 'my best mate's friend's brother's mate who never seems to get a second date and can't stop talking about his crush on the girl he saw at the bus stop' (that entire sentence explains it all). I don't want a pity shag. Or a blind date with somebody who shares my interest in finding the perfect beef jerky (yes, I did meet him at a party), but absolutely nothing else. Or newly divorced Dennis who comes in every Thursday to check out our sci-fi books and has declared he's open to dating anybody providing their boobs are bigger than their stomach and they're up for a curry and beer night. To be honest I think his best bet is to date his buddy Steve; they make the perfect couple.

Anyway, even if they don't, I don't want him.

So, there are a lot of *don'ts*, and I am normally more of a *do* person. But I just want a date with a normal guy.

My big problem is I don't know: a. where to find him, or b. what to say if I do, or c. how to tell if he's interested (as D. B. Tricket will confirm).

So, finding a date online had seemed like a good idea. I thought I would have some control, and also wouldn't have to rely on my dodgy ability to read body language. Normally I don't have an issue with this. I can tell if somebody wants me to piss off, sit down, leave them alone or help – which is why I love working in a shop so much. But my wires just seem to get crossed, or totally fused together, in a potential-attraction situation. Or, well, any one-on-one with a man in a social situation. I get flustered, I panic, I lose my ability to string together sentences, I cannot act like a normal human being.

It is beginning to annoy me.

Using an app, though, I thought I could check for compatibility at least, get the basic niceties out of the way, and we'd both turn up for our first date because we wanted to be there.

Seems I was wrong.

I am now even more annoyed.

* * *

This bar is a bit like a hotel, with a steady trickle of customers coming and going – but not staying for long. Which leaves me feeling even worse. It isn't the type of place I'd normally come on my own (to be honest I don't do bars on my own), it isn't even the type of bar I'd come to with Robbie, or Bea. It's a bit brash, loud, trying a bit too hard to impress.

Trendy shiny stools and uncomfortable seats that don't let you slump, carefully dimmed lights that are supposed to create ambience but just feel false. Not me at all. I'm more a chilled, take me as you find me type of person.

My prosecco, like me, has lost its bubbles. I knock back what is left, and stare at Gabe's profile and have to admit it feels a bit like I've been kicked in the gut. He's not shown up for our date. Our first date.

10

The First Date

Second date I might have been able to stomach (unless I'd really been into him), but first date? Really? He hasn't even given me a chance.

Bastard.

It's that feeling you get when you're six years old and can't see your mum in the audience at the school Nativity.

He has ruined my master plan. He has let me down, just when I thought I was about to make some progress and come out of what Bea calls my 'hermit shell home'. I've been trying, I really have, and I thought this was it.

Gabe Stevenson. Blue eyes, dark hair. Age 32 and ¾ (I'd thought that was cute; who doesn't like a guy with a sense of humour?).

Not famous, a film star or millionaire, but play the guitar (badly), sing in the shower (not quite as badly), cook a mean curry. Like dogs, kids, chocolate and cake. Scrub up okay.

Cute. Slightly serious, but fun. Honest, presentable, can laugh at himself. Perfect. I thought.

Grrrr. Being stood up is bad enough. But this has just got even worse, even more humiliating. I have been ghosted. He will not answer my messages! What kind of inconsiderate moron won't even reply to a simple '*Running late?* 😊' text message?

By the fourth message I may have dropped the smileys and dipped a toe (or whole foot) into the passive-aggressive arena. I did not, however, text '*Where the fuck are you?*' even though I was itching to. I'm rather proud of my self-restraint, so that's one positive I can take away from this.

I turn my phone off and back on again, just in case it has lost connection, or has been hiding stuff from me.

It blinks at me.

'Oh gawd.' I put my head in my hands. 'Why am I even doing this to myself? First dates are the biggest load of shite . . .'

'Then you're dating the wrong guys.'

'Shit!' I hadn't even realised I'd moaned out loud, and the deep voice that sounds like it is inches away from my left ear makes me jump. I start to slither off the stupidly high and shiny stool, throw my arms out wildly to recover my balance, and slap my empty glass with the palm of my hand so that it skids along the bar. 'Fu—' I lurch forward to try and grab it, and somehow instead end up sucking a strange man's chin.

I say strange but mean strange as in 'stranger' not weirdo; he's actually quite presentable. Minty breath (can't avoid it), nice nostrils (no long hairs). I can't see much more of him this close up. And yuk, bristles! Thank God he's just gone for not-shaved-today and hasn't got a full bits-of-food-in beard. Which would be totally gross.

I edge back, so that my nose is no longer pressed against his lips. What kind of germs might I have picked up, licking an unknown man's stubble?

It's then I realise that I cannot move to a polite distance because I am in a weird tango position – one arm outstretched, fingers reaching for my glass, the other hand pressed against his chest.

Em-barr-ass-ing.

I appear to have been in a clinch (but luckily now at arm's length) with a man. But he is not Gabe.

Definitely not Gabe.

'You're not Gabe!'

He chuckles. 'Nope. Not Gabe. I'm not the first date shite!' He raises an eyebrow and grins at me. 'More the first date dream.'

'Really? Are you for real?' *This* is why I don't come to bars like this one. 'Has nobody ever told you how bad that sounds?'

Just as I thought this couldn't get any worse in the humiliation stakes, it has. I am groping my not-first-date. What the hell am I doing? Shit! What if Gabe turns up late and finds me grappling somebody else? And a cocky, confident, sexy, self-assured type of somebody else. A player!

Is it possible to be unfaithful to somebody you haven't yet met? Oh my God, Tinder isn't like TripAdvisor, is it? Can I be rated on true-to-likeness, turns-up-on-time, and likelihood-of-being-faithful?! Is there a noticeboard where I can be branded a bitch and lose forever the hope of a swipe surge? Even though it *is not my fault*?

Well actually it is partly Gabe's fault for picking this place, which is a bit of a pick-up joint from what I can tell, and for not turning up on time.

I have got to get away!

But Not-Gabe has his hand on my waist. And he's got a pretty firm grip of me.

Maybe I need to let go first. My hand is still splayed over a surprisingly firm pec, which I am tempted to squeeze. But I don't. If I shove hard enough, I might catapult myself backwards over the bar and possibly injure myself hideously in the process.

Instead I take my gaze off my twitching fingers and glance back up. Straight into smiley eyes that have laughter wrinkles at the corners.

I wriggle, and his fingers move against my waist but don't go away. So I freeze.

This is a weird game.

What do I do now? No blog I have ever read about first dates has covered this situation. Or rather, how to get out of it. Even Bea, the fount of all man-related knowledge didn't cover this in her pre-date pep talk.

She covered: what to do if he's boring (suggest going to a karaoke bar – he probably won't go, but if he does at least you've got a distraction); what to do if he's ugly (tricky one, nobody likes cruelty, but turn the convo to plastic surgery?); what to do if he's drunk (just sit and wait until he passes out); what to do if he won't stop talking about his divorce/ ex (leave, no argument, just leave); and what to do if he keeps saying he wants to shag you, but you don't fancy him and the thought of seeing his bits in all their naked splendour is making you feel like you need to vom (tell him in a whisper that the infection has nearly cleared up, only a few more blisters to pop – but if he tells anybody he's dead).

Tango-style clinches with an attractive but totally unsuitable man (who wasn't the man you were meeting), and getting out of them, were definitely not mentioned.

'Let me go! What the hell are you playing at?' Attack is always a good form of defence.

His warm fingers close over my hand which is holding the glass. He doesn't move out of my personal space. I gulp. It's weird. Holding hands with a man who isn't Robbie.

Even weirder having his thumb inches from my left boob.

Maybe I should savour the moment, use this as a taster of

what is to come. You know, get used to being touched by a stranger.

Or maybe not. My nipple is stirring uncomfortably at the uninvited attention.

I twitch and can't help but glance down, then he jumps as though he hadn't realised he was touching me, and unhands me. Before very gently peeling my own hand off his chest.

Awkward. Had forgotten about that.

'Well you did throw yourself at me, so I caught you!' He shrugs and grins. 'You can say thank you later!'

'I did not throw myself at you,' I can feel myself turning the colour of a beetroot, 'and I am not going to say thank you!'

'Now there you are wrong. I was standing here, minding my own business, trying to get a drink and you leapt on me!'

'I did not! What is it with some people, always trying to pass the blame? You crept up on me while I was concentrating on my phone, whispered in my ear and made me jump. I do not leap on people!' The cheek of the man. If I did leap on people, I wouldn't have this bloody dating problem in the first place.

He chuckles. I can feel the hairs on the back of my neck spring into high alert. This man spells trouble. Flirt – tick. Twinkly eyes – tick. Womaniser – tick. Smooth operator – tick. Sexy clothes – tick. Hot body – tick (I know I shouldn't have noticed, but it is hard not to). Invading my personal space – tick, tick, tick!

Carefully selected Gabe wouldn't have behaved like this. See, this is the trouble with relying on meeting guys randomly – you end up with womanisers who think they are God's gift.

Not my type at all, no, no.

He's watching me. His steady gaze challenging.

I stare back unwilling to back down and break the contact first (what can I say, I'm a bad loser), and slowly it dawns on me. I could actually use this to my advantage. Just this once, talking to a man like this could be useful. Purely for research reasons, of course. To find out why I'm having the problems I am. He's landed, quite literally, in my lap – so why not take advantage of the situation?

Normally I'd have been off the moment he laid his unwanted hands on me, but one I'm slightly tipsy, and two I'm feeling a bit desperate. Pissed and pissed off is not a good combination.

'You don't?' He raises an eyebrow, then winks. 'Shame.'

Oh God, he's worse than I thought. '*You* should apologise!'

'What for? I'm not sorry. Are you?'

This floors me. Am I sorry? Should I be sorry? What have I got to be sorry about?

'I'm intrigued.' He seems to have taken my confusion for a 'no' and carries on talking. 'Why does dating suck?' He twinkles at me. Positively twinkles. And squeezes my hand! I stare at our joined hands. I'd forgotten we were still clutching my glass. I try and wriggle free again and for a moment there's a bit of a tussle, then he casually let's go, one finger trailing down the back of my hand as it goes and winks. 'Nothing better on a Friday night, or Saturday, or Monday, Tuesday . . .'

'You can stop the winking.' I sigh and climb back on my stool. 'I'm immune.'

'Really?'

'Really.' Being brought up by a man who thought a wink made up for everything, including forgetting your birthday party, has kind of made me wary. It worked when I was five years old, but it sets off warning bells now. 'I'm not like your normal swooning to the floor type of date.'

'How do you know what my normal type of date is? We've hardly met. I don't even know your name.'

'True, I was just taking an educated guess, from the winking and touching,' I try not to glare at him, 'and smart one-liners.'

'I've not even started yet. Those are my warm-up lines!'

'See! You can't not do it.'

He puts one rather muscular forearm on the bar and tilts his head on one side. Then stares. 'You're funny.'

'No, I'm not!'

'Oh you are! Funny, sexy, smart.'

I'm not sure if he's taking the piss now, or it's a chat-up line. See? I don't get the signals. But it doesn't matter. I am immune to men like him. He is not part of my life plan.

Maybe this is going to be too difficult; he's not going to be useful after all. Maybe I should just forget this. Go home, get into bed and bury my head in the pillow. Or fill my romantic well from Netflix.

Except I came here for a reason, a purpose.

I don't want to admit defeat, it's not my style. I can't. Not straight away. What am I going to tell Bea?

He leans in closer. 'You are funny, funny strange, not hilarious.' He grins. 'I've been watching you.' He wags a finger. 'You've been here for ages, sitting all on your own, with a drink. One drink!' This is even worse than being stood up.

Being watched being stood up! 'You look kind of lonely, not like the type of girl who comes out on her own. You've been dumped, haven't you? Am I right, or am I right?'

'You're wrong!' I glare at him. I am feeling uncomfortable: hot, flustered and embarrassed. I brush a hand over my knee, even though there's nothing on it. 'Actually, I was just about to say sorry for being grumpy, it was just you startled me,' and grabbed me, 'but now you've spoiled it!'

'Really? I'm wrong? About you being dumped?'

'Stop saying *really* like that!' Technically he is wrong. I have not been dumped, I have been stood up. Worse, I have been ghosted. On my first date. 'And stop saying dumped!'

'Stood up then?'

Shit. I've gone bright red again; I know I have. I need to invest in a really good foundation that will leave my face the same colour whatever happens. Green's the colour, isn't it? 'Okay smart arse, I've been stood up. So what?'

'So nothing. No shame in that, happens to the best of us.'

'You too?' For some reason this cheers me up slightly.

'Well not actually me.' He grins, then chuckles. It's quite sexy. Well sexy if you had to rate it on a scale. Kind of deep-throated, the type of sound that would make you clench your thighs if you were into this man. Which I am not. See, I am unclenching. And . . . relax. 'I was here for a drink with my mate, Jed. We had a couple of drinks.' He shrugs. 'Then he buggered off early.' He glances away briefly, as though it bothers him, then looks back at me and gives me a bit of a wolfish grin. Whatever bothered him has been dismissed. 'So, I'm all yours.'

'I don't want you to be all mine. I'm fine on my own thanks.'
I half turn away, but he doesn't take the hint.

'But you do want something, am I right, or am I—?'

'Will you stop saying that, it's so, well, so annoying.' I had two
glasses of wine before I came out, to boost my confidence. That's
why I was taking it easy on the prosecco when I got here; falling
over drunk isn't a good look on a first date, is it? And without
the pre-date wine I might well have ducked out. It was my
confidence booster. Without the wine I wouldn't be here now,
talking to a man who thinks I am going to fall for his charm.

'Sorry, babe.' He doesn't look sorry. 'Anything else?'

'Can you drop the babe bit. I'm not your babe, I'm not
anybody's babe. Who says babe these days?'

'I meant anything else to drink, not continue with your
character assassination!'

'I'm not . . .' I pause. Take a deep breath. I'm here, he's here,
he might be useful. He's obviously a bit of a jerk and a lot
of a bad boy. Which strangely enough might be just what I
need. For the next half hour or so anyway. 'Oh God, I'm sorry,
I'm not usually this rude and grumpy, it's just . . .'

'The date?' He tilts his head on one side. 'You were totally
into him? Am I right, or . . .?'

I scowl. 'No, I was not totally into him. I've never actually
met him.'

He frowns. 'I'm usually right quite a lot! Not scoring
tonight, am I?'

'No!'

He sticks his lower lip out. 'Part of my charm? Nobody
likes a know it all, do they?'

'No, it is not charming. Look, do you want me to tell you or not? Unless you have somewhere better to be?' His eyes open wide. 'Thought not.' Normally I'm not this forward with men I don't know, with anybody at all if I'm honest. But I am desperate. And I am also a little bit tipsy.

'Wow, you say it like it is, don't you?' He grins. 'Fire away! Let me order more drinks first though, you need to chill a bit.'

'No!' I can't accept a drink off him. 'And what do you mean, chill?' Chill, I can't chill.

'Yes, drinks all round!' He waves his empty at the barman. 'You need to get this off your chest, I can tell. Call me your fairy godmother or whatever.'

'You are the least fairy-godmother-like person I have ever met!' Which reminds me. 'How long did you say you've been watching me?'

'Oh, a while, since my mate left. Well, while he was still here as well.'

'Wow, that's creepy. Are you some kind of stalker? Should I even be talking to you?'

'Should I even be talking to you? You're the strange one who sits in a bar and doesn't drink.'

I glare at him. 'Look, I'm getting another drink!' I wave at the barman, who has been lurking for the past ten minutes, looking pointedly at my glass, but has now decided to bugger off out of range.

'Haha, gotcha!'

I ignore his triumph. 'Why did your friend go?'

'Things are a bit shitty for him right now.' He shifts

uncomfortably, then changes the conversation. Interesting. 'Why does a girl like you need help from a guy like me?'

Good question; however, I think it's a rhetorical one and he won't welcome a full answer. I take a deep breath and decide to go for it anyway, well at least some of it. After all I will never ever see him again, will I? 'Okay. Do I look desperate to you?'

He studies me for a moment. It's a bit unsettling.

'Don't think about it too long!'

'Sad, lonely, maybe a bit grumpy.'

'Hey, less of the gr—'

He holds a hand up to silence me. 'Though some girls get grumpy when they're not getting enough.'

'Enough?' Even as the word comes out of my mouth, I know it is a mistake.

'You know . . . sex.' He has got a dirty grin, a very dirty grin. He probably thinks he looks sexy and endearing.

'I am not desperate for,' I realise I am talking rather loudly, so lower my voice to a hiss, 'sex.' He could have a point though. I might be. It is so long since I had it, I'm not sure. Maybe my current mood is less to do with PMS or PMT or work, and more to do with my abandoned lady parts!

Oh my God, do I even want sex with somebody else? I hadn't got to this point in my dating fantasy before. The pinnacle of my ambitions so far has been one full evening with a guy who I might like enough to repeat the process with.

Robbie has been my one and only for so long, sex with another man will be weird. Well weird. What if other people do it differently? What if I'm expected to do things, thingy things, with things? Oh shit! If I thought first dates were bad enough, how am I going to cope with third dates – when I might be required to undress? Look a new penis in the eye?

'Are you okay?' He's peering at me.

'I am fine! Totally fine!' I feel sick.

He chuckles. 'You should see the look on your face!'

Luckily, he can only see my face, and not what is going on in my head. 'What look? No,' I put a hand up, 'don't say a word. And stop laughing at me! I meant do I look desperate for a date, a guy, and before you say anything, a date doesn't have to mean sex!'

'If you say so.' He leans in and gently rests his hand on my knee. It's warm, a bit unsettling, but rather nice-unsettling. Bea would call this progress. 'Tell me the story, babe.'

'Please don't call me babe, nobody says babe, and . . .' I look at his hand. I probably should insist he moves it. I might have to flick it if he doesn't remove it soon.

'Well you won't tell me your name, so . . .'

'It's Rosie. Rosie Brown. Okay, satisfied?' I mean what's the harm? He's bought me a drink; we probably should swap names.

'Rosie? Yeah, Rosie suits you! I'm Noah.' He holds out a hand and when I put mine tentatively in it, he bends over and kisses the back. 'Noah Adams.'

'My God, you are such a flirt! Do you never stop? Can you just be serious for a moment? You're not my type, so you might as well drop the act.'

He looks pretend-hurt, but I'm not falling for that.

'Fire away then if you're going to be boring. How can I help?' He takes his hand off my knee and leaves it feeling all cold.

I take a deep breath. I am going to do this. I am going to make the next hour of my life, with this totally unsuitable guy, count. 'Okay, you're a man.'

'Last time I looked I was.'

I ignore him.

'So, you can tell me. What the fuck do men want?' This is the question that has been bothering me since I got here. Well since Gabe didn't get here. Well okay, since well before then. Since I realised that I don't know how to date.

If I knew exactly what they wanted, then I wouldn't have been stood up, would I? I would also be confident about first dates.

'Sex, beer, food, football?'

I am a bit worried about the order of this list but will ignore it for now. 'Can you be serious here, just for one teeny moment? I mean as far as a date goes. How do I find the right guy for me? How do I find a date? What do I say? How am I supposed to know how to do it?'

'It?' He grins. He's gone twinkly again. A little dimple has appeared either side of the gentle curve of his mouth.

'Date! Are you completely sex mad or something?'

'You want me to tell you how to find a date? Really? A girl looking like you do?'

'Really.' I try and grin back, but it doesn't work. My face won't cooperate. I think it looks suspicious not happy. 'What do you mean, looking like me?'

'Cute!'

I shouldn't have asked. He's got a flirt-setting jammed full-on permanently. 'This is stupid. Forget I asked.' I slip my purse out of my bag. 'How much do I owe you for the drink?'

He puts out a staying hand, which brushes against my arm and sets the goose bumps off. 'You're being serious, you want to know what men want in a woman, a date?'

'I said forget it.' I'm mumbling, and fidget so that we're no longer touching; this is getting embarrassing.

'But you found a date, he just . . .'

I look him in the eye. 'Didn't show! Blanked me, ghosted me!' I'm embarrassed because I feel stupid. What kind of crazy impulse had taken over my normally balanced mind and persuaded me that this could work?

Okay, you don't need to answer that. I already know. One word. Desperation.

'People get stood up all the time, Rosie. It's par for the course.'

'Maybe your course, but not—'

'You're upset. Come on, let's get another drink.'

'I should go.' Not talk to strange men in bars about my dating disasters. 'I'm not upset.' Well not much.

'Stay, why go home and sit in the dark eating ice cream and watching people pretend snog on the TV when you can chat to me?'

He twinkles at me, in a nice, not over-flirty way. I am tempted. And, how did he know I was going to do that? If he's a mind-reader this could be useful, but also bad.

'Come on, for my sake as well.' He shrugs. 'I've not got anywhere else to go. You'd be leaving me all alone.'

'You'd soon pick up another girl.' I grin back at him.

He looks around. 'Place seems pretty short of single women right now.'

'True. I can see you're really stuck!'

'So I'll sit here and bother you! Come on, Rosie, spill! If you want to that is, or we can talk about me, yeah me!'

I laugh, I can't help it. He's funny. 'Okay I'll have a drink if it makes you happy, but it's my round, okay? And I'm not upset, I'm angry.'

He chuckles. 'I'd never have guessed!'

I roll my eyes and smile back. He's good company actually, and another drink and a moan is a far better bet than going home and sulking with only a packet of crisps for company. And better than bothering Bea. It's not fair on her, I can't call again.

Chapter 2

'Now you mention it, you do look a bit angry. Feisty! Scares some men! Cheers!' Noah raises his refilled glass and grins. He's easy-going, cheerful, just what I need. And, despite the fact I still reckon he's a bit of a player, he's given up on making moves and I have to admit I do quite like him.

And I know he's just flirting, but the way he's looking at me – intently as though he's interested – is making me feel much better inside.

Nobody looks at me intently these days. I hadn't realised I'd missed that – until now.

I can feel myself frowning. 'Not sure I like feisty, that's what Mum used to call the stray cat she left food out for.'

He chuckles again. 'It's cute, I like it!'

'I'm not trying to be scary, am I really?'

He nods. 'Assertive.' His grin returns. 'Quite a turn on, actually.'

I sigh. 'You can't help yourself, can you? Just forget sex for two minutes.'

'Yes, Miss. So, why the mood?'

This is interesting. I never thought of myself as scary. Maybe because I've been nervous, and under pressure.

'It's just,' I sigh. How do I explain to somebody I hardly know, just how important tonight was to me? Noah is the type of guy who has an endless stream of dates. 'You won't get it.'

'Try me.'

'Okay. You asked for this!'

'Hang on, let me brace myself!'

I punch him on the arm and realise that I don't have to move forward to do it. We've got kind of close again, which is a bit worrying. 'Funny! Haha slipping off my stool, hang on!' I wriggle back. I don't think that was an obvious retreat. Very sneakily done, Rosie! 'Have you any idea how long it took me to get ready tonight? I tried on at least six outfits!' That's two hours of my life spent finding the right outfit that I'm never going to get back.

'Really?'

'Don't say it like that, as though you're shocked! I wanted a bit sexy, but not too sexy.'

'Oh God, no, heaven forbid! Too sexy!' He plants his palm over his eyes. 'Complete disaster on a date.'

He's making me laugh again. I've not laughed this much for ages – well since me and Bea thought that hiring a rowing boat and taking a dog she was looking after in it was a good idea. Bad idea. 'And I wanted to look smart, but not like I tried *too* hard.' I pause. 'Why am I telling you this?'

'Who knows, but carry on.'

'I guess if I stop, we'll have to talk about you?'

'Spot on!'

'Right fine, I'm good to keep going. Then there was the

whole waxing thing. I spent ages thinking about it and it kept me awake last night: how far should I go with waxing?'

He blinks.

'Sorry, too much info.'

'No, carry on. How far did you go?' He's doing the cocked eyebrow thing again.

'I didn't, so you can stop that! Just legs, armpits and eyebrows.' It had bothered me, the whole 'how much hair is too much?' According to some stuff I'd read, a single hair anywhere but on a head was a hair too far these days. Not that I'd been expecting to leap into bed with Gabe, but be prepared has always been my motto – and I'd been thinking of this as a dry run for a second and third date. 'But I don't know what is right!' I flap my arms. 'I've never done it before!'

'Waxed?'

'No. God, I'm not hairy, am I?' I glance down as though I'm half expecting to see tufts poking out. 'I meant I've never had to get ready for a first date!'

He frowns. 'What do you mean, never had to—'

'Well not never, ever, obviously. But not for ages, and last time it was different. It's complicated.' A rush of disappointment hits me, and I'd been doing so well at ignoring it. The whole splitting up, and it looking more and more likely each day that I am never, ever going to find another date. I babble to cover it up. 'And it took ages to get here, and I don't even like this place much.'

'Here,' he clicks his fingers and more drinks magically appear. Had I finished mine? I can't even remember drinking it. The first sip, yes. But, after that? 'O—kay. You're not upset.'

'I'm not upset.' Okay, I am. But I sniff it up and refuse to give in.

'But you did find a date, so that's a good start, eh?' He is looking at me encouragingly, like my mother used to when I'd failed my driving tests but hadn't got minors in absolutely every category.

'I didn't exactly find a date. Not in real life.' I am never going to see Noah again, so I can admit it all to him in this moment. 'I found him on Tinder. I've never actually met the guy. This was supposed to be our first date.'

'And he's blown you out? Wow, what a douche! You see, that's the trouble with matching up with some guy on an app, he's not met you in person.'

'Er, that's the point.'

'But if he's not met you then he doesn't know what he's missing!' He leans in a bit, puts his hand over mine. 'See, it's a bit like when you've said you'll go to a gig to support a friend, but not actually had to pay for tickets. Easy to do a no-show!'

'You've done that?' I roll my eyes. 'What a slimeball.' A tiny glimmer of something positive warms me up inside. Noah seems to have that effect on me. 'I'm just a ticket Gabe never had to pay for, and he thinks he's spotted something better? Like a good film on TV?' I grin.

Noah chuckles and shakes his head. 'I didn't say that! But I'm glad I made you smile.'

I glance at my phone. I can't help myself. Just to make sure there isn't a message.

'Forget him.' Noah booms out loud, slamming his hand

onto the bar right next to my phone sending it skittering to
the floor. 'You've just found a better gig!'

I look at him and raise an eyebrow. There's nothing wrong
with Noah, he's funny, but he's not a date.

'Okay,' he puts his hands over his face, but is peeking through,
'you can't forget him, it's too early.' He does a fake sob.

'God, you are such a clown!' I laugh.

'Go on then, tell me about this . . .'

'Gabe.'

'Gabe. If it helps. Not that I think he's worth even thinking
about, and not that I want to hear about the stupid twat, but
if it's going to help.'

I frown. 'Maybe it won't help. It's not actually *Gabe* that's
the important thing. You're right he's not worth bothering
about.'

'No?' He looks confused.

'It was the date. I just needed a date!'

'Why the urgency?' He suddenly grins. 'It's a bet! I get it,
you've bet a mate you can hook him!'

'No.' I shake my head. 'Who would do something like that?'

He shrugs, looks a bit sheepish.

'God, you're impossible. You've done that as well, haven't
you?'

He doesn't answer. 'Okay, you did it cos you need a hot
date for some party! Am I right? You can't go on your own
because your ex will be there?'

I sigh. 'I thought you'd given up on thinking you were right?
No, it's not for a bet, not for a party, I just . . .' I pause, then
lean in a bit closer to him. He's got very nice eyes. I think I'm

a bit drunk. I have to be drunk or I wouldn't be leaning in or telling him this stuff. 'I haven't had a date for ages and ages; I've not even had sex for ages! Well I've not touched a man, apart from you, of course, but that isn't touching-touching, for eight months and nine days to be precise. Oh God, no! More!' I sit back. Wow, I hadn't realised just how bad this had got. 'Robbie moved out six months and nine days ago, but I hadn't seen him for weeks before that. Does that count as non-date time? It definitely counts as non-sex time.'

Noah pulls a funny face and shakes his head. 'Haven't a clue what you are talking about.'

'I've only ever had one boyfriend: Robbie.'

'Wow.' He does a low whistle, and doesn't sound judge-mental, but I ignore him and bat on.

'And we split up, and now he's gone.' I wave my hands to make the point. 'And I've realised I've never really done first dates and I just wanted to do it, you know, get it over with. A proper date, not somebody I've been set up with, or some weirdo stalker, somebody I picked myself because I liked them! I promised myself I'd do it, and now grunge-faced Gabe has ruined it! Will you stop laughing!'

'Get it over with?' He is still chuckling. Which is kind of annoying, but also kind of contagious. 'Look Rosie, just walk up to a guy you fancy and, well, chat.'

'I can't! That's the point! I walk up to somebody, and, well, freeze and don't know what to say, and end up asking him to pass me a beer mat or something.'

'You're talking to me.'

'That's different, you're not a date. I don't fancy you.'

'Not at all?' He looks a bit put out. 'Not even a tiny bit?'

'Not at all, and I'm drunk or I wouldn't even be talking to you.'

'Wow, you know how to boost a man's ego.'

'You don't need yours boosting! I can tell. Look,' I study him carefully, 'okay, you're fanciable, right?'

'But you don't fancy me?'

'You're just not my type, that's all.'

'Oh.'

'You can't be everybody's type.' I pat his hand; I feel like I need to reassure him. 'Oh, I need to go home before I say completely the wrong thing. You see, I don't know what to say!'

'No, you don't, but you're not shooting off.' He pulls my stool closer to his so that our knees brush together briefly and I forget all about needing to shoot off. 'I don't see the problem.'

'I've not had time to date since Robbie went,' or the faintest clue how to find a boyfriend, 'and, I mean, being serious, you can't just march up to a hot guy and ask him out, can you?'

'You can't?' He looks shocked.

'Nope. You can't,' I say firmly. 'Can you?'

'Well yeah, that's what people tend to do. Well not guys in my case, girls. But I'd be well chuffed if some hot girl came up and asked me out!'

'Well I don't do that. I just wanted to date, and Tinder seemed a good way to do it.'

He shakes his head, suddenly serious. 'Ah, so that's why it's

33

such a big deal,' he says softly. He really has got a nice voice, silky, warm, good for pillow talk. I blink and try and get rid of the picture of pillows, along with sheets and a massive bed, that is in my head. 'You're a first-date virgin. You thought this would work if you didn't have to actually chat somebody up. You could sort it all at arm's length. No risk of being turned down, no checking out for wedding rings,' he's counting things off on his fingers, 'no chemistry, just hard facts.'

'Exactly. Reduce the margin of error.' My voice starts off crisp and tails off. It doesn't sound brilliant now he's put it like that.

'And without knowing whether you'd actually fancy them in real life.'

'But you see their photo.'

'This is about looks then.'

'No, it's not!'

'Yes, it is!' He chuckles and taps the back of my hand. 'You've already said he's gorgeous.'

'Well I wouldn't talk to him if I didn't fancy him at least a bit, would I?' I try not to sound huffy.

'Ahh, but fancying is more than looks, isn't it? You know, the vibe, the chemistry the being with somebody. Trust me, Rosie, you need real.'

'But you talk to people, you send messages!'

'And he said what he thought you wanted to hear. It's easy when you can sit there plotting it out on the sofa at half-time.'

'Huh.'

'Okay.' He obviously decides it is time to change tack. 'What gave you the idea in the first place?'

'Bea. My friend. She came into the bookshop where we work with a dog in her handbag, a little fluffy pompom-like dog.' Honestly, it really was like a pompom on legs, except it also had a cute button nose and tiny black eyes. And it was *in her handbag*, that's how small it was. I found that hard enough to get over at the time, now it seems even more incredible. I wish I could remember exactly how many drinks I've had tonight.

'And?'

'She doesn't have a dog. But,' I lean in confidentially, 'she wants a dog.' She positively pines for doggie cuddles and kisses; she never stops talking about it. 'But Bea doesn't have one because she works long hours, has got a very small apartment, and loves her holidays abroad.'

'O-kay, you want a date. She can't have a dog, but she's got a dog. I'm not confused at all.'

'I did wonder if she'd been dog-napping, but she's really honest, you know, and then she explained about an app she'd discovered where you could *borrow a dog* for a day! Isn't that brilliant! It's genius: you sign up, fill in a profile about your perfect pooch match and all these dog owners do the same and they find you the perfect doggie date. You just borrow them, like a playdate, or a sleepover, or for a whole week!' Bea doesn't like big things. She likes cute, fluffy, clean, portable pups. She loves the idea of a glamorous meal out, with a tiny dog sitting next to her, awaiting morsels of food. This app had delivered exactly what she'd asked for.

It was while she was explaining the genius of this app to me that it came to her. If she could find the perfect pup online, why couldn't I find the perfect first date the same way? One I was matched carefully with, one that I could return the next day and mark as unsuitable if necessary, one I didn't have to worry about house-training or commitment with. We laughed about it. She put her dog back in her handbag, and I went back to tidying bookshelves and forgot all about it for at least ten minutes.

'And then my dad texted me cos he'd heard.'

'What?' Noah looks confused again. 'He'd heard about your mate's obsession with little furry dogs?'

'No.' I frown. 'He'd heard about Robbie!'

'Oh. And why would that make you . . .?'

'He laughed at me!' Normally I would not pass on any of Dad's less than nice comments, but I'm drunk, and I'm never going to see Noah again. So, it's fine. It's like writing it down on a piece of paper and burning it. 'Said it was bound to happen at some point he guessed, me being single.'

'What?' Noah looks indignant on my behalf, which makes me feel a bit warm and fuzzy inside (or that could be the alcohol, at this point I'm not sure).

'He said I'm too loud, too outspoken. Men don't like it. Even drips, his word not mine, like Robbie get fed up of it in the end.' I need to shut up before I get carried away.

'Bollocks! I like the way you say what you think! You're funny, you're clever. Sorry, know he's your dad and all that, but he sounds like a bit of a dick.'

I frown. 'He *is* my dad, and all that. He's not a dick. You don't know him!'

'Sorry.' He doesn't look sorry. 'I didn't mean to upset you, but . . .'

'Did you say I was funny and clever?' I frown at him again.

He nods, grins, and I suddenly feel awkward. So I crash on. 'Anyway,' I take a deep breath, time to move on to the important stuff, 'he pissed me off, so while I was eating my sandwich I signed up for Tinder. If it's that good for dogs, why wouldn't the human apps be as good?'

'Does Bea use it to find men as well?'

'Borrow my doggy?'

'Tinder!' He laughs. A deep throaty, makes you feel like you've swallowed a whisky, laugh.

'Oh God, no!' The idea is hilarious. 'Bea doesn't need an app to find a date, she's ultra-cool, and totally confident. Men just, well, men just,' I haven't analysed this before, but thinking about it now, Bea has never needed to think about finding a date because, 'they just appear out of thin bloody air. They're everywhere she goes! Or she just sees a guy she fancies and goes up and grabs him! Literally! I mean what if he's psycho, or doesn't fancy her, or is married? I don't know how she does it.' Actually, some of them have been a bit psycho, well bordering on it, and married. But Bea has just brushed it off and moved on.

'So Bea hasn't used an app, but she thought you should? Or it was your idea?'

'Well yes, well no, we were just messing, I didn't actually say . . .' I didn't tell her I'd actually done it. I signed up in secret, cos I felt a bit daft, and very embarrassed. 'I told her I had a date. I didn't tell her where I'd found him. But lots of people do it! And I mean it is just like BorrowMyDoggy, isn't it?'

'Please don't tell me you used that line on Gabe!'

37

I decide to ignore that comment. 'It is totally similar, and it worked for her! It's brilliant, have you been listening?' He nods. After a few drinks it seems even more brilliant than it did the first time. 'I mean, POOF,' I snap my fingers, 'Tinder is magic, it's like ordering a pizza off Just Eat. You just pick what looks good and . . .'

'Yeah, you can get laid quicker than you can get a kebab, but do you want a kebab you've not actually seen? Or do you want to go in to town, then decide to pop into Krispy Kreme and look them all over and pick the best?'

'Kebabs? In Krispy Kreme?' I'm confused.

'Doughnuts! Whichever food you want!' He laughs.

'Or you could go into one of those specialist jerky places, and try them all first!'

He raises an eyebrow. I might have lost him. But I'm very tipsy, and I do love jerky. Oh no, I can't believe I'm sitting in a bar with a strange man talking about fast food delivery options. And jerky. 'It's dried beef! It's really nice, and not too fattening, not like crisps or chocolate, or . . .'

'Rosie.' He puts his hands over mine. Leans in. We're both a bit tipsy, which is why we get that perfect eye contact. Just pause for a moment, and stare. He has nice eyes. I could stare into his eyes for a while; in fact, it's hard not to. They've got little wrinkles at the corners, and they're a funny grey-blue colour. It's hard to tell exactly. I lean in a bit closer.

'Rosie!' He jiggles my hands and I blink.

'Sorry.'

'It's not the way to do it, Rosie. You deserve better than some creep who's looking for an easy shag—'

'They're not all like that! Lots of people find other people online!'

'I know, I'm not saying it's not an idea, but—'

'Maybe I need to speed date. I mean all the guys are there then, aren't they? No chance of no-shows, and how bad can it be talking to somebody for ten seconds or whatever you're allowed before the buzzer? I'm sure I can think of stuff to say for that long! Wow, that's a brilliant idea, why didn't I think of it before?'

'Stop!' Noah holds a hand up in front of my face, but he's laughing so much any minute now he could fall off his stool. It makes me giggle back. He makes an effort to pull himself together. 'Okay, let me get this straight. You just want a first date? You want a doggy for a day that you can send home later?'

I frown at him. 'Yes, that's what I said! But a man, not a dog.' Just to be clear.

'Not a husband?'

'Oh my God, no, no. Not yet! I just don't know how to date. I've never had to do it. I need dating practice.'

'Cool.'

'Cool?' I finish off my drink and wonder if another one would be a good idea, or a very bad idea.

'I have the answer!' He nods decisively and pulls a funny, excited face.

'You do?' I am dubious.

'I,' he taps his chest to make sure I understand, 'am your man.'

'What? Oh no, no, no, no. You are *so* not my man!'

39

'I am, I am.' He grabs both my hands again. His are lovely and warm. But that doesn't matter, he definitely isn't my man!

'Listen! I'm brilliant at first dates!' He lets go of my hands but doesn't lose eye contact. 'I'm a serial first dater!'

'I knew it!' That slips out unintentionally, but I don't think he noticed.

'A total whizz at asking people out! Not so hot on third of fourth dates, or second dates if I'm honest.' He shrugs self-consciously and looks all boyish and cheeky. I can feel myself getting all hot and bothered.

'But I don't want to date you!'

'Listen, listen, I'm not saying date me, I'm saying I have expertise.' He taps the side of his nose.

'But you're brilliant at dating women, not men!'

'Thank you.' He grins and mock bows.

'That wasn't supposed to be a compliment! I'm only taking your word for that, I'm not actually saying . . .'

'You really need to polish up your chatting technique you know!'

'I know!'

'Okay, okay, so I'm, allegedly, brilliant at chatting up women, but I know what a guy like me is looking for.'

'But I don't want a guy like you!' Shoot I didn't mean that to come out.

'I think we need to talk about that at some stage. I'm getting a very negative vibe here.' He frowns at me, wags his finger; he looks quite masterful. 'But I know what any guy is after, all guys!'

'Maybe this isn't such a good idea.' How do I tell him

that I wanted somebody like Gabe? Sincere, funny, clever, serious. Or at least that is what I thought Gabe was, maybe I was wrong.

'Oh no, no, stop right there, Rosie.' He puts a stalling hand out, as though he thinks I'm about to make a dash for the bar door. 'You're not running out on me now. This is getting interesting. Come on, come on, show me.'

'Show you what?'

'This bloke. His profile. Go on, show me.' He holds his hand out. Waiting.

'No way.' I grab my phone and hold it to my chest.

'Rosie!' His voice has a warning edge I wasn't expecting.

'Okay, just his profile.' I open up the profile and put my hand protectively over his face, then scroll up. I don't want any comments about his looks. 'You can see what he says, that's all. Not our messages!'

'Oh my God, what a smooth twat.' Noah chuckles, and downs what is left of his drink, then orders another round.

'What do you mean?' I look at the profile again. 'He's really nice!'

'Nice eh?' Noah purses his lips and shakes his head. I think he is trying not to laugh.

'Well, okay maybe he's not actually nice in real life. But he seems kind, funny, look he made a joke here.' I jab at the phone and accidentally close the app, so put it down suddenly feeling tired and hopeless.

Noah pats my hand, as though he understands. Then hands me a glass of prosecco. 'Drink up. Come on, things aren't that bad!' He's not laughing at me now. Smiling, but not laughing.

'Hey, Rosie. I *am* your man. I know exactly what we are going to do. I am going to give you lessons.'

'Lessons?'

'First date lessons. I'll teach you how to seduce a man.'

I laugh, I can't help it. Then I giggle. 'You! Seduction lessons. Haha, that's funny.' I crease over, hands on knees, manage to stop laughing. Look up at him and it starts me off again. He grins.

'I'm an expert at first dates, believe me. Total hero!' He points at his own chest proudly, then raises an eyebrow. 'And, I'm a man. I know *exactly* what men want.'

The way he says 'exactly' makes something inside me shimmy. It's weird. And sexy.

'I will teach you my best seduction techniques.' He grins. 'Oh Rosie, Rosie, Rosie. You need me.' He puts his hand over his heart. 'You really need me.'

'But you're not my type!'

'What do you mean, I'm not your type!' He does the puppy dog eyes thing again. 'You wound me with your harsh words. Anyway, that doesn't matter. I'm not offering to be your date, I'm going to teach you how to get one. We pretend, what have you got to lose?'

'Not actual, proper dates?' I want to make sure. Whatever happens, I must not, I cannot date Noah. I know exactly how men like Noah can affect your life, however cute they are. Well, that's the problem. They're always cute. Or brooding, or magnificent, or sexy, or seductive in some other way.

Or a combination of all of the above.

'And you'd do this for me because?'

'You need help.'

I go to object, but I'm not sure why. Apart from not liking being described as in need of help. But he is right.

'And your dad was a shit to say something like that.'

I sigh. 'He's probably forgotten already, and I won't be seeing him for ages.' But it would be nice to show him that I can get a date, that I'm not going to be a lonely spinster.

'And I want to help you, not shag you. Well I'm quite happy to shag you if you ask nicely,' I glare at him, 'but mainly I want to help.' He holds his hands up. 'I promise, no shagging, not even excess manhandling, or anything.' He starts to get a bit flustered; I guess dating is new territory for me, and not-dating is confusing territory for him.

We stare at each other. He puts his hands behind his back. 'Look, no hands!'

I giggle, I can't keep a straight face. 'You're cute you know.' I grin at him.

'I know.' His eyes are twinkling, seriously cute and hot.

'And modest.'

'Totally modest, it's one of my strong points.'

'I don't even want to go near your weak points then.'

He laughs. He is cute.

'You're quite cute yourself, Rosie Brown. But I think you need to get to bed, don't you?' My cheeks start to burn. He grins. 'Alone.'

I do. Alone. 'Seriously,' I say as I slide off my stool, this time on purpose, 'it's really kind of you to offer to help me, but I don't think it would work.'

'Seriously, I think it could.' He pays the barman, waving

away my attempts to split the bill. 'Here. Think about it.' He picks my mobile phone up from the bar, and taps in his number, then hands it back to me. 'Hang on, I'll walk you home.'

'I'm fine, I . . .'

'I'm walking that way.'

'How do you know? You don't know where I live!'

'You said it took twenty minutes, in your ridiculous shoes, so it can't be far.'

I'm impressed he remembers what I said, in fact I'm impressed he was listening that closely.

'I'll follow you if you don't let me walk with you. Which will totally creep you out!'

* * *

He walks me home, stops on the doorstep and kisses my cheek. 'Thank you for a nice evening, Rosie Brown.'

'You're welcome, Noah Adams. Thank you for a nice, a nice, er, not-date.'

'It was actually more fun than a lot of my real dates.' He wrinkles his nose. 'Weird. Well you've got my number if you want a taster session!'

'You won't be upset if I don't?'

'I won't.' He kisses the tip of my nose. 'But think about it, eh? Now, bugger off to bed before I forget my good intentions, Miss Temptress!'

I stand and watch him go, the tips of my fingers resting on the spot he kissed. He doesn't turn back, but I can't help but grin. Taster session! Gawd, some men will call it anything!

Chapter 3

My head is all jumbled up with thoughts about the totally unsuitable, serial first dater, Noah, and my no-show not so perfect guy, Gabe. This means I can't sleep.

I have puffed up and thumped my pillows about. I have thrown my duvet off, then pulled it back on when I realise my shoulders are freezing. I have been to the loo several times. I have drunk about ten gallons of water, to try and avoid a hangover, and then been back to the bathroom several more times.

I stare up at the ceiling and wonder if Noah's tutorials would be all talk and no substance or involve total practical hands-on stuff. And what about practise? Would I get homework? Oh, hell no, what is my drunken brain doing to me? I do not need to go down this route.

This has to stop.

I kick the duvet off for the umpteenth time and text Bea. She'll be asleep, but it will concentrate my mind on the fuckwit who didn't turn up. Which is good.

'He didn't show! x'

'Who? What? xx'

Bea is not asleep.

'My date x'

I add an unhappy face.

My phone starts ringing almost instantly. Bea is like that – I can rely on her, totally. She is like the big sister I never had. We are totally different in so many ways, but it works. 'You had a date tonight!' squeals Bea in my ear. In the still of the night she sounds even more high-pitched and deafening than she does normally – which is pretty loud anyway when she's excited.

'You knew I—'

'You didn't say it was tonight! Why didn't you tell me, how could you not tell me? That's mega! What did you wear?'

'I didn't tell you cos he wasn't a proper date.' I sigh, sit up and twiddle my hair round my finger, feeling a failure.

'What do you mean, not proper? A man, a date, that's proper!'

'I found him on a dating app.'

'Oh.' There's a pause. I hadn't told her that bit. 'That still counts as a proper date though, you noddle.'

'Not when he doesn't show.' The disappointment of him, specifically Gabe, not turning up ebbed away a while ago, around the time Noah started to act the clown. But it still hurts, the being stood up bit. Especially saying it out loud to somebody.

'Oh, Rosie. You should have called me,' if she was here, she'd be hugging me, she's good like that, 'you could have come round rather than being on your own. Or I'd have come for a drink with you.'

'Aww I know, Bea, but I didn't want to bug you, and you were seeing Si.' Si is her latest boyfriend, but I think his days are numbered.

'I wouldn't mind, you know I wouldn't! I'm getting fed up of Si anyway. Did I tell you he's trying to get me to go with him to watch Man U? I mean, Man U!' His days are definitely numbered. 'I put my City scarf on and staged a protest.'

'Poor Si! I was fine though, honestly.'

'I don't like to think of you on your own. It's the pits when some doofer doesn't show. What a dickhead!'

'I wasn't *exactly* on my own. I got talking to this guy and . . .'

She squeals again. 'A guy!!' I can hear her jumping about on the bed making herself more comfortable. 'Tell!'

If Bea had been there instead of me, it would have been a date. I can't help but smile at her. 'It wasn't like that. He wasn't my type.'

'He doesn't have to be your type, Rosie! He was a date!' I decide not to correct her. 'Was he fit? Cool? Funny? Or old, was he too old?'

I grin. Bea is unstoppable. Sometimes I wish I was more like her, it must make some things so much easier, but mainly I'm happy just being me. I think my life is less extreme, less highs and lows. I'm not sure my emotional state could cope with a Bea-type lifestyle. 'He was fine; I suppose he was quite fit, and funny; you know, just a guy. We chatted, had a couple of drinks. It stopped me feeling sorry for myself.' No way can I go into details, not until I have a clear head. 'He was nice, and he walked me home.'

'Walked you home!'

I hold the phone away from my ear. 'Tell me you kissed! You kissed, didn't you!'

'Bea!'

'But you had a nice time? And he knows where you live. When are you seeing him again?'

I try to stop laughing. 'Oh Bea, no way would I date a guy like that. He was such a player, I could tell. He actually admitted he was a serial first dater!'

'Maybe that's what you need. You know, just some fun?'

And to end up getting hurt. 'No.' I say it more firmly than I mean to, but I've seen what men like that can do, the hurt they can bring even as they're saying they love you. The way they even convince themselves they can change, but they can't. I've seen a man like that cause so much pain to a person I love – and not been able to do anything at all to make it right. A man like that is not for me. 'Why is it so bloody difficult?' I sigh. 'It's not like I'm asking for some wonder boy with a super yacht, Jag and French chateau to his name, is it?'

'Would be nice though.' Bea has a dreamy edge to her voice.

'I'm not even after a totally ripped Richard Madden, Chris Hemsworth, Ryan Gosling, Jake Gyllenhaal mash-up, or a Matthew Goode charmer.'

'It's a good bloody job,' says Bea. 'Has anybody ever told

you that you can be strange at times? Boy that is weird: Chris Hemsworth and Ryan Gosling in one package?' I can tell I'm losing her; she's distracted by the thought of all these hunks merged into one perfect man.

'I'm not strange! I've thought about this a lot, it works if you've got the right bits from each one, honestly!'

'Which bits of Ryan Gosling?'

'The twinkly eyes, the cheeky bits! Look I'm not explaining, it's my fantasy, make your own up! But the point is, I just want a normal guy.'

'Don't we all, Rosie, it's not just you.'

'Noah says I need to pick a Krispy Kreme doughnut, not a kebab.'

'What?'

'And I need seduction techniques.'

She giggles. 'Oh Rosie, I don't know about kebabs, but you just need one date. One date and you'll know you can do it. You can, Rosie. You're so lovely, and kind, and you're funny and clever, you'll find somebody soon.' I haven't told her my father's latest comment on that one.

'I will.' Or I'll give up and get a dog.

'And you did have a date, and you did talk to a man, this Noah. That wasn't so difficult, was it? Next time will be even easier!'

'He wasn't a date, he was just a man who I'd never dream of going out with, and we had a chat and a drink.'

'That, my girl, is what some people would call a date!' She chuckles. 'Meet me for brunch tomorrow, proper catch-up and we can come up with a plan?'

'Sure.' I smile. I might tell her about Noah's offer, and I might not. I haven't decided yet, because the last thing I want is for Bea to try and persuade me to take him up on it. I need a better plan of my own first. 'Night, Bea. And thanks.'

'Night, my lovely.' She blows a kiss then the line goes dead.

I stare at my mobile phone for a moment, then put it down and lie back. Pulling the duvet up to my chin, a picture of Noah pops into my head – laughing and nudging my arm. Maybe it would be okay to have just one taster session with him? I mean, we're not going to end up dating because for one, he isn't interested in actual dating, and two, I know he's not the right type of guy for me. So would it really do any harm?

I think of bar guy who pretended he hadn't heard me, of coffee guy who thought I was a loony, of D. B. Tricket my book buying admirer, of Dennis, the new divorcee who'd settle for anybody. Of all the guys I'd swiped away on Tinder, and gorgeous Gabe, who I was sure would set me off on the path to a new relationship.

I am a dating disaster.

Maybe I really should just settle for a dog.

Chapter 4

I'm early for brunch with Bea because I didn't really sleep that well. All my nearly-dates whizzed round on a carousel in my head until I felt dizzy.

I don't think all the glasses of prosecco I drank last night helped either.

I'm on my second large black americano when Bea grabs me from behind in a bearhug. If I hadn't recognised her multicoloured nails (as in one in each colour) I'd have spat my coffee out and screamed.

'I ordered you another coffee on my way in,' she knows my addiction to caffeine, 'and eggs Benedict.' She plonks herself down opposite me. 'Phew I'm knackered. Si came over all assertive after I hid the remote and wouldn't let him watch the football. He said I needed taking in hand.' She grins, her eyes alive with laughter.

'Shush! Too much information.' I put my hands over my ears in mock horror, and she giggles. Bea isn't a giggly girl normally; whatever happened between the two of them has left her on a high that is better not explained in detail. I'm glad she's happy, though, she deserves to be.

'There can never be too much information! Come on then, tell me about your wild night out and this mystery guy, Noel.'

'Noah. And it wasn't a wild night out.' I sip my coffee primly.

'You could at least make something up just to satisfy my terrible imagination. Oh fab, thank you!' She glances up as our breakfast is put on the table, dazzling the waitress in the same way she dazzles everybody. She is warm and lovely, a social butterfly and natural-giver wrapped up in a slightly zany parcel. 'Go on, talk!' She grins. 'I know you're dying to tell me something!'

'I am.' I take a bite of my breakfast, suddenly starving. Because I have made my mind up about what I need to do. Knowing has made me feel better about the world. And hungry. 'On the walk over here, I made a decision. Well, three of them actually. Learning seduction techniques from Noah is an absolute no.'

'What?' Bea's fork clatters onto the table. 'Seduction!' She squeals, oblivious to all the people who have turned round to stare. 'Oh my God! Hit me with a copy of the Kama Sutra! He's going to teach you—'

'He's not, aren't you listening?'

'But he offered!' She shovels more food into her mouth and looks at me as though she's expecting a revelation.

'Bea.' I sigh. I love her natural exuberance, but sometimes she needs to put the brakes on. 'He said he would, and I said no. He's not my type.'

'You fancy him! You've said he's not your type about five million times, which means he is!'

'I don't fancy him.' I feel my back stiffen. 'He, he . . .'

'He what?'

'Reminds me of . . .' I study my plate, suddenly sad. 'Dad.'
I force the word out, a squeak of a sound that is too small
for a man like him.

Bea knows all about my dad, his female friends, his long
absences from home. The way I always felt I was competing
for his attention when I was growing up. 'Oh Rosie, I'm
sorry. But he might not be like that at all, you hardly know
the man.'

'He will be like that, I can tell,' I say stiffly.

All the warning signs are there. The cheeky winks; the way
he made me feel important, as though I mattered. That sincere
look. And that gorgeous laugh, that disarming laugh that
almost persuaded me that seeing him again would be a good
idea. Dad is like that, he's sincere, appeals to something inside
me that makes it impossible to say no. And before I know it,
I've agreed to God knows what – like cleaning the hamster
cage out. Which is fine when you're ten years old and it's
something innocent, not so fine when you're all grown up
and it's a whole lot more damaging than rodent droppings
and sawdust.

Dad gets under your skin. Just like Noah does. For heaven's
sake, he kept me awake at night thinking about him, and I've
only met him once!

I can tell exactly what he is like and getting involved with
a man like that would be disastrous. Before I knew it, I'd be
caught in his web, believing everything he said, and losing
every bit of independence I thought I had. Like Mum did.

'Not everybody stays the same.' Bea's voice is soft as she squeezes my shoulder. 'People do change.'

'They don't. The heart of them, the real them deep inside never changes and you can either decide to work with it or leave. Mum told me that.' My lovely mother, who had decided that walking away wasn't for her. I stop looking at crumbs and meet Bea's eye. 'I am never going to put myself through that. I am never going to date somebody like that. I can't *work* with it!' She blinks. I think I might have shouted the last sentence out, and I know Bea's preparing to launch herself into a speech about love and risk and highs and lows, so I say something quick to stop her. 'Anyway, we were both drunk, he probably didn't mean it.'

'Well ring him. You said you had his number.'

'Did I?'

She laughs. 'Last night you said he put it in your phone!'

'Ahh.'

'Ring him, find out if he was being serious.'

'No.' That would be almost as embarrassing as a first date. No way am I going to call him.

'It's a ridiculous idea.'

'Why? Give me one good reason. Wow, this sauce is the best.' She licks her lips in orgasmic ecstasy and I have a brief twinge of disappointment that I might never do that again. Orgasm – not eat hollandaise sauce. It would be so nice to find the other half of me to share my life with, even though right now it looks like it's going to be position vacant for some time.

It isn't that I yearn for affection because I've had a rubbish childhood. I had a good, loving upbringing. Mum and Dad (when he was present) have always showered me with cuddles and encouragement, but at school I was always desperate to be like my friends. I wanted to spend school holidays at home and chill out with mates. I wanted to have Mum and Dad at home every night for tea together. I wanted to wake up on Christmas morning in my own bed. But it wasn't often like that.

I always felt like I lived on a wobble board – slightly unstable, never quite safe.

Dad plays in an orchestra. He's a good, well great, musician so he travels all over the country, all over the world. And Mum has always gone with him whenever she can – which meant I went too until I was old enough to stay on my own.

If I'm honest, I've always felt a bit like a gooseberry, because when Mum and Dad are together, they are *totally* together if you get what I mean. They are mad about each other, but that wasn't the full reason for tagging along. It's when they're apart that the problems start. Dad is a flirt, a total idiot who forgets what really matters in the heat of the moment. Mum was scared that if she wasn't there to watch out for the warning signs, then one day he might not come back. I mean, how does that make any sense?

I've never actually been in full-blown, mad-for-you, can't-live-without-you kind of love. And after growing up with that, I don't want to be. It sucks.

With Robbie it was more we-get-on-well, share-a-sense-of-humour and we-slot-together-like-two-worn-wooden-spoons affectionate love. It worked for me. I was happy with that.

More than. Because I've seen what full-on passion, letting the brakes off and bearing-your-soul-completely kind of love can do to somebody. I've watched a person I love having their heart used like a punching bag. I've joined them on the rollercoaster of will they, won't they? I've watched the way they've carefully rebuilt the fragile shell of emotions, only to let the person they love shatter them into tiny pieces again, because they just can't help it. They can't step away. And I've kind of understood, because even though I've hated Dad, I've loved him, too. And like my mum, I could never quite give up on him, never stop thinking that maybe one day he'd change. That it could be different.

I couldn't turn my back and walk away from my dad – so how could I expect Mum to?

So, I get it. But I've learned from it. I am never ever going to leave my heart open to that kind of hurt, to the destruction of love.

I mean, no high can ever be worth emotional lows that are so crashing they leave your body feeling as broken as your heart, can they? Nope.

So yeah, my parents' relationship is a bit of a car crash, a bad addiction.

Which is why my childhood dream has always been to feel secure. To have a normal family life. To have a nice husband who I can trust with my heart, somebody steady, somebody who will always be there for me. Somebody who wants what I want. My other half.

I want a nice normal guy who offers a merry-go-round not a rollercoaster. A guy who offers me safety. I'm not bothered about having my heart beat so fast it is threatening to break out of my chest (sounds a bit icky anyway). I do not want infatuation like Mum had, or a daily dose of lust coming from an adrenaline rush that sends me sky high one moment and crashing to the floor with doubt and insecurity the next.

I do not want the risk of love that somebody like Noah would offer. I'd rather be bored.

Not somebody who reminds me of the best and the worst bits of Dad. Because the two go hand in hand. Noah has twinkly eyes and a captivating grin. Noah is the type of guy who wants excitement, for each day to bring something new. Noah is the type of guy who draws you in and makes you feel special. Noah is the type of guy who is compelling, the type of guy you dream about and can't get out of your head. Which makes him dangerous, and everything I do not want.

Noah is sexy, but that's the point, isn't it? They always are. I know his type and I am not going to get involved. Not on any level. Definitely not.

I am done with that.

'I can give you more than one reason why the whole idea is bonkers!' Bea opens her mouth to speak, so I crash on before she can. 'Firstly, I do not want to learn how to be some kind of scarlet woman who has swallowed a seduction technique manual, I want to be my normal self and just bump into somebody at random and it turn into a fabulous first date. It happens in the movies, quite a lot.'

'Okay, fair point,' she waves her fork, 'though the movies are the movies to be fair. They're not real life. Nobody ever had that holding cards up professing love shit, or the mad dash to stop you getting on a plane, or—'

'Okay, okay, you can stop now!'

'And the drippy one is never going to turn out to be hotter than the flirty, fun one who wants to live on the edge. Totally unrealistic. Who thinks this stuff up? Marriage guidance counsellors?'

'Eat your eggs!'

'I wouldn't use your go-to romcoms as a guide. Just saying, so don't pull a face on me! Carry on . . .'

'Thanks! So, secondly it won't work because it involves going out with him. Almost like a fake date. He might want to demonstrate stuff, you know, want to be hands on.' Bea winks and raises an eyebrow. Now she would get on fine with Noah. She'd be able to handle him. But I wouldn't.

I try and stop the sigh escaping. 'What if learning seduction techniques involves fake kisses, or fake cuddles, or a fake romantic dinner for two? Where does fake end and real begin? At tongues? Hands on bums?' I can practically see Noah leaning in for a kiss, feel the touch of his hands on my waist and it is making me hot and bothered. Oh gawd, I hope Bea hasn't noticed!

'I'd just chill and see where it takes you. You can always cop out when the going gets hot.' She raises an eyebrow. 'Or stay in!'

'I knew you'd say something like that!' It all sounds far too complicated and risky to me, and risky is what I am trying to avoid. 'Anyway, it doesn't matter what you say, I've made my mind up. I am not calling Noah. And,' I hold up my hand to stop her interrupting, as this has brought me to my second decision, 'I am deleting all the dating apps off my phone.'

Noah has made me realise that I'm probably not cut out for this kind of approach. I think it is for the experienced dater, who won't get into a pickle or take being stood up, or expected to instantly drop her knickers, personally.

It has worked perfectly for Bea, with her dog-sitting.

It has not worked well for me so far though, and I think Noah might have had a point. You don't actually know what you're going to get. I'd kind of imagined that it would work a bit like an arranged marriage – but without the parental involvement, obviously. It doesn't.

'Noah was right. People lie, people have dodgy intentions, you order a nice steak and end up with horse. You are lulled into a false sense of security that you will get exactly what it says on the menu.' I look Bea in the eye. 'I acted on impulse.' She raises an eyebrow. 'Cos Dad texted me.' The sigh escapes, before I can stop it. 'He's found out I'm single, that I've been single for *ages*.'

Bea puts her knife and fork down. 'Oh Rosie, forget your dad. This is about what you want, it's not about him; but you can't give up. You'll find somebody, you will.'

'I'm not giving up, I know I'll find somebody one day. I've just decided I need to be cool about it. I don't need to rush just because Dad thinks I'm practically on the shelf.'

Bea nods encouragingly. 'You are SO not on the shelf. If you are so am I, so are loads of people!!'

'It's just a case of being in the right place at the right time,' she nods more, 'so if I make sure I'm out in as many places as possible, then that is going to help.' Dog walking is definitely an idea.

'Definitely!'

'*I* will find me a man.' Somewhere, somehow, even an imaginary man if it shuts everybody up. 'When I'm ready.' I could hire a date. Or I *could* ring Noah. If I get really desperate.

No. I am not going to ring Noah. Noah is bad news. Noah will have already forgotten I even exist.

'You've got a funny look on your face.' Bea nudges me in the ribs. 'Who are you thinking about?'

'Nobody.' She doesn't look convinced, probably because I am glowing.

Bea shrugs. 'Think about it. That's all I'm saying, don't just dismiss him, hun.'

'I don't need to think about it. Even if you are right and he's not going to spend the rest of his life unable to grow up and resist everything in a skirt.'

She touches my hand gently. 'That's not fair, Rosie, your dad wasn't that bad.'

'Don't.' I blink away the prickle at the back of my eyes. I don't want to talk about *him*, about a part of my childhood that I still can't quite come to terms with.

'Rosie, your dad—'

'Whatever,' I interrupt her, 'but this Noah is not my type. He's not serious for a start, I bet he never reads books!'

'Not serious is good, fun! Don't you get it?' She puts a hand on my arm, and looks at me seriously, and caring. 'Not everybody has to be the one, Rosie, or even the nearly one. You just need to get back in the swing of things. He can't be unfaithful if he's just teaching you how to have fun!'

'I don't need to be taught how to have fun. I have plenty of fun, thank you!' I know I'm starting to sound huffy, a bit like a sullen child. But I do know how to have fun. My life might not be a bundle of laughs, but I like it.

'I meant dating fun, Rosie, man fun. I know you know how to enjoy yourself. I'm sorry, I'm not having a dig, I just want to help.'

'I know.'

'He can help you lighten up about this whole first date thing, make it less of an issue. You never find love when you're looking for it. It finds you when you least expect it. Believe me.' She smiles. 'I go out looking for men, but I just find wankers and bell-ends.'

'You don't!' I laugh. Bea has always been able to lighten my mood.

'Now and then, when I'm not chatting people up, when I'm looking the other way, some real gem comes along. I'm too stupid to realise and treat them differently, the way I should. I'm scared to, Rosie. But when that right guy creeps under your radar, you'll realise and you'll know just what to do because you're so much smarter than me.' She hugs me and I feel like I'm holding a Bea I've not seen before. Maybe none of us are as confident as we look. 'It'll happen for you, Rosie. But why not let this guy Noah help you get some first dates you actually enjoy?'

'It's too hard. Too embarrassing, I'm not ready. And,' I search for some straws to grasp, 'he's too thin!'

'Too thin?' I'm getting her 'you are strange' look.

'Well not exactly thin, he's,' I make a totally strange figure kind of body with my hands in the air, 'quite broad in places,' she raises an eyebrow, which I ignore, 'but hard, kind of wiry and firm, and—'

'Boy, you are being weird about this one. Firm is good, girl!'

I try not to scowl. 'I like bigger men, beefier.'

'You mean fat, like Robbie was?'

'He wasn't fat! He was well padded.'

'You can't diss a man for being fit!'

'I can. If he's big then it makes me look thinner!' It does, I swear, I dwindle down to diminutive next to a well-built guy. Svelte.

Bea rolls her eyes. 'You are making excuses.' She stands up. 'I'm going to get us another coffee. And then we'll do some online stalking. If this guy of yours is as hot as I think he is, then I might take him up on his offer if you won't!'

Chapter 5

How can one nice thing be followed by two shit things in the one day? That's not fair, is it? I've never been quite sure whether to sneer at the 'bad things come in threes' saying, or to be worried. Today I am afraid. Very afraid.

Brunch with Bea was fun, even internet stalking Noah gave us a laugh. We found loads of funny things about Noah – biblical and otherwise – and the fact that he is actually, honestly, a real live architect made Bea giggle so much she had to rush off to the ladies lavatories. Who knew that repeating 'good with his hands' combined with 'build me an ark' and 'animals went in two by two' could make somebody wet their knickers? Anyway, I came home with half a mind to ring Noah and go for it, and half a mind to wash the towels and check if I had any sink un-blocker.

Until my mother rang.

'You haven't forgotten that it's our big wedding anniversary soon, have you, darling?'

I think Mum counts every anniversary as a big one because it's such a bloody achievement to evade the divorce lawyers and reach each milestone. I am not being mean when I say that their marriage is a nightmare. Well, more to the point, my dad is a frigging nightmare. If he was a woman, he'd be labelled a slag, a slapper, a nympho or a whore, but he's a man. So that makes him a real Casanova, a bit of a Romeo, or Don Juan, and that's all right then, isn't it? Romantic, funny, a bit of a one.

Funny my arse.

Somehow it makes it worse, and sadder, that they celebrate their anniversaries as though each one means something special.

'*Big* anniversary?' I replied.

'Our thirtieth! Pearl, isn't that amazing?'

'Totally.'

'You are coming, aren't you?' She sounds a bit anxious, as well she might. Each time they have a party like this I am sure there's a niggling doubt in the back of her mind that Dad won't turn up. He doesn't turn up to lots of things – but so far he's not missed an anniversary party. He has missed birthdays, holidays and even Christmas on one memorable occasion – memorable because I have never heard my mum scream so loud or threaten to cut off his goolies and hang them from the highest branches of the tree. Quite honestly, at eight years old this held a morbid fascination and I did wonder what colour string she'd use and if she'd drape tinsel round them.

It didn't happen. He came home and we shared a late Christmas dinner. All bodily parts intact. And he was funny, charming and brought wonderful presents back. Then went off to 'attend to urgent business' two days later.

The First Date

'Of course, I'll be there! I'll put it in my diary.'

'That's wonderful, darling. Now what else was it I wanted to tell you?' There's a long pause, but I wait. 'Oh yes, Robbie! You know young Robbie?'

'My Robbie?' Of course, I bloody know Robbie!

'I think you had a lucky escape there, Rosalie.' I don't know why she calls me Rosalie, nobody else does. 'You'll never guess what's happened.' I'm sure I won't, so I wait again. 'He's moved to Wales.'

Surely that can't be the news?

'He's got sheep, isn't that funny? He never seemed to be keen on animals at all. I remember him going quite pale when your aunt Sal arrived with that terrier of hers.'

'Maybe he's changed.' Changed more than I thought. 'Oh well, must get off, Mum.' I start to do that leaning-forward-as-though-I'm-going-to-put-the-phone-down thing.

'And he's got married!'

What?! I sit bolt upright. Phone glued hard to my ear. How can she add in the married bit as though it's an afterthought? *That* is why she called me by my full name. I should have known she was working up to *really* bad news.

Now I know why Robbie's mum crossed the road when she spotted me the other day. I'd thought she hadn't seen me, or she'd been in a hurry.

My hand clutching the phone is suddenly clammy, my forehead too. I'm having a hot flush, but inside I feel cold. Icy cold and empty.

Robbie in Wales is fine, Robbie with sheep is a bit weird, and quite funny.

Robbie married is not what should have happened at all.

How can Robbie be married? Robbie who less than a year ago had declared he didn't know what he wanted; he didn't even bloody know who he *was*.

How can Robbie have moved out and completely moved on? I've only just hit the 'ready to try and date' stage – and he is bloody married!

I wipe the palm of my hand over my face. When my palm rests over my mouth, it's trembling.

How could he just move on so quickly? How could he be married? We'd laughed about weddings years ago, but it just hadn't featured lately.

Maybe he'd gone off me a long time ago; maybe he *did* know who he was and what he wanted and what he told me was all a load of bollocks. He wanted to be a husband – just not mine.

'Okay dear, you get off, I know you're busy.'

'Fine,' I say numbly, still thinking about the life I'd thought I had. I can't quite get it to make sense in my head.

We'd been together forever. We'd never dated anybody else. We realised that we weren't as madly in love and as totally compatible as we always thought we were.

We parted by mutual agreement, and there was nobody else involved.

And he has a wife.

I feel queasy.

'I'm not sure where your father is, but when he comes home, I'll let him know you're coming to the party,' Mum carries on, totally oblivious to my current meltdown. 'He'll be pleased about that. He doesn't see much of you.'

That snaps me out of my daze. 'That's not my fault, Mum! If he was there more—' Most of my brain is still grappling with the Robbie-is-married scenario, but the remaining bit still makes me indignant when *I'm* blamed for not being there for Dad! For God's sake!

'Oh, I know it isn't your fault, Rosie,' Mum says in her 'shh-ing' tone. 'But you know how busy he is, and the orchestra are so busy these days, and he has to practise and—'

I sigh. I can't help it. 'Please don't make excuses for him, Mum.' It comes out wooden. I feel awful, it's Mum who has to put up with him never being there. Not me.

Our family life has always been on his terms. Brilliant when he's decided to be there, crap when he's decided to go and 'practise' out of hours with the latest violin player, or some groupie who's been swept off her feet by his easy charm and glamorous lifestyle. Ignoring the fact he has a family. Grrr.

'I can't believe Robbie has got married – are you sure, Mum?' It can't actually be true. I must have misheard. I've got myself in a tizz about nothing.

'Positive! I saw his mother in the Co-op, she showed me the photos on her phone. All hippy yurts and fields and flowers, and sheep.'

His mum used to chat to me in the Co-op, but now she pretends she doesn't know who I am. 'Of course. Mustn't forget the sheep!' I laugh weakly. Maybe the thing to do here is concentrate on the sheep. Sheep are nice, sheep are daft, sheep don't walk out of a long-term relationship and declare to love, honour and obey a woman they've known for barely two minutes.

Would he have stayed if I'd had sheep? Or a yurt?

Oh gawd, I'm going bonkers. What have sheep got to do with anything? I didn't want him to stay. We'd reached our sell-by date. But I didn't want him to find somebody else that quickly! Somebody he loved enough to marry. Which means she is the right one for him, and I never have been. And he knew it. Long before he told me.

'I'm glad you're not still with him, darling. I would never have seen you if you'd gone to Wales sheep farming.'

'I'm glad too, Mum.'

'She's pregnant I bet. She had a smockie dress, billowing it was! And lots of flowers, you know, distractions! I bet she was hiding a bump.'

'Not necessarily.' It comes out a bit grumpily. I'm trying to work out how pregnant she'd have to be to be showing. 'She might just like that kind of dress.' How big is this bump? How long has she been bloody pregnant? He's not only found himself, and a wife, he's found fatherhood. But in which order did all this discovery happen?

I think I need gin. A bottle of it.

'Hmm.' That's my mother's version of saying she's not convinced. 'Are you okay, darling? It must be a shock.'

'Of course, I'm okay! Why wouldn't I be okay? I'm fine, fine! Absolutely fine.' I think I'm beginning to sound fine in a slightly hysterical way. 'Why would I be bothered? I am over him, totally over him, we split *ages* ago!'

'It wasn't that long, Rosie. And you had been going out for a long time. I mean, I know he wasn't the one for you, but it's not easy to go out there and date when—'

'It's perfectly easy! No problem. It was so easy I've found

68

a new man, a much better man than Robbie!' Fuck! What have I said? I haven't got a boyfriend. All I have is . . . I bite my bottom lip, all I have is Noah. A man who told me he'd show me *how* to get a boyfriend. Just how quickly is it possible to learn? Does he run a fast-track course?

Shit. She'll tell Dad.

'Oh Rosie, why didn't you say?'

I try and concentrate on what she is saying and try not to think about Noah. And his totally whacky idea. Talk about clutching at straws, I can't seriously be even considering . . .

'I can't believe you didn't tell me. It will be so nice to meet him, and you can bring him to the party!'

I am considering it. The whacky idea. Because how am I going to get out of this one? Mum, despite her own crap-fest of a marriage, is convinced I'll only be happy if I'm part of a couple. And now I've told her I am. And when she tells Dad, I will never hear the end of it if I don't actually turn up arm in arm with somebody.

Great.

'Oh, I am so, so pleased. I didn't like to say, but I was worried, Rosie. You do spend all your time with your nose buried in a book.'

'I work in a bookshop, Mum!'

'I know, darling. But you do need to get out if you want to meet people. I'm so excited, you've got to tell me how you met him! Where was it? What did he say?'

There must be a way out of this. I only said I had a boyfriend so that she'd stop thinking I hadn't got over Robbie. And now this.

Like Dad says, I really should think before I open my mouth. He'll think it's hilarious if he realises that I've sunk to this, *inventing* a boyfriend. I'll never hear the last of it. It will become his new party piece, as yet again I prove I am not the perfect daughter. *Our Rosie still has invisible friends, even though she's over thirty, invisible boyfriends, haha, wink wink . . .*

'It's not serious yet, Mum, not about to get married, haha! I've only just started seeing him, not sure he's ready for the whole meet my family thing!' Dad doesn't even need to hear about it. I'll tell her not to tell him.

'Oh, that doesn't matter he's still welcome, even if he is just a casual fling! And who knows, by the time we get to the party day you might be ready to do a Robbie!'

Great. We have now coined a new phrase. To do a Robbie. Which I presume means to get married in haste and procreate as quickly as possible, preferably with sheep in attendance.

'Maybe not! I'm not sure he wants to move to Wales!' Now she's expecting me to be part of a proper lovey-dovey couple and she'll be disappointed if I'm not. I need to temper her expectations. I don't like disappointing her, she has enough of that in her life. I think she's invested all her hopes for happy-ever-afters in me. Her only daughter. So far it isn't going well.

In fact, it's going considerably worse than even she expects.

How the fuck do I get a boyfriend before the party? I can't even manage a first bloody date. And yes, I do know I'm swearing a lot. It's a reaction to finding myself in a hole that I seem hell-bent on digging even deeper.

So, my fun morning with Bea has been kicked into touch by the news that 1. There is another sham of an anniversary party looming (at which I am expected to have an escort so that Mum can kid herself she still believes in love and romance) and 2. Robbie has a wife. And I can't even get one bloody proper date!

I'm not upset that Robbie has fallen in love. I'm just upset that he's moved on so successfully and I haven't moved an inch. I am still the same girl he left behind. Minus the soft furnishings and other belongings that he took with him.

And minus his lovely family. Robbie's parents are very lovely, especially his mum. She always said I was the daughter she'd never had, and she also said (though I'm not sure if this is good or bad, given the circumstances) that it was wonderful that me and Robbie were together because she was sure I'd want to stay local, which meant he'd never move away. She'd gain a daughter, not lose a son.

So, I've let her down on that front as well. And I tried very hard not to. Maybe that's partly why Robbie and I stuck together for so long. Maybe that's why I didn't take the leap and walk away from him earlier.

It's no wonder that she's avoiding me now.

I miss her. I miss all of them. When I was in my teens, they were the security that I didn't always have. They were always *all* at home on Christmas Day. They weren't touring Europe in the school holidays – they went away for two weeks and that was it.

I saw more of Robbie's family than I saw of my own. And his dad always teased me nicely and made me blush.

Bugger. I've let them down, and now Dad is going to give me his full-on disappointed look as well. If he even turns up for the party, and if he doesn't it will be my fault. Because the neighbours will be gossiping about Robbie, and I'll be standing on the sidelines wallflower style, an embarrassment.

He will point out that I should listen to him, try and act with a bit more decorum and stop being so bloody opinionated. And he'll say, 'look at your mother'. Which will make it all one hundred times worse because I know she doesn't want me to be like her.

She wants me to be happy *all* the time, not just now and again.

I have no choice. I have to grab the one lifeline that has been thrown my way.

Noah.

'Are you still there, Rosie? You've gone very quiet.'

'Yes, Mum. Just thinking.' He's going to have to be a miracle worker. In fact, when I tell him I'm on a deadline he'll probably do what Dad would. Laugh and walk away.

I am doomed.

'Well, darling, mustn't keep you. Don't forget to save the date for the party, and you have got to bring your new man! I insist: there you go, I've written him on the list. Will you be coming over next weekend? You can bring him with you then if you want?'

She has to be kidding. 'Sorry, Mum. I'm working.' All weekend, and the next one. 'But I'll ring.'

Okay, so, I need to get my act together. I am going to have

sex again, at least once, before I turn into somebody who doesn't care.

I am also going to show Dad that he has a daughter to be proud of, one he can show off, who is worth coming home for. And maybe this time he'll hang around a bit longer – at least for the entire party.

The sigh escapes before I can stop it. Last year he left at the same time as the final guests, well ten seconds later for appearance's sake.

I'd got a bit over-excited and loud apparently. Now before you jump to conclusions, I was not rat-arsed. I was just having a lively debate with one of his friends about how a certain massive retailer isn't helping small bookshops, like the one I work in, survive.

His friend was a bit like Dad, and 'always right', and I am a bit like Dad in that I won't back down if I know I'm right. And I was.

Dad's parting words before he left the house were that I needed to calm down, that I was too opinionated, too unlady-like, embarrassing.

Robbie tried, in a very polite way, to stand up for me. Which didn't help.

Dad never really liked Robbie that much. They didn't have much in common. If I find a new, better boyfriend then they might even have things they can talk about. Things they agree on.

Hopefully not that I need to be quiet though. I can't be. I've tried.

'I have got to do it!'

I have to do it. I have no choice. And quickly.

My palms are all sweaty, and slightly itchy as I eye up my mobile phone.

Noah bloody Adams is not my type, but he could be the answer. In fact, he's my first and last resort.

He's like an earworm, a catchy song that I cannot get out of my mind even though I'm not that keen on it. An itch I can't quite reach to scratch. But in his case, he's a funny person with a ludicrous idea. And an infectious laugh. And I can't seem to shake him out of my head.

I'm sure it's not actually his infectious laugh that's the issue here, more the fact that I am now in the 'desperate' arena when it comes to my man-drought. And his off-the-wall idea, though bonkers, is all I've got. I mean, who knows? This dating lark is completely beyond me, so maybe something as whacky as this could work.

A few pointers and I could discover my inner man-killer.

And then, voilà, I will have my pick of boyfriends to take to the party!

Noah was amusing and quite good company, but also slightly infuriating. He seemed too flirty and fun for me to imagine him hunched over a computer creating 3D perfection, and surely a professional like him is far too busy to have any spare time to teach a girl how to seduce other men? And, I have to admit, though I know one should never generalise and stereotype, I always imagine architects to be serious and family-minded, living in large bespoke *Grand Designs*-style posh creations, with perfect wives and possibly a very clean cat, or house-trained child who does not leave dirty fingerprints on the polished surfaces.

But I feel that not only do I need Noah to help, I would also like to see him again anyway just to get some answers, and to find a way to banish him from my head, even if his seduction training techniques turn out to be a waste of time.

I wipe the palms of my hands down my jeans and pick up my mobile. What have I got to lose? I can do this. I am not my mother. I am not going to let him into my actual heart. Or my knickers. Or my head.

No harm in just one little chat, is there? I mean, it's not like I actually fancy him, or he fancies me. It will be like taking acting lessons.

Ahhh . . . The plan has just hit a snag! What if he wants paying?

I put the mobile down.

Although surely an architect will be too rich to want paying? Or he values his time so much he will bill me by the second. Sugar.

Oh, to hell with it. I hit dial and he answers so quickly I don't get chance to change my mind.

'Bloody hell, you're a toughie! Do you realise it is, hang on, nearly twenty hours since you met me, and you've only just rung – you've set a new record!'

'Haha.' I try to keep a straight face and ignore the tremor in my stomach that starts up about a millisecond after his chuckle. I was feeling surprisingly nervous about talking to him again, and the fact he might not even remember me – but strangely enough his warm voice on the other end of the line is comfortingly familiar. 'You do know who I am?' Just to be sure. He might know a lot of Rosies.

'Of course, I do, Rosie!'

'The Rosie, the one who was,' I close my eyes briefly and concentrate on not clenching my teeth, 'stood up.'

'Yeah, the ghostie-ghosted one who walked for *miles* in her shoes, drank gallons of prosecco, spent hours defuzzing—'

'Hours thinking about it, not doing it!' My God, does he think I'm like a monkey?

'Mates for life and loves jerky.' He carries on, ignoring my interruption. 'The gorgeous Rosie Brown!'

I am quite impressed at his recall, but I suppose this is a seduction technique. I'm not sure I can master this aspect; my memory is a bit random at the best of times.

'Were you being serious?' I spit it out before I change my mind and hit 'end call'.

'I'm always serious where beautiful women are concerned.'

I sigh. 'No, you aren't! Can you quit messing about just for one second? You know flattery won't get you anywhere!' If he doesn't stop flirting, I will chicken out, I know I will.

'Oh Rosie, Rosie, Rosie, you are such a breath of fresh air! A bit like an icy wind at times but refreshing.' He chuckles again. I can imagine him sitting on the couch, with his feet up on the table. All chilled and casually sexy. Oh, gawd, Rosie, stop! 'Yep definitely refreshing.'

'Have you any idea how hard it was to call you?'

'Nope.' His voice drops a tone or two, loses a bit of its humorous edge. 'I'm not hard to talk to, am I?' He sounds concerned, and I instantly want to reassure him.

'No.' He's not. 'It's not hard to talk to you.' I blink as the realisation hits. He is not at all difficult to talk to, though the subject matter is. 'It's just,' take a deep breath Rosie, 'were you serious about teaching me how to . . .' Oh God, how do I put this?

'Date?'

'Exactly.'

'Definitely.'

'You're not too busy?'

'I wouldn't have offered if I was. It will be a change.'

'From what?' I can hear the note of suspicion in my voice.

'Proper dating.'

'Oh.'

'That might not have sounded good. Rewind. Honest, I do want to help.'

'Oh.' This is nice, he sounds sincere, and it would be easy to wriggle out now if he had just been messing. But he's not trying to. 'You don't have lots of houses to design?'

'Ahh, somebody has been surfing the net. You're a stalker, too, I knew it!'

'No, I'm not! I just needed to know you weren't, well, weird, or a murderer, or bigamist, or . . .'

'What did you find out?' He sounds genuinely interested. Which I suppose I would be, if somebody told me they'd been googling me.

'Not a lot.' I try not to groan. 'You are so annoying! How am I supposed to vet you, to know what you're like if I can't find anything out!'

'Have you learned nothing from gorgeous Gabe? The World Wide Web knows nothing, Rosie. Throw away your passwords, take the reality challenge! Meet me, ask me in person; you know the old-fashioned way.' I can practically see him, grinning, his eyebrow raised.

'Okay, fine, I will!'

'What?' He chuckles, and it's a rich, chocolatey sound that makes me squeeze my hands together, hunch my shoulders and want to rush round in circles laughing like an excited cartoon princess. I don't, you'll be pleased to know. I try and act cool.

'I will meet you, but we need rules!'

'Ahh, rules of engagement.'

'Or non-engagement,' I say, as seriously as I can, trying to keep a lid on the nervous anticipation that seems to have made me wobbly and inclined to grin like a loony. Nerves can have a funny effect on a person. 'I'm also very busy so I thought I'd combine activities.'

This can be translated as 'I'm scared shitless of being in a proper date situation because I'll freeze up and Noah will agree that I am a lost cause, not even he can teach me seduction'.

'Please, just this once?' I cross my fingers behind my back: survive the first lesson and the second might be fine.

'You, woman, are like nobody I have ever known!'

'And what do you mean by that?'

'I've never been called an activity before.'

'Have you ever done this before?'

'Well no.'

Phew, that makes me more relieved than it should. Why should I care if tutoring women in the art of seduction is an everyday occurrence for him? But I do. 'So,' I am determined to get back into my flow, my pre-prepared script, which he keeps diverting me from, 'I am combining you with Hugo.'

'Oh my God, a threesome! Skipping straight to lesson 73!'

'Seventy-three! I'm so crap I need seventy-three lessons?'

He ignores me. 'Can I pick who we have next? I'm not sure Hugo is going to do it for me.'

I sigh. 'You are so rude! He's a dog, not a man.' I think I've cocked up a bit. Before I met Bea for brunch, I had decided that my plan was to abandon seduction lessons, but to get out more by offering to walk dogs. So I signed up and offered to walk Hugo. It is now far too late to cancel. I can't let him down, can I? Combining my activities seems the best of both worlds. One, I won't have an awkward not-a-date OMG-what-is-he-going-to-teach-me encounter with Noah in some bar: we'll be relaxed, out in the fresh air. And two, he can give me some hints and tips on how to meet my perfect first date whilst out walking (my preferred, relaxed, approach to dating). See, I have devised a lesson plan! 'Anyway, what do you mean, lesson 73?' I can't let it drop. 'How many lessons are there?' What am I committing to here?

'I was joking!'

'Thank God for that! Can you warn me when you're being funny, please?'

'I'm that unfunny?' He laughs. He's not unfunny, it's just this feels so intense I'm finding it hard not to take everything he says literally.

'You're brilliant face to face, it's just hard on the phone when I don't know you! You're hilarious, dead funny, is that enough ego stroking?'

'More than enough, I feel all manly and admired again.' I'm not sure if he's being funny in a dry way, or serious now. 'But I wasn't really planning on woo-ing in wellies.'

'Wellies is how I roll,' I say firmly. 'Are you in, or out?'

'Oh I'm in.' He chuckles again, in a very seductive way. Men like Noah just have it too easy; one chuckle, or cheeky grin, or compliment, from a man like him and I'm thinking of rolling over to have my tummy tickled. Life is so unfair. 'You haven't got all this on a list, have you?' His voice is tinged with suspicion.

I ignore him and don't answer.

'Thought so. Well that's one thing I'm going to have to fix! Right then,' briskness has taken over, which means any second now he's going to hang up, which strangely enough makes me feel like I want to keep him talking just a little bit longer, 'what time and place does your list say?'

'Are you free on Saturday morning?'

'I certainly can be!'

'Oh.' Despite the urgency of the situation, and my determination to try this out, he replies so quickly I am wrong-footed. No way out now!

'Ten o'clock in the park?'

'Fantastic, just around the corner from my place. Look forward to it. It's a date!'

And he disconnects before I have time to correct him and point out that it is not actually a *date*, it is more of a business appointment.

Which reminds me. There is one aspect I have to be totally clear about before we meet.

I redial.

'Bloody hell, woman, you're keen!'

If any other man said this, I would be embarrassed and tongue-tied. But this is Noah and I'm getting used to his teasing ways.

'I need to ask you something.'

'Fire away.'

It needs to be said, before this goes any further. 'You're not expensive, are you?'

'What?'

I cringe and hold the phone away from my ear; he said that with some force.

'Bloody hell, Rosie! What do you think I'm offering here? I'm not some sort of gigolo you know!'

'Sorry, sorry, sorry!' I suddenly feel very hot and bothered and have to waft the bottom of my jumper. 'Sorry, I didn't mean that, I didn't say you were!' What am I getting into? 'Gigolos do sex! I don't want sex! I told you!' Even on a phone, when he can't see me, this is embarrassing. I am worse at this than I ever imagined.

'I gathered that last time we met.' His tone is dry but has dropped to a gentler level. 'Of course, I don't want paid. Hang on, that's something else I need to put on the list.'

'What list?'

'You aren't the only one with lists, my girl. This is going on the things Rosie needs list, diplomacy, tact, you know sneaking in there and not being quite so direct. I can take it, but,' he does a low whistle, 'not every man can. We're a sensitive lot you know.'

'Oh yeah, I thought you said something about this being easy?'

'It is,' his warm voice has a hint of laughter in it now; he's obviously forgiven me for my blunder about payment. 'Dating is easy, look at all the dorks that do it! You just need confidence,' he pauses, 'great looks, sense of humour, smart clothes, toned body, stamina, witty repartee, the ability to look interested in the dumbest people, the—'

'Oh God, I told y—'

'Haha, gotcha! I'm kidding, Rosie! But you do need to tone down the whole direct, honest to the point of blunt thing . . . you just need to . . .' he pauses as though he's wary of saying it, 'lighten up a bit?'

'Lighten up! You do know telling somebody to lighten up has the opposite effect? It's like ordering somebody to enjoy themselves!'

'Okay, it came out wrong, but you need to sneak in under the radar, soothe, caress . . .'

'I think I need a lie down.'

'Really?' There's a hopeful edge to his voice.

'On my own! This is exhausting! Are you sure about doing this?'

'Totally. Stop asking.' The way he says it, it's almost like he's here, putting his arm around my shoulders and giving me a reassuring squeeze. Spooky. 'Are you going to bugger off and leave to me to lesson plan in peace now then? I'll see you and your chaperone, Hugo, on Saturday.'

'Certainly.'

'Oh, and Rosie.'

My end-call finger freezes mid-air. 'What?' I whisper, afraid he's going to back out or worse, set some rules I can't work with.

'You've picked Hugo, so I get to pick what we do for lesson 2. Okay?'

'Okay.' I can hear the tremor of anticipation in my voice and sincerely hope he hasn't. I end the call and can't help but smile. This could be fun!

Chapter 6

My phone is buzzing again immediately, and my heart does a little flip. He's forgotten to say something, or he's changed his mind.

Sound breezy, like I don't care either way!

'Hi!'

'Did you do it?' It's not him. Something inside me takes an illogical dive. Why on earth should I be disappointed that it isn't Noah?

I clear my throat and try and smile. A smile shows in your voice apparently. 'You are so nosy, Bea!'

'Oh God, you're upset. He said no!'

'I'm not upset, this is my smiley voice! And why should he say no? What makes you think . . .'

'You sound funny, sad. Oh my God, you sound funny because you did it, you did!' I think *she* might be doing the Disney princess thing now. I'm sure she just clapped her hands. 'You did it and he said yes!'

'Might have.' Bea knows me far too well.

She laughs. 'This is epic, Rosie! Wow! I am well jel. He is such a catch.'

'One, I don't want a catch; he's teaching me not dating me, and two, you can't know he's a catch because we only found one photo of him online!'

'Girl, I only need one photo! That man is hot, I know it! Admit it, he is HOT.'

'Okay,' I say grudgingly, 'I will admit he is attractive.'

'Hot!'

'Okay,' I sigh, dramatically for her benefit. 'If you say so, he's hot.' I suppose if I objectify him and think of him in terms like this, it might help. I can idolise rather than risk fancying him. Like you might fancy your maths teacher but would never, ever even dream about dating him. Because that would be weird.

'You think so too! And you fancy him.'

Bugger. 'I don't fancy him.' It's only a small, unimportant fib. I do fancy him a bit, but only in the way you can have the hots for some totally ripped movie star that you will never, ever meet. 'But if he was actually my type—'

'As in boring, predictable, safe . . .'

I ignore her. She knows me too well. '—and he looked like that then I might do.'

'You'd drag him off to your cave and have your wicked way, admit it!'

'Well he's not my type, so it's irrelevant.'

'Smokin'!'

'Isn't that sexist? Or objectifying him or something?'

'Oh boy no, I'm interested in his brain as well. I bet he's got pillow talk off to a T!' She laughs throatily. Then there's a pause. 'But, hey, seriously, Rosie? He can't be a total player, or we'd have seen loads more piccies of him splashed all over the internet. Serial daters like people to see their success, they put themselves out there, Rosie. He'd be king of the selfies!'

She might have a point. Noah is rather low profile, unlike most unfaithful men (i.e. Dad) who thrive off attention. 'I admit he's good-looking, okay? I'm attracted to him. Satisfied? But he *is* a serial first dater. He told me.' So, even if he likes to keep his private life quiet, he still isn't the type of man I want to actually go out with. 'We're not going to be dating though, so I can handle him,' I say airily, and suddenly realise I have my fingers crossed, so self-consciously uncross them. But I can handle him. I'm sure I can. I think.

He might be the teacher, but I am controlling this – the where and when, the pace and just how far we're going to go with the practical sessions.

I must be crazy. The man is gorgeous, upfront, gorgeous, confident, gorgeous.

Not my type at all.

This could be like agreeing to enter a shark cage just because you want to look at the pretty penguins that they're about to eat.

'Course you can handle him! Can I come over and help you pick an outfit? Or we can go shopping?'

I try not to sigh. 'No, Bea. I know exactly what you'd try and get me to wear, and that leopard-skin print dress you convinced me would turn me into a feline wonder just makes me look like a constipated, overweight moggie. Anyway, I know exactly what I'm going to wear.' Like I said, Bea and I are like sisters – but very different sisters. She is naturally exuberant, totally self-confident and a bit of a risk taker. And I am not.

We're not the type of sisters who would ever raid each other's wardrobes.

'You do?'

'I do.'

'Wow, whatever happened to indecisive dater Rosie? So, what are you going with? That black dress? Oh no, I know, that dress you bought for—'

'Nope.'

'Tell!'

'Well, I'll give you one clue. It involves rubber!'

'Rubber!' She screeches.

I grin, put the phone down and go off in search of my very gorgeous Joules wellies which I haven't had the chance to wear for ages.

Chapter 7

'Y ou must be Rosie! Ophelia, delighted to meet you, darling.'

I have opened my front door and I am pretty sure there's an elegant tall woman with her hand stuck out, but I can't take my eyes off the dog. 'Oh, my golly gosh he's big!' I do not normally talk like this, but faced with a posh lady, who is talking in a posh voice, and is carrying Barbour accessories, I can't seem to help myself. I also can't help that my voice has the squeak of threatening hysteria. Big is the understatement of the century.

It is 9am on a bright and sunny Saturday morning, and I am suddenly hugely relieved that I am meeting Noah. I mean, I do realise that he's there purely on a dating advisory basis, but surely, he can't object to acting as a dog anchor at the same time?

I seriously hope he isn't allergic to dogs or scared of them – although he didn't object when I mentioned Hugo over the phone.

'Big? Oh, good heavens no, dear.' She laughs, rather heartily. 'He's quite small for his breeding,' she puts her hands over his big floppy ears, 'a bit of a disappointment if I'm honest, after the amount of money we spent,' she removes her hands and raises her voice, 'but you're such a darling, quiet as a mouse, aren't you, Hugo? In you go, sweetie.'

Hugo steps inside what, up until now, I've thought of as a reasonably sized hallway, and flops down. He takes up the entire doormat and creates a pony size barrier between me and his mum. He is like a donkey, but without the sticky up ears.

'You'll hardly know he's here!'

He shakes his head and I have to jump back to avoid a drool-shower. My suede boots, lined up neatly under the coat hooks, are never going to be the same again.

I bloody well think I will know he's here.

On paper, Hugo was the man of my dreams. Well-bred, tall, aristocratic and two years old. In real life he's a bit scary. As in scarily ginormous.

I might have made a mistake. I'd signed up for doggie borrowing on impulse, without thinking it through. It had been a bit alarming how quickly I'd had a response, and once I'd said yes, I couldn't back out and say 'well actually I've decided to stick with the man dates', could I? So now I have a potentially disastrous double date. I might have to call Noah and warn him. Or then again that might be a mistake: he might back out.

Maybe everybody needs a Hugo so that they can test out a man's mettle? The Hugo test could be part of my armoury, if I ever get an actual date. If a guy backs down when faced with this, then I know they lack guts and will be crap in an emergency. I'll be abandoned to my own devices. It's not that I want a man to save me, but a bit of teamwork is always good.

'Oh, totally forgot to mention it on the form, but he's scared stiff of umbrellas! I know, incredible, isn't it?' Ophelia guffaws loudly. 'He's such a baby still, aren't you, Hugh-gy woogy? Just hang on tight if you spot one, haw-haw! But you'll be fine, the sun is out. It's so good of you to do this at such short notice; the girl who normally has him has got flu, and the other one has had to work overtime, and I was beginning to panic!' I think she's talking fast so I can't get a word in. A word like 'no'. 'Peregrine was sure I was going to have to miss the first race, and he knows I can't take Hugo with me as he's scared of horses! Isn't that a hoot? Who would have thought it! Honestly, you'd never know his ancestors could bring down a wild boar, would you?' I don't have time to say he's unlikely to be challenged by one of those as she's throwing food and dog accessories in all directions. 'Right, sorry, have to dash, I should be back by ten o'clock. That is okay, isn't it? Oh, you're a star. See you later, Hugo, sweetie. Be a good boy.' She kisses his noble head, reaches over him so she can press his leash into my hand and dashes off to her sleek and polished Jaguar F-Type, which is parked in the no-parking spot. 'Probably needs a wee, we didn't have time for walkies!' She yells out of her window as she's pulling away.

Bugger. How do I get past him to close the door? I step one leg over, and he shifts. For one horrible moment I have a vision of him rising up underneath me, leaving my feet dangling, so I go for it. Shoot over the top and land half in and half out of the door.

'Well hurdled! Didn't know you had a four-legged beastie!' Yells the middle-aged man from next door, who is putting his bins out. He's taken to dressing, and talking, like an army major lately. I'm not quite sure if he's practising method acting (he's in the local am-dram group) or trying to impress the lady who has just moved in three doors down, but it is weird.

'Not mine!' I yell back, retreating on all fours.

'Damned fine specimen. Watch out for rear guard action, m'dear. Might see that pretty backend of yours as an invitation!'

'What?' I roll over, alarmed. But Hugo shows no sign of any kind of action. He has his large head resting on his enormous paws. Drooling jowls flopping down to the floor.

I think I'm going to have to mop the floor as well as the walls once he has gone home.

I take a deep breath and pat his head. He grins up at me, then abruptly struggles to his feet, wags his tail and nearly takes my legs out from under me. Nobody said doggie daycare involved body armour.

Today could be trickier than I thought. Why on earth didn't I stipulate a maximum size of dog? I think my flamboyant, doesn't really matter attitude, might well backfire on me. Though I hadn't planned on anything as big as a Great Dane.

At least it's taking my mind off Noah.

'I was thinking we could get to know each other over breakfast.' Hugo flaps his tail, but this time I successfully dodge. 'But if you need the toilet, I suppose we should go for a walk straight away? We can saunter round for,' I glance at my watch, it's not far off the time I said I'd meet Noah. I can survive that much time solo, surely? 'a little bit before Noah arrives and do our, er, business?' He cocks his head on one side and stares at me with the most gorgeous brown eyes. 'I suspect a Great Dane size wee would flood the kitchen?'

I suddenly feel slightly queasy at the realisation that he might need a number two whilst in my care. Do I need binbag size poo bags?

Chapter 8

I would never, ever classify myself as a tree hugger. No way Jose. I appreciate a forest as much as the next person, but I have no wish to bond with one. Except right now, I am hugging a tree. I blame the fact that it's a lovely day, and the park is crowded. Absolutely heaving, with picnic goers and small children who seem intent on scaring my dog.

He's not even thought about emptying his bladder yet; he's been far too busy trying to spot scary things. Then he spotted a sun parasol and mistook it for an umbrella and bolted. Who knew I could cover 100 metres quicker than you could shout 'for fuck's sake stop!'?

Anyway, he slowed down, and I was just congratulating myself on passing the first test and not letting go of the leash, when a flaming magpie squawked and gave him the evil eye.

I swear it was nought to sixty in less time than it takes to take a breath. And this time we were heading back in the opposite direction. At least we were en-route for the entrance, where I'd arranged to meet Noah – every cloud has a silver lining – it was just the thought of the gate (he might clear it, but those spikes on the top would be my downfall) and

95

the crowded pavement on the other side that was making me lean back with all my force as though I was water ski-ing.

I lunged for one tree as we passed, soil spewing out from my heels, the branch coming off in my hand, so when he slowed down next to a particularly sturdy specimen ten yards away from the boundary, I thought all my prayers had been answered. I'm not religious, but I have been praying, believe me, repeatedly under my breath as I've been carted from one end of the grassy field to the other.

He'd dived around the tree so fast, my instinct had been to grab his ear with my spare hand as he reappeared on the other side. But before you call the pet protection squad, I did slide my fingers down into his collar.

The problem now is the tree is the filling in a dog and Rosie sandwich, and I daren't let go.

If I let go of his collar, and a squirrel coughs or a leaf moves, he might take off again and I'll end up with my face mashed against my saviour tree, or have my other arm ripped out of its socket. Not good.

But no way am I letting go of the end of the leash and risking him shaking free of his collar. I am taking my duties seriously. Losing my first dog within an hour of taking charge of him will see me blacklisted, or blackballed, or something. Nobody will ever let me borrow their doggie again. Though to be honest that sounds like the most brilliant thing ever right now.

Oh God, what am I going to do? I close my eyes, bang my forehead against the bark and regret it. 'Think, Rosie, think!'

'Is this a new game, here we go round the mulberry bush with dogs?'

The First Date

My knees go all wobbly as the familiar deep voice tinged with laughter breaks through my head-banging reverie, and it is not because he is looking more gorgeous than ever (I can only squint at him out of one eye anyway, as the other side of my face is squashed against the tree), it is because I am about to be rescued!

'Oh my God, I am so pleased you're here!'

Before I can object, Noah leans in so close his breath fans my neck and sends goose bumps down my arms and sets up a quiver in the base of my stomach. 'Wow, I knew you'd be a quick learner, flattery will get you everywhere!'

I fight the groan that is threatening to break out. This is terrible. I am stuck; I can't back off or wriggle out of reach. I am stuck between a tree and a dangerous place! People will think we are lovers!

'You're already getting the hang of this,' luckily he backs off slightly and I breathe again, 'and we've not even started. Top marks for that. Let me just make a note.'

'Don't you dare make notes!' I scream as he reaches for a notepad in his back pocket. 'Just rescue me!' He doesn't seem to appreciate the urgency of the situation here.

'Straight on to lesson 2, Rosie, my girl.' He kisses me on the cheek whilst I can't escape. With the exertion and embarrassment, I didn't think it was possible for my cheeks to heat up anymore, but I think they just have. 'Great to see you again.'

There is something wrong here. The whole Hugo thing has left me weak at the knees. I am not going to be weak and feeble; I am not going to beg. I am also not going to kick him in the shin.

I try not to grit my teeth. I try to smile. 'Please help me!'

'Wow, you really are getting good at this stuff!'

'What?'

'Pleading for help, giving me the chance to act all strong and manly. Are you sure you don't mind me taking notes?'

'I am not pleading!' I should have kicked him. I knew I should. Karate Kid all the way. 'Don't you dare write any of this down!'

'I mean,' he sinks down onto his haunches and looks up at me, his head tilted to one side, 'we all love an independent woman, right? But feeling needed, indispensable, well, woo.' He shoots his hand up in the air, and Hugo flinches. 'Ego right up there moment. Me Tarzan!' He winks at me, beats his chest and Hugo trembles. I lock my knees. I am *not* going to wobble. 'Aww mate, sorry.' Noah leans in and fondles his ears, and just like that the tension goes from his big dog body. Hugo has fallen in love.

'So, I take it this is Hugo?'

'Yup.' I'm fine when he's not directing his kisses at me. Absolutely fine. Just a little bit weak.

'And this isn't some weirdo planned game?'

'Nope. Dropping the lesson stuff for a moment and helping would be much appreciated.' I've felt surprisingly more relaxed since he arrived: reassured, but awkward. Like you are if you're wrapped round a tree in public view.

'You got it. Hang on while I work my manly magic.'

'I can't do anything but hang on!'

He chuckles. I'd forgotten what a sexy, disturbing sound it was. Robbie never chuckled like that.

I do actually want to scream out 'hurry up my boob is getting bark rub' but I don't. That would be flirtatious and possibly encourage the type of response I don't have an answer to.

I wish I had a thicker bra on.

'Let go of the end.' Noah gently prises the leash out of my fingers – which seem to have developed the digit equivalent of lockjaw – unwraps Hugo and gently strokes his head, then runs the palm of his hand over his large ears. I wish he'd do that to me. The head bit, not ears, I need soothing. I am more traumatised than Hugo, I'm sure I am.

'Are you a vet or something?' I ask, surreptitiously rubbing my boob as we set off down the path. Hugo has transformed into the perfect pooch. Totally chilled. He is plodding along at Noah's side with not a care in the world. A noisy kid whizzes by on a scooter, dragging a balloon in their wake and he doesn't as much as flinch. Why do some people breeze through life, and the rest of us have to feel as if we're wading through treacle half the time?

'No, an architect,' he says, one eyebrow raised.

'Oh yes, of course you are!' How could I forget the only fact I knew about him? My cheeks, which had chilled down to normal temperature, heat up to a gentle glow.

He winks to soften the blow. 'But one with special animal powers. Just call me Crocodile Dundee!'

'Croc for short? Or do you prefer Dundee?'

'Mmm, think I might stick with Noah. One sounds a bit snappy and the other makes me sound like a fruitcake.'

I grin, feeling a bit more chilled myself. 'With added nuts

on top!' As a kid my nana always bought Dundee cake, and I'd take the nuts off the top. It took longer than eating the cake.

'Sure.' He gives a wry smile. 'Seriously though, my kid sister's always been animal mad. She's a vet now, but when we were kids, she did her best to fill the house up with four-legged furries. Guess getting them on my side was a survival instinct!' We walk on in companionable silence until we reach the gate. 'Do you fancy a coffee, or . . .?'

'Do you mind if we head back? I can make you a drink?'

'Sure.' He smiles. 'Guess the big fella's shaken you up a bit. Not nice being taken for a ride.'

'Nope, not nice at all,' I say, and just like that an image of my dad jumps into my head. It's like a slap in the face, which kind of ruins the happy vibe I'd been feeling.

If I carry on seeing Noah, then I'm heading into shark-infested waters. I don't want to be the sprat that is swallowed whole.

To be honest though, Noah untangled me from the tree pretty quickly. Dad would have still been taking photos of my predicament and sharing them on Twitter. He's also being really gentle and nice and seems genuinely concerned that I'm okay.

'Aww don't be sad.' Noah's arm has snaked round my shoulders somehow and he squeezes me into his side. 'It could be worse!'

It could. 'Ouch!' As hugs go, it was a nice gesture, but bloody painful. My skin smarts all the way down my left side. At least it's given my dad a firm kick up the backside and out of my head!

'Close encounter of the tree kind?'

'Haha you're such a comedian!' We share a grin and I feel myself relax again. Despite the pain. Noah's easy company.

'Moving over to the bark side?'

'Stop!' I cringe and put my hands over my ears. 'No more! Eek, that is seriously bad. Hilarious you are not.'

He gives me a thumbs up. 'Can't beat a bit of Yoda!'

'Whatever, you do promise me you won't give up the day job and move onto stand-up.' He has, however, made me laugh, and forget (well almost) my dad, and my raw, prickly skin.

Oh, bugger my bloody dad. He's done it again. Why can't I just forget about him? Never quite banished. You can guarantee that every time I start to chill a bit he will pop into my head and I'll remember not to get carried away and fall for a charmer.

I guess you could say that my relationship with Dad is complicated. He does and says things sometimes that should make it easy to hate him, but he has a knack of making me feel important (well I bet he does it to everybody he wants to charm) when it suits him. He has always been able to make me feel like I am the centre of his world, that I matter to him. So, when I was a kid, it didn't matter that I was mad at him because he hadn't been home for days, or upset that he'd missed my birthday (again). All of that was forgotten when he turned the charm full on, when he tickled me, or told a funny joke, or laughed in a way that I had to join in with. Or gently smiled, cupped my face in his big, warm hands, looked me straight in the eye and told me he'd always love me.

And now Noah is making me laugh at his ridiculous puns, just like Dad used to do.

And all I can see is that Noah is not for me. That I'm heading for danger if I carry on playing this game.

Except I want to. Well to be honest, I have to if I stand any chance of taking a date to my parents' anniversary party.

I know that Noah is not my type at all, but right now, just at this moment, I'm enjoying forgetting my quest for the right man and just enjoying being with the wrong one.

Really enjoying it.

It's not like being on an awkward date; it's like being with Robbie, but better.

And to be honest, he seems unselfconscious when it comes to his bad jokes. Dad never makes fun of himself. Everything is pretty measured and about making you laugh in the right places – not about making you feel better.

I concentrate on Noah's hand, which is swinging in time with my own. Parallel, not quite touching. Agony and ecstasy, pain and pleasure. Yin and yang. Oh lordy, I'm going all existential. I must be in shock. It must be the pain. And it is going to be a pain, literally. I like to sleep on my left side; my right side doesn't work the same.

'Are you sure you're okay, Rosie? You seem a bit quiet?'

I glance up and he is studying me with his clear grey eyes.

I want to blurt out, don't look at me like that. But instead make do with, 'Don't take your eyes off Hugo! He might bolt.'

'He's fine, aren't you, mate?' He chuckles, and Hugo guffaws back and a bit of normality is restored. 'My sister's still got a right menagerie now. I'm used to them.'

'I thought I was,' I say, then realise I sound a bit sulky. 'I've had lots of dogs, but they usually only come up to my knees, and they're not scared of everything. Hugo is a complete wuss.'

'He's a boy.' He ruffles the hair on the top of his head. 'Needs reassurance,' he winks at me, 'to be kept close. Body contact.'

I try not to meet his eye, and instead look at Hugo. Who is glued to Noah's thigh.

'I thought he'd like a long lead; you know, a bit of freedom.' I see now the error of my ways. A dog on the end of a very long leash is pretty hard to control, unless it is so small you can just reel it in like a fish. I don't think the retract button on an extendable lead would work with Hugo.

I'm beginning to think Dad might have more in common with Hugo than Noah.

'He needs to know you're there for him, don't you, boy?' Hugo looks up and for a moment they stare at each other, complete love-in. I'm beginning to feel a bit jealous.

'Huh, well.' I think I have discovered why Ophelia's other dog-sitters were unavailable – even if Hugo is in fact a big sweetie. Which he is. 'I'm not convinced dog sitting is one of my special skills. It's trickier than man-dating!' I sneak a sideways look at Noah. 'I thought I'd try it instead, dog sitting, doggie borrowing; I thought I might meet somebody nice in the park or something, with a common interest.'

'Hugging trees?' He chuckles, and I punch him lightly in the ribs. Mates-style. 'You did meet somebody nice, me!'

'This is my place,' I say slightly surprised as we slow down near my gate. We've somehow got home without me noticing.

And Hugo hasn't stared at anything with suspicion or threatened to shoot off.

'I know.'

I feel myself blushing. Of course, he knows. He's been here before, when I was drunk, feeling sorry for myself. 'Sorry about that.'

'It was fun, so,' he rubs his hands together, 'I pick the next scenario!' He draws out the word scenario. It makes me smile back at him, forgetting my total embarrassment. He has this knack of knowing the right thing to say, lightening things up. 'You'll never get past the first base with Hugo. He'll be a crap kisser, all drool and big tongue!'

'Eurgh, shut up.' I punch him and laugh; I can't help myself. Even when I'm sober, Noah makes me laugh. A lot. 'I don't want to snog him or you!'

'Well, here you go.' He hands the end of the leash over. Hugo sits down and looks up at him, then at me, then back at Noah. He doesn't want him to go. Noah does something I've failed at: gives him confidence.

'Thanks.' I unlock the door but don't step inside. I'm not sure I'm ready to let Noah go either. 'I'm sorry we didn't get much time for, you know . . .'

'Seduction techniques?' He's got the most gorgeous dimples. How come I've not noticed them before? Grrr! I've not noticed them before because I don't want, I must not, notice things like this. We have a business arrangement. 'Don't worry, it gave me a bit of,' he pauses, eyes twinkling, 'insight!'

I take a deep breath. This bit is trickier now we've drawn to a halt. In my head 'come in for a coffee' was easy as we walked back. But I've now hit that awkward silence on the doorstep. The one that is scared of letting him in to my house, letting him see 'me'. I take a gulp and go for it. 'You fancy that drink?'

'Look, Rosie.' He rests his hand on my arm. 'You don't have to do this you know.' He shrugs. 'But it could be fun.'

'I know.' Oh lordie, this is embarrassing. 'But I want to.' I think. 'I have to,' I blurt out before I can stop myself.

'Have to?'

In for a penny, in for a pound as they say. 'I need a date for my parents' wedding anniversary party. I told Mum I had a boyfriend,' Noah raises an eyebrow, but I crash on, 'and she'll tell my dad.'

'Ahh, your dad. You can't do this just for your dad, Rosie.' His tone is soft. His gaze is soft.

'I'm not, I'm doing it for me.' My voice has gone wobbly.

'Well that's fine then.' He reaches up. He's going to touch me, he's so close. He's going to do that fingers along the cheek thing they do in the movies, then tangle his fingers in my hair and . . . 'Twigs in the hair might work for some, but it's a bit of a niche audience.' He holds up a leaf and grins, but it's a grin with soft edges that match the tone of his voice and makes me feel even more awkward than I did before, if that's possible. 'Lumberjacks, tree protesters, hobbits maybe.'

I gulp, try and clear my throat. 'Not many of them round here. Hobbits that is. There's a very nice tree surgeon in—' I'm rambling to fill the silence that I'm expecting any minute, but he puts a finger on my lips, so I freeze.

'What are you afraid of?'

'Nothing,' I squeak. But I am. I'm petrified that if he touches me, I'll end up crushing on the wrong guy. This would be the worst kind of failure. I do not want to discover that I have been conditioned to fall for somebody like my dad, that I'm going to repeat the pattern of behaviour I've seen as I've grown up.

If I get this wrong now, not only will the chance of taking a date to the party be doomed – so will I. Well, maybe not doomed. But it is not going to happen.

'Shall we start again? You know, in a conventional kind of setting. You, me, man, woman.'

Hugo groans and flops down. 'No dog?' I bite the inside of my cheek. I need a prop. What do I use if I can't have a dog?

'No dog. Let's hit this head on, off the nursery slope, straight onto the black run.'

I never did fancy ski-ing.

'Stop avoiding me, Rosie.' His voice is soft. 'I'm not the one making you do anything. Skip out if you want, it's your life.' He holds his hands up in surrender.

I don't want to skip out; I don't want him to walk out and not see the best of me. Oh bugger, why am I thinking like this? I'm doing exactly what I've always done with Dad – desperately wanted him to see the best of me. Tried to please him.

Take a deep breath, Rosie. You are not doing this so Noah can see the best of you. You are doing this for yourself. Because you can do this.

It is my life. And I'm not too stupid to ignore the fact that right now it's a life that needs a bit of added-spice, and a companion – but not of the four-legged furry type.

'Tomorrow?' My heart is pounding like billy-o.

'Oh, afraid I've got . . .' He looks uncomfortable.

'A date?' Gulp! Why does that make me come over all possessive? He's allowed dates, I'm allowed dates, that's the point!

'To see my mate.' He suddenly looks all deflated and sad. 'It's the anniversary of his wife's death.' Noah blinks; he's looking my way, but not at me any longer. He's looking into the distance. 'I don't like him to be on his own,' then the moment passes as he snaps himself out of it and gives a crooked smile, 'bloody miserable company though, he's a real sad sod.'

'Oh.' I try not to be relieved that he's seeing his friend. That's horrible, being pleased when his poor friend is heartbroken. 'I hope he's okay.'

He shrugs, and I want to hug him. Not because I'm pleased that he's not proper dating, but because he cares about his friend. The lump in my throat catches me by surprise. This is a side of Noah that is nothing like my dad. My father wouldn't put himself out like this. He's a good-time boy, like I'd presumed Noah was. Out to have a great time, but never sticking around for the bad times.

'He's a bit broken.' That twisted smile flashes briefly again. 'That's what love does for you. Anyway, Thursday?'

'You're not busy, you know, proper dates?'

'I can fit them in Wednesday or Friday.' He winks. Not funny. See, what did I say about not being impressed by winks?

'You are okay? Sure?'

I think he has mistaken my silent, and totally inappropriate, simmering for dog-induced trauma. It is not that at all. I am in shock. Shock that I am the slightest bit bothered about him dating alongside our tutorials. Which is ridiculous. Why should I care? In fact, it is a bonus. He obviously doesn't fancy me, and so all my fears about pretend-dating the wrong kind of man are groundless. I am safe. Phew.

But also slightly miffed. Why doesn't he fancy me at least a tiny bit? Am I really that unattractive that even a serial first dater (who, let's face it, must get through a helluva lot of dates) isn't interested? Huh!

'I don't need to check you over for damage?' He raises both eyebrows suggestively, his dimples deepening.

'You never stop, do you!' I grin at him; I can't help myself. Maybe he does find me just a teeny-weeny bit attractive after all. He shakes his head, then pats Hugo.

'Noah?' I stop him on impulse, about to ask him why he's doing this.

He pauses. Raises an eyebrow.

I can't do it. I can't ask because I don't want to hear an answer that might be crushing and will make me slam the door and never dare date again.

'Thursday?'

'Thursday. I'll text you the details!'

'What? You can't . . .! You need to tell me.' He starts to step backwards down the path, away from me. Smiling. 'I don't like surprises!'

'My turn!'

'Don't be mean! Give me a clue? Where?'

The First Date

'Laters! Oh, and Rosie, if you haven't got a date sorted for that party, I can always step in!' He winks, waves a hand and is gone.

Hugo stands up, shakes and strolls into the house as though it is his home.

I push the door firmly shut and lean against it. What have I done?

Then I look at my phone. I could cancel! No, I can't cancel. I can handle this. I can.

Hugo barks. When I look, he wags his tail then sits down looking very pleased with himself.

Why am I doing this? I stare at my reflection in the hall mirror, and I do know deep down, even if I won't say it out loud. It's not just the party, or my dad.

I *like* the idea of being in a relationship. And I like being in love. I miss it. I don't want to just watch it on Netflix, or read about it, I want to do it. I want to fall in love.

'Am I mad?' I go in search of Hugo, who has flopped out on my sofa, and left me a tiny corner to squeeze into. 'I know I have to get a date for the party, but I really want a boyfriend again.' I fondle his ears. Like Noah did. It seems to work: he sighs. 'Am I being pathetic? Is it just FOMO?' Hugo cocks his head. 'Do I really want a date or am I just scared I'm missing out?' He rests his large head on my lap. 'Oh my God, Hugo. I've just agreed to meet up with a serial dater again! Twice!' I feel a bit sick. But I think it's excited sick. Jittery, nervous, can't sit still kind of sick – not head in a toilet bowl. 'Would I be better off staying safe, finding the right dog?' He wags his tail lazily, with a thump, thump, thump. 'You do realise this is all your fault? If you hadn't liked him so much, I wouldn't be doing this. I trusted you!' There's a loud slightly disturbing noise from my lap, and a woomph of warm air towards my crotch. Hugo is asleep, snoring and blowing bubbles between my thighs.

I edge up, trying not to disturb him.

Hugo is lovely, and I like dogs, but really? Am I really ready to skip snogs and cuddles from a sexy man? I guess the answer is no.

It's probably impossible to find the love of my life before the party, but once it is done and dusted, I will politely dump my desperate date and use everything Noah is about to teach me to find the man of my dreams.

Watch out world, Rosie Brown is about to find out what a man really wants!

Chapter 9

I went to bed feeling very positive and determined and woke up humming to myself as I brushed my teeth and made a coffee.

The door slams behind me and I practically dance down the street on my way to work. I've got this. I have a plan.

Stage 1 is to learn how to first date and with Noah's help nab a man before the party. I will not have to resort to taking Noah, despite his kind offer.

He's too easy to like, which makes him dangerous. And what makes being with him even more dangerous is that while I was lying awake in bed last night it dawned on me that although he reminds me of Dad in tons of ways, he's also different in quite a few lovely ways. He seems to genuinely care about people for one, and he also seems to quite like me as I am. But letting myself fall for a man who loves his carefree life and having fun would be bad for me. So I am not going to let it happen. Introducing him to my parents would be a massive mistake. And Dad probably wouldn't like him anyway, as they're so similar.

Bugger. Dad. I don't care whether he does or doesn't like

my boyfriends. I have to stop thinking this way. I've spent too much of my life trying to please him.

Except I do care.

Anyway, Stage 1 is about letting Noah teach me how to get a date, then getting one. Before the party.

Stage 2 is about using my new-found skills to find the right man. A man I really want to be with. Obviously, this might take time, but that is fine.

My mobile beeps as I'm putting my handbag in the back room of the bookshop.

Morning, sexy lady! This is your sex god calling!'

I can't help the smile that teases at the corners of my mouth. There's a pause, then a second text.

Noah, in case you were wondering!'

I laugh. I can't help it; he has that effect on me.

'Good morning, Noah. I did realise! Rosie.'
'I need help! Noah'
'Don't you just!'

I add a smiley to show I'm joking.

'Haha very funny! ☺ Look, I need to get something straight in my head here. You keep (again and again) telling me I'm not your type (soul-destroying, but I'm trying to cope). So

what is your type? What kind of man are we after? Noah'
'ps still can't believe I'm not your type, I'm everybody's
dream!! Noah'

   'So glad you asked! I want somebody who likes me as
I am, solid job, kind, wants to plan for the future.'

I'm sure he's getting the gist by now, but just in case he
isn't . . .

'Not interested in charm, don't want somebody who flirts
with other people, or men who spend more time in the
bathroom than me (not long). Don't need flamboyant
gestures or exotic holidays.'

I just want to be loved and love back. But I can't say that.
There is a long pause after I hit send.

   'Wow!'

I am not sure if this is a good wow, or a bad wow.

   'Somebody who wants to commit.'

I add for good measure, just in case there is any doubt in
his mind. There is another long pause. Maybe I've overdone
it and scared him off. Bugger. I really need him to help me.

'Long term this is! Short term, I'm looking for a few fun
first dates to get me on the right track.'

'Are you sure you want safe, secure, boring??!! You're fun, clever and full of life!'

I am just starting to type a reply, saying that flattery will get him nowhere and what's fun now might not turn out to be after the wedding bells have chimed, and that some people do believe in deep, honest love that doesn't necessarily jingle their innermost organs and give them palpitations, when there's a new text.

Dad.

Why does my heart sink before I've even read it? It's not right, is it? This is so different to the excited feeling of anticipation I had when I spotted that Noah had texted.

'Thought about a makeover?'

Straight for the jugular, don't mess about with niceties, Dad!

'Less provincial bookworm, more interesting catch. Dad x'

For all his faults and similarities to Dad, I can't ever imagine Noah sending me a message like this.

What?! I glare at the message.

'Sorry? R x'

Maybe he meant to send it to somebody else.

'You can be a bit off-putting. Too, how do I put this,

strident? Challenging? A new sexier image could help. Try a bit harder! Just a thought! Dad x'

Strident, challenging? Try a bit harder?

'I'm not a fish, I'm not a catch! R x'

His next text starts with a crying with laughter emoticon.

'Not yet you're not! Get your skates on, darling! Only trying to help. Dad x'

There's another laughing emoticon after the 'skates'. I hate him.

'Love you, darling, must dash. Conductor has his baton poised. X'

Does he love me? Do I love him? How can a relationship with your dad be so screwed up? I've always tried to please him; I've always thought that if I tried harder, if I was better, if I was the daughter that he really wanted then he'd come home. Spend more time with me, with us. I guess I'm still harbouring that stupid, childlike dream.

'Everything okay in there?' Yells Bea. 'I've got you a coffee!'

'Out in a sec.' Dad thinks I'm too loud, too boring, and now apparently too staid and unsexy. I'm also going to get the sack if I don't actually start work soon.

My phone rings. Despite myself, I can't ignore it. Maybe he's going to apologise, tell me I am okay as I am after all.

'Rosie? Everything okay? You didn't text back.' *Noah*. 'Did I say the wrong thing?' I can hear the smile in his voice, and it makes me want to cry. 'Overstep the mark?'

'Apparently,' my voice is slightly shaky, 'what I think I need isn't important. I need to be somebody different altogether. I need to find myself like Robbie did, haha.'

'Rosie, what's happened? Where's the bubbly Rosie I know and love?'

'Being bubbly is half the problem, the other half is my appearance.'

There is quiet and for a moment I think he has rung off. 'Your dad again?'

'How did you guess?' I sigh. How can he be so perceptive? How can he just know? 'He messaged with a few home truths.'

'Oh.' There's a whole lot of 'knowing' in that one syllable. 'And?' His voice has an edge I haven't heard before.

'He asked if I'd thought about a makeover to make myself look more attractive, sexier . . .'

'Rosie,' his tone is gentle. My eyes well up. I mustn't cry, I really must not. I have customers to deal with, and I'm being silly. 'I think you're totally fine, more than fine, perfect, exactly as you are. You just need to see the girl I see and believe in her. Listen to me, I'm your resident expert, remember?'

He's trying to make me feel better, to smile. It works.

'It's what makes *you* feel good, Rosie. Not what I think, not your dad. You! Yeah?'

'Yeah.' I repeat in a small voice.

'You just kicked off your list saying you wanted somebody who liked you as you are. So, do you?'

'Do I what?'

'Do you like yourself as you are? Do you feel good about yourself?'

'Well yeah, well no, well I don't bloody know!'

'Maybe that's what we need to talk about, who you are, not who you want this ideal man to be.'

'Sounds complicated to me.' I sigh. I'm tired. This whole relationship is hard work, even when I've not really started. 'Look, sorry, I need to go. I'm supposed to be working. It's not fair on Bea.'

'Sure.' His voice is soft, the nearest thing to a hug I can imagine. It's making me feel sorry for myself again, so I bite down on my lip hard. 'I'll catch up with you later then, okay? You are okay?'

'I'm fine. Don't worry, I am, really. He's always like that, he doesn't mean to upset me, it's my fault.'

'Rosie, it is not your fault!' In my head I can practically see him rolling his eyes. 'You're lovely, you really should be proud of who you are,' there's another pause, 'and so should he.'

Oh God, he is *so* nice it is making me sniff. If I ever feel the urge to date a charmer, he'll be top of the list. 'I do have to go.'

'I know.'

Bea doesn't say anything when I finally step into the shop and target a pile of books that need sorting. She ignores my flushed face and just raises an eyebrow. I nod and smile weakly. She knows what I'm like after a message from Dad.

* * *

'Somebody,' Bea says, just as I am trying to decide which of the Tolkien covers deserves pride of place in the display, and I'm still debating whether I do like myself just as I am, 'is asking for you.'

'Hang on a sec.' Am I happy? Do I feel good about myself? It's not something I've really thought about. I've just drifted on. Tried to ignore Dad's barbs, been soothed by Robbie's casual acceptance.

'Rosie!' She sounds unusually impatient for Bea.

'I said hang on! I'm coming down in a sec.'

'Really, you're saying hang on when *that* is calling your name?'

The way she says 'that' makes me twist round on the step-ladder, and I nearly fall off my perch. Not because she is fanning herself and making wide-eyes (I have excellent peripheral vision), or because she is mouthing 'is it him?' I am feeling like somebody has turned me upside down and is shaking me because it *is* him. Noah.

'Hey!' He winks.

Bea puffs up like a cat that's about to wind herself round his long legs and smiles as though he's said 'hey' to her and not me. 'And hey to you too!'

Where the hell has that sultry voice come from?

Oh my God, it really is Noah and he's about to talk to, or more likely be pounced on by, Bea.

I'm in such a hurry to get between the two of them that I dismount in much the same way a fireman goes down a pole and end up staggering around, still clutching J.R.R. 'Here.' I throw it at Bea and rush towards him, making herding gestures until I've got him cornered next to 'Software for Geeks'.

'What are you doing here?' It comes out as a bit of a hiss. 'You can't be here!'

'Ah, but I am. You didn't answer my last message!' He wags a finger at me and looks very amused.

'The message you sent about two minutes ago?' I'd felt my phone vibrate whilst I'd been shifting Harry Potter to a more prominent position. 'I was up a ladder!'

'That's the one.'

'I haven't had time to read that. Don't you have any houses to build or anything? It's not Thursday yet!' I need time to prepare in my head. He can't just be, well, spontaneous!

I suddenly realise he has stopped talking and is studying me intently with a concerned look on his face. I shut up.

When he speaks, his tone has lost its earlier teasing quality. 'I was worried about you.'

'You don't need to—'

'I know I don't need to. I just was! You sounded really down, subdued.' His tone is so gentle, and his gaze so steady, it's making me feel all tearful again. This is not good, feeling tearful. I am used to standing up for myself and coping, not crying because somebody is being kind.

'I'm fine. How can you think that, just from a quick phone call?'

'One of my superpowers.' His eyes are twinkling again; there's a ghost of a grin hanging round his mouth. He's trying to cheer me up. 'Am I right, or . . .'

'Don't you dare start that again!' I can't help but smile back at him though.

'That's what I like to see! My feisty Rosie is back again.

119

Right, I've got a free hour, so why don't I start to rebuild you instead of some derelict building?'

'Rebuild?!' I've gone a bit screechy. He's beginning to sound like Dad. I have also just spotted Bea creeping closer. 'Out, out, now!' I've got him by the front of his T-shirt, and he allows himself to be dragged towards the door. I scowl at him and fold my arms. 'Right, I thought you said this was about confidence!'

'It is!' He touches my elbow briefly. 'I'm not talking about changing you, Rosie, I'm talking about changing the way you see yourself.' I squirm under his steady gaze. 'Everybody else sees the person that *you* choose to see; if you know you're great, and you love yourself just as you are, then so will they.' He winks. 'Works for me.'

'So why doesn't my dad?' The words are out before I can stop them.

'Because he's a shit who just wants to mould the world around himself?'

'You can't call him a shit! You don't even know him.'

He shakes his head, holds his hands up. 'It was a question. But hey, I'm not your boyfriend, I'm not family, so I can say what I see, can't I?' He pauses. I don't say anything. I don't know what to say. 'For fuck's sake, Rosie!'

I blanch. I've not really heard Noah get angry or swear like that.

'Sorry, sorry, I just don't get why anybody would try and . . .'

'Yes?'

'Undermine you like that, let alone your own bloody dad! Aren't parents supposed to look after you?'

'He doesn't mean . . . you don't understand, you don't know him.'

'No, I don't.' He sighs. 'Don't do this for him, Rosie, don't go trying to get a date, or think you need to be glam for your dad. Do it for you, do what you want to do. Eh?'

'I'm not doing it for him,' I mutter. But in my heart, I know Noah's got a point. And if I batter him with the nearest Jamie Oliver cookbook and chase him out of the shop for daring to say what he thinks, then my hopes of a date for the party are zilch, and even the chances of a date before this time next year are severely diminished. 'Fine, yes, sure. I am.' I unhand him. Straighten the front of his clothing. Pat him down, then stop abruptly when I realise people going into the shop are staring. 'So, how are you planning on changing me? Are you going to tell me I'm,' I wince, 'more stay-at-home bookworm than sexy seductress?' If he says 'yes' I might have to sack him on the spot. However kind he has been.

'No, I'm not! Why the hell would I say that?'

'Well some people might,' I say huffily. 'I'm probably not making the most of myself, because I like—' I look down at my sensible flats, 'being a bookworm.' Dad might have had a point. Dress to impress has only been for special occasions for me. 'And I am at work, in a bookshop.'

'Which is perfect, it's you! I'm not planning on changing you. If there is going to be any change at all, you're going to do it.' Noah is giving me a quizzical look, as though he's not sure where I'm going with this. He's not the only one.

'But maybe it's not me.' I sigh. 'Maybe I don't feel one hundred per cent happy with myself.' This is what time up a ladder with Tolkien does for you. 'Maybe I don't always like myself just as I am.'

'Okay, so ignoring what anybody might say to you. If you could wear anything you want, do your hair how you want, whatever . . . what would you do?'

I stare at him. He looks straight back.

My mind is completely blank.

What would I do? I've spent most of my life trying to be what I think Dad wants me to be. I've never really stopped to wonder what I actually want myself.

But Noah is telling me that this isn't about changing myself for Dad, or possible dates, this is about whether or not I'd actually quite like to change myself for *me*.

I look at Noah, who is waiting patiently. And being buffeted by customers pushing their way in and out of the shop.

In my teens I used to spend hours flicking through magazines, looking at the latest trends, the wild fashion shoots. Wondering what I'd look like with green hair and a black leather jacket. I did it in my early twenties as well. Not the green hair thing, but I still loved the magazines.

Then somehow it stopped. I flicked on past the handbags and shoes pages: I couldn't afford it. I bought soft furnishings with Robbie instead. Invested in our future, ha!

'The more outrageous the better!'

A little flicker of something strange tickles at my insides. It's like the feeling I had as a kid, just before I was allowed to start opening my Christmas presents. Anticipation.

'I'm not sure, I might need to window shop!'

'Your wish is my command.' He chuckles and bows.

'I quite fancy a bit of remodelling; no structural work though!'

'Fantastic!' He rubs his hands together. 'I can't wait. Let's find out who Rosie really is! I've got an hour, lead the way, let's shop!' Then he frowns at me. 'We'll examine the rest of your man-requirements another time,' he says darkly, which sounds ominous.

'What do you mean?'

'All that boring shit about steady job, clean chin, flosses twice a day.'

'I did not say that!'

'Close enough! Oh Rosie, Rosie, Rosie, you want the right guy, not some make-believe . . .' He stops himself short, probably because he has seen the look of disbelief on my face. 'Okay, okay, that's for another time. Lead me to the shops!'

'But I'm work—'

'You must get a lunchbreak!'

'I've only just started, it's nowhere near lunchtime!' I'm torn, I would actually quite like to go shopping. It's kind of exciting, being with somebody who doesn't have any preconceptions, or expectations. Somebody who thinks anything is possible. But I'm supposed to be working.

'Coffee break?'

'She does, she does. Off you go.' Bea has caught up with us. 'I'll hold the fort.'

I look at Noah. Hesitate.

'Go!' Bea has booted us out of the doorway and pulled it firmly shut behind us. We turn round and then I glance back. She is wiping her brow with the back of her hand, then does a dramatic swoon. I can't help myself. I snigger.

123

'And I thought *you* were weird!' Noah chuckles. 'Come on, call this lesson 2. Riotous Rosie rediscovered!'

'I hate to disappoint you, but I've never been riotous.' I think about the black leather jacket and green hair.

'I bet you have,' he taps the side of his head, 'in here! Right where do you want to start?'

'Small? Something not too noticeable.' Then I'll work up the courage to go wild.

'I've got just the thing! Start at the bottom and work up as they say!'

I hope this doesn't mean high heels. I can't do high heels; they make my bottom stick out and my legs go rigid.

'Oh, and I've come prepared,' Noah continues, unaware of my fear of footwear.

'You thought I'd say yes!'

'I knew you'd say yes. I'm irresistible!' He grins, dips into his pocket and pulls out a slightly squashed chicken wrap. 'Here's lunch. Never say I don't give you anything.'

I sigh. 'Okay, I'm all yours.'

He chuckles. 'Well I never thought I'd hear you say that!'

'Stop it.' I give him my severe look but feel a little bit – as my gran would say – chuffed. 'You know what I mean. Lead the way.'

We've taken approximately fifteen steps, I've only taken one and a half bites of my wrap, when he stops.

'Oh my God, no!' I splutter a mouthful of Southern fried chicken in all directions, and a dog leaps at my hand – which has dropped to my side. 'Shit!'

'What?' Noah blinks at me.

'That bugger took half of my lunch!' I swear that bloody animal winked at me, before trotting on alongside his owner, who is totally oblivious to the fact that she has the canine equivalent of the artful dodger in tow.

'Never mind, I'll get you another one, after we've . . .'

'No way, I did not mean that! I am not going in there. Is this what you meant by riotous? You have so got the wrong girl!' I dig my heels in and gesture at the shop window. Wherever my search for self-confidence had been taking me, it was not here – a lingerie shop. 'It's that shop! Nope, big no.'

Noah carried on walking after I'd stopped, and we're now stretched at arm's length. Did I mention the fact that he'd taken hold of my hand just after he'd handed over lunch? Well, to be honest I'd hardly registered it, well I had registered it, but not in a horrified 'oh gawd, what's he doing, how do I react? Is my hand sweaty?' kind of way. It had just felt natural, fine. Until now. He tugs gently, persuasively. I don't want to be persuaded. I tug back, then try and shake myself free. 'Forget it. I am NOT going in there with you.'

He frowns. 'But you said start with something small! And, we should start at the bottom.' He waggles his eyebrows. 'I thought this was perfect! You're not telling me you don't wear undies?' His eyes are positively twinkling, deep dimples frame his mouth. I stop myself staring.

'Of course, I wear knickers! I don't wear them with you, no, no I don't mean that!' He's enjoying this far too much. 'I don't buy them when you're there, and I don't go in shops like that!' My knicker buying is online, from the privacy of my bedroom – or from Marks and Spencer or Matalan – multi-pack bikini style. Tried and trusted. 'I was thinking jewellery when I said start with something small!'

'You're kidding me.' His face falls, puppy-dog style. 'Confidence starts from within, and this is as close to within as I'm going to—'

'Stop it!'

'Can't you just go and browse for—'

'No!'

'You're such a spoilsport.' He heaves a sigh of resignation and I'm not sure if he's genuinely upset or winding me up. 'This was the fantasy part.'

'It's about my fantasies not yours!'

'I don't even have to see them on, off is fine, it's just the thought . . .' I growl at him. 'Okay, okay.'

'Hey, Noah!'

Shit, the door of the shop is open and we're being waved at rather vigorously by a girl with immovable boobs (good advert for the job), perfect lipstick, perfect eyebrows and even more perfect flicky eyeliner.

I need to point out at this point that this is no discount knicker store. This is the works, the type of place I normally sidle past and pretend not to look. The one time I did look and leaned in closer to look at the quite pretty camisole top (wondering if Robbie might appreciate a bit of Christmas glamour), the accompanying price tag made me hyperventilate. I'd been thinking 'there's not much to it, but I don't mind stretching to a tenner', reality was I'd have had to cancel the hairdresser, my festive nails and most possibly the turkey. We'd have been left with stuffing, sprouts and a sexy top he might not have even noticed.

This is an expensive, silk and satin, flimsy lace, red and black stuff type of lingerie shop. The type where glamorous assistants insist on measuring you and pulling 'I wouldn't if I were you' faces when you eye up anything skimpy, before they offer the type of bra that could keep a blancmange immobile for the duration of a 100 metre hurdle sprint.

'Are you coming in?' This is getting awkward. Miss Perfect boobs and eyebrows is waiting.

Noah raises a questioning eyebrow at me.

'You go if you want, I'll er go and look at shoes next door. I like shoes!' I say brightly.

'What?'

'My inner self is not lurking in my crotch,' I hiss at him, while trying to smile at the girl, 'nobody is going to see my . . .'

'Really?' He looks shocked. 'But I thought that was the point?'

'Not the whole point.' But maybe it is.

'Come on.' He tries to tempt me over the threshold as though I'm an unwilling puppy. 'It's my favourite shop!'

That figures. I scowl at him. The most daring I've been in the past, when it came to knicker choices, was to go for black and a hint of lace. If you've been with the same guy since puberty, spending this kind of money on sexy undies isn't really on the agenda – a new sofa seems more important.

'Aww please.' She smiles at me. 'I'm Rach, by the way.' She looks from Noah to me and back again. 'I want to see what you think about this stuff I was thinking of getting for my wedding anniversary, but I wasn't sure if it was too much.' She grins at me. 'Don't want to give Darren a heart attack! I need a second opinion.'

I glance at Noah, who has actually gone a bit of a funny colour. Bloody hell, he's blushing! Which makes me giggle. And it makes my mind up. Despite all the flirty comments, if undies can make him blush then he can't be a complete womaniser, can he?

And then I think about that Christmas. The one time I did nearly go in this shop. I'd wanted to because I'd thought that camisole was going to make me feel sexy, desirable.

And then common sense had won the day.

'Okay.' I take a deep breath. This feeling good about myself could seriously damage my bank balance. Then I hold up a hand to block Noah. 'Not you. You can sit over there on that bench.'

'I'll bring you a coffee, babe.' Rach laughs out loud at him. 'Looks like you've finally met your match, Noah!'

'Oh no, no, he's not met his match,' I follow her in, trying to explain, 'we're not a couple. We're just—' Oh flip, we're just what? I can't explain to a complete stranger! 'Friends, we're friends.'

Rach isn't listening. She is standing next to a display of very flimsy undergarments which she grabs and waves in the air.

'Oh, I don't think those will . . .' I suddenly realise I'm boosting my boobs up in my hands, 'work,' I say, letting go abruptly and feeling my skin heat up.

'Ahh but they're Noah's favourites, aren't they?' She frowns. 'I wouldn't know, like I said, I'm not, we're not . . . I'm not sure they're me.'

'You'd be surprised how much of a firm hold you'll get.' Rach carries on. I'm not sure if her comment is a double entendre, or just praise for the manufacturing standards. 'Look what they've done for me!' She jiggles her own rather ample chest and I have to admit to being impressed. If they can hold that, they can certainly cope with my offering.

'Might be a bit of overkill for me.' I edge off to look at something that has caught my eye.

You'd have to be colour blind for it not to have done.

'Wow, this red is so, red.' I touch the nearest satin bra tentatively, and my fingertip slides across the luxurious material in such a way that leaves me unable to resist. I need to feel it properly. I don't know about seduction, I wouldn't be able to keep my hands off myself if I bought this. 'Oh my God, this is far too nice to let somebody rip off!' Just the thought of the beautiful bra being flung onto the floor in a heap is horrible, but the sound of ripping would kill dead any lustful thoughts I'm sure of it. I'd be out of bed and trying to work out if there really was such a thing as invisible seams. 'I can't.' I can hear the longing in my voice. I want to. I really want to.

Luckily the ping of my phone cuts in. Unluckily it is Noah.

'You can't buy that!'

How the hell? I stare at the text, then spin round and he's at the window.

129

'Have you turned into a dirty old man!' I've flung the shop door open and am yelling out of it before I can stop myself. People stare. So I grab him and drag him in.

'Oh, I can come in now?'

'No! This is temporary, you're out again in a moment! You can't look through the window like that. There's names for people like you!'

'Horny?'

'Stop it! Has anybody ever told you what an infuriating man you are?'

'Infuriating, sexy, good-looking.' He winks. 'Helpful?'

'No, you are not helping. Why can't you go and sit on the bench? I've only been in here for two minutes!'

'Well one, I'm not a dog, you can't just tell me to sit.' Reasonable. 'Two, you've been in here at least ten minutes and don't seem to be getting anywhere.' I glare. 'And three, I just came to see what had happened to that coffee, and I couldn't help . . .' He grins. 'You can't blame a man for looking!'

Rach hands him a mug of coffee. 'I love this girl, Noah. Love her!'

I'm about to launch into an explanation of the situation again, when it dawns on me that I'll be wasting my breath. Instead I wave my mobile at him. 'What do you mean, I can't buy that?'

All of a sudden, I really do want to buy that lingerie, more than I've ever wanted to buy an undergarment in my life. I'm tempted to clutch it to my chest and refuse to let go. 'Why not?'

Noah laughs. 'Pink.'

I frown.

'You need pink, not red.'

'I want red!' It really is the most gorgeous colour. 'I thought we were after seductress.'

'Are you two setting up an escort agency?' Rach has folded her arms and is watching us with a bemused look on her face. Noah ignores her.

'More temptress.' He waggles a finger at me. 'Don't want you to scare them off, do we?'

'I'm not scary!'

'You're awesome, but you don't take prisoners, do you, Rosie-Posie?'

I roll my eyes. 'Please don't call me that, or I'll call you.' Why don't many words rhyme with Noah? 'Or I'll think of something!'

'Just call me Mr Wonderful. Now come on, hurry up and get your knickers off,' he looks at his watch, 'we've got a lot to cram in.'

Rach chuckles, I glow like a well-prepared barbecue, and Noah takes a sip of coffee.

'Not too scary, remember? You're far too big a personality to need red. Red is for the meek and mild.'

'Really? That doesn't sound right! Nobody meek would wear . . .'

'Pink. Believe me.' His voice has a firm edge; it sounds pretty seductive actually. He takes a step closer and studies me with a dark, smoky gaze that makes me feel a bit topsy-turvy. He puts a finger under my chin, so that I can't help but stare back into his eyes. 'You've still got to be you, Rosie.

Honestly, this isn't about me getting my kicks from knowing you've got new knickers, it's about you feeling good. Don't sexy knickers make you feel, well, sexy? Pampered?'

I nod. My vocal cords don't seem to be working.

He makes me feel sexy. Pampered. He makes me feel like what I want, who I am, matters.

'Good.' His voice has a husky edge that makes me shiver inside.

We stare at each other for a moment. My throat is parched. 'Pink?' I dampen my dry lips.

'Pink.' Oh my, how can a voice be that sexy?

My heart is hammering, and his eyes seem to be getting darker by the second.

I can imagine his finger sliding down my neck, straying along my breastbone. There's a prickle of awareness down my spine and I can practically feel the heat of his touch.

I want to flap my top and let some air in, but I can't move.

Oh my God, what if he kisses me now?

'Good, great, glad we go that sorted out. I'll wait outside.' He nods, then rather abruptly breaks eye contact, spins round and heads towards the bench, pausing to look over his shoulder. 'Tell me when you've picked.' The soft tone has gone, we're all business again, and I feel strangely abandoned.

It's weird, like he's thrown a bucket of cold water over things. Just as I was starting to get into the whole sexy undies thing. Rach is an expert though, she knows just what will work.

'What *have* you done to him?'

'Er, nothing. We're not going out, we're friends, kind of.'

Why did I start this? It's far too complicated to explain but I need to make that clear. I am not a girlfriend he is treating to new knickers that he will enjoy ripping off. I am also not investing in a brothel. I am investing in a makeover that other men will benefit from.

I am investing in *me*. I try on the pink undies. They caress my skin, boost my boobs and make me feel, well, special.

Annoyingly, Noah is right. The pink suits my skin tone. They are me.

I have an impulsive urge to rush out and show him. But I don't. I give them one last stroke before they're popped into a bag.

* * *

'Oh my God you've got legs!' And just like that, the jokey version of Noah is back, and it is so unexpected and nice it makes me grin. There are definitely certain sides to him that are nothing at all like my dad.

'I'd fall over otherwise!' I grin, then pause. 'Not too short?'

'What do you think?'

I shake my head slowly. It doesn't feel too short. 'It feels just right.'

After our lingerie shop experience, we'd wandered down the high street until I'd stopped abruptly because of *the dress*. You know how sometimes you can spot clothes that you instantly fall in love with, but then tell yourself that they're too expensive, you'd never wear them, your boyfriend wouldn't like them or something like that? Normally I'd stare for a few minutes, then walk on. But today, with Noah by my side, it's different.

Clothes shopping with Noah is amazing. 'Go on, try it. You know you want to!' He'd nudged me.

'I suppose I could, I mean I don't have to buy it.'

'True.'

Okay I admit that my standards might have slipped, I wear nice not sexy. Lived in. Com-for-table. I like that word. It is one of my favourites. Even the sound of it is nice. Relaxing.

I guess when I was younger, I did make an effort. But you don't really think 'sexy' when you've been with the same guy forever, do you? I've never had to put a massive effort in to impress anybody. I've forgotten how much I used to enjoy dressing up, looking good, *feeling* good about myself. Robbie never even seemed to notice what I was wearing, how I looked.

And his mum, though wonderful in so many ways, wasn't exactly a style guru. She was more interested in crocheting cardigans for poorly animals.

But Noah *does* care how I look. And now I am wearing this beautiful dress, I can't help but show him.

'If it feels right then it is right. Sensational legs!' He whistles, which makes me strangely pleased. So I dive back into the changing room and study my legs.

We do a tour of town. Shops I've never been in – I tend to buy off the internet, it's easy, no embarrassing changing rooms, no wasted time huffing and puffing and feeling hot and bothered. And I know what I like, what fits me.

The First Date

Apparently though, now I've been let loose and encouraged by Noah, I seem to have discovered that what I like and what I need are two different things.

'Bloody hell!' shouts Bea, as I stagger back into the bookshop fighting a losing battle with all my carrier bags.

'Sorry I'm a bit late,' I say breathlessly. I can't get near my watch to see the time, but it has to be late.

'No probs. Where's the hunk?'

'He's gone back to work.' I drop my bags behind the desk. 'And don't call him hunk.'

'When are you seeing him again?'

'We have an appointment,' I say primly, 'tomorrow.'

'Wow, look at this.' Bea is delving into my bags, lingerie first.

'Stop it.' I slap her hands and try and grab the bag off her, but I'm too late.

'He really is taking this seriously!' She giggles. Holding up my new satin bra and knickers. 'Oh my God, Rosie! This guy is thorough.'

'He didn't pick them, I did! He's not even seen them!'

'Yet! Is he going to test out ripping them off?'

'Shush.' I bundle together all my bags and back away from her holding them protectively close. 'I'm putting these in the back room, and no peeking!'

'So, he might?'

'No, he will not be ripping anything off! Have you any idea how much this stuff costs?'

'Speculate to accumulate, as my dad used to say! So, what is he going to do if he's not allowed to rip this stuff off?'

'See what the results of my makeover are.'

'What, and if he gets a hard-on, you've passed?'

'Eurgh, you are so disgusting at times! It's not all about sex you know!'

'I think you'll find it is. Sex, power and money!'

'Bollocks! I'm going to re-order the religious section and clear my mind of your filth!'

Unfortunately, my mind does not clear of filth. I have to apologise to the books, because every time I think about my new sexy underwear, I think of him. Noah.

The look he gave me when he asked me how my luxury undies made me feel is branded across my brain. For that moment, it was as though my answer was all he was interested in, I was all he was interested in.

I close my eyes and can feel the warmth of his hand against my chin.

And then he lets his hand drift down my neck, my chest.

I can feel Noah tracing a finger over the lace of my bra, sending a shiver down my spine and making me beg for the touch of his mouth. Noah devouring my pink knickers with his eyes, then slowly stripping them off (he is of course doing this with due reverence – no ripping involved – they cost a fortune) with his capable warm hands.

I blink. Put my hand over my throat to chase away the fantasy of his touch. I'm being ridiculous, like some silly schoolgirl with a crush on her teacher.

I must not think about him in that way.

It is wrong. Very wrong. Noah has no place in my knickers.

So is Bea. Wrong that is, about it all being about sex. If life really does just boil down to sex, power and money then I'm screwed (though not in the sense she means).

My phone pings with an incoming message.

'A* for that lesson! Homework – decide what else you'd like to change and do it! Noah.'

Chapter 10

Devastated.

Noah texted to say that he had to cancel our lesson on Thursday. Up to the eyes in redesigning a building due to planning objections was his official line. But maybe he doesn't want to do this? Maybe after our shopping trip he realised I was either a. a lost cause, or b. he wanted to go out on proper dates.

I spent two hours berating myself for being so pathetic and caring about a cancelled *lesson*, then another hour drinking wine and eating popcorn before the second longer text came in saying he was really sorry, and he'd make it up to me.

'I'll add in an extra free lesson! Noah'
'But I don't pay!! Rosie.'
'Aha, on the ball as ever! Have to make it up to you some other way.'

He signed off with a winky face that made me disproportionality happy.

Totally out of proportion. I mean, why should I care this much either way?

Apart from the fact that I have told Mum I will be bringing a date to her party and Noah seems to be my only hope at the moment, and every time he cancels a date, he decreases the probability of me achieving my aim. So therefore, him adding a bonus lesson in has to be worth celebrating, yes? Great!

But the initial disappointment is bothering me. My heart used to plunge like that when I'd been waiting for Dad for three hours, only to be told that he'd had to cancel his flight.

I'm beginning to depend on him. Rely on him, like I relied on Dad.

This is not good.

If there is one thing I've always been determined to be, it's independent. Well, at least where men are concerned.

But he's not Dad. He did apologise, and he didn't need to.

Oh hell, am I making a massive mistake? Would I just be better hiring an escort? One from out of town that nobody will know (can you imagine the embarrassment if I hired him sight-unseen and he turned out to be the plumber, moon-lighting for some extra cash?). I mean, I really do suck at this adult relationship lark. I'm a capable woman. I have a good job, friends, a nice home – isn't that enough?

It's not though, is it? I liked having a boyfriend, I just did. Like some people like having a pet, I suppose. I just wish I could work out why I'm so rubbish at this and then maybe I could sort it out. Myself.

Without risking getting too involved with somebody like Noah.

Chapter 11

This seduction business is bloody hard work. I'm not sure I've got time for it. The past few days have passed in a bit of a whirl. It went like this:

Monday

I was woken by a deep vibration, of the mobile phone incoming text variety.

'How's the homework going? N x'

Noah has taken to signing off on his texts with a kiss: this happened at some point during our exchange after he'd had to cancel Thursday. This is just like me signing off to Bea with one. We're friends now, we (or rather I) have got over the awkward 'is this a good idea?' phase, as I'm positive he has absolutely no interest in me at all (on a proper date front) so I am safe.

'Slight blip. R x'

'*???*'

'*I need to find a new hairdresser.*'

After a long think yesterday, while soaking in the bath with a glass of white wine and my Kindle for company, I realised that one thing I had fancied doing for ages was getting a new really good haircut. Nothing too drastic, but maybe a bit shorter, and a bit more shaped, and maybe a few highlights, and well . . . okay, something that made me feel a bit sexier.

My current hairdresser doesn't really do sexy. She seems to specialise in trimming split ends off. Which, to be fair, is what I've been happy with. But I don't come out feeling all swishy-haired and fabulous.

'*I'll ask Sadie. Nx*'

I *am* safe. One hundred per cent safe on the 'he's got no interest in me' front. Unfortunately, I've still got a few issues with getting my imagination under control. But I suppose fantasising about him is okay, if I know that it is completely one-sided. Which I do know. So nothing will happen. Even if I sort-of wanted it to. Which I don't.

'*Sadie?*' Okay I know it's none of my business, but I'm still slightly miffed if he meant what he'd jokingly said, that he had plenty of days to proper date around our lessons.

Although I suppose I am being a bit hypocritical here – I'm going to be off dating other people as soon as I'm ready. Which hopefully will be soon. I'm running out of time.

The First Date

'Went out with her on Friday. Hang on. N x'

Oh. Right. I try not to be cross. But what's Sadie like? Is she prettier than me? I bet Sadie isn't direct and challenging. Or over-bubbly.

I'm beginning to think he's disappeared off to see Sadie. The texts seem to have stopped. She probably gets several kisses on her texts, not just one.

'Okay. Sadie's given me the number of the guy she uses, said he was good at sexy-seductress stuff. N x'
'You told her!!!'

Oh my God. The swine! Now Sadie knows he's been enlisted to help out poor desperate dating disaster me. Is he going to tell everybody? I want to send an emoticon that says 'I will kill you' but can't find anything even close, so send a devil face instead.

'Chill. Said my sis was after a new sexy style, she mentioned him, I said yeah but can he do sexy? She kicked me and said, "what the fuck do you think mine is?" She also said "since when do girls ask for their brother's help?!" I think I've been dumped, solves the problem of her thinking we might get serious! But I did get the hairdresser's number first. Here it is. N x'
'I am impressed at your devotion to the task, and the sacrifice. R x'
'Not a problem. She was a bit scary, as in "can I move in?" scary, not scary like you. We'd only had one date! N x'

> *'You always have to spoil it, don't you? You're supposed
> to say I was worth the sacrifice! R x'*
> *'Always!! N xx'*

I think I better stop texting. So instead, I call the hair stylist
and make an appointment; apparently if Sadie recommended
him then he can squeeze me in on Wednesday.

Noah has sent another text, seeing as I didn't reply. It
consists of three crying with laughter emoticons and no kisses.
Phew! Two kisses had definitely been scary.

> *'Hope you're not doing anything too drastic? I like your
> hair as it is! N x'*
> *'You'll have to wait and see! R x'*
> *'Tousled, bed hair?? Nx* 😕*'*
> *'Red, pixie cut? R x'*

There is a long pause. He's obviously trying to think of a
suitable not-too-crushing response.

> *'Anything would look good on you! N x'*
> *'You charmer, you! Might get matching nails as well! R x'*

I am smiling stupidly. It's a long time since I can remember
smiling at a text from Robbie. Although, 'can you get more
shaving foam, please?' doesn't really give you the warm and
fuzzies, does it? Although, thinking about it seriously, I can't
remember a smile-inducing text exchange at all.

The First Date

'Isn't it the first thing a girl does when she's dumped, you know, go for the new-me look? Not that I really know. I've never split up with anybody before. R x'

Obviously that's one upside of staying with the same guy – no unexpected expenses. Downside is you turn into a stay-at-home frump.

'Oh yeah, so I've heard. I mean, I tend to go out and buy a new T-shirt when I've split with somebody. N x'
'You must have a helluva lot of T-shirts.'

I add a crying with laughter face and grin.

'What can I say? I like T-shirts, you can never have too many! N x'

Tuesday

'Meet me for lunch in half an hour, across from your place? N x'

Strangely I have missed Noah despite the texts (not that I'd inflate his ego further by telling him) and am stupidly pleased at the prospect of seeing him again. Winky emoticons are not the same as seeing the real thing: the way his eyes wrinkle at the corners, the laughter that dances in his eyes. One grin from Noah and I seem to feel so much better about myself.

No last-minute doubts about having my hair restyled and lifted from the boring but safe sameness I've seen every time I look in the mirror since I was at school. His chuckle warms me up inside and the way he looks at me makes me feel I can do (almost) anything. Even find a date.

Or it could be the fact that I've been told the window display at the shop needs doing and I've finally been trusted to do it again, so I'd be pleased for any excuse to get out of here for a bit.

The boss has insisted on Bea doing the window since my near disastrous Valentine's Day love-you-to-death style showcase. Did I not mention it? Robbie did his runner two weeks before the big day.

Well, anyway, I wasn't in the mood for hearts and flowers exactly, and I bet there are a lot of other people who aren't. So, I went for an alternative approach. You have no idea how many books are about crimes of passion, vampire kisses, and love lost.

'Fucking hell, Rosie, are you off your head?' Was Bea's reaction. 'This says love me to death. Nobody wants to be given their lover's heart literally!' she yelled, holding up a book with a particularly gruesome cover.

'Well that's how I feel! And I think you'll find that is somebody's liver not heart.'

'Eurgh.' She dropped the book. 'I am off to find something pink!'

So anyway, my first attempt *has* to make up for the last one. I must not fail, which is a bit daunting. Coffee with Noah will be much less of a challenge.

The First Date

Wow, who thought I'd ever say that?

'An hour, I've got some spines to dust. R x'

'Sounds sexy, want to try it out on me? N x'

'You're chuckling! Must be the sex god on the phone!'

'Don't call him that!' I shake my head at Bea. 'Haven't you got some books to tidy or something?'

'It is him, isn't it? You go all girly when he texts you.'

'No, I don't!' I don't, honestly. 'He's just funny.' He makes me smile; he makes me feel all warm and happy.

'Yeah, and then some. You know what they say about a man who can make you laugh! You keep that chastity belt on your knickers locked, girl!'

'Shush!' I wave her away, but a little niggle of unease teases at my heart. I fear my chastity belt is not as firmly attached as it should be. It is in danger of slippage.

How can I miss somebody *so* much? I need to find a real boyfriend quickly, one that is steady and reliable. One who I can work with and live with, and love in the way I loved Robbie.

Without the irrational head-over-heels hormonal side.

That's a slightly depressing thought actually: losing Noah's corny jokes and naughty sense of humour. And dirty grin. And the way my heart kind of flips when I realise he's on the phone. And the way he can bring goose bumps out on my arms just by staring steadily at me in that 'I can see everything in your head' kind of way.

It's a bloody good job he is still dating the Sadies of this world. Women who are happy (well maybe not happy, but

147

happy to go along with) that he will never commit. He will never fall in love. Because he doesn't want to.

I admit he's not just like my dad, he has lots more positive points, and he does care. But that makes him more likeable, more dangerous – because he still is like him in some ways. I'm not daft, I know you can't change a person.

We are too dissimilar; we want totally different things in life and all his flirting is just that. Flirting. He can't help himself. I can't let him get under my skin and into my heart – and I'm really worried that he's starting to.

* * *

I needn't have worried about any possibility of my relationship with Noah taking a wrong turn, because the first thing he says when I sit down in the café is: 'I've got the number of a brilliant nail salon if you're interested! You said you were thinking of getting them done?'

'How do you know it's brilliant?' I say suspiciously. 'You don't get yours done, do you?'

'No.' He grins. I imagine if he did decide to get a manicure, he'd get away with it.

'Don't tell me.' I hold up a hand, 'Sadie's back!'

'Nope. This was Helen.'

'Who's Helen?'

'Keep up, Rosie! I went out with her last night.'

'Sadie?'

'Definitely gone.'

'What is it with you and women?'

'I like them.' He grins. 'A lot.' My stomach does a little dive. Okay, I know he's not the man for me – but right now he's reminding me of that other man in my life. Dad. Just when I was starting to think that he isn't actually much like him at all. 'Can't blame me, can you?'

'But you don't stick with anybody.' I give him my disapproving look. 'How can you know what somebody is like if you don't hang around and get to know them?' I suppose the one big difference is that he's not actually being unfaithful, but why can't he just be more, more, well . . . Not more like Robbie. Maybe it's easier to say why isn't he less like Dad?

'You'll get lines if you frown like that!'

'You can't distract me that easily.'

'Look, Rosie.' He puts his menu down carefully and looks me in the eye. 'I know your dad is a bit of a shit—'

'I never said that!'

He puts his hand over mine. 'You didn't have to I've seen the effect he has on you every time he gets in touch! Look, Rosie, I care about you.'

'Huh.' I scowl.

'You're cool, you're cute, but I reckon you might have some,' he pauses and studies me for a moment as though he's unsure whether or not to carry on.

'Go on.' I say stiffly. 'Hit me with it. I'm immune to personal insults.'

'No, you're not.' His tone is soft. 'And you shouldn't be. You also shouldn't have these trust issues with men. We're not all the enemy. Give us a chance.'

'I don't have trust—' I'm getting hot under the collar, and practically bristling.

'You—'

'Can't you just be nice?'

'Look I'm trying to be.' He looks slightly indignant. 'I'm always nice!'

'No, you're not. You can't call my dad a shit!'

'He's not exactly nice and supportive, is he?' he says reasonably. Then leans forward. I scowl. 'Anyway, the point here is, I'm not your dad. I'm not married, I'm not offering commitment, I just like women, I like having fun, and I like to date. Okay? It doesn't make me enemy number one, just not the man for you. We're all different, Rosie. I'm not the enemy, I'm just a guy with his own reasons for doing what he does, and I don't need you to judge me.' His steady gaze is a bit unnerving, so I look down at my own menu. He puts a finger under my chin. There's a minor tussle while I try and keep it down and he tries to make me look at him, but the power of his finger wins. 'Okay?'

'Fine.' It's not fine though. He's right, I shouldn't be judging him. I just wish he wasn't like he was. 'So, what are your reasons?'

'What?'

'For being like you are! All this,' I wave a hand, 'not, not . . .' his words come back to me, from when he was selling his services at being brilliant at chatting people up, at first dates, 'not being so hot at second dates, or third dates!'

'It's the way I rumble.' He shrugs. 'Not everybody believes in happy-ever-afters, Rosie.'

I raise an eyebrow.

'I've just, just,' he hesitates as though he doesn't know whether or not to say anything more, 'I realised it wasn't for me a long time ago, Rosie. Love is fine until it goes wrong, until you lose it, isn't it? So sometimes it's just better not to . . .' He stops talking.

'Get involved?'

'Yep.'

'Hmm. Fine.' He's got a closed look on his face. There's an awkward silence. It's not nice. We've never had awkward silences. 'Why did you want to see me?' I say grumpily. I'm unreasonably cross with him which is silly. It's none of my business. 'Not just about nails?'

'Thought having a bit of fun wouldn't do you any harm.' He says the last bit under his breath, but it seems to resound round the café.

'I heard that, I know how to have fun!'

'Sure.'

'I do.'

'You just need to loosen up a bit.'

'If I loosen up any more I'll be on my back!'

'Exactly!' He grins cheekily and I can't help myself, I smile back.

'You're so annoying at times. I was trying to stay grumpy with you!'

'I know, on both counts. Like to keep you on your toes.'

It's almost a cosy moment, but the waitress chooses this moment to gate-crash, which is probably a good thing.

'Which pizza do you recommend?'

'Depends how odd you are.' She is the first woman I've met who seems immune to Noah's charms. She is staring at the table, not at him.

'This one? Bit of everything?' He's not giving up.

'Oh my God, you must be kidding me? I am so not a fan of cross-cultural contamination on a pizza, putting Mexican chilli right next to American hotdog is like gross.'

'But Mexico is next to the States,' he says reasonably.

Our waitress rolls her eyes. 'But there are borders, yeah?'

'Have you never heard of fusion?'

'Fusion? I'm not some kind of nuclear scientist! Look dude, I just want . . .'

'Fusion food. Forget it. What do you fancy?' He looks at me and I don't know if a dare say.

'Well, I, well you're not exactly selling . . .'

'Selling?' She looks from me to Noah and back again, then shakes her head. 'I'm not some kind of waitress man, I just wanted to borrow the salt.' She points. 'If that's okay?'

Noah nods, and looks uncomfortable, and apologises. A lot. It's quite cute actually. I smother my giggles in a napkin as she walks off shaking her head.

'I'll just have a Caesar salad I think.' We've got over the tiff. We've got over the dangerous 'moment'. We're back where we should be. Mates.

'Maybe you should throw in a gym session.'

'Why?' I pull my stomach in involuntarily. Not that the flabby muscles are really listening; they quiver a bit then relax back into their normal positions. 'Are you saying I look fat?' I fold my arms and manage to cram a fair bit of indignation into my voice, because if I want floppy bits, what's that got to do with him? 'That's chauvinistic,' I count off on my fingers, 'patronising, rude—'

'And not true.'

'I'm not fat?' I look at him suspiciously. This is tricky, trust is in the balance: if he says no he's smooth talking, if he says yes then . . .

'I didn't say that. What I said was that it's not true that I was saying you looked fat. You assumed that part.'

'So you do think I'm fat? Chubby? Over rounded? Well built?'

He holds up a hand. 'Woah, woah, woah.' Then heaves a sigh of relief when I stop talking. 'Can we rewind here. You look fine, perfect even, squishy in the right places.'

'Squishy?'

'Though I'd know better if I could put my hands on—'

'No hands!'

'Purely for research. Look, before you bite my head off again and feed me to your young, the gym is about confidence. Not wobbly bits.'

'Confidence? We're back to that.'

'No escape from it! Because that's all dating is about. Love yourself and the whole world will join in.' He waves his hands expansively. I think the whole world, well the female side, had joined in with him. Apart from the waitress that wasn't a waitress. She was more interested in salt.

'Hmm. So dating isn't about sex, power and money?'

'No, that's what life is all about, not dating! The gym isn't just about toning up though, it's about stamina.' He winks.

'Don't you ever stop thinking about sex?'

'Who said I was thinking about sex?' My face heats up faster than you can blink. 'And it's a great place to meet hot guys, chat over the bench press.' He raises an eyebrow. 'Try out your chat-up lines while you're eyeing up—'

'Seriously? You're mad! How can you eye up anyone when you're going through hell? I don't chat and exercise.' He's seriously over-estimated my fitness levels here – talk and exercise? Pffft. 'Anyway, that rewind thing, can we do it again. Why are we here?'

'So I can see your lovely face, hear your . . .'

'Noah, concentrate! Nails! We're here to talk about nails, not sex and workouts.'

He sighs. 'Sometimes you can be such a let-down. Okay, nails. Here you go.' He hands me a business card. 'Now can we talk about—'

'No!'

'The gym? Honestly you have a mind like a sewer. Won't you at least think about it? On your day off?'

'Sure.' I nod. But I might be telling a little white lie. Tomorrow is my day off, and I'd much rather have my nails done, in fact I'd rather have a Brazilian wax and my eyes poked out than try and master talking, breathing and pounding a treadmill all at the same time. Lethal.

'Great.' He grins. 'Better get back to work I suppose! Love your top by the way, is it new?'

It is. His words make me preen. Then I remember, it's all in a day's work for him.

The First Date

Wednesday

'Surprise!'

'This has to be a nightmare.' I blink my bleary eyes. I must be losing the plot. I've blamed late night cheese for Noah's appearance in my dreams; cheddar can't be responsible for the fact he's on my doorstep.

'I know you're pleased to see me really. Are you going to let me in, or shall I stay on the doorstep and yell 'wow Rosie, that was the best sex I've had for years' at the top of my voice, then stagger off down the street?'

'Don't you bloody dare.' I grab the front of his top, drag him in and glance furtively up and down the street. It does not look good, a man on the doorstep when I'm still in my PJs.

'Oh my God I had no idea that pyjamas with rabbits on could be so sexy!' He groans, and I suddenly realise I'm clutching him to me, so shove him away.

'They're cosy!' I glare at him. 'And they're not rabbits, they're dogs!'

'Really?' He leans back in to peer more closely, rests one hand on my scantily clad waist and the warmth of it burns straight through. It's like he's found direct access to the deepest part of my body and I seem to be melting. And fizzing. And a little bit scared and far too excited. 'Stop it!' I think I might have leapt rather over-dramatically into the air, like a rabbit.

His eyes open wide.

'Sorry, sorry, I was talking to me, not you.'

'What?' He's even more confused now. I don't blame him, so am I. I'd had a split second to choose between rubbing myself against him like an over-sexed cat or bouncing about like a puppy. I go 'puppy' every time.

See, this is what happens when I'm caught out half-asleep by a man with a sexy smile and warm hands. Sexy smile, where did that come from? Boy it's got hot in here, even with the front door open.

'Can you excuse me, just one moment?'

He nods. I go into the kitchen, flap the bottom of my pyjama top, splash my face with ice cold water, bang my head on the fridge door and plaster a smile on my face.

'Are you okay?' He's followed me into the kitchen.

I nod.

I'm not okay at all.

He's caught me unawares, literally walked out of my dream and in through my front door in real life. In my dream he'd got considerably further than my front door, he'd also got considerably less clothes on. And he'd got his fingers tangled in my hair, and his lips burning a path down my neck. He'd reached the sensitive spot on my neck that makes me shiver. And unlike Robbie, Noah is lingering in a way that's made me all hot and bothered.

I'm still hot and bothered. Just not being kissed. Dream fantasies and reality are not supposed to mix. It's confusing. Too confusing.

'You've got wet hair.' He frowns.

'I know. Forget it, it's nothing.' It's my turn to frown as I back into the corner next to the cooker. I never realised this kitchen was so small. One more step and we'll have moved onto another of my fantasies.

Stop, Rosie!

'Why are you here? It's eight o'clock in the morning, and my day off! You woke me up!'

'You're so cute when you're sleepy but angry at the same time!'

'Why?'

'I don't know, something about the tousled hair, the spark in your eye and—'

'You know what I mean! Why are you *here*! Now, in my kitchen.' I self-consciously touch my hair and try not to look pleased.

'Oh yeah, well it's your day off!' He grins triumphantly.

'Er, yes. But it's not yours.' How did he remember it was my day off? Nobody remembers stuff like that. Robbie didn't, not even Mum does. Well, I guess *Robbie's* mum sometimes did. She had it all written on the calendar – a column for each of them, and even one for me. It's sad realising nobody is that bothered in my life any more. That the nearest thing I had to a family has disappeared into thin air. Or Wales.

Except now Noah bothers. Damn the man, he's just so nice, so thoughtful, so . . .

'Cooee it's only me! I've got a parcel for you!' A loud voice slices straight through my thoughts. Which is a good and a bad thing. Good because I've got a horrible feeling that I'm starting to like Noah far too much, and not just because he's undeniably hot, bad because it's my nosy neighbour.

'I closed the door,' mouths Noah, frowning.

'I know,' I mouth back.

He raises an eyebrow. I open my mouth to continue the silent conversation, and a small wiry woman bustles in like a terrier who has scented a rabbit. She is clutching a brown box in her hands and stops a foot short of shoving it into my arms.

'Oh! You have company!' She fixes him with a piercing stare then beams – if she had a tail, she'd be wagging it. 'Oh, my goodness me, I'm not surprised you've got your mouth hanging open.' I close it. 'What a fabulous sight first thing in the morning; they should do it on the NHS. This one is so much better than the last one, Rosie!' She circles him. 'Bravo, well done!'

'He's not—'

'What a gorgeous physique, such lovely legs. I can't stand spindly ones, can you?'

'I've never really thought about it,' I say lamely and glance in the same direction she is.

Oh God, she's right. He's even got sexy knees! How did I not notice . . .? I think I was so obsessed with trying not to look like I'd been having fantasy sexual relations with him I'd blanked everything out below the waist. 'You've got legs.' He grins. 'I mean shorts, you've got shorts on!' I point.

'I could take them off?'

Rhonda squeals, and I glare at him. She doesn't need encouraging; she's 'popping in' far too much as it is.

'Maybe not.' He winks at me 'But you need to get yours on, come on, shoo, go and get dressed. I'm taking you to the gym!'

'The only place for a spindly leg is on a table I always say!' Interrupts Rhonda, sliding between us and shoving her hand out. 'I'm Rhonda.'

'Delighted.'

I can hear them, but from far away. All I can see are his legs. I'm fixated. I shake my head and finally find my voice. 'Rhonda's my neighbour.'

Yeah, I know, knees shouldn't be such a big deal – everybody has them or they'd fall over – but when they're like this, and they're in my kitchen, they are quite something to behold. Rhonda is right, his legs are rather shapely, in a manly way. 'She has a key, to er . . .'

'Feed the cat!' announces Rhonda with a big smile, still giving Noah the once-over as though he's a juicy bone. I can understand now why her husband spends all the time in his shed.

'You've got a cat?' He's looking confused.

'No.'

'The previous occupants had one, such nice people they were. Always had time for a chat.' Smiles Rhonda. 'They gave me a spare key so that I could help out when they were away and keep an eye on the place. I kept it when you moved in, didn't I, dear?'

'Well yes, but there really is no need.'

'She's not got a cat!' says Noah.

'But she's got plants that might need watering, and I take parcels in if she's away, and you never know she might get a cat one day! Always handy if a neighbour has a key, in case you lock yourself out. I do like to be neighbourly, not enough of it around these days.'

'I don't think I will lock myself out.' I shake my head and cross my fingers at the same time – because it isn't an impossibility. 'And my mum does have a spare key.'

The key is a bit of an issue if I'm honest. I'd only been in the place one day when there was a brief knock on the door, followed by a 'cooee it's me' and there she was. Rhonda. She has a whole cupboard full of neighbours' keys. I mean, it is a good idea in some ways, but it's her habit of knocking then letting herself in without waiting that's the issue. Not even my mum does that.

'Well there you go. Brilliant!' says Noah. I give him the evil eye. 'Perfect timing, you've just saved us a whole lot of bother.' He smiles, full wattage aimed straight at her. I swear I see a start of a swoon; any second now she'll be fanning herself.

'I have?' She's preening, looking proud of herself even though she doesn't know what it is she's done.

'You certainly have. We need a spare key and you've saved us a trip to get one cut.' He holds his hand out, and she drops the key into the palm without a murmur. 'And there's no cat to feed yet, or parcels due, or imminent holiday, is there?' He looks straight at me.

'No.' I mouth. How did he know how desperately I wanted my key back? How can he think of a way so quickly? How can he make Rhonda putty in his hands like that?

'Of course, dear. You only have to ask!' I have asked, several times; we have been at a key impasse. 'Anything to help. It's so nice to see Rosie with a man again. Did she tell you about Robbie? He went a bit strange. I mean, what kind of man wanders off with a rucksack on his own for months on end

160

like that? At his age as well! He used to have a proper job, you know, and now look at him! It's all yurts and sheep. Did you know he got married?' I'm not sure if she's asking me or Noah, but I nod anyway. 'Well, that's my good deed for the day, so I'll be off! I will see you again, won't I?' That comment is definitely aimed at Noah.

'I'm sure you will. You're a star.' And he somehow manages to usher her out of the door at double fast speed while kissing her on the cheek. I can hear her humming as she walks down the path; any second now she'll be skipping.

'How did you do that?'

'They don't call me the charmer for nothing.' He smiles, but this time it's not cheeky, it's soft at the edges. 'She just wants to feel needed.'

'I know but thank you! That was pretty,' I try not to grin, 'masterful.'

'Wow, compliments!'

'Don't let it go to your head!'

'You'll be saying you like me next.' He chuckles, but luckily doesn't wait for a response. 'Anyway, we can't risk having her dropping in on you once we've managed to get a load of hot dates lined up, can we?'

I feel faint. 'They don't have to be hot,' I say weakly. Hot men are bad for me. Lukewarm is better, much, much better. Lukewarm with only moderately sexy legs.

He winks. 'They will be though; they'll be beating a path to your door! Now come on, let's get a sweat on.'

I'm so glad Rhonda wasn't here to hear that. 'But you've got work to do, you can't, I can't . . .'

'I knew you didn't mean it when you said you'd go on your own, so I said I'd be late in work this morning. I'll make it up this evening. Come on, chop chop or we won't get a proper workout!'

Oh gawd. A workout. I'm going all hot and cold at the idea.

'You took time off just to help me?'

He rubs his hands together. 'I thought you had a target of your parents' party?'

I can almost feel the blood drain out of my face. Yeah, I admit Dad is on my mind far more than he should be, because how can I not keep comparing the carefree Noah to him? But I had been trying not to think about THE PARTY which is hanging over me like a black cloud hangs over a picnic. What on earth made me tell Mum I had a boyfriend?

'No time like the present to get their daughter prepped and ready for action!'

'I'm not the main course.' It's sweet. He's taking this seriously, but I'm slightly sad that he obviously wants to get it all done and dusted.

'I think you probably are!' He grins his cheekiest smile. Dimples on full strength. 'I said I'd teach you how to seduce, I promised I'd get you dating again, and I like to keep my promises.'

His words land like gentle thuds inside me.

Being with Noah is like being on a roller coaster: one minute I'm feeling all good about myself, and on some weird kind of high, the next I'm reminded why he's here. And the fact that he'll walk out of my life as casually as he walked in. 'It's not going to happen, is it? Me getting a date in time?'

'Of course, it's going to happen!'

'I'm a challenge, aren't I? A project and you're one of those people that hates to fail.' How come I feel so disappointed? I knew this was what this was all about for him.

'Hates to? Oh no, Rosie. I *don't* fail. Never fail!' He chuckles, which softens the blow. It's hard to dislike him. 'I'll do whatever it takes.' He winks. 'But you're not much of a challenge, you're far too seductive and sexy just as you are.'

I gulp down the lump in my throat. It's just words, Rosie; he's a flirt, he knows what to say. That's all. He doesn't mean anything by it. Look how he just got Rhonda to do exactly what he wanted!

'You're good,' I say as brightly as I can, trying to ignore the heat of his fingers as he tucks a tendril of my hair behind my ear, sending a shiver down my back.

'And don't let anybody tell you otherwise!' He grins, then walks over to look out of the window and luckily the moment has gone. Thank goodness for that. All this shivering and tingling and flushing is playing havoc with my head as well as my body. 'Right, let's step things up!'

'That sounds ominous.'

'If we run out of time, you'll have to take me to the party remember!'

For a second I do actually think about it. I mean, he's presentable, fun. Mum would love him. Although he seems to think my dad is public enemy number 1, so that might not go well. And even if he pretended to like him, well we'd both be pretending. And I can't spend the rest of my life trying to kid Mum and Dad (and me), can I? For a start they'd probably wonder why we never ever snogged or even held hands, and then they'd wonder why we hadn't moved in together, and then somebody would spot Noah out on a date, and . . . well it doesn't bear thinking about. I need to get my act together.

'You need to teach me faster!'

'So you don't have to take me?' He puts on his sad face.

'You know what I mean!'

'Let's go fast-tracking at the gym then, best place to up the pace!'

'Haha, you're so funny. I am being serious though.'

'So am I. This is the next lesson. Find out how easy it is to chat somebody up when you've got something to focus on.'

'What?'

'You don't need to think up any fancy chat-up lines, or what to talk about, you can get straight in there and talk dumbbells and crunches.'

'I can?' What is there to say about somebody rocking about on the floor like an infant who's forgotten how to stand up?

'Admire a guy's rowing technique, ask him if you're doing it right.'

I glare at him. 'I don't need help!'

'Apologise for taking soooo long to fill up your water bottle, and then accidentally tipping it over them!'

'You've done that, haven't you?'

He grins. 'Just chew the fat about the best tracks to pound to on the running machine then.'

'I'm not a cow!'

He suddenly chuckles. 'They chew cud not fat, herbivores?

Your practical exercise for today is to chat to at least two men you don't know, and extra marks if they ask for your phone number or share their playlist!'

I groan. 'Practical exercise? Practical? Aren't I doing enough exercising on the bloody machines?'

'That, my dear, is a means to an end. Come on, stop trying to delay the inevitable. No snogging though.'

'What?' I squeak. Oh my God, he's been reading my mind! My cheeks are burning. He's putting snogging down on the lesson plan, with him?

'Hands-free encounter in the gym, though you can do this.' He rests his hand on my forearm and my mouth is suddenly dry. So is my head. I can't think of anything to say, so I nod dumbly as we stare at each other. It's weird. How can the lightest touch feel so intimate?

Then he lets go and steps back. 'Right then. I'm all yours, but only for a couple of hours, so get your skates on.'

He's not all mine, not all mine, not all mine, I chant as I head up the stairs, doing my best to hold in my quivering tummy muscles.

'Only me dear!' I freeze. Rhonda is shouting through the letterbox. 'You can drop the key off when you get back!'

Wednesday a bit later

'Buggering, flaming, stop, please stop, stop!' I let go of the rail for a split second to jab at a button, then grab it again before I fall off the running machine backwards. Just in time as my legs start getting left behind, and my armpits feel the stretch.

'Shit, shit.' I put on a sprint so I'm upright again then risk glancing round. 'No-aaaaaah!'

Okay so this could be partly my own fault. I did insist I knew what I was doing, and that he could go off and do his own thing and leave me alone. I practically pushed him away. But that was because 1. I have been here before and never had a problem; after all how hard can it be to programme a machine like this? and 2. Having his body that close to mine when he is only dressed in gear that clings to his torso and his rather well-toned bum (you'd have noticed too, it was unavoidable) was bringing me out in a sweat before I'd even started any kind of exercise. Panting before you've started isn't a good look.

I spot him pretty quickly out of the corner of my eye. I've got a kind of Noah-radar which is horrible because I nearly forget to keep moving and my feet are off in the wrong direction again.

It would seem he meant it when he said it was a good place to chat people up. He is standing by the water cooler, casual and sweat-free, a broad smile on his face as a blonde goddess flicks her immaculate hair in his face and leans forward to take a cup of water from him. Her hand brushes his, I'm sure of it, even at this distance, and I feel a twinge in my chest.

I turn back so abruptly I nearly give myself whiplash.

'Are you okay?' The soft voice nearly sends me off the machine sideways. I'd been concentrating so hard on trying *not* to watch Noah, not to think about what he was joking about, that I didn't hear anybody come close. 'Hey?'

I try and smile. I probably look sick; I feel sick. My feet have got a mind of their own, and Noah has buggered off to enjoy himself. Then I look.

The guy is still there, and he's got the nicest, softest green eyes.

'Do you need a glass of water? You look a bit—'

'No!' I shout. No way am I going near that water cooler. Unless it's to throw a cup of water at Noah's crotch.

He's looking even more concerned now.

'I don't think I am okay, but I don't need a drink.' I am sure I sound slightly, okay a lot, pathetic. 'I'm normally fine on this machine,' I try not to pant, 'but it's doing weird things.'

'Hang on.' He leans in. 'Here, let's decrease the incline, and er, speed. Somebody has set a challenging programme.' He smiles. 'It might have been me actually, sorry!'

'You!' I smile. I am now capable of normal expressions and breathing now the machine has slowed down. 'My fault though, I should have reset it.' I should; if I hadn't been in such a rush to jump on and impress Noah. My God, why am I trying to impress the man?

'Hope you didn't mind me jumping in.'

'Oh God, not at all. You saved my life!' I think he's set it to super slow now, which is fine. I can do tortoise speed.

'Your, er boyfriend just looked a bit busy.'

'He's not my boyfriend,' I answer quickly.

'Oh, right, good.' He half smiles.

'He's a friend, like a brother. Well, not my brother, but you know what I mean. We're buddies!'

'Boyfriend doesn't mind?'

167

'No boyfriend!'

'Oh.' His hand is next to mine on the rail as the machine comes to the end of its performance and slows to a halt. We stand and stare at each other.

He's nice. Not buzzy in your tummy nice, but nice-nice. Not Noah nice. But I don't want Noah nice, do I?

'You wouldn't fancy a drink some—?'

'Yes!' I blurt out before he finishes his sentence. Then feel like punching the air! I have just been asked out! On a date. A proper first date! 'How can I say no when you just rescued me?' I have completed my practical with flying colours, and a bonus – an actual date with a nice guy!

'Great. Friday any good?' I nod. Speechless. A date! 'Pop your number in my phone, I'll text you.' He smiles, no doubt at my slightly dubious look. 'Look forward to it. Steve, by the way.'

'Rosie.' I hold his phone out. We're still kind of both clutching it when I feel the warmth of Noah's hand on my back.

'Everything okay?'

'Sure.' I grin at him. 'Never better! But I think I've had enough exercise for one day.' I wipe my sweaty hands down my leggings. Mission accomplished, exercise over!

Noah looks from Steve to me, then back again. 'Did I miss something?'

'We were just.' Steve motions with his phone and looks flustered. 'I didn't think you two . . .'

'We're not,' I say firmly.

'She's busy this week,' says Noah at the same time.

'My bad.' Steve takes a step back.

I kick Noah on the ankle bone and am totally gratified when he gasps.

'No, it's his bad!' I glare at Noah, daring him to say anything. 'I'm not busy at all, I'd love to go out.'

'Well, if you're sure?' He looks doubtfully at Noah.

'Positive.' I grind my heel into his toe for good measure. What has got into the man?

'Great, er, I'll be in touch later. Tonight. Bye. See you!' Steve waves a hand, flings his towel over his shoulder and saunters off whistling.

'Who was that?'

'He's called Steve. I've got a date. A proper date! I can't believe it, I've done it!' I hold a hand up to high five. Noah doesn't. Which makes me feel a bit stupid, and angry.

'What's the matter? You should be pleased for me! You've done it, succeeded. After hardly any lessons!'

'Fine. I am.' His voice is stiff. 'But you didn't tell me.'

'What do you mean, tell you?'

'That you were going to, you know.'

'No, I don't know. Anyway, he saved me, when you were too busy pressing that blonde's buttons to notice.'

'Saved you? Oh, come on, don't turn him into a knight in shining armour. We're in a gym not a jungle.'

I frown at him. 'You could fool me from the way you're prowling about like a tiger with a sore head. What is the matter with you?'

'Nothing.' He stares back and looks slightly sullen.

'It's only a date! You told me to, you said it was today's lesson!'

'I told you to chat a guy up, not arrange a date! He's not your type.'

'Meaning?'

'He takes boring and weak to a whole new level! I know you want safe, Rosie, but really?'

He might have a point, Steve does seem a bit, well, uninspired, even for me. But I'm not going to admit that to Noah. 'I think I'll decide that, and how do you know what my type is?' I say coldly, trying to keep the quiver from my voice. 'And anyway it's a date not a lifetime bloody commitment!'

'You need somebody who's your equal.'

I glare at him. 'Like you, you mean?'

He ignores that comment. 'He's too weak, too nice. It'll be yes Rosie, no Rosie until you're screaming out for him to contradict you just once.'

'What? Are you having me on here? He was fine until you butted in, Mr Macho!'

'Or it could be a cover, devious.'

'Oh, get lost, have you any idea how much of a dick you sound at the moment?'

'He could actually be a bit of a player. If you punch above your weight you—'

'What!' I can't help myself. I yell at him. 'How dare you say—' I'm so angry I'm speechless. 'What the hell is that supposed to mean?' Okay, I'm not completely speechless.

I fling my own towel over my shoulder, nearly flicking his eye out, and push past him. 'You're being ridiculous. Don't you want me to be happy?'

'Rosie, stop overreacting.'

'Me! Overreacting. Me? Ha.'

'Come back. I just don't want you to lose confidence, to get hurt.'

'I won't,' I say, not even turning around. I won't. I'm more likely to be hurt by Noah than Steve, but I don't voice that. I'm too angry, and my triumph has completely died away to be replaced with the feeling that I am about to burst into tears.

This is just like so many times Dad has undermined my decisions, told me I've got it wrong, even when I've been trying to please him. Just like I was trying to please Noah.

They're two chips off the same bloody block, and I've done it again – thought if I tried hard enough it would all be okay.

I hate Noah. I wish I'd never met him. I don't know why I thought I could do this, why I was beginning to think he might actually not be as bad for me as I'd originally thought.

Always trust your first instincts don't they say?

Wednesday night

'I'm sorry. Truly. Still on for tomorrow night? N'
'I just don't want you to get hurt. N x'
'He looks okay, I was just taken by surprise N xx'
'You're doing great, amazing. You've got this cracked – just sorry I'll soon be losing my best student far too soon. I've taught you too well ☹ *N xx'*

I sigh. I can't just ignore Noah, but he has truly pissed me off. The whole purpose of our seeing each other was for me to get a date, wasn't it? Shouldn't he be happy I've managed to do that? I don't get him at all. And I don't get why it's upset me so much that he's been such a miserable git.

I'm normally quite a rational, logical person. This is the point at which I should just tell him that he's achieved what he said he would, and I should just walk away. I am now a graduate of the school of seduction. I am a fledging seductress.

I just don't feel like one.

But I am vaguely hopeful that Steve could be the first of many. Or at least one or two. Not that the hordes will be beating a track to my door. But just the odd one would be nice. And if dating one happened to tie in with my parents' anniversary party then that would be even better.

I think it might be pushy to try and book Steve in for that now though.

'Sorry, just seen your texts, been in the shower. Rosie'

I have been in the shower. I've also been stomping around my place muttering under my breath and swearing quite a lot. And eating.

I am still not quite sure why Noah was so stroppy about Steve. I was so pissed off when I left the gym that I went into the supermarket, bought three pastries that were on offer and a pack of Pringles that wasn't. I then binge watched Netflix and wished I had a cat to cuddle.

And screamed at my mobile phone every time it beeped with a message. That wasn't from Steve.

I feel sick. Probably nerves because maybe Steve won't text after all. He did say he'd text and confirm our date, so it probably isn't going to happen. He must have got home and realised he'd made a mistake, or already had a girlfriend.

'Forgiven me? Seeing you flirt made me feel possessive! N x'
'I'm supposed to flirt, I thought that was the point, teacher? R x'
'Full marks on that, A grade student. But maybe take it slow?'

I sigh, the texts had been going in the right direction, and now he has to say that.

'Why can't you just be pleased for me? I've been going slow all my life, I need to speed up before I die. And before the party.'
'I am pleased for you. I'm sorry. I'm an idiot.'
'Did your blonde brush you off?'
'No, we've got a date on Friday.'

This is followed be a smiley face.

'Hypocrite.'

There is a long pause between messages.

'Ouch, but fair. Ignore me. N'
'Impossible. R x'
'True! I meant ignore what I said at the gym, not what I just said. I don't take being ignored well, I'm a me-me-me type of person. N x'

173

I can't help but notice that the kiss is back on his message.

I flick through programmes and wonder if I should watch *The Good Place* again for some tips on deception, and redemption, and 'soulmates'. With Noah I'm not quite sure if he's a bad guy pretending to be good, and this is all a joke. Or he's actually the good guy he really seems to be, with double standards when it comes to relationships.

I've never been able to work out what Dad really is, so what chance do I stand with Noah? It's not that I'm torn in two ways over my father, it's like my brain is buzzing with a whole ant's nest of conflicting messages. I mean, he's my dad! When I was young, I believed with a capital P that he was perfect, that he'd always love me, that he would have been there if he could have been. Then the doubts started to creep in, the thoughts that if I could be better then I'd deserve him more.

Bea says I shouldn't need to earn his love. He should give it. Unconditionally. Even if I'm his worst nightmare – like she is to her parents (she said that, not me, she's not a nightmare – but her parents love her to bits).

I've never really judged Dad. I hate that he flirts his way through life because it hurts Mum. It's selfish, it's cruel, and a buzzing in my head tells me that Noah is right – he's a shit. Because he's not just flirting, he's actually not always very nice. Even though everybody thinks he is. I used to think he was. So whilst one little buzzy voice (which is getting quieter by the day) is saying he's okay, he just can't help himself so, it's not entirely his fault, there is another, louder buzz telling me it *is* his fault, and he could just ACT NORMAL. And another buzzy voice is telling me that maybe I'll never be good enough, because he keeps moving the 'good enough' bar so he's got an excuse to never be 'good enough' himself.

I'm confused and torn. My dad is a part of me. I can never quite not believe what he says to me. That's what love does to you, isn't it?

Noah is not a part of me though. And am I being stupid putting him in the same categories I've been measuring my dad against?

If he'd just settle down, let himself have a proper relationship, then maybe I'd know what type of man he is. Except then I wouldn't be happy, I know I wouldn't; I don't want to see Noah exit my life because he's madly in love.

Arghhh.

More to the point, because my head really isn't up to finding answers right now, how can he be so cross that I flirted? I am *supposed* to flirt! It was part of the lesson.

'At least let me help you before your date, even if you brush me off after? Still on for tomorrow night? N x'
'How can I say no? R x'

I can't actually. The thought of a possible date, with a very nice guy, should be making me less desperate to see Noah. But he's like a drug. I don't want to stop seeing him. Maybe Steve will cure me of that. If he ever texts.

'Glad I'm still irresistible! N x'

I can't help but smile. We've been bickering like brother

and sister, or a couple in a relationship, and falling out with Noah leaves me feeling anxious. I want to be friends. He's the one person (well, the one male person) in my life who has been there to help me find a date. Okay, he's been there even more than that. I have started to rely on him. I chat to him more than I chat to anybody else.

Oh my God, I'm not using him like some kind of father substitute, am I? Don't they say women go after a man who reminds them of their dad – and in my case I'm doing that, even though I'm hoping like hell he's a modified and improved version.

Oh bugger, I am really screwed.

I must not feel anxious. This is scary. I must not rely on him. I can cope without Noah, I can, I can.

He is just a friend, and people cope with losing friends. I hardly know him, it's not like he's Bea. Or even Robbie's mum or dad.

'p.s. you don't have to reply to that! N'

I must keep it light.

'You are incredible! R x'

I pick up the debris of crisp packets and cake wrappers and wonder if I should turn my mobile off. Steve still hasn't texted. What if I am still totally un-dateable?

'Hey!'

176

The First Date

Oh my God, an unknown number! It's him, it's Steve.

I sink back down on the sofa with a sigh of relief. It's official. I have got a first date.

Chapter 12

'Wow.' Noah gives a low whistle that makes my skin shiver as he slips off his stool and leans forward to kiss my cheek.

I'd been dreading this, seeing him again. I've had butterflies of anticipation and have been a total wreck all day, worried that we'd spoiled everything. That we'd lost our easy friendship. Which I like. I realised last night that I will miss Noah so much when he decides he's taught me all he knows or is just too busy to see me.

But just like that he's made everything better.

'Aren't you the sexy lady? Give me a twirl!' He grins, dimples framing his generous mouth, and I blush, feeling happy. Then I have to remind myself that he's a pro. He's doing his job.

'I look okay?' I ask as I self-consciously turn slowly on the spot. My makeover was completed after work by a new haircut, with added colour, and I am now everything Noah told me I should try and be. Me.

I have completed my homework to the best of my ability. I have bought clothes that I have always longed to wear and have changed what I want to change – my hair. Ignoring what anybody else might think – including my bank manager. Who is going to think I have been abducted by aliens, and been forced to divulge my pin number.

I have been primped and poked (not in that way) like never before. I was afraid that the inside of my wardrobe looked strangely alien. It would seem the clothes don't look quite as alien on me, unless Noah has really weird taste.

'Bloody hell. You are looking so gorgeous you've just made me forget my pick-up line!'

'Well what a crap teacher you are going to be!'

He chuckles, and the moment that could have been awkward is suddenly quite chilled. 'I ordered you a drink, is that okay?'

'How do you know what I like?' I can't help it. I give him my suspicious look.

'Rosie, Rosie.' He takes my hand in his two warm ones. One finger tapping the back. 'Tip number one, give a guy a tiny bit of the control, let him make a decision now and again. You know, not rule your life, just tinker with the simple stuff that doesn't really matter.'

'Hmm.' I twist my mouth and ponder that one. I don't like letting other people control anything in my life – unless they're a plumber and I need a pipe fixing, or something like that. Fixing stuff that I can't, or don't want, to do.

'You'd let a waiter recommend the best dish on the menu, wouldn't you?'

'Maybe. As long as it's not bull's penis, or crispy ants, or something like that.'

He raises an eyebrow. 'You seriously go to places that serve stuff like that?'

'No, I watch *I'm a Celebrity*, but I mean, you never know.'

'You are a bit strange, you know, lesson 16,' he waves a finger, 'don't scare the shit out of the guy. If he looks like he survives on worms and roadkill then fine, otherwise,' he shakes his head, 'don't mention eating dicks, not of any kind. Not dried, salted or skewered, definitely not skewered.'

'It was just an example.' It was. And I could actually imagine Noah eating weird stuff for a dare. Maybe not a penis, but we all have our limits. 'Are we really on lesson 16?'

'At least. So, er, let a guy make a decision now and then?'

I nod, slightly sheepishly. How on earth did I get onto eating willies and worms? He waves a hand.

'Come on, we're sitting over there.' I think this is his demonstration of a man making a decision, so I nod dutifully and smile, and follow him. I am trying my best to listen to *everything* he is trying to teach me. Even if some points seem a bit misguided.

'Some men like women to make the decisions, you know!'

He shakes his head. 'Not the type of man you need in your life.'

'Meaning?'

'You don't want a doormat, Rosie! You need a challenge!' He winks. 'Trust me!'

I mock-sigh. Trouble is, I am beginning to trust him quite a lot. Well at least his judgement on how to catch a guy, I'm not sure about his picture of the actual guy.

When all this is over, I can tweak things to suit though.

Nobody sticks one hundred per cent to what they've been taught, do they?

Noah chose this place, it's a bit off my beaten track, a bar I've never been to before, and I think we'd got a kind of unspoken agreement that our meetings would be away from my normal haunts.

I'm impressed now I get a chance to look around. I'd got tunnel vision when I walked in; my tummy was full of butter-flies, my legs on the wobbly side (partly down to the heels) and my knees practically knocking (blame the skirt). I'd been concentrating on making it to the bar – and Noah – without either falling over or chickening out.

Now I can actually understand why women going down the red carpet hang on to a partner. They are literally hanging on; it's got more to do with balance than attraction. It reduces the risk of falling over due to temporary lack of shoe control, or lack of leg control linked to the nervous shakes.

Anyway, I had nobody to hang on to, so I settled for deep concentration. Luckily by the time Noah commented on my new look, I'd been able to grasp the back of a chair and no longer had my tongue stuck out (apparently this is a habit when I'm concentrating – thanks for that Robbie).

The bar is relaxed and erring towards traditional. Not what I'd expect as Noah's first choice – though maybe he's off his beaten track as well. He probably doesn't want to put off potential dates by being seen cosying up to me.

Talking of which . . .

Oh God, he's steered us straight to a cosy romantic corner! I stop dead. I can't help it. Maybe I should have had a bottle or three of wine before I attempted this. Is this really what he thinks we need to do before I meet Steve tomorrow?

'Thought this would be good, where we won't be disturbed and you can say what you want,' the corner of his mouth quirks, 'not that anything would stop you doing that. No hands I promise! Here we go!'

The drinks magically arrive at the table the second we're sitting down. My cocktail actually looks quite nice. Very nice. 'Good job.' Oh hell, that sounds like I'm praising a toddler who's conquered potty training. 'I mean, er, lovely, I'm impressed.' Ouch, where did that come from? I sound like my mother. I can feel the colour start to leach into my face.

'What do you call a sad strawberry?'

'I have no idea. Is this a chat-up line, or part of the lesson?'

'A blueberry!'

'That's terrible!' I laugh despite myself, and instantly the embarrassment disappears. Noah grins and I realise him being happy makes me feel happy.

'Courtesy of a nephew. Sorry. I've got more?'

'I'm not sure how many I can take.'

'What do you call a strawberry playing the guitar? No?' I shake my head. 'A jam session!'

I groan. 'Another nephew joke?'

'Oh no, that's all my own work! It was my comeback joke. I think I've peaked!'

His grin is decidedly naughty, and I don't know if I can totally blame the glow in my cheeks on the cocktail.

'When I got here and you said I'd made you forget your chat-up line, that was a chat-up line, wasn't it?'

His grin morphs into a big smile. 'You're a quick learner. Guilty as charged! Hang in there though, they get better!'

'Nobody ever tell you you're cheesy?' I roll my eyes and take a sip of my cocktail.

'And you're the sweet chutney that makes me complete.'

'Oh, pu-key. How far will you go?'

'As far as it takes.' His eyes are twinkling. I'm enjoying myself. This isn't hard at all. Being with Noah is fun, and chilled.

I tip my head on one side and study him. 'You don't even mind if I laugh at you, do you?'

He shakes his head. 'Not at all. This is about you, not me.'

'You're good at this.'

'I am, I told you.' The cheeky grin comes and then drops away. 'So are you. It just has to be about the person you're with, that's all.' He leans in closer. 'Yeah, I've got an ego the size of an elephant, but I just put it on hold. The only secret is to forget *you* for a moment. Let's face it, Rosie.' He takes my hand. 'Most of the time you're thinking about other people, aren't you? You're kind, considerate.' Blushing at the moment. 'I've seen you at work, or with your mates, and you're more interested in other people than yourself. You just get hung up when you're with a guy you don't know.' He smiles, but his thumb is stroking the back of my hand. It's mesmerising and I'm liking it far too much; I feel like he's hypnotising me, drawing me into his world. 'If you go in feeling confident that you look your best, you are your best. It's easy, Rosie. It's only hard when you're thinking about how you feel, not how you can make the other person feel. So,' he lets go of my hand, leans back and twinkles again, bringing me back down to earth and back to lesson-land, 'if you weren't ridiculously lucky and able to be here with sex god Noah, name three top qualities your perfect date must have.'

'Reliable.'

'Woah.' He holds a hand up. 'I knew we had to get back to your man-requirements and get real.'

'Do you remember everything?' I sigh.

He grins. 'When it comes down to you, I do. Strange eh?' The wink makes me all gooey inside. Then I twig what else he said.

'What do you mean, get real?'

'It's a rubbish list!'

'There's nothing wrong with wanting somebody reliable!'

'Well no but, number one requirement? You're kidding, me?' He grins.

'Shut up, this is my list!' I screw my face up and think. 'Considerate.'

He groans. 'Twenty-five going on fifty? Safe job, everything in moderation.'

'You're impossible!'

'You should be having fun, you deserve it. I consider it my duty to turn you around, to make you forget that boring list and come up with a new one!'

'Don't I deserve somebody good, faithful?' Somebody *not* like my father.

'Are we talking about Hugo again here?'

'Shush!'

'Rosie, somebody can be fun and faithful, if they're the

right person! I'm going to prove that to you.' He taps the table to make his point. 'Look, you deserve somebody,' he hesitates as though looking for the right words, 'somebody who brings out the best in you, somebody who makes you feel good, who makes you feel like you can do anything.'

'I do?'

'We all do. Nobody wants their other half to be just part of the fixtures and fittings. Don't settle for a doormat just because you think it's the safest option. What if one day the doormat wakes up and realises you're too good for it?'

'What exactly have you been drinking?'

He doesn't respond to that. 'Work hard, play hard, jump off a cliff now and then.'

'Okay, I give in, what are your three?' He might have a point though. I'd never call Robbie a doormat, but he had been what I'd thought was the perfect guy for me. And look what happened there. He sloped off to Wales and found sheep.

'Confident, brave, fun. Like you.'

I ignore the 'like you' bit. 'Not sexy?'

'Sexy comes with the other three. Have you not been listening to a word of today's lesson, Rosie-Posie? Tut, tut. Right, I dare you to close your eyes and the next drink you point at on the menu is your pick.'

'I'll be drunk.' I grin back at him.

'It doesn't matter.'

'It does, I have—' I'm about to say 'a date' tomorrow, but something stops me. I don't want to spoil the mood. 'Work tomorrow!'

'You'll be fine. Right next question.' He pauses, then looks me straight in the eye. 'What would you do if somebody cheated on you?'

'Walk away.' My shoulders stiffen. There are some things in life I have solid views on, and this is one of them.

'No backward glance?'

'Never. Nothing. Just walk away.' I motion to demonstrate.

'But what if you'd made a mistake? What if they hadn't actually cheated? You just thought they had? Or what if they'd just made a horrible—'

'One, I'd ask them straight out, so I'd know I hadn't made a mistake, and two, cheating on somebody is not a mistake. If you love somebody you don't do it, do you?'

'True.'

'It's disrespectful, cruel, hurtful. It can ruin somebody's life.'

He puts a finger under my chin, looks into my eyes. 'Don't ever let anybody ruin your life, Rosie. Only you have permission to do that.'

'That's an odd thing to say.'

'It's true. It's your life, make the rules, change the rules, do whatever it takes.'

'Do you?'

'Always. Right, next question.'

We chat about dates, good dates, bad dates, about my fear of flying, and his spider phobia. Light fun, nothing serious or tricky, and it's as easy as chatting to Bea.

'So, you approve of my makeover?' I'm not fishing for compliments. Okay, I might be a bit. But somehow, it's important what he thinks, that he does find me sexy. Not because of him, of course, but that if he does then somebody else might.

187

'It was a few tweaks, not a makeover.' He twiddles a strand of my hair in his fingers, so that it tugs ever so slightly at my scalp and sends a funny feeling surging through my body, which shocks me so much I freeze. I vaguely remember a sensation like this, a hollowing of my stomach, a feeling of delicious anticipation. It was the first time Robbie and I had a proper grope in the porch at my parents' house. Before Mum switched the light on and asked if we were going in 'before we caught our death'. After that all I felt was that it was nice and meant to be. Not quite the same. 'You're practically perfect as you are.' He is still twiddling, and his mouth is so close to my neck I can feel the warmth of his breath, and I forget about Robbie and squirm a bit.

'Only practically?' I laugh to cover up the fact that I need to shuffle away.

'Seriously.' He puts his hand over mine, gazes into my eyes. 'I'm the lucky one here, thanks for giving it a go.'

'That's a line as well, isn't it?' I can hear the strained edge to my voice. The words are forced, but if I can joke, say normal things then I can keep this how it's supposed to be.

Instead of letting it turn into something so tempting I want more.

'Partly.' He grins and sits back, and I know I should be heaving a sigh of relief, but instead feel disappointment. 'Ready to hit the road then?'

'Sure, fine! Lovely evening.' Shut up, Rosie.

He holds the door open for me and I take a step out into the perfect night. Warm air, a beautiful clear sky.

As we set off down the road, his hand brushes mine. There's

a tingle, a strange need inside of me to catch hold of his fingers. Is this how it's supposed to happen? Falling for somebody, wanting to date? Is this what I really want to happen – letting fate step in and lead me to a man who makes me tingle, rather than trying to pick the perfect guy?

Our forearms briefly touch, the hairs on mine prickle, we're walking in step and I realise I'm holding my breath. That the rest of the world no longer matters. If he kissed me now, I wouldn't care who saw. I wouldn't care that it's wrong. It's as though there's just the two of us. Nothing else matters.

He slows the pace. 'Rosie?'

I swallow. Is this it? Is this the moment when I throw out my rule book and let him kiss me, because I want him to so much and I'm prepared to risk being with a man who might be just like Dad? My heart is hammering, I can hear the thud in my ears.

'Yes.' I clear my throat, try to ignore the shivery anticipation that is threatening to break out of me.

'That Steve guy, you're going through with it?' And just like that he's burst the bubble.

It's not the two of us. It's a man and a girl striding along a dirty pavement.

'If you mean, am I seeing him? Then yeah, tomorrow.' I can hear the defensive edge to my voice.

I'd got carried away. I'd forgotten that he's doing this because of some other guy, not for me.

He's turned the heat up because he couldn't help himself. Because he didn't like the fact I'd been chatted up. Even though that's what we are here for.

Dad is like that. He can't help himself. He'll be off on tour, flirting and romancing his way through concerts, through life, but he only wants Mum to want *him*. To have *him*.

As the thought runs through my mind for the first time, I realise it is true. The slightest mention of other men in Mum's messages to him and he'd be home.

Not because of her, not because of us. But because he couldn't bear the thought of her being happy with other people.

He couldn't stand the thought of her doing to him what he did to her.

He was possessive, he got jealous – because to him, he was the only person who mattered. I don't want a guy who's like that. And I don't want to feel like that about a guy – because every time there was somebody, something, who demanded Dad's time and took him away from us, I was jealous.

I got angry. I felt hate.

I don't want to feel like that.

'I'm looking forward to it,' I say stiffly.

'Where are you meeting?' There's a gulf opening up between us that is far wider than the physical gap on the pavement.

'Stacey's.' It's a bar not far from where I live, and the moment Steve suggested it I knew it would be perfect. Casual, open, the type of place you have to shout a bit to be heard. Not the type of place that is uncomfortably intimate, or stiff and starchy. Fun.

'I'll go there with my date, then I can check you're okay.'

Eurghh, why do those words 'my date' annoy me so much? 'I'll be fine. But thanks for the offer.'

'You need me there, in case it turns out he's a psycho.'

'Gee ta, now I feel a lot better, big brother.'

'Be careful, Rosie, I don't want anybody to hurt you, to stop you believing in love.'

'It's only a date.' I don't get him, I don't get what he's so . . . well, scared of. What did he say? Love is fine until it goes wrong, until you lose it?

He stops, standing in front of me so that I have to look up and meet his gaze. 'I'll be there. It's the least I can do. Make sure you're safe.'

Safe from what exactly? Steve isn't a threat, I'm sure of that. So, is it him, or myself I need protecting from?

'And Rosie?'

'Yeah.'

'Your homework is to write a new list: the type of man you'd really like to have in your life. Not the one you think you should.'

'I—'

He puts his finger on my lips to shut me up. 'You don't have to hand it in, it's just for you.'

Chapter 13

Noah was right. Steve isn't exactly my dream date. He doesn't really tick any of the boxes on my new (not even committed to paper) list.

I thought I wanted, no correct that, *I know* that the type of man I actually need is all the things I said at the start. Some of those things are non-negotiable, like being faithful, a guy I can trust blah, blah . . . but I've had to add on 'funny'. Noah can be wickedly funny; he can make me smile when I don't even want to.

With Steve I've just smiled to be polite, like you do at a party of colleagues or family.

Robbie did make me laugh sometimes, but not belly laugh; it was more because of something that had happened, than something he did on purpose. We'd shared a sense of humour like I probably do with Steve. But with Noah it's different.

With Noah it's more like with Dad. Dad could make me laugh when he wanted to. Which was usually to deflect attention away from the fact that he'd just missed my birthday or forgotten to bring something home that he'd promised.

So naughty sense of humour had definitely not been on

my list. Until Noah. Noah does it because he wants to make me laugh – not because he feels he needs to for his own ends.

I thought cheeky laugh and winks went hand in hand with addictive personality and getting what you want. I think I might have been wrong.

So yeah, when Steve asked me out, he did fit my safe, secure, nothing-like-my-dad list.

But after spending time with Noah, this is all a bit, well, boring.

He's incredibly kind, incredibly nice, incredibly all of those overused words that are pretty meaningless.

Meaningless.

Like a pretty picture when I'd actually like something a bit edgy, a bit more nuanced. Though obviously not too much: I've not had a personality change, just a tweaking of expectations.

Noah is right (gahhhh). I need somebody who has a bit more about them. Sadly. But this is only a *practice date*, not a lifelong (or even day long) commitment.

Steve just happens to be very good at controlling runaway gym equipment. For which I am grateful. But not grateful enough to agree to a second date. But, hey, I'm having a first date at which the guy turns up, and stays, and we've had a lovely time. So that's a big win in my book.

Part of Steve's nervousness could be down to the fact that he spotted Noah at the other end of the bar about three seconds after he sat down – even though it is heaving and noisy. Noah isn't one to merge in with the crowd.

'He came over and said you'd probably want olives?' Steve says, sitting down with our second round of drinks.

'Sorry?'

He inclines his head in Noah's direction, and Noah winks.

'He what?!' I am going to kill him!

'You don't like olives?'

'He told you to get me olives?!' This is just the type of controlling thing Dad does. Something so minor nobody notices.

Like when you turn round and say that you'd been looking forward to choc-chip ice cream for ages, not the vegan coconut and lime new one he's insisted you have, he turns round and says, well it's not worth making a fuss about, is it? So you don't. You eat the ice cream that you didn't really want. And Mum drinks the wine that gives her a headache, but that Dad says everybody who knows anything about wine is drinking.

'Are you okay?' Steve touches my arm lightly, as though he's not sure if it's safe to. 'I can get rid of them. To be fair he didn't exactly tell me to get them, it was more an "olives are good here, mate, she devoured a whole bowl last time! Might get you extra brownie points" wink, wink, thing. I didn't know if he was trying to help or drop me in it!' He looks even more nervous now.

'Oh, hell, I'm sorry.' I want to hug him and tell him it isn't his fault. 'It's like going out with your big brother watching!' I laugh weakly. 'Always you, know, butting in? He's on a date; you'd think he'd be busy doing his own stuff.'

Steve raises an eyebrow. 'Maybe you two guys should actually get together.'

'Who?'

'You and your gym buddy of course.' Steve inclines his head to indicate further up the bar.

'Oh Noah? Oh no, what makes you say that?'

'The way you keep watching each other.'

'We don't! Well, he looks out for me, he's just a bit . . .'

'Possessive?'

'Protective,' I say stiffly, wondering why I'm defending him. 'Sorry about the other day. He behaved like an arse, he's not normally like that. He's quite friendly normally.'

'I'm sure he is. He could lighten up a bit on the bodyguard act though.'

'Bodyguard?' I frown.

'Look, I'm not being funny, but being smiled at when you're at the urinals is kind of off-putting.'

'He followed you to the toilets?' I don't know whether to be angry or laugh. 'He came up to you at that bar, *and* he followed you to the toilets? You're kidding?'

'Well, it could have been a coincidence.'

I raise an eyebrow. 'And he smiled?'

'In a kind of, well not menacing, more warning, like "don't mess with my woman" way. It made me a bit nervous if I'm honest!'

After deciding he wasn't being controlling – like Dad – but more caring – like Mum – and not possessive – like Dad – but more protective – like Bea, I am now cross again. There's protective, and there's 'this is getting downright over the top'.

Following my date into the toilets suggests the kind of quality control that is totally uninvited. Was he checking he measured up in all departments?! 'Oh, you have to be joking me. And I'm not his woman, honest!'

'I get that.' Steve shrugs. 'But maybe he wants you to be.'

It's not the same after that. The conversation doesn't quite flow. It's like going out with your dad in attendance. Well worse.

Dad, when he was present, always gave my friends a bit of a once-over to see if he approved, but he was actually quite distant most of the time now I come to think about it. He kissed, cuddled, joked, called me his girl, but emotionally he was actually quite closed off.

Which is weird now I come to think of it. Because I haven't thought about it like that before.

In fact, I've only realised it right now, because Noah is the exact opposite. He's managed to get right under my skin for all kinds of different reasons.

Steve leans in and kisses my cheek. 'Honestly, I'd give it a go. That girl he's with is well pissed off.'

'I hadn't noticed.' I have though, and I know it's totally horrible, but I've been pleased that they've not been all over each other.

'Thanks for this evening, I've enjoyed it.'

'Me too.'

He smiles. It's not a sparks-flying what-comes-next type of smile. It's just, well, nice. 'Maybe we could do coffee some time?'

'I'd like that.' And I mean it. I would. As homework goes, this date has been pretty good. Apart from the interfering-Noah bits. I obviously don't want Steve to realise I've categorised him as 'homework' and not 'red-hot date'.

'You sure I can't walk you to the bus stop or anything?'

'She's sure.' Noah's silky-smooth voice makes me jump. I could hit him! Or, I could go with Steve, just to spite him.

Or I could be mature and stand my ground and give him a piece of my mind.

'Okay?' Steve gives me a questioning look.

I sigh. 'Sure. I'm sorry, I had a lovely evening, thanks. And I would really love a coffee sometime.'

'Great. See you round! Keep up the training.' He makes a running motion and I smile.

'Will do!'

'I'll text you!' He is watching Noah nervously, but then plucks up enough courage to kiss me on the cheek.

'Great! See you soon!'

'Is this seat taken?' The instant Steve turns away, Noah points at his empty seat.

'The standard of your chat-up lines has dropped dramatically.'

'It can go either way after a few drinks. I'm either hilarious, suave and a total catch, or a bit cheesy. So, he had an early night?'

'Steve? Yeah, he had to get off.'

'Good evening?'

'Great, he's really nice.'

'Reliable and considerate?'

'Yep, and kind, easy to talk to.'

'Boring then?'

'I didn't say that!'

'Ahh but you didn't have to,' he waggles a finger, 'go on admit it, he didn't light your fire.'

I sigh. 'Just how drunk are you?'

'Not that bad. Can squeeze a couple more in; are you game, Rosie-Posie?'

He's not exactly swaying, but he's definitely had a few more than me. And all of a sudden, getting slightly sloshed with Noah seems like quite a nice idea. There's been an edge between us since Steve asked me out, and I've missed our easy closeness. Noah and I just kind of slipped into a jokey double-act effortlessly from the first time we met. I can't remember ever having that with anybody, not even Robbie.

I've missed Noah.

I've also missed the little fizz when his arm brushed mine, the lump in my throat when he held my gaze for just a nano-second longer than a casual friend would do.

I'm stuffed, aren't I? I think I might be in danger of rewriting my 'suitable guy' list so that he has a chance of sneaking in. Shit. Let's face it, I am talking about fancying the pants off a guy who has just spent the evening *with another woman*. While I've been dating another man.

'He was fine, we had a nice evening, but no, if it makes you happy.' It needs saying, honesty is the best policy. 'He wasn't the most exciting guy I've ever been out with.'

'Haha! I knew it! Didn't I say that, was I right or was I—'

'What do you mean, haha! Come on, Noah, it's actually none of your business if I fancied the pants off him, is it? You're just here to help me make guys fancy the pants off me. And he seemed to!'

'He did.'

'So, you got a result.'

'I suppose so,' he says slightly sulkily.

'Anyway, what happened to your date? Was she pissed off

199

because you were interfering with Steve at the bar, and following him to the toilets?'

He flinches and pulls a funny face.

Okay, maybe that didn't come out right. 'You know what I mean! Why did you have to stick your nose in? I didn't come over there and give you advice, did I?'

'Like what? I'm the teacher here!' He smiles.

'Like asking if that's the way to go – full on brassy-blonde hair extensions. I could have found out where she had them done!'

'Woah, woah, woah, my little Rosie!'

I'm being bitchy. What is he doing to me? This is *so* not me. Shit, he is making me sound jealous. Okay, honesty time, he is making me feel jealous – and I *hate* it, because I've spent a large part of my life feeling it. I've watched Dad move in a little too close to other women, spend a little too much time with other women, and this conversation is reminding me of that.

I must stop.

I don't want to be with a man who makes me feel like Dad did.

'Don't call me little! And I'm not yours.' Take a deep breath, do not let him make you angry. 'You really don't need to keep an eye on me, you know!'

'True, you're not mine, are you? So you keep telling me! Anyway, for your information, delightful Daisy was not pissed off with me talking to your date. She started to ask about my job, my house, my five-year plan.' He grimaces. 'Boring. I told her I wasn't the guy for her, and I had business to attend to!'

'I'm not *business*.' I can hear the sullen edge to my voice. This is why my 'man requirement' list must not allow a Noah-shaped spot in my life. Even if I am happy to have a few casual dates right now, I'm a Daisy through and through. My question checklist includes all those details that Noah finds so boring. *Why* does he have to be so not-the-right-guy for me? Sometimes life is so unfair!

'Yup you are. Saw he was about to go—'

'You chased him off!'

'Hang on!' I suddenly feel slightly more cheerful. 'You're jealous!'

'I am not!'

'You are.' I grin. He grins back and looks a bit sheepish.

'Okay I admit it, a teeny-teeny bit jealous that a guy who is completely wrong for you is getting to spend the evening with you. When you could be sitting with me, making me laugh and helping me polish my ego.'

'Oh yeah? So I'm your cheap entertainment?'

'Not so cheap.' He grins. 'But definitely entertaining. I'd rather,' the grin drops, and he takes my hand in his, 'be here with you talking about Hugo and dating disasters, than be with anybody else in the world.'

I know he's taking the mickey, but it'll do for me.

'So here I am ready to help you reflect on lessons learned.'

'Haha. So forgetting all the flannel, basically you ducked out because it got personal with Daisy?'

'Ooo I'm being analysed!'

'Did a girl break your heart, Noah?' We're still in jokey-mode, and the question has come into my head from nowhere, but it has suddenly hit me. Why else would he be keener to spend time teaching a girl like me to date, than actually getting stuck in with a girl who knows the score and wants to play by *his* rules?

'Haha, amateur psychologist, Rosie.' He slumps down beside me and gazes up. Then reaches out and strokes my cheek with the back of his hand. It's so tender and deliberate all the antagonism between us disappears; it brings a lump to my throat. I must have drunk more than I thought. 'Guys already fancy the pants off you, you're beautiful.' I shiver involuntarily, gulp. I should move, I should go now. 'Look, Rosie.' He puts a hand over mine and leans in even closer, confidentially. 'Before we go any further, there's something you need to know about me.'

'What do you mean before we go any further?' I whisper back, my throat all sandpapery.

'With the lessons, before we get to the real nitty gritty and you fall madly in love with me.'

The way he says it, so matter of fact, hits the intense moment on the head. It's gone, just like that. I laugh. 'I'm not going to fall madly in love with you! Big head!'

'You are, unless you know. You see,' he leans in even closer, until his nose brushes against my skin, lowers his voice to a very loud whisper, 'love is horrible.' He sinks back onto the seat as though the announcement has exhausted him. We're still shoulder to shoulder, our fingers close enough to entwine, but he's miles away. 'A total ball-breaker. You never recover from it.' He nods his head. 'Honest, cross my heart. I know. It is evil, so,' he taps the back of my hand, 'don't do it, Rosie-Posie.'

'Oh, Noah.' I want to hug him, but I resist. Is this what he was talking about, love that went wrong? 'It can be evil, but it doesn't have to be.' I mean, I know exactly about the bad side of love, don't I? The totally in lust, passionate, destructive type of love that can practically remove all common sense and replace it with a lack of impulse control and make a person put up with crap they really shouldn't. This is what I've been trying to tell him – that safe, sensible love is a much better option. 'It doesn't have to be like that, not all kinds of love are evil. You just have to find the right one, who won't hurt you, or cheat on you . . .' My words drift off, he's giving me a funny raised-eyebrow look. I'll save that speech for another time. 'Who did this to you? Who was she?' I know it's not really any of my business, but I feel like I want to know who's hurt him so hard he feels he has to veer away from any woman he might fall for. Because maybe he's not the same as Dad at all. Maybe he's more like me. Afraid to fall too deeply for somebody who might hurt him all over again.

'Who?' He blinks.

'The girl you loved.'

'I didn't love a girl!' He frowns. 'I've never been in love really, have you?'

I am confused. Very confused. He looks confused as well.

I take a big gulp of the drink he bought for me and decide to play along, then steer things back to him. Subtly. Although I'm not good at subtle when I've had a few drinks. 'I thought I was, but it wasn't proper love, it was—'

'Safe! You went for somebody you just liked. Very wise. But,' he looks around as though he's expecting somebody to be eavesdropping, 'I know somebody who was totally in love! Off his head, completely, doo-lally, bonkers in love.'

'You do? It wasn't you; it was somebody else?'

'Oh God, yeah. And it ruined him. He's ruined. Totally ruined, a mess.' He shakes his head and looks genuinely upset. 'Broken into little bits. That's what love does. Do you want another drink? I'm parched. Back in a minute.'

I watch him weave his way to the bar. I've never seen Noah drunk. And I've never heard him use the 'L' word before either. I feel a bit tipsy myself, but not so tipsy that I don't need to hear the rest of this.

'So,' he plonks himself back down, and takes a swig of his drink. 'Drink up, cheers!'

'Cheers! This guy?'

'Jed! It's Jed!'

'Jed?' I frown. The name rings a bell. 'Oh Jed!'

'You know him too?' He looks confused. 'What a bloody coincidence. Miserable git, isn't he?'

'I don't know him. The day we met, when I'd been stood up?' He nods. 'You said you'd met him for a drink.'

He nods violently. 'You sure you want to hear this? It's sad. Very sad.' He pulls a sad face, it's a bit of a pantomime face, but there's more to it than that. His eyes look sad. It's important, I'm sure of it.

'Tell me about Jed.'

'O-kay.' He draws the word out, swigs his drink and takes a deep breath. 'I met Jed at uni and he was dating this girl he'd grown up with. Millie.' He smiles. 'She was lovely. Pretty and funny. Bit like you.' He glances at me, twirls a lock of my hair absentmindedly then lets his hand fall away. 'They were so good together, they got married as soon as we graduated, and they were still just as loved-up.'

'What happened?' I whisper. 'What did she do?'

'She died.'

Whatever I'd expected him to say, it wasn't that. Then I remember his comment before, about going out with Jed because it was the anniversary of his wife's death.

'She went and fucking died. Car crash. Over. Gone.' He waves his hands around, then rests them back on the table.

'Oh my God, no.' I put my hand over his; there's pure shocking bitterness in his tone.

He nods. 'I envied them, you know. They were so bloody happy together, properly in love. I watched them sometimes and it was the way he watched her, you know?' He looks my way, but I don't think he really sees me, he doesn't seem to expect an answer. 'It was like at times nothing else mattered; he literally only had eyes for her.' He laughs, a short laugh, but it isn't harsh, it's fond memories, I think. 'I used to tease him, but he didn't care, he'd just shrug.' He studies his hands for a moment. 'When it happened, he seemed okay at first, he went through the motions, coped at the funeral; you know, one day at a time stuff. He coped, that's the word everybody used, coped. I thought give him space, support him, don't rush. You know?' He looks at me properly now, his eyes darting as though he's looking for answers in my face. I nod. 'Six months after she died, we went to a footie match. We'd always gone to the football together and Millie used to come too. He cracked, completely,' he shakes his head, 'he wasn't bloody coping at all. He fell apart, right there in the ground before the game had even kicked off.' He takes a long swig of beer. 'And that,' his voice is stronger now, his normal tone. Decisive. 'Is what love does to you. To think I was bloody jealous of him.' He laughs. 'Wrecked him. Never had a date since. Never been the same happy guy again. And that is why it just isn't worth it. I am never going to be like that. Happens once, happens twice, never going to bloody catch me out a third time.'

'Oh.' I try to get to grips with this in my slightly drunken brain. Noah is a serial one-night stander because he's scared? Scared of falling in love? Big, brave, confident Noah isn't incapable of being faithful, he's just frightened of what meeting the right woman might do to him? And what did he mean, it happened twice?

'You don't have to be *madly* in love though, you can just be . . .'

'A bit?' He guffaws, but then it gradually morphs into his normal deep chuckle – sending mixed messages to my tummy. He's so gorgeous, he's so nice, he's so . . . wrong. He stops laughing and gazes at me, his face serious. 'It's the real deal, or nothing at all.' He leans forward, intent. 'How many songs do they sing about being a little bit in love? Or how many of your movies tell you to settle for the nearly-guy? Eh, eh? How many,' he taps my hand, 'settle for boring?' Then he sits back triumphant while I wriggle uncomfortably. 'All or nothing.' Then he grins. 'Though nothing can be pretty damned good sometimes.'

Noah is never going to understand my version of comfortable love. How can he not see it doesn't have to be total passion, it can be more about companionship, somebody you *like*. That you trust. I think that is a conversation for when I am sober and can think straight, and he is sober and might listen to my logic. 'How is he now? Jed?'

'Better,' he pauses, 'coping. But he's never gone back to being the Jed I knew.' He stares at me. 'There's a bit of him missing. There's a bit of all of us missing.'

'You were fond of her as well?' I ask tentatively. This goes beyond him just feeling sorry for his friend.

'She was gorgeous, just like you are. And she's gone, just like, just like . . . You want another drink? I want another drink!'

'Or shall we go back to mine?'

'Will the nosy woman with the key be there?'

'She hasn't got a key, you took it off her, remember?'

'Haha, yes! We have the key! Come on then.'

We wobble our way down the road, and it just feels right to slip my hand into his. A moment later he pulls free, and I feel like I've lost a part of me, then his arm is around my shoulders and it feels like it belongs there. We're offering each other support – mentally and to stop ourselves falling over.

We stare at each other when we get to my front door.

'This is me.'

'I know.'

'Coffee?'

'Maybe not a good idea.'

I think the walk has sobered him up. He's right, maybe not.

We both know that this could go horribly wrong if one of us should take a step forward, if one of us should reach out. If he puts his hands on my waist, or I put mine on his shoulders. If our lips were to meet. I know it would be perfect. I know it's what I want.

I know it would change everything. Spoil everything. Be the beginning of the end.

But oh my God I wish he would.

Because maybe he isn't the man I thought he was. Maybe he's not like my dad at all.

But it would still end in tears. Mine. Because I'd just be another girl who wants more than he can give. Like Daisy.

He gives me a gentle shove. 'Night, Rosie.'

'Night, Noah.'

His words are soft, and mine match, but I don't think he hears. He's already turned away, waving briefly at the bottom of the path without looking back.

Chapter 14

Noah has gone a bit strange on me. You know when you get up in the morning and you have that empty feeling in the pit of your stomach, because you know things aren't right?

That.

I suppose it's my own fault. When he didn't reply to my first text, I should have taken a deep breath and left it. But I didn't.

It's just I find it so frustrating if I text somebody about something and then I don't get a reply. Even though the original text wasn't *that* important. I text again, then start to panic that things aren't right, that I've said the wrong thing. So, I text again. And before I know it, I'm getting more and more wound up about something stupid and there is no way back.

I couldn't just leave it.

Anyway, he's not replied.

I think we might have spoiled everything. This is what happens when you get drunk with somebody and share your innermost thoughts. You cock things up, because there is no going back to the person you wanted them to see. They can see the other, naked you.

Noah is naked, and he never wanted to be with me. I'm not stupid, I know it's not me personally. He doesn't want to be stripped bare in front of anybody. So, he grins and flirts and gets along just fine.

I understand, I truly do. I have my own barriers. I know the version of Rosie that I want the world to see. But this does hurt: the feeling of loss, the feeling that we might have spoiled things and can't go back to the way we were. If he'd just reply to my bloody texts it would be okay.

It is making me feel sick and churned up inside.

I stare at my reflection in the bathroom mirror. It's not just the thought I've lost Noah that is making me feel a mess, it's everything.

I am so glad I don't have to go into work today. It's not just that I have an alcohol induced hangover, I've also got a mental hangover – total brain ache. I zonked out the moment my head hit the pillow, then was awake two hours later feeling slightly sexually frustrated and majorly annoyed with myself. Sending texts that I shouldn't.

What was that last night? I really could have grabbed Noah and kissed him. As in totally snogged his face off. Tonsils, tongues and tits as my mate at school used to say when we were young and hormonally challenged.

We were drunk; definitely, totally smashed. And I was sad for him, so it would have been wrong; it would have been a pity snog. That's it!

No, it wouldn't, who am I trying to kid. I really wanted to

snog him. I wanted to feel his hands on me. I wanted him to rip off my new sexy underwear and ravish me.

Oh shit.

I put my hands on my hot cheeks.

This is not good.

If he hadn't been the gentleman he is, then last night could have ended in disaster.

Or would it? I mean, from what he said he's not the player he comes across as. He's just scared of love.

Although isn't that what players are? They're not all shits who like the chase and the power. Some of them just can't commit.

I lay my hot forehead against the cold glass. It helps for a split second.

I can't date somebody who can't commit. I can't. I can't be like my mother. In love with the fantasy version of a man.

I'm in dangerous water. Noah was seriously upset last night; he genuinely cares about his friend Jed and it nudged something deep inside me. He's a good man, a nice man. He'd make a brilliant friend – but how do I make sure I don't try and make him out to be more in my head?

Maybe the fact he's not talking to me is a good thing. If he was, I might make a complete jerk of myself.

My phone buzzes and I scurry back into my bedroom at an indecently fast pace. Just in case it's him.

Bugger. I've stubbed my toe on the door jamb and it bloody hurts.

I take a deep breath and force myself to stop and rub it. Slow down. It doesn't matter if it is him; it doesn't matter if you miss the call. I'm turning into the desperate woman I swore I'd never be.

It's not him.

The surge of disappointment is scary. And my head hurts. Even my eyeballs are smarting.

'Hi, Mum!'

'Hi, darling, it's me!'

'I know it is.' I sit on the bed and force a cheery note into my voice.

'Is everything okay?'

Ha! That didn't work then. 'Fine, just stubbed my bloody toe.'

'Don't swear dear, how many times have I told you to wear slippers?'

'Plenty. Everything okay, Mum?' I inspect my foot. It's not bleeding, but it is throbbing. Like the rest of me, haha.

'I can buy you some.'

'What?'

'Slippers, dear.'

'I've got some.' Five pairs in fact. Four unworn. One pair under the bed. Mainly Christmas and birthday presents from my parents. 'I just didn't put them on.'

'We're not having the party—'

'Oh thank—'

'—in the house this time.' She carries on as though she hasn't heard me. 'We're going to have a marquee. Sorry, darling, what did you say?'

'I said oh goodness.' Bugger, for a moment then I thought she'd come to her senses and abandoned the idea. 'Does that mean there are lots of people invited?'

'More than normal; some of your dad's friends from the orchestra are coming. I thought it would be a nice surprise for him!'

Oh hell, this is getting worse. 'Surprise?' I say faintly. Does this mean he doesn't know?

'Surprise. So anyway, it doesn't matter if you're bringing a plus one, or not; you don't have to tell me in advance as we'll have lots of room.'

'Great.'

'But you *will* bring your young man, won't you? You are still seeing him, aren't you? The fling.' She chuckles.

'I am.' Am I?

'Well whatever you like to call him, we'd like to meet him.'

'He might not want to come. He might be too busy.' At the moment he's too busy to even text me to confirm that he's still alive. 'But who knows I might have another guy by then, haha.' Why on earth did I say that? We've not progressed beyond beginner's level lessons, and it doesn't look like I'll ever get to the practical sessions.

The only man I have had an actual date with is Steve. And I can't ask Steve, because there really is no future in that, and I don't really want to ask Noah because things are tricky enough in my head as it is, without introducing a 'meet my whacky parents' scenario. Not that he'd reply anyway.

I need to get a move on. I need to go out and try out my fledgling seduction techniques. Find myself a real boyfriend. I mean, Steve fancied me and that worked out fine as a date, so I've definitely made progress, haven't I?

'Darling, are you still there?'

'Of course, I'm still here.'

'Have you got a contact number for that pretty cellist that your father is fond of? You know Stella, Sarah, the young one?'

'Serena?'

'That's the one.'

Shit. Simpering Serena who was so thrilled to play in Italy with Dad. I think she took a personal tour of his own less monumental but similarly inclined tower of Pisa.

'I know he was *exceptionally* fond of her, but he moved on, and if I don't invite her it will look like I'm bothered.'

'But you are bothered, Mum. Of course, you're bloody bothered.'

'Don't swear, dear,' she says mildly. I think it's from force of habit rather than her being bothered.

'Mum, is this really a good idea? Can't we just invite friends, you know, real friends?'

'Rosalie, darling, you really don't understand, do you? I don't blame the girls, I blame him.'

'Oh.' There really is no answer to that.

'It takes two to tango, and I can't blame those silly deluded girls if they're taken in. I was!'

'But that's different! You fell in love with each other, and he—'

'We did, darling. And I still love him a lot, but he loves himself and the thrill of the chase even more. If he wants to collect pretty things, then we might as well put them on show rather than hiding them in a cupboard, don't you agree?'

'Well, yes, but . . .' If I thought my head was spinning before, it's hit a whole different level now. I sit down heavily on the floor and rest my forehead on the palm of my hand. 'Not at your wedding anniversary party, and not at our home!'

'Well I don't see why not. That's the problem, he puts things in different boxes, and I think we need a reorganisation.'

I'm not sure if she's lost it or come to her senses.

Is this a menopause thing?

'I feel very guilty about dragging you halfway round the world with us when you were little.'

Mum has never, ever said anything like this before, but the last thing I want her to feel is guilt. 'I loved it!' I did, in the main. I loved the new places, even if I was lonely at times when my parents only had eyes for each other. But it was better than being at home with a mum who was sad and anxious.

'It was selfish, but I couldn't let him put his family in a box to come back and play with when he got tired of his new toys.'

'I'm not sure I like being classed as an old boring toy.'

'You weren't an old boring toy, he loved playing with you, he always came back – you were his favourite.'

I feel a bit queasy. Is this what it's like when you take hallucinogenic drugs? Wow, that must be what happened last night. My drink was spiked, none of this is real.

Was I really just an entertaining plaything for him? A novelty.

'But he couldn't resist new shiny toys; he still can't, and to be quite honest I've grown too old and wise. I haven't got the time and patience to be running after him waving my travelling toy box.' She sighs. 'He thinks we'll always just be here when he fancies coming back to us.'

'But we will, won't we?' A note of alarm has crept into my voice. I can feel a shiver of fear in my throat. She's not going to leave him, is she?

I've never thought about Dad this way, and I'm shocked that Mum does.

But maybe she's right.

Maybe however hard I tried to be perfect, I'd still always only be the daughter he came back to see when it suited him. When it was convenient, and there was nothing more exciting on offer.

I feel ill. Is that all I ever have been, convenient?

Is he something worse than just a bit of a womaniser and cheat?

Does he deserve to have somebody as wonderful as Mum waiting for him?

'Oh, course, Rosie,' she says firmly. 'I'm just knocking the safe walls down so that we can all see more clearly what's what. I refuse to hide! You can only listen to the same old promises about changing so many times before you start to get immune to the sugary charm that they're coated in. Now, that's enough of that. It's entirely up to you if you bring a boyfriend, though I would rather like you to fall in lust at least once.'

'Mum!'

'I let your father give me stress and frown lines I don't

deserve, but when we were younger, oh goodness the passion was worth anything. I'd forgive him anything at that moment when—'

'Lalala, hands over ears, can't hear you!'

She laughs. 'You're a funny girl at times! I was about to say when he looked into my eyes and I felt like I was the most important thing in the world to him. I want that feeling again, Rosie.' Her voice softens. 'There's no better feeling than being loved, than being somebody's entire world, not just a small square-shaped hole they'd like me to wait quietly in. You'll know when you get it.'

'I—'

'I'm not being nasty, Rosie, but your Robbie wasn't that. He was a nice enough boy, but you're not really bothered he's gone, are you?' She doesn't wait for an answer. 'Now, I am arranging this party because I want a good party. I like the excuse to dress up and dance, but I am also not going to pretend these flings don't exist, so if you can track Serena down for me that would be wonderful. I'm sure you can find her on the internet quicker than I can. Are you going to tell me why you've got a hangover?'

'No, I'm not!'

'I hope he was worth it.' She laughs.

'I could have been out with Bea!'

'Ah, but you weren't, were you?'

I don't quite know what has happened to Mum. She's being weird, weirder than normal. 'You're not, well, ill or anything are you, Mum?'

'I'm not planning on dropping dead any time soon, if that's

what you mean. I just want a bit of fun, to live a bit. I'm thinking of Botox, and bootcamp.'

Oh God, she has got more energy than me.

'I've been telling you all your life to do things for yourself, not some man, and everything I do is for your bloody father!'

'Don't swear, Mum!'

'Oh he makes me want to swear at times. I mean, I went out with him in the first place because my friend said "go out with him and you'll never have a boring life!" I mean she was right, we didn't, but now I even watch what he wants on the TV, you know. Even when he's not here! So he's only got himself to blame for this.'

'What, Mum? You've lost me.' Normally Mum is pretty lucid, but she seems kind of hyper today. Everything is at double speed.

She sighs. 'I saw him on this documentary thing.' She has slowed down and sounds a bit defeated. It was nicer when she was speeding. 'I only got a brief glimpse of him, at this opening night of some opera or something. He wasn't featured or anything, just a face in the crowd.'

'And?' I can hear the blood pounding in my ears, it's just the way she says it. Matter of fact but so deliberate it's scary.

'I double checked the date, but I was right, it was my birthday. He told me he had a life-changing audition and so I forgave him.'

'Oh.'

'I've turned into a right doormat and it isn't who I really am. Be yourself but better is my new thing!' Her voice has lifted again, and she sounds genuinely happy, not put-on happy. Strong.

'You're beginning to sound like Noah.' I can't help but smile.

'Noah? Ahh! He's your man. I like him already! And he gave you a hangover and made you all wound up, which is more than Robbie ever did.'

'I am not wound up!'

She laughs again. 'I do love you, Rosie.'

'I love you too.' I say, not quite able to hide the fact I am slightly miffed.

'I didn't give you a shit upbringing, did I?'

'Only when you wouldn't let me have supersize popcorn at the cinema.'

'I shouldn't have followed your dad round like I did. I could have scarred you for life.'

Scared for life more like. 'I wouldn't have seen him if we hadn't! And you wanted to be with him.'

'God knows why I've put up with him for so long.'

I stare at my feet. 'Because of me?'

'Oh heavens, none of this is your fault! I mean, I did want you to have two parents when you grew up, that was my decision. But honestly, Rosie,' her tone softens, 'he wasn't the best example of fatherhood, well manhood, in the world. A man can be fun and flirty without feeling the need to get into every passing pair of knicker—'

'Mum!'

'And think it's right to lie to and deceive the people who love them. Anyway, when you were born, we were the adults and I was determined to try and make it work, but I honestly wonder if you'd have been better off without watching our sham marriage.'

'It wasn't a sham, Mum.' I've always given Dad excuses, blamed me, blamed work, blamed a million and one things, but never really blamed him. Maybe I need to face up to it, like Mum has. Dad has, like Noah said, been a pretty shit father.

And Noah was right when he said that I should be the person *I* want to be, not the one I think Dad wants me to be. And Noah was right when he said that my list of requirements isn't all it should be.

I don't want a 'Robbie', I want somebody who is fun and makes me laugh. I want a little bit of the good things that Mum had.

Maybe there's some truth in what she's said though, about the sham marriage. Maybe this is why I'm so totally crap at adult relationships. If I'm so confused about who my parents are and what they want from each other and expect from me, how can I possibly know what I want for myself?

I take a deep breath. 'You wanted to be with him, and I did too.' Sharing more time at home would have been nicer, but that had never been the life Dad had mapped out, with or without his 'Serenas'. He'd never have been a nine-to-five man.

'True, at least you weren't left with some stranger, or your grandparents I suppose! Who knows what effect they would have had on you! Oh heck, is that the time? I'm supposed to be going rollerblading. Better go.'

'What?' WTF? Rollerblading?

'It's good for the thighs, you should try it. Thunder thighs your dad used to call me when we were younger!'

I smile. I've been wrong. Whatever Mum's been through

hasn't really changed her. She's bounced right back. Maybe I need to take a leaf out of her book. Be me. Be brave. Maybe falling in love with the wrong guy wouldn't be the end of the world after all.

Chapter 15

Two hours after Mum called, when I'd had a chance to shower, drink several cups of black coffee, and google HRT to see if it can cause extreme personality changes (the menopause has a lot to answer for, but I'm not sure it can be held totally responsibly for Mum), my mobile rings.

'Ropes.'

'What?' This was not the first word I thought Noah and I would share after our intense evening together.

Maybe he is one of those people who doesn't recall anything they say after several drinks.

'Our next lesson, I've decided we're going to do it with ropes.' He chuckles. Why has this made my mouth go indecently dry, and my body feel all hot and bothered?

'Ropes?' It comes out all high-pitched. I swallow and try again. 'What do you mean ropes? And what do you mean next time, we haven't done it a first time!' For some reason my mind has taken a detour down a very dirty route.

'Rosie, Rosie.' He tuts, but he's smiling. 'Mind like a sewer, and I thought you were such a nice girl.'

223

'I am a nice girl!' A confused girl, but a nice girl. 'I thought we were going to meet at that café by the park?' Cake, not ropes.

'Change of plan. I've decided we need to fast track!'

Oh no, he can't wait to get rid of me. 'It's okay if you're busy, you can just stop, I do understand.' My fingers are crossed, I'm not quite ready for Noah to walk out of my life. Not yet. 'I have learned quite a lot, I'm loads more confident than—'

'Don't be daft, it's not that. But you've still got to be party-ready, yep?'

'Yep!' This is even more important now, after my chat to Mum. Not only have I kind of reinforced the idea that I have an actual boyfriend, and I have somehow managed to drop the name 'Noah' in, I am also determined to turn up on full supportive terms for her, and to stick a metaphorical two fingers up at my wayward Dad by being with somebody *I* want to be with. This is tricky, as I am now beginning to think I do actually want somebody who is fun and flirty (like Noah) – and where the hell am I going to find somebody like that with such short notice? I think we need to jam as many lessons, and practice dates in as possible. Quickly.

'I was thinking last night about what it is that we're missing, and I got it.' WTF? I lie awake wondering if he's okay, and if not kissing him was a mistake or a good thing, and when and if he's going to get back in touch, and he's thinking about bondage and fast tracking me? 'I set some objectives. You need to take a few risks in life, step outside your comfort zone.'

'I do?'

'You do. You need to let go of control a bit.'

'What do you mean?' I try to push the note of suspicion out of my voice.

'Well, er you're a bit reserved.'

'No, I'm not!'

'Well, not always.' He's grinning. 'You're a bit of a conundrum, more than direct enough when it comes to speaking your mind, but you need to dice with danger a bit – find out that it won't kill you.'

'Is this about me not letting you pick a drink for me!'

'Something like that, and the fact that you picked a boring git like Steve to go out with.'

'I was practising! It was just a date!' I pause. 'Oh right, I see, you're getting me back for sorting out my own practicals!'

'He was a safe bet.' He chuckles again.

'I was actually quite proud of myself actually getting a date, until you butted in and—'

'Oh.' There's a long pause. 'Sorry, I'm being a git. You did do well, brilliantly, but you need another date, better dates.'

'Hmm.' Lots more dates: he read my mind. 'Mum says I need passion.' I'm not going to tell him what else she said – that would have him running for the hills.

'Exactly! Wise woman. So, tomorrow we'll get you up in the air. Then I'll take you for a drink after to recover.'

'Recover?' I'm not sure I like the sound of that.

'Trust me. I know what I'm doing.'

Do I trust him? I think I trust him – I mean he's never given me a reason not to, has he?

'Oh, and sorry I didn't reply to your texts, forgot to put my phone on charge when I got in last night. Too much to drink; sorry if I got a bit OTT, dunno what got into me.'

'But you're okay now?'

'Of course, I am, why wouldn't I be? I'll pick you up at 10am.' He ends the call before I can say anything else.

I call an emergency meeting with Bea. This calls for coffee, cake and some logical thinking.

And an escape plan.

* * *

'Why are you looking so worried?' Bea nudges me in the ribs as I drop my mobile phone back in my bag.

'I'm not looking worried.'

'Okay, pensive then? Come on then, spill. Tell me about him! Did you shag?'

'Bea! You know it's not like that!'

'No, I don't! Hang on,' she peers at me, 'you're talking about Noah, aren't you?'

'Why, who are you talking about?' I frown at her.

'Steve! Your date, remember?'

'Oh him, yeah.' I'd pretty much forgotten about Steve.

She laughs. 'Come on then, what's happened now? Honestly you spend more time talking to Noah that you did to Robbie!'

She's right. I hadn't thought about it before, but I do talk to Noah and text him a lot. When we go our separate ways, it will leave a big hole in my life. Though the whole point of this it to fill any holes with a new man, or at least the ability to get one.

'So?'

'Ropes.' I stare at her. 'He wants to do it with ropes!'

'Wow.'

'That's what he said. What does he mean?'

'Ropes, oh my God, Rosie! He's a dream! Honestly, why you're not shagging him yet I will never understand.'

'Stop it, he didn't mean that!' I say, even though that *was* exactly my first thought. 'And we're not like that!'

'You've gone pink!'

'He said I need to step out of my comfort zone and let go of control.'

'I bet he means climbing walls, or that jungle place.'

'Oh shit, why didn't I think of that?' I didn't think of that because hanging suspended above a forest with only a rope to hang onto is not something I even think about, let alone consider doing. 'No.' This is really stepping out of my comfort zone. 'I'm scared of heights!' I am. Just seeing somebody else stand on the edge of a rock face makes me feel queasy.

'You can cling on to his manly body.' She chuckles. 'Though you have to admit, if you survive that then it will make dating people a piece of piss.'

'Very nicely put,' I say, madly googling 'rope climbing'. 'Frig, you could be right.' My heart is pounding as I look at the website with the tag line 'go wild'. I put my phone down. I feel sick. 'Let go of control AKA scare myself shit-less.' I am now feeling weak at the knees for totally different and unromantic reasons. 'I think I'd rather he just tied me up,' I say glumly.

Bea laughs. 'You're funny.'

'You know I don't like it!' This doesn't date from some experience in my childhood. It's like spiders. But less irrational. Falling from heights can hurt you. I've seen enough murder movies to know that.

'I know.' She smiles softly at me. 'But you do trust him, don't you?' She says encouragingly.

'Well, yeah, but . . .' I do. I have never trusted anybody in my life like I do Noah. Something about him makes me feel safe in some deep-down part of me.

'Then try it. What can go wrong?'

'I die?'

'These places don't let people die, except—' She grins. 'Except in extreme circumstances, or,' she pauses, 'sabotage.'

'Thanks, I feel much better now. I think,' I stir my coffee slowly, 'I need to get another date quick. I can tell him I don't need to do the ropes!'

'But you haven't got a date!'

'I'll pretend!'

'You could just say no.' Bea is giving me her piercing look.

'He might dump me.'

'Ha!' It's a triumphant shout which I choose to ignore. I carry on calmly, reasonably. 'This isn't about you needing dating help, you're scared of losing him, aren't you?'

'No.' I am. If it wasn't for the party, then I'd be willing these lessons to take longer. I'd be a klutz of a student, demanding extra sessions. I suppose if I do fail at getting a date, and he does come with me as my 'fake date' then it will mean that we carry on doing this for a bit longer. But then that will complicate life soooo much, and I'll be lying to my mum.

'Admit it! Oh Rosie.'

'Don't oh Rosie me,' I say crossly.

'Well just say no to him.' She sits back. It sounds like a challenge.

'Okay, I like seeing him. Satisfied?' She waits for me to carry on. Bloody hell, this is frustrating. 'I'm using him to pretend, aren't I? While he's in my life I'm stalling; I'm not having to go out and do it for real.'

'Or you're hoping?'

'Will you just drop it? We're not compatible, you know that. There is no way I'd date him for real, we're friends.' Except since he told me about Jed and his view of falling in love, and since I chatted to Mum and realised I need to be braver, and since it started to dawn on me that Dad never coming home wasn't my fault, and that even Mum believes that faithful and fun aren't mutually exclusive . . . since all of that I've had a little niggle in my head saying that maybe dating Noah wouldn't be such a totally bad idea after all.

Except then, it might just be one date and I'd have lost him as a friend.

'Of course, you are.' She touches my hand gently. 'And friends can say no.'

Chapter 16

When I get home, I make the mistake of googling Serena the cellist. I know what my mother is like, she won't forget that she wants to invite the woman. If I don't do it and get it out of the way now, she will escalate the pressure – with texts, emotional blackmail and may resort to leaving pleas on my social media.

This is another reason why I didn't understand my parents' marriage. Mum is so determined and efficient in all other aspects of her life but failed miserably when it came to sorting out her love life. Why has she always let Dad get away with things?

Except maybe all that is about to change.

Anyway, it doesn't take much effort to find Serena. Mainly because the second result that comes up has a photo of her with my father.

They are so close together they have to be touching. In fact, I'm sure his hand is on her bum. But it isn't that which upsets me.

Even after chatting to Mum, even after thinking I'd got what kind of man he really is sorted out in my head, this stings.

It's the look on his face. He is laughing down at her and his face, even in a picture, is alive.

It is the look he used to give me when he decided to come home and grace us with his presence. I used to long for that look, wait for that look. That moment when I felt like I was important. I was his everything.

And this image is that look frozen in time.

With some floozy.

I slam the lid of my laptop down as a feeling of revulsion and anger runs through me. I hate him. How can he do that with somebody else? How can he not come to see me, us, and be looking at somebody else that way?

I mean, I do know he's a total charmer, I do know he flirts his way through life, I do know he's had what Mum calls 'stupid flings', but I've never had the evidence shoved in my face.

This is everything that Mum didn't spell out. The man she knew, but I was shielded from.

Googling my dad is not something I've done before – because he's just my dad. I've always taken his career for granted, just thought about it as an ordinary job. He doesn't make the nationals, it's not like he's famous. You have to dig out the 'arts and culture' pages of the Sunday supplements and search with a magnifying glass to find some mention of him. So I don't.

But apparently, he does help fill the digital columns.

Particularly when he messes around with ingenues and prodigious talents that the world of music is watching.

My fingers are trembling slightly as I re-open the lid, take a deep breath and look again.

Was I really just another person in his life to charm? I gulp down the lump in my throat, then hit the cross and close the photo. The next result is a newspaper report. There's another photo of the two of them. It looks like they're shouting at each other.

I don't read the story, I can't. Instead I try not to throw up over my keyboard (I'd never get the bits out) and flick down the screen with tunnel vision until I find her contact details.

It's not that hard. Mum could have done it herself. It's not like she's not capable of using a laptop. Maybe she asked me because she wanted me to stumble across some of this crap; maybe she thinks I'm old enough now to know more, be able to handle the truth that is my parent.

'Mum, I've found Serena's details, but are you positive you want them?'

'Of course, I do.'

'Are you sure you couldn't have got them yourself?'

'You know you're much quicker at finding things than I am. I bet it took you two seconds flat and I would have been messing for ages. My laptop is so slow as well these days, I think I need a new one.'

Should I tell her? Surely, it's better to know? If she doesn't already. 'I found this photo in Rome.'

'The cosy one? He always was very good at hankering to the press.'

'And an online article in the *Daily Mail*.'

'Ah that one, I heard about that, but I don't bother looking these days. I know what your dad looks like, especially when he's arguing. That journalist seems to be rather keen on featuring your father; does make me wonder if he's had a bit of a thing with her. She seems angry, doesn't she? Didn't you think that? A woman scorned?'

'I didn't read it, Mum.'

'Serena was a child prodigy, that's why she gets the coverage.' She sighs. 'You'd really think he'd be a bit smarter about who he picks, wouldn't you? Stupid, arrogant man.'

'Why not ditch the anniversary party, Mum?' Please I pray inside my head. Why not ditch him as well, I want to add.

'No, trust me, Rosie, I need to throw this bash. Do you want to text me the details? Is that easier than reading it out? I want to make sure I've got it right.'

'Yes, Mum.' I sigh again. 'Oh Mum, I hope you're doing the right thing. I don't want you to get hurt.'

'I've already been hurt, Rosie. We both have and I'm sometimes worried it's affected you more than me.'

'Look, Mum, we've been through this. I'm fine.' We blow kisses and exchange 'love yous' and I put my mobile down. One down, one to go.

This has put me off Noah and his ropes even more, if that is possible, for two reasons 1. is Noah, and 2. is ropes. I am worried that because of 2 I will end up clinging to 1, and that is not acceptable at all.

Much as I want to, clinging to charming, flirty Noah could lose me everything.

Bea is right. I just have to say no. So, I am going to call him and explain that as I have dates, I don't need to do this.

* * *

'Oh no, you can't get out of it like that.' I can hear the background chuckle in his deep voice.

'But I've got a date lined up, a proper date, I don't need—'

'Nope,' he says firmly. 'That doesn't change anything, this will still do you good.' I've got a horrible feeling he wants me suspended from the ground so that he can interrogate me about my next date.

'I can't.'

'What do you mean, you can't? You'll be fine, high ropes are totally different to climbing a rock face. Hey,' his tone softens, it travels seductively across the airwaves and aims straight for my heart, 'I'll look after you, you know that, right?'

I nod. Strangely enough, I do. 'It's not the climbing, it's the heights.' And *you*, I say in my head. And I can't get any closer than I am already to you.

Oh bugger, I should not have said yes.

Chapter 17

The weekend started off very ropey, haha, but has just got decidedly better. I am being manhandled by a very dishy guy, and it isn't Noah. He's dishy in a quiet, unassuming serious manner, which is lovely. And has very large, warm capable hands, which is even lovelier. And, like I say, he isn't Noah, which helps put our relationship back on a professional (if it's wise to call it that) footing.

Noah wouldn't back down on the whole rope idea thing; we had a bit of a tiff to be honest. I felt a bit raw after the whole Serena thing, which didn't help. But even using my logic and reasoning to tell myself that Noah is not Dad, and that this isn't a romantic involvement anyway, the whole idea was still making me queasy.

It's not that I didn't want to watch him romp about on a rope Tarzan style, I've just got a thing about being suspended high up in the air, my feet dangling and lots of spiky things below waiting to, well, spike me, if I let go. Or something breaks. I don't want to end my days resembling a raw kebab.

He did mention kayaking (honestly? You must be joking, all that water all around and who knows what weeds lurking ready to drag a body down), skydiving (too expensive, thank God), and wild swimming (see kayaking, above, plus this is England and even though it's summer it's not exactly the same as swimming with dolphins in sun-kissed sea, is it?). I counteracted with motorbikes or a gallop on the beach, which he said wouldn't work as a. I'd suggested them so they obviously didn't scare me, and b. if I thought he was getting on a horse I had another think coming. His sister apparently put him on her pony when he was eight, then hit its bottom with her whip. He's never got over the indignity of being galloped off with then dumped in a smelly ditch. She thought it was hilarious.

Anyway, we settled on a compromise. He insisted on ropes but did say we didn't have to do it in a forest. We could do it indoors, full health and safety regulations in a controlled environment. I don't think it was quite what he was aiming for. Not exactly wild and exhilarating, but still scary and pulse-raising. And involving stepping out of my comfort zone and letting go (not that I'm going to physically let go, are you kidding me?).

We're at a climbing wall. In an old converted church. And I am in Stuart's capable hands, which is slightly exciting, and not at all scary. But I'm not going to tell Noah that. I know the scary part is yet to come.

'This isn't supposed to be a date!'

'Shit, ahh!' I am so shocked when Noah pops his head up over the other side of the wall that I nearly forget to hold on. 'What are you doing up here?'

I have got to the scary bit. I am miles up from ground level, clinging to frail bits of plastic and a far too thin rope. The last thing I need is somebody popping his head over from the other side like a flaming meerkat.

'Keeping an eye on you. What are you playing at? Making eyes at him?' He hisses.

'Who?'

'The instructor!'

'I'm not—'

'Yes, you were! You were,' he struggles to find the right word, 'simpering!'

That is so not the right word. I nearly laugh, except laughing would involve relaxing muscles, and at the moment I have everything tensed against disaster. 'I do not simper!'

'You were flirting!'

'That's what you do all the time,' I fling back at him, 'now get down, go away.' I'd wave him away, but I'm too busy clinging on.

'Everything okay up there, Rosie?' Stuart's voice rings out loud and clear.

'Fine, fine.' I daren't turn round, or look down, or basically move in any direction. I can hiss though. 'Go away, Noah!'

'Promise me you'll stop flirting.'

'I'm not flirting, he just likes me! And isn't that the point of all this?'

'No! It's not a flirting workshop, today is about you, and taking risks!'

'I am taking a frigging risk, and anyway aren't sex and danger linked?'

He glares at me. In fact, he's more glower-y today than I've ever seen him.

I tilt my head on one side – well as much as I can with a helmet and load of gear on while I'm hanging on for dear life. 'Anybody ever told you you're quite sexy when you scowl?'

'Trust me, you shouldn't flirt with him.'

'Trust you? I did trust you and now I'm stuck at the top of a bloody wall! This is worse than being in a bloody relationship!' I don't think this comment has helped.

'Fine.' He lets go with one hand.

'Don't, oh God, don't. Hold on properly!'

'Rosie.' He looks me in the eye, still not holding on. I'm trembling and I don't know whether it's because he is staring at me so intently that I'm sure he can see exactly what I'm thinking, or because I'm scared he'll fall. 'Do you want to be helped or not?'

'Do you mean off this wall, or in general?'

He rolls his eyes. I've never seen him this huffy. 'Fine. I'm going down.'

'When I froze, he said look into his eyes, so I did! That's all! And he was nice, nicer than you're being.'

'I'm not bloody surprised he was nice the way you were pawing him.'

'I was not pawing!' I give him my evil eye. 'Why are you being so nasty?'

He sighs. 'Honestly? Well I don't know what's got into you. You need to chill, be yourself, not pretend to be, to be . . .'

'Some seductress?' It comes out stiff, cold. 'Every time I'm getting somewhere, doing what you told me to, you say it's wrong!' I wish I was in a position to prod him with a finger, to make my point, but I'm not. 'And it's not wrong! It's working! I'm working, people are asking me out!'

'Just chill, be yourself. Don't pretend you're somebody who wants, who wants to be with a jerk who'll give you the run-around!'

'But that's the point! This is not me, I'm not being myself! You made me different. I don't climb ropes!' I realise I am glaring at him. 'You're never happy, are you? You find fault with everything I do!'

'No, I don't! I just don't want you to date twats who won't respect you.'

'Fine, anyway he asked me out,' I say, smiling smugly, but actually not feeling smug. There's a hole in my stomach, an emptiness because I don't want to do this on my own. I want Noah to be happy for me.

'He what? When, when did he have time—'

'You've been watching us?'

'I was just checking you were okay. I feel responsible,' he says stiffly.

'Noah!'

'So what did he do, follow you to the toilets or something?'

'No,' I sigh, 'I was stuck up a rope, remember? Your idea? I had a panic attack the first time. I told you I didn't like heights and he helped me down, then we were kind of looking at each other . . . and he got me a drink of water and told me to sit down for a minute.'

'And?'

'Well then I felt better, and he told me when we tried again to just listen carefully to his voice, and,' I take a deep breath,

'I said he had a lovely voice I could listen to all day, which made him laugh. Then he told me about his cat.'

'His cat?'

'Yeah and how he's saving for a house, which is why he's doing these lessons. It's not what he normally does. I listened, made it about him like you told me to and you were right! I forgot all about being nervous cos I made it about him.' I smile, he doesn't smile back, so I blunder on. 'Then he asked me out.'

'Great.' He rests his head against the wall.

'Glad you're pleased for me,' I say stiffly. 'I better ask him to rescue me again, get me down.'

'What's the big rush, Rosie?'

'I don't like it up here. I'm starting to feel weird.'

'I don't mean to get down! Dating! Why not take your time?'

'Oh, Mum and Dad's party, me, my life, you know. Normal stuff.' I glare. 'Old age!'

'You're not old.'

'I will be by the time I get off this bloody wall.'

'Oh, for fuck's sake, Rosie, don't mess it all up just for the sake of a party. I can always go with you if you're desperate.'

'Gee ta, desperate Rosie. Is that how you see me?'

'No, you know what I mean. Men like him are the worst, all strong and masterful, holding on to you, saving the poor damsel in distress.'

I laugh. He doesn't join in. 'I chatted him up, you dork!' He still doesn't laugh. 'You mean it, don't you?'

'Shit. I'm being a jerk, again.' He stops talking. His steady gaze on mine, then he looks down at the top of the wall. 'I don't want you to get hurt. Really. All this seduction stuff, maybe it's bollocks. You're great just the way you are, Rosie. You'll get a guy whatever you do. You don't need me.'

'Oh, don't be ridiculous, of course—'

But he's gone, sliding down his side of the wall and I'm suddenly scared that he's gone out of my life as well. I take a deep breath and force myself to look over the top.

'Noah, Noah, don't go.'

He looks up. How the hell did he get back down to ground level so quickly? 'I'm not going far.' He sighs. 'Don't worry, superman Stuart will get you down. I'll see you in the café by the entrance, okay?'

Phew, at least he thinks I meant 'don't go and leave me up a fake wall', not 'don't go and leave me for ever'.

Chapter 18

'Fuck, no!' All thoughts of whether I do or don't need Noah are emptied from my head.

Which is pretty amazing considering by the time I'd managed to get down from the wall, thanked Stuart profusely, arranged a date, and worked out how to walk on terra firma again (I was very wobbly) there was no sign of him. I was pretty sure he'd walked out of my life for good, and then I'd spotted him. Sitting outside the café with his eyes shut.

I felt like crying with relief, but I resisted the urge to skip over at high speed and instead did a rapid saunter (I was too happy to do a normal saunter) and squeaked a 'hi'.

He opened his eyes and smiled. Then high-fived me and suggested walking back through the park.

Phew. We are okay! Even if we are walking a few more inches apart than we normally do. Which is fine, absolutely fine.

Anyway, my wonderings about whether or not I'll ever brush arms with Noah again exit my brain abruptly.

That is what shock can do for you. For a moment I fly catch, then realise Noah is squeezing my shoulder. Rather hard.

'Ouch, stop it.' I flap him away.

It can't be. I must be imagining things.

'Rosie!' I might also have closed the distance between us, and be leaning in so close to Noah, I'm standing on his foot.

'Nooooo. It can't be!' I peer over his shoulder and squeeze my eyes into a squint. Which is sod all help, apart from adding a film-worthy softness to the surroundings. And out of the blurriness the monster in the blue top keeps coming. It's like watching a horror film: every second brings the enemy closer.

'Can't be what?' Noah turns and looks, then turns back to me. 'What's going on, what's up?'

'Will you stop shaking me,' I say angrily, focussing on him for a moment. To be honest I've got a feeling he is working up to slapping my face, and I'm not having that. 'It's Gabe.'

'Who?' He looks puzzled for a second, then it dawns on him. 'Oh, Gabe. Christ, really? Where?' His eyes open a bit wider, and he turns back round to where I'm looking.

'Over there, the guy with,' I swallow, 'a pram.'

'I can't . . . where exactly?'

'For God's sake, over there, by the entrance to the park. The one with a fucking big baby-carrying machine!' I hiss. 'I'm not exactly going to point.' Throw a sharp object maybe, but not point. 'Stop staring, he'll see you looking.'

Gabe is getting closer and now I can see him quite clearly. At first, I thought, or hoped, it was just somebody similar, that I'd make a mistake, that we'd laugh it off. Once my heart rate returned to normal and I'd stopped hyperventilating.

No mistake. He's quite distinctive.

'I really can't . . .'

I cannot believe Noah can't spot him. Okay, he's never seen the guy (I made sure he only saw the messages) but there isn't exactly a surfeit of male pram-pushers. 'Oh, fuck's sake.' I mutter under my breath. 'Forget it, sorry, I've got to—' It's a split-second decision.

Gabe is heading straight towards us. Him and his bloody *children*. A baby *and* a toddler. Any second now he will spot me, and my humiliation will be complete.

I can't let him catch me staring at him. I can't. I need time to take this in, to process it. To decide whether kneeing him in the groin in the street will have me carted away for GBH. And whether it will be worth it if I am. At the moment I am leaning towards 'maybe' and 'yes'. Bastard.

I yank Noah round so he is facing me, and put one hand, palm flat on his chest. 'Sorry, really sorry. Here goes.' The last bit I mutter to myself.

'What are you?'

'Shush.' Gabe is close. Any second now he will be right up to us.

I look at Noah and take a deep breath. You can do this, Rosie. You have got to do this. I close my eyes, then open them again – just to check. Gabe is even closer. Any second now I'll be able to see the colour of his eyes. Shit.

Noah is looking bemused.

Gabe is pushing the pram with one hand, the other arm cradling the cute toddler that's balanced on his hip. The perfect father.

I stare into Noah's eyes. For once he's not grinning. He's sexy when he's serious. Looking at me so intently. Even sexier than normal. Gorgeous. Full lips. I run my tongue over my own. This is no hardship. This is fine. I can do it.

His hip nudges mine, any other time I'd pull back, his crotch nestles . . . oh my God.

I grab his T-shirt and go for it.

For a moment his lips are firm, unyielding, like his firm chest beneath my palm. And then his mouth softens. Oh boy, does it soften. I can't help myself, I melt into him, close my eyes (which I really need to keep open) and let my hands do what they want to do. Which is move to his shoulders, slide to his neck, allow my fingers to thread their way into his hair.

He smells amazing, he tastes amazing. He's holding me firmly now, his mouth moving beneath mine. He is taking control and, oh my.

Kissing Robbie was never like this; kissing Robbie didn't leave me desperate to get even closer, to explore his mouth with my tongue, to groan in an indecent demand for more.

A low wolf-whistle breaks into my consciousness. 'Well if it isn't the old devil himself! Still up to your old tricks eh, Noah! Hey, it is Noah, isn't it, buried under that lovely lady?' There is a laugh. It's a bit like a chuckle, but not a proper one, not an earthy one like Noah's. Oh shit. I keep my eyes closed and think about burying my bright red face in Noah's chest. Seems like a good idea, so I do, briefly, then surface and look round at him.

Gabe.

In the eye.

He hardly registers me, he's too busy catching up with his old buddy, Noah.

The First Date

The baby makes a mewling noise. 'Shush.' It cries louder. 'Sorry, can't hang about, he doesn't like it if I stop! But we should get together some time, mate!' He thumbs up, pats Noah on the arm and is off, walking backwards briefly, then turning to look where he's going.

I count to ten under my breath, listen as the crying dies away. 'Mate?! You bloody know that, that, that . . . man?'

Noah grimaces. 'Yeah, sure, well slightly. I don't know him that well. He's a mate of my sister's husband. They both work at this PR firm; it's just down the road from my office.' He gestures, as though showing me where.

'His name isn't Gabe, is it?' I say weakly as I realise my hands are still on his chest, so I let them drop and take a step back. Concentrate on not touching my swollen, throbbing lips.

'That was Gabe?' He stares after the sauntering Gabe, or whatever his bloody name is.

I nod.

'Your Gabe?'

I nod again. It is not that words are not coming easily. I have plenty of words in my head, but if I open my mouth they will burst out – and they contain a load of abuse and loud screams.

'I was looking for some other guy with a pram, I never thought you could mean him. Oh no, I don't . . .' He runs his fingers through his hair and stares after the guy. 'Really? You're kidding me.'

I shake my head. 'No, I'm fucking not! And he didn't even recognise me!'

'He has only seen your pic on Tin—' He stops abruptly when I give him my stare. 'Shit.' I don't think this is because I've scared him.

'What do you mean shit?'

'What do I tell my sister? Gavin's wife is her friend.'

'I don't give a f—' I break off as what he's said sinks in. 'Haha, Gavin?' I laugh. For some reason the fact that he's a Gavin not a Gabe is funny. I laugh louder. It's a hysterical cackle that makes people turn round and stare.

'Are you all right, love?' A woman touches my arm.

I nod, but I'm not. I'm so not all right.

'Is he giving you grief?' She inclines her head towards Noah.

'Oh no, no, he's fine, he's nice. I kissed him!' Oh God I kissed him! I lean forward, put my hands on my knees and take a deep breath so that 1. I don't have to look at Noah, and 2. I can hide my inane grin from both of them. 'It's somebody else.' I glance up at her.

'You're sure, duck?' She gives Noah a hard look then sidles away, glancing back over her shoulder, not convinced.

'He's married!' I look up at Noah, who nods. 'He's got, he's got, a, a.' I don't think I can say the word baby.

Fuck, he's got kids! The tears prickling my eyelids catch me unawares and for a moment I'm on the verge of blubbing, so I do a bit of swearing under my breath and get a grip.

'Are you okay?' Noah looks worried.

'Don't look at me like that!' I croak. Sympathy is a killer. If he keeps on being nice then I'll crumble. If I stick my nails into the palm of my hand and ground myself with pain, then I'll be fine. Absolutely fine.

I straighten up. 'How old is it?'

Noah pulls a funny twisted face. 'Well . . .'

'Go on!'

'Not very.'

'As in just popped out?'

He waggles a hand, palm down, the way you do to say 'more or less'. In this case I'd guess we're erring on the less rather than more side.

'His wife was preggers and he was on Tinder!'

Noah nods, he's gone pale.

'And he'd have bloody recognised me if I was the only one! He'd have remembered, wouldn't he? Wouldn't he?' I challenge Noah, who nods again. Then shakes his head.

Oh my God. If he'd turned up for our date, if he hadn't ghosted me, I could have ended up dating a man just like my dad. Exactly the type of man I'd been trying to avoid. And, I gulp, I could have ended up being the other woman.

I feel so tense I could explode. I'm so angry I could kick something. I'm angry at Gabe, and I'm angry at me for falling for his chat online.

And yet he didn't seem like that. He wasn't overly charming, he wasn't flirty. He just seemed nice. Normal.

He just . . . Oh shit, what did I so nearly do? 'What's he doing to his kids, his family?' I don't wait for an answer. 'Dad did that.' I point wildly in the general direction Gabe has taken. 'He didn't give a monkey's arse about us.' Okay he probably didn't go out looking for people on Tinder, but he did take every opportunity he could when he was working. He just did whatever he wanted. Took whatever was offered.

In my heart I know he did. Even though at the time in my head I was always giving him excuses.

'Un-fucking-believable. Gavin. Bloody Gavin. I'm going after him, I'm going to tell him who I am, show him his poxy messages.' I need to hurl every insult I didn't throw at Dad at him.

'Rosie, hang on.' Noah catches my arm. 'Just hang on a sec, let's think this through.' He puts his hands on my shoulders. 'He's got his kids with him, I mean his daughter, she'll . . .' He pulls me closer. 'She'll understand, or at least hear it. It's not fair, is it?' His voice is soft, and when I look up, his gaze is even softer. Worried. 'We need to do this right.'

I deflate abruptly as his words sink in. 'You can let go. I won't run after him.' My words slightly muffled against his torso. He's right. I also can't stay in his arms. I'm getting all hot and bothered again; the blood is pounding in my cheeks and all I can think about is nestling in for a while and letting him hold me while I hang on like I never want to let go.

It's not right. I can't. I wriggle. 'Promise. No way would I want to upset his kids.'

He lets go. I make a big fuss of brushing myself down and straightening myself out so that I've got time to get my pulse rate down to a normal level.

Kissing Noah was so such a bad idea.

His skin is so smooth, like velvet draped over a hard rock. Oh hell, I'm going all mushy and dramatic.

I'm all over the place with the shock of seeing Gabe, with knowing he's not just some stupid guy who doesn't turn up for dates, knowing he's a married man. With the kick in the gut that he's yet another man just like my dad. With kissing Noah.

I need to get control.

'Get a grip, Rosie.' I mutter under my breath.

'Are you okay?' Noah tucks the hair behind my ear which makes me flinch away.

'Fine.' Oops that might have been a bit snappy. 'Sure, thanks. I am fine, just in shock.'

'I'm sorry you had to . . . It was bad enough the git did what he did to you, without you finding out he . . .'

'It's fine.' I smile at him.

'It's not though, is it?' His voice is soft.

'I'm fine. Honest.' Being in his arms was far more of a shock than seeing Gabe with his family in tow. I try not to stare at Noah's mouth. He's got such nice full lips, well not too full, firm, but just right for kissing.

'Rosie?'

'Sorry.' Must stop staring. 'So,' I clap my hands together and aim for brisk, 'what's the plan then?'

'Let's go and sit down, grab a coffee from that van. Come on.' He leads me over to a bench, fusses around as though I'm a trauma victim, then goes to buy us a coffee. He hardly takes his eyes off me.

It's so sweet I feel like crying again.

'Right.' He sits down. 'Tell me about your date with your climbing instructor then. You shouldn't date your teachers, you know.' He wags his finger and gives me a stern look, that's also supposed to be funny.

'I know,' I say miserably. Oh, I definitely know I should not date my instructors. Either of them.

I also know that I don't want to go on a date with Stuart.

It doesn't matter. He was nice, easy-going but I don't want to date for the sake of it. I want to kiss Noah again. Which is scary and stupid. 'I probably won't do it.'

'Oh?'

'I'm not that into him.'

We both stare into our coffee cups. 'So, tell me about your dad then.' His voice is soft, the words unexpected. 'Please, if you want to.'

I don't say anything, I'm too busy trying to gather my thoughts, put them into words that make sense. 'Not a lot to say.'

'Oh, Rosie. Gabe didn't bother you, did he? It was the kids, the thought of kids getting tangled up in this and hurt, like you were.'

'How could I have got it wrong, how could I have nearly . . .'

'You didn't know him, Rosie. You hadn't even met him.'

'But I should have been able to tell!' I'm shocked that with all the layers of self-protection I thought I had draped around myself, with all my determination to make sure I found the right man, I still could have got it wrong. I stare into my cup. 'Dad cheated, *cheats*. He's done it all my life, I think. He travels round with his orchestra and shags who he wants and has always come home when he's bored or wants a change.' I shrug and try and pretend it's easy to say.

'Those girls he sees must know he's got a family though, it's totally different to you meeting somebody online. You can't blame yourself.'

'I know.' I sigh. 'I've built my whole life around protecting myself from the charmers of life and trying to build something safe and secure. Something boring and risk-free, so that I'd feel safe. Have a normal life.

And I've jumped to conclusions about people like Noah. Somebody who has always been honest, somebody my instincts have told me I can trust. Somebody who has always given me one hundred per cent of his attention while he's been with me. When he's been with me, he's been with me – if that makes sense. He's never been watching other people, flirting, or finding his phone or a conversation more interesting. Even though all I am is a girl he's decided needs a helping hand.

'Dad wasn't an easy man to grow up with. Not that he was there much.' I sigh heavily.

'Okay, start with your mum if it's easier, and I'll try and fill in the blanks.' He smiles at me disarmingly.

Mum *is* easier. Well her relationship with me is, I'm not sure about the one she has with Dad. 'Mum is lovely.'

'Like you.' He smiles.

'Flatterer! She is though, lovely, but a bit batty at times. No, don't say it! She was stunning when she was young, really gorgeous in her wedding photos, and of all the men she could have married, she had to fall for Dad.'

It's hard, he's my dad. You don't think nasty things about your dad when you're young, do you? They can never do any wrong. Annoy you maybe, but you don't see the real flaws. I'm starting to see the real flaws. It's horrible, it's casting a shadow on my childhood, a longer one than noticing he wasn't there at the time. But, I mean, how bad is it when you realise that you're comparing possible boyfriends to your dad and instantly binning any that show any similarities *at all*. When I started to date Robbie I did it self-consciously, pompously aware that they were very different, and quite proud of myself and my wise choice. Since I've been a single woman again there's been a beacon flashing in my head shouting out loud and clear that trusting any man with a flirt gene is impossible for me.

I hate him. Dad. He has effectively stamped out any desire (well, maybe not *desire*) to follow my heart in a search of passion. Mum might think I'm missing out, but really? Is passion really that great, great enough to risk a broken heart?

'She's still pretty okay.' I flick through my phone, as a distraction, show him a recent snap of the two of us.

Noah peers closely. 'More than pretty okay. She looks beautiful. Obvious family resemblance, though you of course aren't quite . . .'

'Cheeky bugger.' I play thump his arm, then stare at the photo again. 'She was so glamorous, so confident and bubbly when I was little.' I smile to myself. 'The coolest mum at school pick-up time. But,' I've only realised this bit recently, 'she was doing it mainly for him I reckon. She was chasing him, trying to make sure he still loved her.'

'Is that so bad?' he says softly.

'What do you think?' I square up to him. 'Was love worth it for your mate, Jed?'

'I'm talking about you, not him. He's not here to say.'

'Look, I reckon Mum was dead sexy, really confident when she was younger. Well, that's what I get from what my grandparents say. They actually thought Mum and Dad were a really good match, and even though she was brilliant, fun, everything a man should have wanted,' I glare, challenging him to contradict me, he doesn't, 'he still cheated on her.'

'It happens, Rosie. I'm really, really sorry it happened to your mum, but some people are shits.'

'He's made a fool out of her.'

'It was her choice, Rosie. And she tried to do her best for you, didn't she?' I nod, ignoring the lump in my throat. Noah leans in. 'This is why you had a go at me, isn't it? The player? You think I'm like your dad.'

'I didn't say that.'

'You didn't have to. You think I'm like him, you think Gav is like him.'

I make a harrumph sound.

'Okay, okay, maybe you're right, about Gav not me.' He gives me a warning look and waves a finger. 'But it could just be a one off.'

I raise my eyebrows. 'You believe that?'

'Maybe not. But he didn't actually turn up for your date.'

'Don't give him excuses, Noah.'

'I'm not, honestly.' He puts his warm hand over mine. 'He's a shit whether or not you were the only person he talked to.'

'I gave my dad excuses. He must be the only bloody musician working a regular 24 hours a day, haha.'

'He was never there?'

'Not often. He'd come back now and then, but it didn't always tie in with when we needed him. It was just,' I try to keep the heavy sigh inside, 'when it suited him.' I nod to myself. 'Because he had nothing better to do, nobody more exciting to be with.' I half smile. 'For a rest.'

'Oh Rosie.'

'Or when somebody had shown an interest in Mum.' Some of the memories come back. 'She'd say on the phone that some old friend from school or college had popped in, some old boyfriend had been in touch, and he'd be there the next day. He hated her getting attention.'

'Not the best dad in the world.'

'Nope.' But worse than I'd remembered. I'd given him the benefit of the doubt. Like you do, when it's your dad.

Noah squeezes my hand. 'We're not all like him, you know.'

I nod. 'I know. Robbie wasn't.'

'Is that why you were with him for so long?'

'Maybe. I did love him though.' Just not fancy the pants off him, I could have added. 'I can't let Gavin just do what he likes.'

Noah kisses my cheek. 'You can't, and nor can I. Right then, if you're sure you're okay?' I nod. 'Have you still got his profile on your phone?'

I nod again. 'I don't care about me, it's not about me. I don't care he stood me up.' It's true I realise. It was a shock seeing him in the flesh, an even bigger shock seeing him with a pram, but now the shock has blown over I know I'm not bothered. That date with him seems like it was years ago, a different life. I'd been far too busy with Noah to even think about being stood up. It had been like it never happened.

Until now.

'I need to show Gemma, my sister. See what she says. I mean his wife has just had a baby, she'll be emotional enough, won't she?'

'Guess so, don't ask me though. I have zilch experience of birth-mother hormones.'

'Will you come? Show her what you've got?'

I take a deep breath. I'm going to do this. 'Only if you come to my parents with me, to the anniversary party.'

'I said I would, you don't have to blackmail me.' He grins; the flutters start up in the base of my tummy, which makes it impossible not to smile back.

'It makes me feel better!' It does, I feel better if I can tell myself it's a deal. It isn't any kind of a date, it's not me getting more personal than I should. It's just one favour in return for another.

'Right, let's go then.'

'Now?'

'Now.' He takes my hand in his, and I dig my heels in. Shocked.

'But, but . . .' I am not dressed for visiting. 'I have my rock-climbing gear on, and my hair in a ponytail, and very little make-up.'

'So do I! Well not the ponytail or make-up.'

'That's different, she knows you. She's probably seen you naked.'

'Gem won't mind.'

'But I do.'

He stops pulling. 'Rosie, you're gorgeous as you are.'

'You're just saying that to get your own way.' I sigh. 'Okay,

okay. Fine. Lead the way, it's not like you're my boyfriend or anything and I need to impress anybody.'

He gives me a slightly weird look that makes me wish I hadn't said that bit.

Chapter 19

Gemma doesn't live far away, but it feels like miles when I'm thigh to thigh with Noah in his sporty little car. I should have said I'd get the bus, because I swear my heart is ticking over more loudly than the car engine.

Luckily, he seems oblivious. He doesn't say a word until we pull up on the driveway outside a rather imposing Georgian-style house.

He pauses as he lifts a hand to knock on the front door. 'I wasn't just saying it by the way. You are.'

'What?' I'm trying to resist the urge to smooth my hair down and am concentrating on what is going to come next, what I'm supposed to say to Gemma. How I explain me and her brother, and hardly register what he's said.

'Gorgeous.'

'Oh.' I stop dithering and look at him. He smiles. Touches the very tip of my nose with his finger. I grin back, like an idiot.

'That kiss by the way.'

'Oh God, I'm sorry.' I stop smiling. 'I didn't mean, I just couldn't think of anything . . .'

261

'Awesome. No lessons needed there. Shame really, I was looking forward to moving on to that bit.' He winks. Too gorgeous for his own good, and mine.

Luckily the door swings open at this point. Otherwise I might have felt the need to insist on extra-curricular activities.

'Noah, this is,' she glances at me, then back at him, then back at me again. It would be odd if she didn't look so surprised. 'A nice surprise. Hi!' She waves at me. I wave back. 'Hi!'

'Come in, come in, wow, aren't I rude?' She's got Noah's eyes, his lovely easy smile, his gentle manner and I instantly like her. 'You'll have to excuse the mess, been putting a dog back together all morning.'

'Back together?' We follow her in; the place looks fine to me. Tidier than mine anyway.

'Hit by a car.' She winces. 'A bit smashed up, but who needs legs that all point in the same direction anyway?'

'Ignore her,' says Noah. It's pretty hard to ignore his hand in the small of my back as he steers me towards the kitchen. 'She's ace at straightening them up, all the right bits in all the right places.' He kisses her on the cheek.

'Okay, okay, enough of the being nice big bro, what have you done now?'

'I haven't done anything.' The hurt tone of his voice makes us both laugh. Then I remember why we're here and stop laughing, and fish my phone out. 'It's Gavin.'

'Gavin?' She frowns.

'Gavin,' I say, scrolling through until I find the profile pic of him. I hold the phone up; Gemma nods. 'Gabe,' I say, pointing to the name.

'Gabe?' Gemma looks from me to Noah. 'Am I supposed to be following this?'

'He's been on Tinder.' He pauses, Gemma still looks confused. 'It's a dating—'

'I know what Tinder is, you idiot. What do you mean, he's been on Tinder? Of course, he has!' She frowns. 'Though the Gabe bit is wrong.'

'What do you mean, Gem? Of course, he has.'

'That's where Linda met him.'

Noah looks at me, as though he's asking permission, so I nod. 'That's where Rosie met him. Recently.'

Gemma narrows her eyes. 'What do you mean recently?'

'As in around the time Linda was about to give birth.'

'Let me just check I've got this straight. You,' she inclines her head my way, 'are on Tinder and chatted to Gavin, who called himself Gabe.'

'More than chatted,' I add glumly, 'we arranged to meet. But he didn't show!' I add this as though it's a positive.

'Linda probably went into labour,' Gemma says, surprisingly calmly.

'Wife in labour' wasn't one of the excuse scenarios that had run through my mind when I'd been running through possible reasons for his no-show. No wonder he ghosted me, he'd been too bloody busy shouting push and mopping her brow. I'd been thinking more along the lines of 'my cat got stuck up a tree', or 'flat tyre'. Similar I suppose.

'What are you going to do?' Noah asks Gemma.

'Do? Me?' She frowns at him. 'Why do I have to do anything? Why is it my problem and not yours, brother, darling? Honestly, talk about shifting responsibility.'

'She's your friend.'

'He's Dan's friend. I'm going to tell Dan. He's my husband,' she explains to me.

I'm starting to feel a bit awkward. Soon everybody in the town will know about my disastrous non-dating experience. Well, everybody that Noah knows will. Still, this isn't the time to worry about my huge embarrassment, this is about Linda, and Gavin-the-Gabe. And their children.

'Maybe we shouldn't,' I blurt out, surprising even myself. 'Mum protected me when I was little, and my dad cheated. I never knew and their children shouldn't have to know, or suffer, or, maybe he's only done it the once.'

'He's still got a profile up,' Noah points out. Squeezing my hand.

'I could tell him I know! I could threaten him, make him stop.'

'And what if he just signs up somewhere else?' Gemma chips in. 'I know it's not fair on the kids, but Linda's a good mum, she'll make sure they're okay.' She squeezes my other hand. 'Don't worry, it's not your problem, but,' she looks me in the eye, 'she needs to know, doesn't she? It's up to her what decisions she makes, not us.'

'Oh hell, I feel so responsible, this is partly my fault, if I hadn't . . .'

'Bloody hell, Rosie, it's not your fault! You didn't know when you arranged to meet him.'

'Maybe he doesn't actually meet anybody, maybe he just likes chatting and arranging the dates,' I say glumly.

Why did I ever decide online dating people I didn't know was a good idea? Noah was right when he said it wasn't the way to meet people. Things could have been so much worse for me, what if I'd ended up dating a married man?

'That is immaterial.' Gemma folds her arms. 'He shouldn't even be chatting. I mean an affair doesn't have to be *physical*, does it? And what about all those poor women he's been leading on? It's disgusting. And to think that's how they met! What a shit. I'm going to ring Dan now. Don't worry.' She pats the back of my hand. 'Leave it to me, we'll sort this out. Right, so,' she rubs her hands together and looks at Noah, 'you are coming to the barbecue, aren't you?'

'Er.'

'You forgot! Bloody hell, Noah!' She is laughing. 'What's he like?'

'I didn't forget!' He shoots me a quick glance that says it all.

'I bet.' Gemma has spotted the look. 'He always comes up with an excuse if I text him, better to just put him on the spot! You will come, won't you, Rosie? Tomorrow? Nothing formal, just us, some beers and burgers, and I promise Gavin won't be here!'

'Well.' I look at Noah, he shrugs. 'Sure, I'd love to!'

'Great! So,' she frowns, 'how did you say you two met?'

'We didn't!' Noah says firmly, 'and you know it!'

'Oh my God, you met on Tinder as well!' She puts her hands over her mouth, but I can see the laughter in her eyes.

They're dancing with the same kind of merriment Noah often has on his face.

I laugh. 'No, we didn't! Oh my God, Noah on Tinder!'

'Do you two mind discussing me in front of my face?'

Gemma grins. 'Not really. Though we can do it behind your back if you want?' She waits for me to say more.

'It's complicated.'

'I bet! You'll have to tell me the whole story over a glass of wine and a burnt sausage! Oh heck, you both need to bugger off, I'm on call and that's my pager going off. I really hope it's something easy. I'm so knackered I'm not sure I can do any major putting back together things.'

'You'll be fine, little sis.' Noah grins and kisses the top of her head.

'Er you're a bit sweaty smelly, what have you been doing? Where've you been?' She eyes him up and down.

'Climbing wall,' I say, when he remains silent.

'Haha, Noah up a climbing *wall*, that's hilarious. The man who wouldn't be seen dead in some pretend, health and safety infected . . . Hang on, you're being serious? Really? Wow, you must be keen, big bro! Wow, wow, wow, I am so going to corner you, Rosie, so you can dish the dirt when he's not listening in!' She's still sniggering and saying 'climbing wall' and 'Tinder' under her breath as she sees us to the door, follows us out and gets into the car. 'Go and shower, get changed and come back tomorrow – and don't forget to grab some beers! I'll let you know what Dan says later. See you tomorrow, nice to meet you, Rosie!'

The First Date

I glance at Noah; he doesn't look bothered, he doesn't look cross. He shakes his head and winks. 'Sister's eh?'

Oh bugger, this is getting complicated though. Awkward. How do I tell her? Obviously, it is dead easy over a burger and sausage to say 'your brother is giving me lessons in seduction. We met when I got stood up by your mate's two-timing husband. Then he rescued me from a Great Dane who'd wrapped me round a tree, and that clinched it.'

Sure, I really am going to say that. Uh oh, weirdo alert. She'll probably think I've created the whole Gavin/Gabe thing and am now going to ruin her brother's life.

'We better do as instructed then and bugger off, then I better go shopping for burgers and beers or I'll forget and never hear the last of it. Ready to go?'

I am, so I say so. I need time to regroup. To think about Dad, Gabe and how on earth I've managed to get invited to Noah's family barbecue.

We travel most of the way in silence but have just turned into my road when Noah clears his throat. 'Fancy popping home, freshening up,' he holds a hand up as though he expects me to object, 'though you look fine to me, and going out for a drink? I was wondering if you needed some prep before you meet climbing man? I can pick you up in an hour, if that's enough time?'

I think this might be a tentative olive branch after he was nasty to me at the top of the wall. 'You mean Stuart?'

'Him.'

'It's okay, I don't—'

267

'No, it's fine. I want to help,' Noah says in his firm, listen to me voice.

'But I'm not going on a date.'

'Oh.'

To be honest, it was a confidence boost being chatted up and asked out, but I've been feeling less and less in the mood for dates lately. There doesn't seem much point. The only reason I can really think of for doing it is to take my mind off Noah. Which is wrong in many ways. I should be dating for myself, not because of him, and it also isn't fair on my dates, is it? I can't even say I'm doing it for a bit of fun.

'Oh.'

'I thought you'd be pleased, at least you can't accuse me of being too flirty, or tarty, or—'

'I have never accused you of being tarty!'

'Close!' I say, as he drops me off outside my place.

'How about I do some major grovelling, and throw in a free lesson to make up?'

I roll my eyes. 'They're all free!'

His cheeky grin is back. 'Top tips not revealed in my normal curriculum?'

'You're incredible!'

'So I've been told. Not usually before the advanced practicals though.' His chuckle sets up a warm glow right at the base (and I mean base) of my stomach.

I shake my head and try to keep a straight face, but it's difficult. I'm buzzing – on a dangerous high, no substances involved. Who knew a normally sane person (me in case you wondered) could be this high on nothing but hormones and happiness? Not wise.

'An hour is fine. I'll see you there?'

Chapter 20

Okay, I must be totally bonkers. I agreed to getting showered, changed and return to ground zero in an hour after the day I've just had.

Today has been a day of many ups and downs (in all senses of the words), and it's got me in more of a turmoil than a ride at any theme park could. And I do mean *any* ride.

I mean, I've been up a scary wall, and down several times (result!), chatted up a guy and got myself a date, practically sucked Noah's tonsils (still making me feel hot and bothered), and been invited to his sister's house (giving me palpitations).

But how could I say no to a Saturday night date, even if it isn't a proper date? At least I can gaze into a man's eyes, let his gorgeous rumbling laugh bring out goose bumps on my arms, and remember how his firm, dry lips felt against mine.

Has to be better than an evening in with a packet of crisps, doesn't it? Okay, more dangerous, but hey, maybe that shows how far I've come. I am willing to face the fear and do it anyway.

I've never forced a kiss on anybody before, not even Robbie.

Maybe it has unleashed a new, more powerful side of me that has lurked deep down waiting for its moment. Maybe this is the start of the new me!

Or maybe I just want a night out.

'Busy day!' Noah grins.

'That has to be the understatement of the year!' Oh boy, am I in trouble. Just seeing him has made my pulse rate go into overdrive and my vocal cords to switch to gushy mode.

He's too cute. I think kissing him has released some kind of sex hormone in me that is making me want to jump him. I'm on some kind of adrenalin rush that can only have one satisfactory conclusion.

'Drink?'

'Large one.' Maybe alcohol will calm me down, take the need to hang on his every word, hang on his arm, hang on his body, away. Or, oh my God, it might just dissolve the shred of inhibition that is remaining, and I will ignore my latest rule. The only rule that is important tonight – no making moves without an invitation.

'Are you okay, you look . . .'

'Fine, fine, I'm fine. Just a bit . . . tired.' I finish lamely.

'You don't look tired.' He gazes straight into my eyes. 'You look incredibly sexy.'

'Oh!' I squeak. Taking the drink that he pushes my way and taking an unwise gulp. Unwise because it burns its way down my throat and makes me splutter. Unwise because I need a clear head or I will forget my new rule.

'Here.' He takes the glass from me and puts his hand between my shoulders. Oh boy is it warm. 'Better?'

272

'Much.' Don't gaze back into his eyes, don't.

'Let's make tonight all about how it should feel.' He puts his hand over mine.

Help! 'Let's not!'

Oh gawd, that chuckle. I have unleashed that dangerous chuckle. His eyes are alive, I can't not look into them.

'I want you to let go of your inhibitions like you did at the top of that wall, like you did,' he leans in closer, 'when you saw Gavin.' His finger traces a line down the back of my hand, and I tense. 'I'm not going to mention him again. This evening is all about . . .' he's even closer. The light citrus-hint of after-shave surrounds us. 'This evening is all about desire.'

Oh boy I want to kiss him.

'Right.' He snaps back into his seat and jolts me back to reality. 'Let's get down to business, Rosie. That's what you're not paying me for! Extra-curricular activity.' He winks, but this time the wink isn't seductive, it's mate-y.

Noooo. How does he do that?

My head, my body cannot cope with this. I'm back on that bloody big dipper ride again.

'We are going to get you chatting people up.'

'Well, I know that, but . . .'

'Here, now, right now! Speed flirting!'

'I thought you said you weren't a pimp!'

'I'm not pimping, this is just a bit of light flirting practice. I can rescue you if you need me to!'

'Are you mad?'

'No. Go on. Try. Go up to the bar, I'll pick a man.'

'Get lost, you are not picking a man out for me!'

'You'll be fine, I'll watch you.'

'I don't want to be watched. You did that with Steve.'

'I did not.'

'Yes, you did, Mr Stalk-y man. You might have put him off dates for life! You definitely put him off dating me.'

'No loss, haha.'

'Don't be mean, he was nice.'

'Sure, but it doesn't matter, this is just about technique. I can let you know how it goes!'

'I think I'll be able to tell how it goes, by whether or not they want more! And that's spooky, chatting someone up and being assessed is too weird.' I give him my interrogation look. 'You've not got a marksheet, have you?'

'Yup, approach, one-liners, body language, confidence, all of the stuff I've been teaching you!'

'You have not!' I am worried now, what if he has? I was all prepared in my head for a cosy non-date with him, flirting optional.

'I have, it's in my head! Think of it as facilitating.'

'Think of it as stalky man! No way, no. I am not just going up to the bar and chatting some random guy up. And anyway, I did that at the gym with Steve, and I did it at the climbing wall. I—'

'The right people. I don't want anybody to take advantage, to—'

'I'm not a baby, Noah! This is supposed to be about fun, about getting a date, having fun like you do.' It's my turn to put my hand over his. 'Come on, how many dates have you got lined up for the next week? 'Fess up!'

He looks down at our hands, then back at me. 'None.'

'None? Oh, come on, don't mess, tell me!'

'I'm not messing.' He sits back, sliding his hand out from under mine. 'I'm free all week actually, you can have as many lessons as you want!'

'Wow. I'm stuck for words.'

'So much me you can't cope?'

I want to kiss his dimples, or at least touch them. 'I meant I'm in shock you've not got a date lined up!'

'I wanted some time to myself. It's exhausting being perfect and sexy all the time, you know!'

'It must be,' I say drily. 'Actually,' I put my head on one side and study him (ignoring the dimples), 'I think I'm starting to understand you! You're a bit of a control freak yourself, aren't you?' I hold up a hand to stop him talking. 'Stop right there! I know you'll say I am, and I admit it. I like control, there, I said it! But so do you. You need to stage things, control the dates, decide when you need to make a quick exit. You,' I pause, 'need to control me – that's why you hated it when I took the initiative and arranged a date with Steve, then chatted Stuart up!'

'Woah, woah, woah, Rosie. You're overreacting a bit here! I just feel responsible. I started this, so I don't want you to get hurt, not on my watch!'

'Your watch?'

'Okay, I don't want it to go wrong.' He comes back a bit closer, puts a finger under my chin and studies me. 'There are a lot of pricks about, I don't want one to use you just to boost his own ego.'

'Is that what you do?' I ask softly. Knowing it's not fair to even ask.

He shakes his head. 'I try not to hurt anybody, Rosie. I go out with girls who know the rules, who know it's about having fun.'

'It doesn't always work like that, Noah. I think they sometimes forget.'

'Maybe that's why I need a break.'

'Is it?' I peer more closely at him. Has Noah decided that first-dating his way through life isn't so perfect after all? 'Have you, Noah Adams, seen the error of your ways?'

'The only error,' he grins, 'is that your glass is empty.'

'My round,' I say, standing up.

Luckily the barman recognises me this time, and I'm not standing waving empties at him for ten minutes.

He smiles. 'What have you done to Noah? Not seen much of him lately; he used to be a regular feature in here, propping up the bar.'

'Nothing to do with me! I think he's been busy at work.'

'And there was I wondering if he was settling down.'

'Settling down?' It comes out as a croak. I open and close my mouth. Has Noah moved on from first-dating? Is he going steady?

'You guys seem the real deal.'

'What? Oh, haha.' I cackle in relief. 'You mean us?' I point at my chest. 'Us? Me and . . . Oh God, no. No! No we're not dating, we're friends.'

'What a jerk.'

'Jerk?'

'Missing out on a girl like you! If you ever, you know . . .' he leans on his forearms on the bar, 'if you've not got a boyfriend, or girl—'

'No! No, no boyfriend, girlfriend, any friend! Sure, great, maybe!'

'Here, I'll put my number in your phone if you like, just in case you fancy . . .'

I sashay my way back to the table and put the drinks down.

'I did say I'd pick the guy for you to chat up!' Noah shakes his head and raises his glass. 'Guys like that are . . .'

'I know, I know. It's his job, pull a pint, pull a girl.'

He smiles. It's like the sun coming out. Really. When he full-on smiles he makes the world seem a better place.

I expect him to chuckle, but he doesn't. The smile fades and he looks slightly sad. Serious. His voice is soft, gentle. 'You've got this cracked, haven't you, Rosie? You really don't need me anymore; you don't have a problem chatting *anybody* up. And if I'm going with you to the party, then there's no urgency . . .'

'Oh, I don't know.' I match his tone. 'I haven't got a clue how to chat up the person I really want to.' Or whether I would, even if I knew how to. 'Noah?'

He nods.

'Can we just forget me chatting anybody up, just have, I don't know . . . just have a drink? As mates?'

He shrugs. 'I don't see why not. Could be nice.'

'You can tell me about your sister.'

The smile comes back then. This time affectionate, not naughty or dazzling. 'Our Gem, very aptly named! Not that she isn't a pain in the arse at times, but you know, sisters.'

277

I don't. But I get it, seeing the look on his face. 'You're really close, aren't you? It must be nice.'

'We are, though we don't always see that much of each other. But I know she's there for me, and I think she feels the same. Her and Dan make a good team.'

'So, it is possible.'

'What?'

'A happy ever after!'

'Ahh, that.' He studies his glass, then fixes his attention back on me. It should be unnerving, being inspected so closely, but it isn't. He raises his eyebrows and gives me a twisted smile. 'I guess it is, when all the planets align, and all that stuff. Possible, but not very good odds.'

'I guess you can shift them in your favour.'

'But fate has the final word. Another?'

I nod. Watch him at the bar. Not flirting. Despite the girl who is standing next to him making a comment. It's odd. He just smiles politely then turns away. I've not really watched him when we've been out together, but now I think about it he has never flirted with anyone else. Smiled charmingly maybe, been polite. But never messed around, even though we weren't on dates.

A man you can maybe trust not to cheat on you, a man who always leaves with the girl he arrives with.

His long legs covering the ground between us easily, his gaze never shifting from me.

'So, enough about the serious stuff, my lovely Rosie-Posey.' He puts the drinks down, and this time comes to sit next to me. 'Shall we resume the lesson of the day? We've done the talking to death, so let's do this bit. Part one,' he turns so that he's half-facing me, 'the smile.' I nod, the corners of his generous mouth lift. Just enough. 'The first touch.' He tucks a tendril of hair behind my ear and sends a delicious shiver of anticipation down my spine. His fingers trail with the gentlest of touches over my cheek, until the tip of his ring finger rests on my lip. He studies my mouth for an age. I dampen my dry lips. 'Is it okay, if I . . .?'

I swallow hard and I know my lips have parted, I know I can't stop myself from leaning in. But I can't speak, I can barely nod.

And then he does.

He kisses me.

The contact is so gentle, so light at first it is more of a caress than a kiss.

His fingers cradle my cheek.

His body is warm against mine.

I'm holding my breath, waiting in case he pulls back. But he doesn't. His teeth tease at my bottom lip, tentative at first then more demanding. And then his mouth covers mine properly.

It can only have lasted seconds, a minute at most, but I feel dazed.

I run my fingers through my hair and blink. His eyes are dark.

'Oh Rosie.' His voice is husky as he strokes his thumb over my lips, then moves away. He shakes his head. 'You do know this will never work, don't you? It can't, not properly, not long—'

'It'll do for now,' I say, at the same time as my heart clunks down to my feet. 'For today.' I straighten my clothes and avoid looking at him. Because I don't want him to see inside my head. I don't want him to realise that I wanted that to be so much more than just a kiss. I don't want him to see just how shaken up I am.

'Good.' His voice is soft. 'You deserve the best you know.'

Chapter 21

You know that 'Gavin won't be here' line? Not true. Gavin is the second person I see when we wander into Gemma's back garden the next day for the barbecue.

The first person is her husband, Dan, who puts out a delaying arm and says, 'You're not going to like this.'

I don't. Gavin-Gabe is no longer adorned with a toddler and a pram, he now has jeans, a T-shirt with the slogan 'No ketchup, just sauce' and a beer. What a dick.

'He turned up on his own five minutes ago, says he left Linda at home with a crying baby and just fancied a beer and a break. He didn't realise we'd have company.'

'I can help with the breaking part.' I realise I am growling through gritted teeth. 'Will you hate me for ever if I go and punch one of your guests?' I say to Dan. 'Hi, by the way, I'm Rosie.'

'I heard you were direct,' says Dan, smiling. Shaking my hand.

I look at Noah, who holds his hands up, 'not guilty, must have been Gemma!'

'Feel free.' Dan waves us through. 'He denied everything;

in fact he laughed in my face and Gemma has been seething ever since. He did this "Tinder? Not been on it since I met the woman of my dreams, must be an old account that's somehow popped up" thing.'

'I'll give him old account!'

'Be gentle, Rosie.' Noah looks concerned. 'It's not him I'm worried about, it's you. Don't let him get to you.'

'I won't,' I lie. I already have let him get to me. But I know what Noah is getting at. He doesn't want me to mix this slimeball up with my dad, to let all the frustrations and anger that have built up over the years suddenly spill over the brim and leave me a soggy mess. 'I'll be fine, honest.'

I do, in fact, feel fine, as I march towards the man who a day ago made me snog Noah's face off. He owes me big time, 1. For not turning up to our date, and 2. For making me kiss a man I really shouldn't have.

Although maybe I owe him one. If it hadn't been for that kiss in the park, then would the kiss in the bar have happened?

Although I still haven't worked out if that was the BIGGEST MISTAKE OF MY LIFE. Noah hasn't mentioned it. I haven't mentioned it. We are moving on as though that tender moment never happened.

As if.

Anyway, Noah is a problem for later.

'Nice T-shirt!' It isn't actually, it is naff particularly given the circumstances, but saying this stops me punching him in the mouth or calling him a two-timing bastard. I smile sweetly. My face is stiff and my teeth are gritted. 'I want to thank you.'

'Really?' Gavin smiles slightly nervously.

The First Date

'If it hadn't been for you, I wouldn't have met Noah.' He glances at Noah, who has followed me over, rather furtively. 'Or realised that dating apps are a crap way of meeting people.'

'Haha, really? Have to disagree there, that's how I met my wife.'

'And it's how you nearly met me.' My smile is so fixed my face is about to crack. I can feel the fault lines forming.

'Ah, I don't think we've met, have we?' He peers closer, then grins. 'Aha, in the park earlier! We've not met properly and been introduced though?'

'Not quite.' I hold up my phone. 'Though we got pretty darned close.' My dramatic moment is slightly marred by the fact that my fingers are actually trembling. Which riles me even more, how dare he make me tremble!

Gavin makes a move to the left as though he's going to leave, but Noah puts out a hand.

'I think you should see this, mate.'

'Yes, Gabe,' I say, holding my phone up so he can see himself, and his wonderful smile. 'Great photo, isn't it? Really good likeness.'

'Oh shit, I've been cloned!'

'Oh.' This thought hadn't occurred to me, and my stomach takes a dive. Oh my God, have I unfairly accused an innocent man? Shit, in front of his friends!

Then I look at his face. All the colour wouldn't have drained from his cheeks if he didn't know exactly what I was talking about. His hand is shaking slightly as he hands my phone back to me. To give him credit, he's a quick thinker. Although I suppose he had been prewarned by Gemma.

'Really?' I try and sound concerned. 'Oh wow, that's awful! Isn't that terrible, Noah? Let's work out who it is who's done it and you can confront him.'

'It doesn't . . .'

'It's terrible, isn't that fraud or something? I know!' I punch the air. 'I've got it. I can arrange to meet him, and you can tag along, and we can tell the police. Like a honey trap! A bastard trap! I mean, this kind of thing can get you in all kinds of trouble. Hang on, hang on a sec I'll message him right now and—'

'Stop.' His face is stony, but his voice is low and he's looking round anxiously.

I stop pretending. I never have been good at keeping an act up for long. 'If you don't admit this to your wife, Gabe, Gavin or whatever you're called, then I will!'

'Why don't you just fuck off home, Gav, and sort your mess out?' The deep voice makes me jump. I spin round and a slightly chubby, average height guy with mussed up hair and tired eyes smiles at me. 'He's not worth getting worked up about.'

'But, he—'

I turn back round, but Gavin is very wisely doing as suggested, and fucking off. He's walking backwards across the lawn as though backwards means nobody will notice. Then he bumps into the fence, spins round and finds himself face to face with Noah.

Noah doesn't look amused. He's gone a bit shouty if I'm honest and is waving his mobile around, and prodding Gavin in the chest.

'We never liked him,' says chubby guy. 'Always seemed a bit too blokey.'

'You don't like blokey?'

'Not OTT blokey. Only put up with him because of Linda. She's sound, and Gemma loves her to bits, and well, what can you do?'

I nod, not sure what to say to that.

'I'm Jed by the way.'

I find myself smiling with pure pleasure. So, this is tragic Jed, who I'd imagined looking devastated, a worn-out shell of a man. Instead he looks quite normal. He hasn't got *tragic hero* tattooed across his forehead. 'Rosie, pleased to meet you. Noah's talked about you.'

'Oh really?' he says in slow motion.

'Nothing bad!' I add hastily.

'Don't panic, I meant oh really, as in you're Rosie. I've heard about you too.'

'Really?' I suddenly feel nervous. What has Noah said to his best mate about me?

'All good, promise. We can swap notes! Fancy a burger?'

'Sure.'

I smile back at him and it feels like I've met a long-lost brother. My heart rate has already gone back to normal, and I'm sure in a few minutes' time I'll have lost my beetroot hue and smoke will have stopped coming out of my ears. 'You can protect me from Gemma.'

'Oh?'

'I think she wants to interrogate me!'

'Ahh. I'm sure she does, she's very fond of her big bro, whatever she says. Protective instinct kicks in.'

I laugh. 'Noah doesn't need protecting!'

'You'd be surprised.'

'Why?' I am genuinely interested. This is something that I would have never thought could be true. Noah looks after number 1 quite capably.

'He'll tell you himself when he's ready! Right, are you a beer out of the bottle girl, or do you want one of those disgusting paper cup things?'

* * *

'Jed's lovely, isn't he?' I say to Noah a couple of hours later when some very good burgers have been consumed, washed down with several beers and we are wending our way home.

'Lovely. You two seem to hit it off.' His tone is dry.

'Hey, what's wrong with that?' Then it hits me. He's warning me off. He's been a bit on edge since he picked me up to come here.

Why would he want his best mate and the girl he's teaching to date to get on together? Our worlds weren't really supposed to collide like this. We are on separate tracks.

'I just.' He stops dead. 'I've not seen him laughing like that for ages, it was almost like the old Jed was back.'

'So, that's good, isn't it?'

'Good, except he'll feel duped when he finds out we're not actually dating, and he'll probably never see you again. I don't want anybody to get the wrong idea.'

Ouch. Great. Spell it out loud and clear, Noah! 'Oh, stop being such an arse. I told him.' He frowns. 'What kind of a girl do you think I am? And what's that look for now? Worried he'll think you're screwing me over or something.' His mouth opens and closes, flapping fish style. 'Oh, stop worrying for God's sake. He thinks the sun shines out of your arse still. It amused him.' That isn't one hundred per cent true. He did laugh, so I'm not lying, but then he said, 'oh yeah pull the other one. It might have started out like that, but I know Noah. Boy do I know Noah. Fancy risking a kebab and another beer?'

'He looked after me, he was nice.' I pause. 'What is it with you? Every time I'm having a good time you come over like this and spoil things.'

'I don't.'

Luckily, we are now outside my place. The perfect timing to say my piece and part company. 'Yes, Noah, you do.' He opens his mouth to say something, but I stop him. 'But don't worry, I'm not after getting cosy with your friends, you, anything. I can kiss somebody and not think I'm falling in bloody love!'

I close the door on him then go through and flop back on my bed. I feel like I have been steamrollered.

I also think I might have just told a lie.

Chapter 22

I have a text message from Dad. This is odd because he very rarely texts me, apart from when he's making up excuses for not coming home, insulting me, or when he wants me to do his dirty work for him.

This started when I was fourteen years old and he brought me my first mobile. I didn't realise at the time, but apparently, even though I am now all grown up and have moved out, he still thinks this is acceptable in emergencies.

'Hi Ro!'

He's the only person to call me Ro.

'Can you do me a favour, darling? Dad x'
'Sure, I'll see you at the party, we can sort it then! R x'

Signing myself off Ro has always seemed kind of weird, so I settled on R quite a long time ago. Once I'd realised that his texts usually were the lead up to him letting me, or Mum, down. Ro suggested we were in it together, camaraderie, co-conspirators. Even as a teenager I recognised the need for distance to protect myself.

'Need to sort it now, darling. Dad x'
'Call me.'

I know he won't. Dad hardly ever calls because 1. He's too busy living his best life, and 2. He hates confrontation. He prefers distance. Texting. I think he is partly, okay mainly, responsible for my non-confrontational, logical approach to life. Except I do it with better, more honourable intentions. I am beginning to think he doesn't know the meaning of honour, especially not in the 'love, honour and obey' context.

I'm also beginning to realise that he is one of the most emotionally detached people I know, despite being one of the most charming and flirtatious. Oh, and one of the most deceitful. It's funny, isn't it, how easily you can be tricked by what people say, and who they appear to be? How you can mistake touchy-feely and smiley for close and open. How you can mistake platitudes for honesty and doing things in your best interest with controlling.

'Sorry, rehearsal, shouldn't have my phone on. Can you find out how your mother got Serena's contact details? Dad x'
'That's easy. I got them for her. Why are you rehearsing, you should be on your way home, shouldn't you? X'
'Mix up, long story, will do my best to get there. Dad xx'
'Do my best had better mean you will be, I'll kill you if you aren't! Ro x'

The First Date

I put the 'Ro' to counteract his two kisses. It is text sarcasm. Dad, I've realised, is an emotional manipulator. See, something else I've worked out. It's taken me a while, but there's no stopping me now. I'm on a roll.

'Haha you're just like your Mum! Dad x'
'No, I'm not actually, I'm a mix of the two of you.'

God help me.

'No excuses – you've known about this date for 30 years!!
☺ *See you later R x.'*
Please don't mess this up, Dad.

He doesn't reply. He's probably working out just how big an excuse he'll need for not showing. Or how quickly he'll be able to leave afterwards.

I can't let Mum keep punishing herself like this. After this party we are going to have another mother-daughter chat. I am going to put my foot down. This is the last time.

'Be five minutes late, sorry. Noah x'
'Early compared to Dad then! Rosie x'

I add a crying with laughter face because that's how I feel.

Smiley because Noah is coming. I haven't heard from him since we went to his sister's barbecue. It was all a little strained on the way home. I'm not sure what we're doing any longer, or why.

Crying because I think maybe he's trying to work out how to tell me he doesn't want to do this any longer. His pointed comment about how comfortable I was chatting to Jed proves that. I just put the bravado on and said 'sure' but the point is, Jed wasn't a date. I can talk to men who I don't fancy, have no plan to go out with, and who are friends of friends. It's the date bit that sends me into a panic. Not that I have any interest in going on a date at the moment anyway, but I'm not going to tell him that.

Anyway, he was a bit huffy and sharp, so I was a bit sarky and short, so we parted company on much the same terms you do when you fall out with a sibling and you're ten years old. But without slamming the bedroom door or saying, 'I'll tell Mum it was you who let the hamster out'.

I'm a bit (okay a lot) scared about Noah walking away and leaving me to tackle the dating scene alone. Okay, truth bit here. It is not fear, I'm not scared. Even if I'm not going to admit it to anybody else, I just don't want him to walk away. Full stop.

I knew this would happen. I knew it was a total mistake getting involved with a man who was sexy as fuck, confident, funny, fit, loves dating, doesn't want commitment arghhhh. I knew I'd fall for him. And end up wishing I'd never met him. Or wishing that I wished I'd never met him, because now I know him, I can never imagine forgetting him.

And we haven't even slept together.

The only upside that I can cling on to, is that there is one massive, inescapable difference between him and Dad. He doesn't believe in love, and he won't ever get married. Haha lucky escape.

The First Date

There are so many downsides though. So many other differ-
ences between him and Dad as well – he's not self-obsessed;
he's caring; oh and he doesn't shoot me down, he likes me
just as I am. And he's not distant, he's the first person I've
felt I could share anything with (and that covers the whole
gamut from the last slice of pizza, to my innermost secrets).

So, anyway, despite my head being royally screwed up and
having a love-hate relationship with him that he knows
nothing about, I am pleased he's still coming to the party.

Though I suspect this might be our grand finale. But I am
determined to make the most of it.

Maybe if I play this right we could actually go out with,
as Bea suggested, a bang?

However, I am exasperated to the point of crying with the
other man in my life. Dad. Because although I *think* he'll show
up to the party, his heart obviously isn't in it. This could be
because some other part of his body is in somebody else, if
you'll pardon the crudeness.

The phone rings. 'Are you okay? What's happened with
your dad?' Noah's concern makes me want to blub it all out.
So I do. I never blurted things like this to Robbie because it
was somehow different. He'd grown up with them, criticising
my parents to him would have been like criticising his. Okay,
yeah, we were normal kids who had a moan, but we didn't
come out with anything really damning. It was 'I hate him
because he won't let me stay over at yours' not 'I hate him
because he's a heartless shitbag who's trying to ruin my life
and makes Mum cry'. See? There's a difference.

It's different with Noah, I seem to be able to talk to him

about anything. We don't have the emotional history that screws it all up, puts the brakes on.

He also actually listens and doesn't brush me off with an 'it'll be fine, can you move to one side, the game's about to kick off'.

'How can he even think about not turning up?'

'You're kidding? Your dad's not turning up to his own wedding anniversary party?' He gives a low whistle.

Cool down, Rosie, breathe. 'He's been texting, trying to give me excuses. I reckon he's panicking cos Mum has invited some of his, his,' I can't call them girlfriends, or flings, 'some of the people he plays with.'

'Ahh, nicely put.' There's a pause. 'Has she really invited them all?'

'I wouldn't say all, I don't think you can hire a marquee *that* big.'

He chuckles. 'Your Mum is so cool, calling his bluff,' I can hear the smile in his voice, 'good for her, I can't wait to meet her.'

I've never thought of Mum as 'cool' before, or the fact that she's bravely calling his bluff – but maybe he's right.

'I've always thought of her as having all her spark knocked out of her by dad, but you could be right. Maybe she's tougher than I gave her credit for.'

'I'm sure she is, just like her daughter. She's lucky to have you; you're lucky to have each other. How does the song go, together you're indestructible?' He chuckles.

'Invincible, Muse,' I say, smiling. This calms me down a bit. 'I think he's bricking it actually.' He wouldn't have called me otherwise. 'Serena's name came up.'

'Serena?'

'Top of the bill in Rome. She's a cellist,' I'm not quite sure why my brain fixates on things like that, 'we thought that was over a while ago but maybe not. She was thrilled to be invited; maybe she wants to eye up the opposition, or crow, or wrap her bow round his neck?' I end on a hopeful note, and Noah laughs again.

'Maybe your mum is hoping they'll all turn on him! Batter him with a double bass?'

'Funny!'

'Clobber him with a clarinet?'

'Haha.'

'Flay him with a flute?'

'I think you're getting your wind and string section confused.'

'Help me out here, I'm struggling.'

I laugh, then sober up. 'I hope he behaves, for Mum's sake.' He'll turn up. He has to. I'm worrying over nothing. How can he not turn up now Mum has invited all his friends? Letting his family down is one thing, standing his wife up on their thirtieth wedding anniversary is fine. But showing the whole world he's a selfish git? No. Not his style. 'He'll be there, it will be fine.'

'It will, and you'll be there for her if she needs you.'

And who will be there for me, I think.

'And I'll be there for you,' he says as though he's read my thoughts. There's a silence while we both take that in. 'Right,' he's gone all brisk, 'I'll be with you shortly. Just had an issue with the car, all sorted now.'

Chapter 23

Dad is not here. I can tell, even before we walk up the steps. Because if he was, he'd be flinging the door open before we knocked, before we'd got out of the car. It's what he does.

Makes it all about him.

We have arrived at the party ten minutes late and he is not here. Surely the host is supposed to arrive before the guests.

I glance nervously at Noah and try not to bite my bottom lip too hard. He squeezes my hand. 'Okay?'

'Oh Rosalie!' Before I can answer, the door is flung open and Mum wraps me in a hug. She's good at hugs, which people who don't know her don't expect – as she's so glam on the outside. New friends kind of lean in tentatively for an air kiss and are swept off their feet (sometimes literally). 'You're here!'

'Of course, I'm here!'

'Well you never know.' This is the only indication that all is not one hundred per cent well in mummy-land. 'Come in, come on, introduce me to this gorgeous friend of yours. Good heavens, how on earth can you resist him? You're a stronger woman than me!'

I have found this to be increasingly challenging. The resisting bit. But I'm not going to tell Mum that. I was nearly turned into a melty mess when he knocked on my door earlier. My legs as well as my tummy had a kind of wobble thing going on, and I was so tempted to leap on him for hugs in the manner of my mother that I scared myself.

I'm sure this was because 1. I've not eaten, and 2. have got myself into a state about the possible repercussions of this party, and it is absolutely nothing to do with the fact that I've been starved of seeing him for several days and he's now turned up looking even hotter than ever.

It's like being taken to an Italian restaurant when you're on a carb free diet. Excruciating. I have to keep reminding myself that in the long run the abstinence will be worth it. My heart will thank me.

I could cut this off at the knees by explaining the prosaic and boring reason why Noah is here. I could explain that despite being my father's daughter I am incapable of tackling the dating game without backup, that Noah is only here as a favour and because he's such a nice man, not because he fancies me in the slightest, and that despite the fact that I cannot ignore the fact I fancy the pants off him, I will not be actually removing them as my head has told my heart to stop being such a jerk.

'More to the point, how can I keep my hands off a girl who takes after such a glamorous mother.' Noah grins his cheekiest smile and I inwardly groan, and outwardly roll my eyes at him.

'A charmer as well!' Her smile broadens. 'I do love a charmer.'

The First Date

'Don't I know it.' I mutter this into the bouquet of flowers I've brought her, so she doesn't hear. Unfortunately burying my nose in lilies is not a good idea. I come out sputtering.

'Rosie, are you okay?'

'Yes, Mum. These are for you.' I shove them at her. I'm not okay. I'm so wound up I might spontaneously combust at any minute. For a girl who doesn't like emotional conflict (or real passion on any level), this is a nightmare.

Let's just spell this out. I've come to a party to support my mother, against my father who I've started to realise is a complete shit not my knight in slightly tarnished armour, who it looks like isn't going to turn up (but I didn't know that so have worked myself into a tizz about what I'm going to say to him) anyway. I have brought a fake boyfriend, who I wish was my real boyfriend because he's so hot my nether regions start to tingle indecently the moment they see him, and I feel sick that after today he might exit my life forever.

So, no, I'm not that okay.

'I'm great! You're looking very glam for a party in the back garden! You look amazing.' She does. In fact, there's an edge to her I haven't seen for a long time. I remember when I was little, watching her put the finishing touches to her make-up before she went out for the evening. She glowed. She was like a princess.

I'd never noticed how much her light had been dimmed over the last few years; it must be exhausting trying to hang on to a husband who is so good at being elusive.

'Thank you, darling.' She touches my arm lightly. 'That's a lovely thing to say. Now come on you two, let's go and get you a drink.'

Noah's fingertips rest on the small of my back as we walk through the house, and it's impossible to ignore. I want him to walk his fingers up my spine, to kiss the nape of my neck to . . .

Stop!

I stop abruptly and turn around so that I can hiss in his ear. 'You can stop the flattery while we're here.' I can't help myself, my self-protection mode has kicked in, to override my 'I want to jump on you' mode.

'What do you mean?' he whispers back, his closeness sending goose bumps down my arms. Maybe getting this close wasn't the brightest idea I've ever had.

'That comment about me taking after Mum! She knows we're just friends.' Oh shit, why am I doing this? Why can't I just go with the flow rather than trying to create an argument that I know I'll regret? Hitting out at him will change nothing. Except I suppose then he might realise I need lots more lessons, so hang about a bit longer.

'It wasn't flattery, you do.' He moves from my ear, his warm breath fanning my cheek, until he's facing me. Nose to nose. Looking straight into my eyes. Gulp. 'You're beautiful, fun and clever.' He pauses. 'But still a bit scary.' Then he grins.

'Here you are, darling, a nice champagne cocktail, and you can have a Tom Collins, is that okay?' Noah nods, and takes the drink, looking slightly bemused. Knowing me hasn't prepared him at all for meeting my mother. 'Oh, your dad isn't coming by the way,' I am aware the smile has gone from my face and I'm gripping her hand as well as the stem of the glass, 'but I bumped into Bea in town earlier and asked her to come along, isn't that nice? I do hope she does, the more the merrier, we've got lots of food!'

She says it all matter of fact-ly. The Bea bit in the same tone as the Dad bit.

'Dad isn't coming?' I glance at Noah, his lips are pressed into a thin, hard line.

'No darling, he sent me a message. Oh Rosalie, I hope you're not too upset.'

'I'm upset for you, Mum, not me!' I'm fuming. I have come to the realisation that 'pearl' anniversary may be strangely appropriate as Dad is the irritant, the dirt that crept into her life and she's wasted the best years of her life doing her best to cover the irritant up, protect herself, make something beautiful.

She sighs. 'I asked Bea to come, because I thought you might be upset, and I didn't know if you'd bring Noah along. Oh Rosie.' She hugs me.

'What do you mean, you thought I might be upset? You didn't know . . .'

'I just had this feeling that your dad might pick this moment to finally burn his bridges. He's a coward, Rosie. I'm sorry but he is.'

'Burn his bridges?' I know he's a coward. I've never really wanted to accept it, or say it out loud. But those texts? I mean, really.

'Shall we sit down?'

'Mum, tell me!'

'I forced him into a bit of a corner if I'm honest. I know it's underhand, but . . .'

'Mum! What's his excuse this time?'

'Oh Sally, so pleased you could come! Catch up with you in a moment!' Mum stops for a moment to hug her neighbour, and I wait, worried. 'Where was I? Oh yes, he got Serena pregnant.'

'What?' Whatever I was expecting, it was not that.

'Serena. You know, the *when in Rome* girl.'

I didn't know she knew about Rome.

'But, I got her email for you and—'

'Oh, I already knew, darling, or I wouldn't have been so keen to invite her, would I?'

I'm pretty sure I'd have fallen over, if it hadn't been for Noah's hand on my waist. He kind of neatly caught me, and now I seem to have wilted against his side. 'Oh my God, she's pregnant and you *knew*. And you invited her to your *anniversary* party? And he's leaving us for Serena?' Are you mad? I could have added, but I don't.

'He's not leaving us.'

'Not?' I manage to separate myself a bit from Noah.

'Well no, that isn't his style, dear. He refused point-blank to do that when she asked. Poor girl.'

'What do you mean "poor girl"? Mum!'

'Well she is a poor girl; she's young, naïve, like I was once. He's never going to go, Rosie,' her tone is soft, 'the next woman might not be so forgiving, and then he wouldn't have the security he wants.'

'But you can't . . . oh Mum. Why did you invite them all if you knew . . .?'

'So your dad could pick, out in the open. In front of everybody who matters to him.'

'What?' I am flabbergasted, is she stricken with grief? 'How can you make him pick . . . even though you know he'll pick you.'

'Oh Rosie, I'm sorry.' She strokes my hand, not looking at all upset, then looks at Noah as though she expects him to understand something I've missed. 'I'm not one of the choices, darling. I am off the menu and he's not even had the decency to turn up so I can have my moment!'

I frown.

'Honestly, that man would never let me win. Not once! I want them all to know who he is. It's always been on his terms, and just for once I wanted it to be on mine.' She sighs. 'He won't even let me have that. It's not about revenge though, it is about getting a decent settlement! Now come on, it's a party, off you two go, have a dance!'

I am confused. Very confused. I also feel that my mother has set down the gauntlet as they say. She's in a feisty mood today, and if I refuse to dance with Noah, she might get even worse. And what did she mean by 'settlement'?

'Oh look, there's Donald! Give me a moment, darling, you circulate, I'll come back and explain properly later. I'm sure we'll get a moment before you go. Donald, Donald!' She waves madly and is off at the double. I don't know how she balances and manages to look fabulous in those heels. I think I need to ask for lessons.

'Wow, I thought you were direct, sexy and a force to be reckoned with, I can see where you got it from now.' Noah puts a mock startled look on his face, and I laugh. 'Great cocktails though.'

I take a big gulp of mine, then realise the error of my ways. By the time I've stopped spluttering Noah and I seem to have been squeezed against the wall by the crowds queueing for the buffet.

'You look like you need another?' He expertly lifts two more glasses off the tray of a passing waiter, and I drink the second one a little more cautiously.

'I haven't got a clue what's in this, but it's pretty potent!' It is, I've not eaten all day and it has gone straight to my head.

I look at Noah and all of a sudden all I can smell is him. His grey-blue gaze is fixed on me.

'Okay?'

'Fine.' I whisper back.

I want to kiss him. I have to kiss him again. Just once more.

'Dance?'

'I'm okay here.' I don't want to move. I don't want to end this moment, in case I never get it back again.

'You're swaying.'

'I like this track.' I can't help myself.

'Cool.' He offloads the glasses, and both his hands are on my waist.

I really want to kiss him. I want, I need, to know if that feeling I got when I assaulted him in the park, used him as a Gabe diversion, was real. If our kiss in the bar was as eye-wateringly good as I thought it was.

I've dreamed of that moment our lips touched; I've fantasised about what would have come next if Gabe hadn't stopped and talked to him. I've tormented myself and convinced myself it just seems like it was incredible because he's forbidden fruit. I can't have him, and that has to be why I think it was so good.

'I like your mum, she's cool.'

'I know.' His shirt is so light, I can feel the warmth of his skin beneath my palm, feel the beat of his heart. 'She is.'

'And beautiful, like you. I meant that, when I said it earlier. I wasn't just flirting.'

His eyes have darkened and it's so sexy I honestly feel like I've stopped breathing. How can he make me lose the power to breathe just by looking at me?

'Really?'

'Really.' He moves his hand against my back and the need starts to build. I've never, ever thought of myself as somebody who *needs* sex, but right now I'm re-categorising.

His hard thighs are pressed against mine and still I'm moving to the music, which makes him gasp when my hips sway against a part of his trouser that, let's just say, wasn't jutting out like that before.

'Oh Rosie.' He brings one hand up between us, rests his finger under my chin, then very slowly, very deliberately he leans down. I still can't remember how to breathe, my whole body is tensing, my lips parting and then abruptly he closes the tiny gap between our mouths and comes down crushingly hard.

I was expecting a delicate brush of the lips, expecting a chance to object, to move away, but this is so much hotter. This is irresistible, this is something that I never imagined could be like this. This is bloody hot-and-panting heaven.

I don't think I've ever been kissed like this in my entire life. My whole body has gone into overdrive. Super sensitive to his touch and the shudder runs right through the core of me as his hand cradles my face, his fingertips caressing that sensitive spot behind my ear that makes me whimper.

Oh my God, his other hand is cradling my bottom. He's just added a whole new dimension to this, and I don't know if I can cope. His fingers are curled round, and I'd clamber all over him if I could.

Who knew nibbling lips was so erotic? Oh my, his mouth is on my throat. I need, I need . . .

Oh. My. God. I need to get away!

'It's my, my . . .' I can't even say the word. 'I need the loo!' Apparently, I can run very fast in high heels. I'm across the lounge, up the stairs and locked in the en-suite quicker than I thought possible. I sink down on the toilet seat and pant. And cover my burning face with my hands.

Okay, I think I have found this passion that Mum was so keen for me to experience. I don't think she meant me to feel it at her party though.

Shit. I actually wrapped my leg round him.

I bit his lip; I sucked his tongue. I pulled my fists through his hair.

I wrapped my leg round his thigh, almost round his bloody waist.

All to the rocking beat of 'Simply the Best'.

Tina Turner would have been proud of me.

And then I saw MY DAD.

My father is here, and the look of disdain on his face said that he'd just spotted his daughter acting like a tramp on the dancefloor and was disgusted.

The First Date

My dad saw me eating a man. I feel sick.

I need to take a deep breath. Breathe, breathe, calm down. I have done nothing wrong, who is he to judge me? He's the one who has made another girl pregnant. He's the one who goes shagging his way round Europe as though he's on a mission to unite the world.

I am grown up. I am allowed to kiss men.

'Hey, hey!' There is a banging on the door.

'Go away, it's taken!' Who on earth has had the gall to invade my parents' en-suite?

I close my eyes and put a finger to my bruised lips. Whatever Dad thinks, I can't regret what just happened though.

I'm never going to be the same again. Obviously, my mouth will recover, but how do I go back from this? A kiss that was close to orgasmic.

And I still had all my clothes on.

It's worse than that though, much worse. It was the moment before, those minutes before he kissed me. When we could have been the only two people that existed. When there was this frisson of anticipation between us and I'd felt closer to him than I ever have to anybody else in my life.

I hug my arms around myself.

'I know you're in there, Rosie, open this fucking door before I kick it down.'

'I know you wouldn't do that.' I open the door with a sigh. 'Hi, Bea.'

'Hi back at you, Rosie girl.' She grins. 'I didn't think you could move that fast.'

'Nor did I,' I say glumly.

'You two were getting cosy!' She raises an eyebrow.

'Don't! Oh Bea . . .'

'Is that an "oh Bea, what a lovely kiss I've had"?' she says in an airy tone, totally interrupting my revelation that my absent parent has reappeared, 'or an "oh Bea I think I'm falling for him"?' Her voice has dropped to a sultry growl and she's clutching her chest with her hand.

'Sod off.' I am trying not to grin, it's not working.

'Haha! I knew it!'

I close my eyes. Noah's 'am I right' sayings from that very first evening are loud in my ears.

'You've got it bad, girl. I prescribe a light buffet and several of your mum's toxic cocktails. Come on.' She holds out a hand. 'This is for your mum, not you. We'll scrape you back together again later.'

I sigh and let her haul me to my feet. She's right. I do need to get my act together for my mum's sake. Dad has done his normal trick of sneaking in round the back so that he can pretend he arrived on time. Hell, she probably doesn't even know he's here! 'You'll be fine, girl. At least you know what a proper snog is supposed to feel like now, instead of a snuffly sloppy one.'

'Robbie was not snuffly!'

'Well, he wasn't like that, was he?' She raises a knowing eyebrow. I glow red hot and decide it is safer not to object further.

'I think I've OD'd.' I sigh. 'It was incredible.' And Dad managed to spoil it.

'And now you're just trying to make me jealous. Come on, your mother was asking where you'd got to.'

I groan and pull my big girls pants up, metaphorically. In reality I'm wearing indecently skimpy lace things that couldn't contain a big girl if they tried.

Maybe if I go back to waist high M&S specials my life, and emotions, will revert to normal.

'And Noah was a bit concerned, said he was worried you'd got cystitis.'

Oh God, I will never revert to normal. 'He didn't!'

'Maybe not, he was looking a bit lost and confused though. Not himself at all.'

'Bea.' I put a staying hand on her arm, just as she heads for the stairs. 'It's not just Noah.'

Maybe if Dad was that disgusted with me, he will have just barged out, back to his latest girlfriend. Nobody else will ever know he was here. Except me. That look will be branded on my brain forever.

'What? Rosie, what is it? You look a bit . . . you don't feel sick, do you? Shall we go back . . .'

'I do feel sick, and I would like to go back in the bathroom.' I take a deep breath. 'Dad's here.'

'Your dad? Fuck me? Where?'

'I don't know! He was watching me, watching me . . .' I can hardly breathe let alone speak, I think I might be hyperventilating. 'Snog Noah!' There, I've said it. I feel slightly better now it's out in the open. 'I've got to warn Mum. I don't think she knows.'

'I think she might.' Bea's voice is soft. We're halfway down the stairs and we stop, and I follow her gaze.

Dad is holding court, centre stage with a large group of

their friends around him. And Mum is standing quietly on the side-lines watching. Like she always does. A glass of champagne in her hand.

'Oh look, cocktails!' Bea grabs us both one, then slips her hand through my arm. Solidarity.

And then Dad spots us, and I just know he's going to head me off and try and spoil my magical moment with Noah. He will douse it with disappointment and ruin it forever.

'Bea, I need to . . .'

'Here.' She is already steering me away from my parents. 'You need time to get your shit together before you talk to him.'

Chapter 24

Noah hasn't let his concern for me spoil the party. He's propping up the makeshift bar, talking to Laurie.

Laurie is the doctor's daughter. She is five years younger than me, one foot taller and ten times more confident. She is also thinner. And never looks like she's fallen asleep on her plate.

Natural she's not. Coquettish she is. Now there's a word I never thought I'd use.

He's flirting: the casual hand movements, the leaning in, the grin, the way he tips his head on one side to listen properly. Oh yes, Noah has taught me well. I know the signs.

I can't criticise him, he's doing what comes as naturally as breathing to him. Charming the opposite sex – just like Dad has always done.

There's a twinge in my chest. It aches, a physical hurt that makes my throat constrict. I've fallen for him. I know I have. Bea was nearly one hundred per cent correct, but not quite. I'm not *falling* for Noah Adams, I've already fallen for him. Hook, line and sinker.

Soon I'll be in too deep, which means I've got to stop this

311

right now. I've got to do what my mother didn't. Turn away from the charm. Walk away. Not be like her.

I never want to be the girl who gets stood up on her wedding anniversary: getting stood up on a first date was bad enough.

Let's face it, this is a man who doesn't even believe in love. He's not just a commitment-phobe, he genuinely believes it ruins lives.

The moment he spots me though he turns away from her and I can almost see him brace – ready for impact. Then he smiles tentatively. Bea nudges me, hard, with her elbow.

Oh heck, the man is heading my way. We're on a collision course.

'If the mountain won't come to Mohammed.' He twinkles at me.

'Are you calling me a mountain?' Keep this light, Rosie.

The twinkle fades. 'Have I done something?'

Kissed me. Touched me. Done everything that some tiny part inside me wanted you to, but the sensible on the outside couldn't cope with.

Yes, Noah, you have done something. It was amazing.

'No.' I smile.

'That's not a real Rosie smile! Come on, you're avoiding me, which is a pretty awesome accomplishment in a back garden.' He tries a grin again. But we both know it's strained. 'Why did you run?' His tone has softened. I love the way he does that, the way he can make me feel like I'm important.

'I saw Dad.'

He frowns.

'He was watching us and . . .'

'And?'

I swallow down the lump in my throat. Try and work out how to explain.

'And who do we have here?' The loud voice booms out behind me – so that everybody can hear, and a fair number turn and glance our way.

I wish the ground would open up and swallow me.

'Dad, this is, er my friend, Noah, Noah this is my father.'

'Friend?' He laughs, but it's not a nice laugh. 'At least this one has got something about him, I suppose.' Then he looks me over. 'Well Ro, I see you took my advice and finally decided to try and make something of yourself, change your hair.'

'I did it for me.'

He smiles. 'And have you managed to find a job that's a bit more interesting?'

'I like my job, Dad.'

'Hmm well, we'll talk about that later. And your, er, man.' He gives Noah a final once-over and marches away before either of us can say anything.

I feel exhausted. Worn out. Drained. I want to cry.

Noah is looking at me. 'How can you let him talk to you like that?'

'He's my dad!'

'And you're an adult, Rosie! He's got no right to slag you off, you deserve better, and so does your mother. He's just got another woman pregnant, and he's having a go at you for kissing me?' There's a note of incredulity in his voice. 'Come on, Rosie, you can't let him run your life like this.'

I know he's right. He is. And I'm angry at Dad, and I'm angry at me for letting him affect me the way he does, and now I'm angry at Noah. Because. Well because he's here to be angry at. And I'm not quite ready to be shouted at about not letting myself be shouted at (even though, to be fair, he's not really shouting). And I still feel so bad about Dad catching me behaving like a sex mad teenager. And still, and this is what I know deep down it really is, I'm scared. I'm scared that I got so carried away with Noah, that I enjoyed so much, that I want so, so much more.

And I can't.

He might not be as bad as Dad, but he doesn't want to settle down. He doesn't want to fall in love. He hates the whole idea of love.

I feel so sad now I want to cry.

The gorgeous Noah just wants fun.

Noah doesn't want somebody like me. He's kind, and he's nice, and he's gorgeous, and he's everything I didn't want but have just found out I'd like to try.

But he'll never be mine.

'Noah.'

'Oh God, don't you hate every sentence that begins with your name?'

'Look, I wasn't avoiding you before. I just ran, cos I saw Dad, and . . . Why don't you just, just,' I don't want to say this, but I have to, 'go back and talk to Laurie? You looked pretty taken by her.'

'Unfair! Hang on, you're cross with me because I was talking to, to . . .'

'Laurie, the one with the hair extensions, implants and peroxide. Be yourself, be natural you said, haha!' Hot tears are stinging at my eyes, but I crash on saying all the wrong, unfair things. I know I'm pushing him away. I have to. I can't change Dad, I can't change the way he sees me, but I can make sure my own life is okay. The way I want it.

'Rosie, I said be natural because that's how I like you! As you. I'm not interested in her, or anybody else, we were just chatting.'

'Fine. Anyway I wasn't avoiding you, you didn't exactly come looking for me, did you?'

He blinks. I'm being horrible. I know it, he knows it.

He didn't come though. It was Bea, my *friend*, who came to see where I was. To check I was okay.

'It was Bea,' his voice is low, 'who told me to stay put; she knew where you'd be!'

'I'll miss the way you do that.'

'What?' He frowns. Even his frowns are cute.

'Read my mind.' And I'll miss lots of other things as well. The confidence boost, the grins, the banter. The kisses.

'Look, I'm sorry but I think we've gone off-piste a bit. This isn't what it's supposed to be.' I avoid his gaze. It's too hard to look at him.

'It was one kiss, Rosie. I'm sorry, look, I thought you wanted . . .' He runs his hand through his hair. 'I'm sorry, I was a jerk, I misread.'

'I can't do this anymore. I don't even want to date right now. At all. Nobody.' I do look him in the eye then. 'I can't do this, I don't want to!'

I'm fizzing with anger.

'And you can't talk about my dad like that.' My voice is shaky.

I'm so angry. Angry at Dad for turning up late, angry at Dad for being such a two-timing cheat who couldn't change his ways, angry he's flirted his way all through his adult life and my parents' time together, angry for all the times he promised her things would get better then went right out and repeated his performance (clearly as a musician he works to the mantra that practice makes perfect), angry that the only times he was home with us was when it suited him.

Angry that I've only just admitted all of this to myself.

Angry that I'm taking it out on Noah who hasn't done anything wrong, apart from be himself. The totally unsuitable man I fell for.

'This is about your dad, isn't it?'

'Of course, it is!' I want to cry, but I must not. Mum isn't howling in a corner. She's putting a brave face on. A mask. I can do masks.

'Your dad is nothing to do with me, with us.'

'But he is!' Despite everything I can't separate the two. I can't let myself believe, trust, that this could be worth the risk.

'I am not your father, Rosie!' His eyes are glinting. 'I have never, ever given you reason to doubt me, not to trust me! That, that,' he waves towards the bar where he'd been standing with Laurie, 'was called being friendly. I have never, ever even looked at anybody else while I've been with you, have I?'

I can't look him in the eye. Instead I bite my lip. 'But we're not an us, are we, Noah? You don't believe in love. I don't believe in taking chances. I think I've learned all I can from you. I think I've just learned my last lesson. Thank you.' I end on a whisper. I've run out of steam.

'You're being serious? You're really pushing me away; you're sending me home like some naughty schoolboy who's over-stepped the mark?'

'We both have.' It comes out all croaky and small.

'Fine.' The word is forced, stiff. 'But,' his eyes are narrowed, hard, 'don't you dare pretend you didn't want that kiss as much as I did.'

I stare at him blankly.

I can't deny it. I don't need to though. He's taken a step back, he's already on his way, marching out of my life as fast as he came into it.

Shit. Why did I do that?

Because of Dad. How could Dad turn up late, how could he have a go at me for just kissing a man, how could he *impregnate* a bloody cellist? I don't have any answers to those questions. But I do know that I can't kiss Noah again.

And I really don't want to watch him dating anybody else. It might damage my battered heart irreparably.

'Listen up everybody!' My dad's voice is booming out. I turn around miserably to look at him. All happy and preening, centre stage. 'As you all know we've asked you here to celebrate our wedding anniversary. Come on, come on, darling. Join me. Who would have thought this lovely woman would still be putting up with me after so many years?'

I blink back the tears as my mother makes her way over

to him. She looks so elegant, so beautiful. So poised. I don't feel poised at all.

A solitary tear plops gently on to my cheek, but I try to smile as she glances my way, meets my eye and winks.

I wipe the tear off with the back of my hand and try and smile brightly back.

He drapes a possessive arm over her shoulder.

How did I never notice that my dad is looking a bit, well, fake these days? His hair is too dark, the wrinkles that should fan out from his eyes and mouth are practically non-existent, his clothes are just that bit too trendy. He's trying that bit too hard. The handsome charming man hasn't faded, he's been remade. It's wrong. Far more wrong than what he's accused me of. All I've done is tried to be more me. Dad has tried to be somebody else.

'Now the question is, will she still be at my side after another thirty years?'

'No.' My mother's voice rings out, clear and bright. 'No, she won't.' The room was fairly quiet before, now there is a deadly silence, then a few nervous titters. 'In fact, she won't be at your side for another thirty minutes. Victor, darling, consider this advance warning of divorce papers being served.' She takes one step away from him. 'Now everybody, plenty more champagne at the bar – grab it while you can, I might be penniless this time next week! He's all yours, Serena!' She raises her glass in Serena's direction. 'Oh, and Dinah! And Bella, oh and I mustn't forget Julia, and Elizabeth, oh dear I think I'm going to have to put a list up!' She grins, and it is genuine. Mum looks more relaxed than she has in ages. 'Cheers girls!' And with that she strides through the crowd, who part but lean in to kiss her cheek and pat her on the back. I'm sure I hear a few muffled 'bravos', it's all frightfully civilised.

I don't feel civilised at all.

I watch her go, and my gaze is drawn to a solitary man. Noah. He looks back for a second. A steady stare. No smile, no raised glass, no wink.

And then he turns and walks away.

'Oh dear, has Noah gone already?' Mum slips her arms through mine as I watch him cross the lawn and go out through the side gate. Not even glancing back.

'He had to er, go somewhere,' I say lamely. Not wanting to actually lie to my mum, but not wanting to explain either. 'Are you okay, Mum?'

'Well surprisingly enough, I am, darling. Here, you look like you need a hug.'

We have a hug. It makes me want to cry again. The only person I've ever met who gives me a better hug than Mum is Noah.

'What a bastard!'

'Noah?' I say, startled.

'Noah? He seemed rather nice to me!' She laughs. 'Your father. I couldn't believe he hadn't even turned up so that I could tell him I'm leaving. I thought I was going to have to WhatsApp him, which seems so impersonal. So, it was brilliant when he did turn up! And trust your father, he gave me the perfect opportunity to get my own back and show him up like he's always shown me up!'

I think my jaw has dropped.

'I think what she's saying is he's a bit of a shit.' Bea has her chin resting on my shoulder, then sidles in so that she's standing in between us.

'Bea!' Mum says rather loudly, shocked. Then she looks at me. A hint of a smile curling her generous mouth. I smile back, she grins, and then she tips her head back and laughs. 'Oh, you are a lovely girl!' She gives her an impromptu cuddle. 'Bea's right! That is just what I am trying to say.'

My mum just called my dad a shit. And she's smiling, triumphantly if I'm honest. 'Did you really mean it then, you're leaving him?' Is this why she's been glowing, looking brighter and happier? Had she already got all this worked out?

'I am! I deserve better, and so do you, darling. You've put up with far too much crap over the years.' I blink. 'Oh dear, I'm sorry, I've never wanted to upset you.'

'You've not, I don't think, it's just a bit of a shock. You never gave me any idea you were about to . . .'

'Well you're so busy, and then you've had the Robbie thing to deal with. I didn't want to overload you. But it's been coming for a while; I suppose I was just waiting for the final push. You know how hard it is to take that step, even if you know things aren't right.'

I nod. I do. 'I was almost relieved when Robbie said it was over, well I was when I'd got used to the idea. Oh Mum, what will you do?' I was in a relationship for a lot shorter time than my parents, how on earth will Mum cope? How will she ever find anybody to share her life with?

'Oh, don't worry about me, Rosie. I'm fine.' She grins, and winks at Bea, 'I've found a man!'

'Mum!'

'Oh honestly, you don't think I'm cut out to be a brave and battling single woman, do you? Now before you give me your judgemental look,' I squeak an objection, 'I didn't find him until I knew about Serena. That really was the last straw.'

I feel slightly queasy. What is going to happen with Serena? 'Is he going to?' I bite down on my lip, not wanting to say the words out loud.

'What?'

'The baby.' I am going to have a half-sibling. Dad is going to run off and take care of it. I am also going to have a new stepmother, who is younger than I am. Will a stiff drink make me feel better or worse right now?

'Oh no, she lost the baby. She was so upset that he'd offered her money for an abortion, then devastated when she miscarried.'

'Oh no, poor Serena,' I say without thinking. 'Sorry, I mean, I know . . .'

Mum smiles, it's a sad smile. 'No, you're right, you lovely girl, it is poor Serena. I mean, I know she shouldn't have slept with a married man, but I do feel sorry for her. It must have been awful; I wouldn't wish that on anybody. That's what they were arguing about in that photograph! She pushed him in a fountain. She'd gone to do the decent thing and let him know she'd lost their child and he was totally insensitive, said it was probably for the best or something like that.'

'What?' How could he say it was for the best? What kind of man does that? I could never imagine Noah saying anything like that. Although thinking back, things Dad didn't approve of always went wrong 'for the best'.

'Poor girl.' Mum shakes her head. 'Oh, Rosie. Why did I never realise he was such a total hard-hearted bastard?' I think that is a rhetorical question. 'But it still shocked me that he could treat somebody else like that, so carelessly, somebody he'd slept with!'

Why, oh why didn't I listen to Noah when he tried to show me what my father was really like? He could see him clearly; he could see beyond the father figure I'd always been desperate to love and look up to.

Love is blind, don't they say? And a child's love for their parent has to be the most innocent, pure, and easy to influence of the lot.

Not even Noah could have known he was actually this bad though.

I'd never realised quite how badly he'd treated me, the mental abuse he'd thrown at me – because I'd always thought he knew best. I'd always trusted him, believed in him. But it is nothing compared to the way he's treated the girls he's gone out with. He hasn't cared about them at all. Maybe he hates women. Maybe he just doesn't care about anybody but himself.

If I told Noah, he'd . . . I can't tell Noah. He's gone. There's a yawning gap. I won't be able to tell him anything ever again. He'll never forgive me, because I said so much that wasn't true. I hit out because it was easier to hit out at him than Dad. I've been a total idiot.

'Did Dad really show you up, Mum?'

'Oh yes, he was subtle mind you, nothing other people

would pick up on. He's very good at undermining your confidence.' She gives me a knowing look.

'He just more or less called me a slut,' I say. Shown me up in front of Noah, in front of everybody listening. In fact, he used to do that when I was with Robbie. Little digs.

'Well he had no right, you're not, and even if you were, he shouldn't do that! I'm sure your Noah put him in his place, didn't he?'

'Well he tried,' I sigh, 'and I told him to shut up.'

'Oh Rosie.' She hugs me again.

'I didn't want to . . . I hadn't wanted to upset Dad, cause an atmosphere, you know.'

'Oh, I know, that's what he relies on!'

But why hadn't I wanted to stand up to him, why, when I finally had somebody at my back who'd have looked after me?

It hits me. I've always felt a kind of comradery with Noah. We've been fighting together. Until for one moment I lapsed back into my old deeply ingrained habit of never standing up for myself and risk upsetting Dad.

I've let Noah down. I've let myself down.

'Honestly the man is unbelievable.' Mum shakes her head. 'How he has the neck to do that, when all those girls are here! Heaven knows what he'll call me then when he finds out about my new man!' She giggles. 'I am off for some fun with somebody much nicer!'

'Where did you find this, er, man?' Maybe I should have just come to Mum for help, rather than risking Noah's attractions.

'Don't sound so surprised! I'm not completely over the hill. How old do you think I am? No, don't say it!'

I am so glad Noah has gone otherwise he might be making a play for her. He thinks she's cool, glam, wonderful – unlike her daughter. 'Sure.'

'I found him on a dating app! When I was at salsa.'

Since when was she at salsa? The other week it was roll-erblading, now it's sexy dancing. Who stole my real mother?

'I got talking to this couple who found each other online; they gave me the details! Oh my God, it's hilarious, you should see some of the men who sign up, they live in a complete fantasy world; honestly, how on earth they think any sane woman would be taken in! They must think we're stupid!' I inwardly cringe, at least I hope it's inward. Maybe she'll put my pink cheeks down to having too many cocktails. Which I undoubtedly have had. 'You should try it, Rosie.'

Bea sniggers, so I shoot her the evil eye.

'You'd be amazed at the interest I got and the number of men who were keen to help me with my judo.'

'Mum, where are you finding time to do all this stuff?' She gives me a blank look. 'All the new hobbies.'

'Oh that,' she waves an airy hand, 'well I don't bother about your dad, and I've stopped washing and ironing his stuff, plus I've given up on cleaning the house.' I glance round in alarm. 'I get a cleaner in. I mean he can afford it. I don't know why I didn't do it earlier. I got to thinking about it, at yoga, all that lying about relaxing nonsense gives you plenty of time to think. I'm in my fifties still, not my bloody seventies, what am I doing wasting my life cleaning?'

'Er . . .'

'*She kept a clean house* isn't what I want on my headstone;

The First Date

I'd prefer *she led a dirty life* to be honest. I think I've reached that age they talk about, when you couldn't give a monkey's what anybody else thinks.'

'Right.' My vocabulary has shrunk to almost non-existent. For somebody who makes a living out of books this is not good.

I can, however, see why my father was dazzled by my mother thirty years ago. I'm not sure she can actually be my biological mother, but she certainly is amazing. She'd make a great mate.

'That's why I decided that this would be our, sorry *my*, last party, and so I wanted to go out with a bang! Though I might be doing that with Art later as well.' She winks.

'What? Oh no, no don't explain! Too much information,' I shout as she makes an 'oo' face. 'What kind of a name is Art?'

'It means Bear man.' She pulls the wide-eyes grinning kind of rude face you should never see on your mother. This party is going to remain with me for a very long time.

'Oh God, why did I ask?'

'He's nice, a bit unconventional, but very nice.'

'You are being careful, Mum?' What if he's a weirdo, or an axe murderer, or bigamist, or, oh my, what if he's a swindler?

'No, I'm not being at all careful. That's the point. But you don't honestly think I'm ready to shrivel up and die, do you? I'm not that old! Don't you worry about me though; after living with your dad for so long I'm immune to smooth talkers. And Art isn't some young boy preying on older women, not that I'm old.'

'No way are you old!' I'd forgotten Bea was there. She's been quietly hanging on Mum's every word. 'Look, do you two

325

mind if I go and grab another drink? This is kind of a mother-daughter thing, I feel a bit of a lemon.'

'Oh, you're not! You're welcome to stay,' Mum says, but Bea just smiles, blows me a kiss and sidles off with her phone in her hand.

'Anyway, I'm not about to elope with Art, it's just lovely to be with a man who's interested. There's life after a split after all! Your dad will be furious; he always used to be if anybody showed an interest in me. The slightest sign and he'd be there at my side, pulling faces!' She sighs. 'Such a hypocrite. But I believed in him, in us, believed we were meant to be, but,' she brushes her hands together as though wiping him away, 'we're not. And if a man can still turn me on when he's two hundred miles away . . . well he's worth meeting, don't you think?'

'You haven't met him yet?' I feel faint. What if he lets her down? What if she's ghosted like I was? What does she mean, turn her on from two hundred miles away? Exactly what kind of messages has my mother been swapping with this stranger?

'Oh, good Lord, no. He lives in Cornwall! How do you think I've had time to meet him? And talking to him is one thing, but it would have been wrong to actually meet him, wouldn't it?'

'I suppose so. I can come with you if you like, when you meet him?'

She laughs and pats my hand. 'I'll be fine. Have I ever offered to come on a date with you?'

'Well, no, but . . .'

'Exactly.'

Noah has. It was nice having Noah around. I felt safe, secure. Happy. Maybe Mum needs a Noah.

'All those years I chased your dad round the globe I was always on my own, darling. I'm used to it.'

'Oh.' I hadn't ever really thought about what her life had involved. 'It must have been lonely.' Dad really is a shit.

'It has been, but it's made me remember how independent I used to be. Look Rosie, when life comes relatively easy, and I have to admit it has with me, the downs and failures hit you harder. Admitting to myself that something was wrong, that I'd failed at something has taken a long time to come to terms with. That's why I've waited until now. I wasn't waiting, I just hadn't been prepared to give up. And I did love him.' She stares at her hands.

'He loved you too, Mum.'

'I know. We were good together, when we *were* together.' She pulls a wry smile. 'I always got what I wanted I suppose; things went my way when I was younger. But I realised a while ago that I can't change the way he is and how he treats me, but I can change the way I respond to it.' She glances my way and raises a cheeky eyebrow. 'I read that on the internet, one of these self-affirming wotsits.'

I grin back.

'I let him do it to me, to us, Rosie. It was, is, *my* life and I gave him permission to hurt me. That's the one thing I really hope you understand. People only do what you let them do.'

I nod. 'Is this why I'm so rubbish at dating, Mum? All this, Dad and everything.'

'Probably, darling.' She hugs me. 'But when you're ready

327

you'll let somebody else in, and as long as you own who you are, then you'll be fine. They can't hurt you.'

All I can do is nod, feeling sad. Have I done the wrong thing with Noah, is that what Mum is telling me?

Well if I have, it's too late now.

'Right, let's go and shake, shake, shake our booty!'

We do. And I feel slightly cheered up, but not much if I'm honest.

Has Mum just delivered the final lesson that Noah couldn't? That I'll be fine, whoever I'm with, whatever I'm doing, as long as I stick to my guns and live the life I want to.

I'm not her; any man I meet who flirts isn't necessarily like Dad. But even if he is, I'm strong enough to know when to say no. To walk away.

To own my life.

Chapter 25

I have not heard from Noah for days. Three weeks, two days, and fourteen hours to be more precise. Not that I'm counting, or have it marked off on the calendar on my phone. Or seared into my brain.

Not that I expected him to get in touch. I just hoped. I just thought maybe there was a remote possibility that because he took his duties so seriously, he might insist I finished the course and send some worksheets, or at least get in touch to tell me I'd failed.

Okay. I'm crazy.

'I am *never* going to suggest you write review comments about romance books again. This is just like when you did that bloody window display for Valentine's Day!' Bea rips up the little card I'd put in front of a pile of books and drops it in the bin with a flourish.

'It's not *that* bad.' I say sulkily, straightening a pile of books.

'"Not quite as unrealistic as a lot in its genre and with a great unexpected killer twist", is not going to entice romcom readers to part with their money, is it? "And if you like predictable and as sweet and sickly as a kilo of fudge then this could be for you." Really, Rosie?'

'That was a joke. I didn't actually put that one on the shelf.'

'What is the matter with you, girl? You need to get out, get a flaming date, for heaven's sake, and stop moping!'

'I'm not moping.'

'Yes, you are, you're worse than when Robbie left, tons worse.'

'I'm not.'

'Go and try out your seduction skills, get laid and let go of some of that tension.'

'I can't!'

'Get laid?'

'Chat people up, flirt, whatever you want to call it!'

'Oh, come on. What do you mean you can't? Are you saying Noah did a crap job, that he didn't teach you a single thing about seduction?'

'No,' I say sulkily.

'This is about your dad, isn't it?' Her tone softens, and she puts her hand on my arm. 'Your mum's already moved on.'

Yeah, she has, to Cornwall to be precise. She's had the locks changed at home – to make sure Dad can't move back in undetected while she's away, packed her new rucksack and buggered off to walk the Cornish Coast Path. I have already had reports of seals, King Arthur and the new tattoo on her left arse cheek. My mother is having more fun than I am.

'It's not my dad, all right? This is not about him. He's old news.'

'Oh.' She pauses. 'This is about Noah then, isn't it!'

330

The First Date

'Can't I just not want to date?'

'And waste all that lovely new underwear?'

'I'm quite happy without a man.'

'Yeah, right, you're totally happy without sex just like I'm totally happy when I cut out booze, or carbs, or breathing.'

'You're being silly now! Are we really expecting to sell this many copies of *this* book?'

'Rosie!' She's losing patience. 'Talk to me.'

I stop putting 'signed by the author' stickers on the pile of books and slam down the copy I'm holding. 'Fine. You're right. Okay?' I hold my hands up. 'The problem is Noah, totally Noah. He was a great teacher, brilliant, he taught me all the right moves and when I flirted with a guy when he had my back it went fine. I was sexy, and confident and all those frigging things that make people want to go out with you, okay?' The words are starting to catch in my throat. 'If I go on a date and do all those things he told me to do, then it will just remind me of him, okay? And I don't want to be reminded of him right now. I need some space.'

'Oh.' She pauses and frowns. 'So the whole seduction lesson thing was a crap idea then, cos you can't stand to do anything he taught you?'

'Spot on. Totally crap idea.' I suddenly feel exhausted. 'It's just a game, isn't it? Dating? And some people are better at it than others.'

'Oh Rosie, it's not a competition, there's no right or wrong way.'

'Just right and wrong people. He scared me, Bea; for a moment there he felt like the right person, and he wasn't.'

331

'Maybe he's not . . .'

'He doesn't believe in love, he thinks it's terrible, will ruin his life.'

'You could persuade him it's not?' she says, an optimistic lift to her voice.

'Like Mum persuaded Dad?' I fight to keep the sarcasm out of my voice.

'I don't think your dad ever believed in love in the first place, Rosie. Noah did. He just lost faith in it. That makes him totally different! And like your mum said, people can only do what you let them do to you.'

If she wags her finger at me, I might have to grab it and bend it back.

'I can't change him. I don't want to.'

'But he might not be like you think! He's already changed because of what happened to his friend, maybe he just needs help to change back to who he really is.'

'I better finish sorting these books,' I say softly.

'I'll go and get us a coffee, and some carbs, shall I?'

I look at the pile of books. I need a plan. I need something to take my mind off Noah, because it's doing my head in, and whatever I said to Bea I'm just not into the whole idea of dating right now. I don't want to be sitting opposite a man who isn't Noah.

Which kind of sucks.

Maybe I should go back to dog sitting? Hugo's mum, Ophelia, sent me several messages after our first disastrous date telling me he was the happiest she'd ever seen him when she picked him up, that he pined for me, that he whimpers when she says my name. That maybe I could just look after him for two hours while she has her friends round for brunch? Because if he's there he'll try to hump her best friend, Sophie, and a Great Dane wrapped around you can play havoc with your new top, and your hair, and, well, everything.

It is tempting. Hugo would be a diversion, wouldn't he? And I'm sure I could handle him the way Noah did . . .

Bugger. Bloody Noah is in my head again.

I will cat sit. Cats have nothing to do with Noah. There is no link at all.

'Hi.'

'Hi, oh hi, Jed!' Arghhhh. I am going to have to move house, work, everything. Why does *everything* link back to flaming Noah? What is his best friend doing invading my workplace?

'Nice to say you again, Rosie!'

Yeah, sure, act surprised now you've gate-crashed my refuge. You have never been here before, that means you have searched me out. 'And you, Jed! How are you?'

'Fine, fine.' He shifts slightly nervously.

Despite myself I feel I have to speak the name that should not be spoken. 'Great, and Noah?? Have you seen him lately?'

'Last night actually.'

'He's okay?' I want to ask how many dates he's had, if he's mentioned me, if he can even remember me; you know, needy stuff like that. But I manage to stop myself.

Jed shrugs. 'Bit grumpy, Rosie,' he hesitates, so maybe this isn't an ambush; he doesn't seem to have a speech planned. 'He's a nice guy, you know, underneath all that, that . . .'

'Bravado? Charm?'

333

'He just likes to chat, to talk to people, to help. What can I say, he's a friendly guy? Look,' I hate it when people say 'look' it suggests they are going to say something I don't want to hear, 'I don't know what happened between you guys, but it's hit him.'

I do a goldfish impression, before managing to squeak. 'Him? It's *hit* him.'

'He's a,' he looks round as though to check Noah hasn't crept up behind him, 'he's a sensitive guy. He was really close to my wife, Millie, known her years. She introduced us actually, and if it had been anybody else, I wouldn't have trusted them.' He concentrates on the book display. 'It really knocked him sideways when she, when it happened.'

'Hang on, *he'd* known her for years? I thought *you'd* grown up with her?'

'Me? Oh no, no I wished I had, but I met her in Freshers week at uni, in a queue to join some society. She was with Noah. I thought that they were going out, but they were just good mates, like brother and sister. Jokey.' He smiles to himself. 'I was jealous of him at first, until I realised there really wasn't anything else on either side.'

'He was jealous of you,' I say softly, trying to get this all straight in my head.

Jed laughs and glances back up at me. 'Oh yeah, he was, after six pints he always used to moan about never finding a girl that he got on with like Mills, and wanted to sleep with as well. Said it was always one or the other. But he didn't let it stop him from trying!' He suddenly sobers, and his steady gaze makes me wary. 'He really felt it when Mills died; he'd lost her, and he'd lost me for a while. I just couldn't cope.' He shrugs. 'Grief can be a bugger. I didn't deal with it well, I admit it, and I pushed him away. I never thought about his feelings and how close they'd been. I don't know if I should tell you this,' he pauses, 'oh bugger, no, no it's not my place. But look, he's an okay guy, right?' He shakes his head and looks so genuinely sad I want to hug him. 'I reckon he feels like every time he puts his feelings on the line, he loses.'

'He said you were really broken up.' I try and stop my voice cracking.

'Totally. Every time I did something that I used to do with her it came at me, bam. It's shit, you know, you're up and down all the time. I forgot that it was probably hitting him in exactly the same way, and we should have supported each other.' He wrinkles his nose. 'Not a very "guy" thing to do, mutual support, is it?'

'I suppose not.'

'We all lose people,' he picks up the nearest book, stares down at it but I'm sure he can't even see it. 'That's life, isn't it? People can die, people can just walk out of your life. But I'm coming out of the other end now. I guess I'm trying to say,' he looks me in the eye again, 'I am there for Noah now. I can see him clearly again. It's none of my business, but he likes you, Rosie.' He nods. 'Really likes you. Do you like him?' He holds up a hand to stop me talking. 'Because if you do, tell him. Please, for my sake, he's being such a miserable bastard he's doing my head in!'

'Call him! Listen to the man,' Bea shouts across the shop as she strides towards us.

'Big ears!' I say lamely, because I can't think of anything else to say.

'Er hi!' Jed grins at Bea as she reaches us, balancing two large coffees. She grins back. Grins! Like, girlish grin, not normal everyday are-you-buying-a-book-or-not preying grin.

I seem to have been forgotten. Weird!

'Hi! You're early!' She beams.

'I'll browse, while you drink your coffee. I was just chatting to Rosie about Noah.' They share a conspiratorial look.

Early? What does she mean early? I stare at Bea looking for answers. She shrugs and laughs self-consciously. Bea is not a self-conscious person. Jed takes a backward step at my scrutiny.

'Okay, what's going on? Is this some kind of strategy to get Rosie a date, it won't wor—'

'Why does this have to be about you, Rosie?' Bea passes me a coffee. 'Get that down your neck. I think you need it you're being so grumpy this morning.'

'So,' I frown at Jed, 'you didn't come in to see me?'

'Er, no,' he looks slightly confused, 'I came to see Bea, though it was great to see you, and I did want to mention Noah if I did, er bump into you.'

'You didn't know I worked here, did you?'

He looks bashful. 'No, not really.'

I laugh. He looks like a naughty child that's been caught out.

'So, what exactly are you two up to?'

'A date,' says Bea still grinning, 'we met when I saw him and Noah out for a drink, and we had a chat – that *was* about you by the way if you're feeling left out – and well, ta-da date time!'

'You met Noah out, you never said! What did he say, did he—' Ask about me is on the tip of my tongue, but that is dangerous ground. 'Look okay, Jed said he's fine, I'm sure he—'

'You're blathering. Stop it! He was fine,' she looks me in the eye and raises an eyebrow, 'a bit subdued, but fine. He asked how your dating was going, and I told him it was shit, and he must have been a shit teacher.'

'You didn't!'

'I did. I told him maybe you needed more lessons, and he said you'd chickened out, dropped out. Quit.'

I can feel myself bristling. 'I don't quit things! I'd finished, we'd finished!'

'Oh yeah. Course you had. Well, that's my coffee done. I'm going to winkle Jed out of the sci-fi corner and introduce him to my fantasy section!'

'Fine. I'll go back to putting stickers on books, shall I?'

'Perfect, back in an hour.' She pauses, her tone softening. 'He did say he was open for sign-ups to a new course, advanced, if you were interested.'

Chapter 26

Bea is right. Noah is right. Even though I'm not a quitter, I just quit. Though it doesn't really matter if I'm not planning on dating any time soon, does it?

I want to send Noah a 'sorry you lost Millie' message, but that would be plain weird, wouldn't it?

But I am. Sorry that it hit him so hard. I can't imagine what it must be like when you care about somebody that much.

'Saw Jed earlier, didn't realise him and Bea were an item!'

Is that a bit pass-agg? I ask the potted plant on my windowsill, and then delete the text. It has kind of 'why didn't you tell me?' connotations. And it was me who insisted we were done.

I have spent the last half an hour picking my mobile up and then putting it down.

What if I have made a mistake?

I could just send a 'more lessons needed!' message, couldn't I? Bea did say he had an advanced course in mind.

Or would that be, what's the word, disingenuous? Insincere. Because he would be doing it to help me, and I would have ulterior motives. I would be doing it so that I could spend time with him, stare at him, feed my rude and not so rude fantasies.

Or I could just apologise for tarring him with the same brush as my father. That wasn't fair at all. Even if he is like Dad, I have absolutely no proof at all. He's not married, he's a free agent. And he's never done anything but be nice to me.

I could just say 'sorry, hope everything is okay with you', couldn't I? And maybe add 'do you think I'd be mad to take Hugo on?' I mean he is the only friend I've got who knows about Hugo, so he'd be the ideal person to ask.

Oh God, I am really clutching at straws now, aren't I?

I need to be brave. Just say sorry. Get it out of my system. Then he can say bog off you witch, and we can both carry on with our lives.

My phone vibrates. So, as it is in my hand, I open the message. It will be Mum depressing me even further by demonstrating how adventurous and open to fun, love and sexual adventure she is, despite the last thirty shitty years.

My heart did a blimp the other day when she Facebook messaged to say 'Met Art's friend Mike, he's lovely, we had threesome after lunch. Fantastic experience, you should try it!'

I was fanning myself and trying to remember how to breathe normally when the dot-dot-dot told me she had more to say. 'Sorry, hit enter by mistake when I was editing that, silly machine! Threesome kayaking! It was breathtaking. White-water sandwiched between two strong men, I was just the passenger! Are you eating proper meals? Shall I bring some fudge back?'

I think she is going to outlive me.

Anyway, it is not mother texting me. I slide down the wall and sink on to the floor.

All thoughts of Mum disappear from my head.

'Thought you'd like to know I saw Hugo the other day! He's got even bigger ☺ *Hugo the huge! N x'*

There is a photo attached.

Fuuuuck! I close my eyes, clutch the phone to my heart and try not to sob. Not because of Hugo. But . . . Noah!

I look at the message again.

Definitely Noah. Oh gawd, what do I say? How do I say it? My hands are shaking too much. I need a full-size keyboard, not a stupid miniscule mobile one that is difficult enough when I'm sober and of sound mind.

'You're not kidding! R x'

It's the best I can do; it would take years to type in all the things I actually want to say.

'Made me think of you. N x'
'You're comparing me to a huge, slobbering dog? R x'
'Fun, clever, mad, gorgeous. N x'

Oh.

Gorgeous.

And the other stuff. But gorgeous. He wouldn't say gorgeous if he hated me, never wanted to see me again, would he? For a moment I am speechless.

'Ophelia has asked me to design a house for him – apparently he can be a bit of a handful! Want to preview the blueprint, see if you think he'd approve?'
'You're building dog houses now?! R x'
'Alongside her extension N x'

Ahh.

'Love to. You do know he's a bit crazy x'

And sex-starved I nearly add.

'Like us?'

Totally like us.

'Tomorrow lunchtime? Park? I'll bring squashed sandwiches? It will be like the old days? N x'
'Great. R x'

Lunch is good. No over-high expectations. No awkwardness. No risk of getting drunk and doing what I shouldn't.

Oh my God, just how dressed up can I be for work tomorrow, without Bea getting suspicious?

Chapter 27

'How've you been?'
  'How's your mum?'
We both speak at the same time.

'You first.' He grins; I knew I'd missed that grin. I didn't realise how much until now. The laughter lines around his eyes seems more defined than they were, maybe it's because he's a bit more tanned. But his eyes look wary, he looks like I feel.

Wanting this to be nice.

Hoping we can be friends.

Well I am. He's probably worried he'll get a repeat performance of my clambering all over him, then having a minor meltdown. Embarrassing.

'She's good. She's in Cornwall doing all the things she wishes she'd done earlier. Including threesomes—' His eyes open wider. 'In a kayak!'

'Haha, very funny.' His voice is dry, then he chuckles. Oh my God I'd forgotten what that does to my insides. From being all dried up and curled up like withered lettuce leaves they spring back to life, unfurl. I feel lighter. It's impossible not to

343

smile back. To laugh with him. Then he stops laughing and stares at me. 'She's fabulous, your Mum. You're lucky.'

My throat is dry. 'I know.'

'You should make the most of your time together.'

'Oh, she's way cooler than me these days, I'm not sure I can keep up!'

'You know what I mean.' He touches my hand briefly, and I suddenly feel like grabbing him and crying, because I know from the tremor in his voice, from the dryness of his lips, that it's important. 'Look,' he takes a deep breath, glances at me, then down at his feet, 'there's something I probably should have told you. A reason why losing Millie hit me so hard, and probably, well probably brought out all that shit I laid on you when I was pissed, about love being so crap, and destructive, and . . .'

'I know you were close to her, I know she meant—'

'It wasn't just losing Millie.' He looks back up and this time his gaze locks on to mine. 'My mum died when I was twelve years old. Twelve.'

'Oh God, oh Noah, I—'

He holds a hand up to stop me talking. 'I reckon it's shit to lose your mum at any age, but it just seemed so complicated then. It kind of destroyed my faith in everything a bit, and screwed me up when it came to getting close to people. Then I met Millie and she was cool, she really helped me, and I guess she gave me a get out. An excuse not to get involved with other girls. I was too young to have that "regret not doing more with her" thing, but I wish I'd been older; I wish I'd known her better. You need to forget your dad, make sure you love your mum enough.'

The First Date

It would be wrong to hug him right now, try and chase the hurt away. He needs to talk this out, *we* need to talk this out. 'Do you remember much about her?'

I can't imagine what it was like for him. I'd be devastated if I lost Mum, and I get now why he said we were lucky to have each other.

'A bit. The hugs, the smell of her,' he looks at me steadily, 'I loved the smell of her, it meant I was safe.' I swallow, blink, try to just sit still and listen. 'And the love. She loved everything so much, she loved life.' There's a sheen to his eyes; my heart aches at the break in his voice, but I just rest my hand over his and wait. 'She seemed to have this never-ending capacity to love, everybody, everything, the flowers, the sky, ice cream, the man in the street, stray dog, smelly tramp, traffic warden.' His voice is steady again now as he digs into the memories, brings her back. 'She used to tuck me in bed at night if I'd had a bad day and tell me kindness costs nothing and we're all much the same inside. We all need love, hugs and hope.' He stares up at me, as though he'd forgotten I'm here. 'I've not talked about her for ages, not to anybody.' He squeezes and I realise his fingers are threaded through mine.

'You should do. She sounds wonderful.'

'She was. So was Dad, he was a hugger before it became popular! Mum's fault.' He grins. A lopsided grin that is a little bit sad and fades from his face as quickly as it appeared. 'But he found it hard when she went.'

'Like Jed did?'

He nods. 'Like Jed did. And after losing Mum, losing Millie

345

seemed like somebody was telling me that falling in love is an idiot's game.'

We sit in silence for a moment. Watching people stride past us through the park. Seeing the children play, but I don't think he really hears or sees any of it.

He'd watched two men he admired, with a huge capacity to love, lose it all. Which led him to draw his own conclusion that it was safer not to give your heart away in the first place.

'Losing Mum was the most painful thing that had ever happened to me.' He says the words as though he's shocked, as though he's never said them before, never thought them before. 'It kind of ripped something out of me,' he says as though he needs to make it clear. Then he looks at me, his direct gaze clear and unflinching. 'I missed her. I've never stopped missing her.' Oh God, I must not cry. I must not. The heat of tears burn inside my eyelids, I bite down on my bottom lip. Nod. Try to keep control.

His own eyes well up; there's a tremble in his fingers as he twists his hand in mine. 'I missed her like hell, and I miss Millie too.'

I do hug him then. I can't help myself. I throw myself at him and hold him tight. He nuzzles against my neck, his tears damp on my skin and he clutches me so hard it feels like he's never going to let go.

'Sorry.' His voice is muffled against my skin, then he pulls back slightly. Awkward. A strained smile on his face. He takes a steadying breath, wipes his palm over his face. 'God, I don't know what came over me, sorry, I've been doing too much thinking lately, not enough work. This wasn't what I had planned when I texted you.' His normally even voice still has a heart-breaking tremble in it. 'Must be the weather, or my age, or something.'

'It must be.' I try and match him, lighten things.

'Or you.'

I swallow, not able to take my eyes off his face. Can I say I've missed him, or is that too much?

He edges away slightly, conscious of our touching thighs, our linked fingers. 'Jed said he'd seen you.'

'Oh yeah, yeah, he came in the shop. He sounds like he's feeling better these days?' He nods. 'He's even dating Bea!'

'Mad man!' He laughs, and the mood brightens. 'So, what about you? How's the dating going, anything to report back on?'

'No dates.' He raises an eyebrow. 'I've been busy, and, er, not in the mood. What about you?'

'Nothing to speak about. Okay, no dates, none. Not the kind I'd speak about or the kind I'd keep to myself.'

'Do you keep some to yourself, dirty secret?' I grin, I can't help it, and nudge him in the ribs.

'Plenty!' He rolls his eyes. 'Come on, eat your lunch, I went to a lot of expense and trouble!'

We grin at each other. Both take a bite of our sandwiches. Sit in silence.

'Rosie, I've not dated because I realised how shallow and pathetic I've been.'

'What?'

'Spending time with you made me realise what a waste of time it all is.'

'Dating?' I gulp. This is not how I expected this to go. I'm all geared up for making up and maybe, just maybe, another kiss, and he's telling me celibacy is the way forward. Talk about messed up timing. 'O-kay.'

'No, not dating. *My* way of dating, all this making the right moves, seducing people. Okay,' he puts his hand flat on his knees and leans forward, 'confession time: everything I've taught you is bollocks.'

'Everything you taught me?'

'Exactly.' He tosses what's left of his sandwich at a pigeon. 'I watched you do it and cringed.'

'Cringed! Don't hold back the punches! I made you *cringe*?' I might have to thump him, not kiss him. This is going from bad to worse. I've put him off for life!

'Oh no, no.' He chuckles. 'Oh Rosie, I don't mean that. It's me I was cringing at, not you. The way you did it, you were amazing. I watched you chatting up all those guys and I was jealous as hell.' Jealous, Noah was jealous? 'I cringed because you made me realise how false I was, how much of a jerk I've been. What I've been doing is crap.'

'A jerk that women still fall for though,' I say reasonably. 'You didn't make *them* cringe.'

'I made you cringe though.'

'No, you didn't.' I smile at him, move slightly closer on the bench. 'You made me laugh, you made me,' I frown, 'made me more me.'

He shakes his head slowly. 'I was a complete twat thinking I could teach you anything; you're perfect just the way you are. You are the real deal, Rosie.'

The First Date

'So I'm not rubbish at dating?'

'Oh no, you most certainly are not rubbish.'

Oh my, this is sexy. His voice has this gruff edge to it. If this isn't a move, if this is the real Noah then he's making me all hot and bothered without trying.

I realise that we've both somehow moved inwards, and now we're almost touching again. Well, at least I hope we've both moved, and it's not just me who has scooted along the bench like a heat-seeking missile.

If anybody is watching this must look like a weird mating ritual the way we're sliding along the bench, touching then retreating.

Actually, it would be quite nice if it was a weird mating ritual.

Some higher-level obscure dating thing that he's not explained to me yet?

'Watching you doing what I told you to, using all the moves I do made me cringe because I had to see those guys all wanting a piece of you.'

'A piece?'

'They thought you were hot.'

'Hot?' I say, pleased with myself. Result!

'And it was doing my head in.'

I raise an eyebrow.

'I didn't want other guys to want you, Rosie. I wanted to keep you for myself. That's why I kept blowing them off and telling you you'd got it wrong!'

I let this sink in. 'You really were jealous?'

Noah nods. 'And even if you don't want me, Rosie. I don't

want you to hook up with some guy for all the wrong reasons because I fed you a load of shit.'

'It wasn't . . .'

'It was.' He holds a hand up. 'Just listen eh? This is hard. This isn't a chat-up line; this is a whole speech I've got prepared.' He actually looks sheepish, awkward. More like the person I am when I'm faced with a potential date, than the person he is.

It's cute. Endearing. 'I've fucked up and I don't want to fuck you up as well. Rosie.' He takes a deep breath. 'I've missed you. I've not been on a date since you blew me out cos I realised I didn't want to. It's meaningless if I'm not with some-body I want to be with, who means something. And you do.'

'I do?' Our thighs are actually touching now; I feel a bit heady and faint if I'm honest.

'You do. Mean something. It's you I want to spend time with.'

'Oh.'

'I've been using those lame moves and chat-up lines to keep myself from getting close to anybody; it was strictly a first date thing, but then being with you fucked it up.'

'It did?'

'It made me realise I want to be close to somebody, at least take the risk, try it.'

'You do?' I squeak.

'You're the first woman since I grew up, apart from Gem and Millie, that I've spent real time with, talked about real things.' He rests a finger on my lips briefly. I want to lick it. I don't. 'That I've been *me* with. That I've missed like hell when I've not seen you.' He's gazing at me with such sincerity in his eyes I'm trembling inside. 'That I've wanted to be more than mates with, that I've fancied.'

'You fancy me?' I say, my voice distant even to my own ears.

'Oh God, do I fancy you, Rosie Brown. I can't stand seeing you going out with all those idiots, unless,' he pauses uncharacteristically, unsure again, 'you're into one of them?'

I smile and a strange feeling of warmth starts to seep through my body and make me feel like laughing out loud. I repress it. There's plenty of time for him to find out just how loopy I am later. He needs easing in gently. 'I'm not into any of them.'

'That's handy seeing as,' he trails his finger along my cheek, and I lean into it, 'I need to start again. Dating. Do it right this time. Will you help me?'

'Well, er yes. If I can.'

His warm hand is on my knee. 'I don't half fancy you, Rosie Brown.'

'Maybe you should kiss me then?'

Oh boy, talk about anticipation. I'm practically quivering as he turns to face me properly, cups my face in his large capable hands.

'Maybe I should.'

I can taste him before his lips touch mine.

This kiss isn't like the last time, or the time before. Or the time before that. Wow, just how many kisses have we had while we've not been dating?

I've lost count. But I don't care. Forget them, they're not important.

This is gentle, this is touching, this is so intimate and searching I lose all track of where we are, and why I ever doubted.

I feel like crying, but not crying, like laughing, but not laughing. I feel happy and sad, but most of all I feel like reaching out, showing him how I feel with my touch. Most of all I don't feel afraid that I'm going to get it wrong. That I have more to lose than I have to gain.

'Wow.' He rests his forehead against mine. His finger on my lips.

'Wow.' I mouth back.

'I need to ask you something.'

There's a long silence, as though he is waiting for permission. So I nod.

'Rosie Brown, will you come on a date with me? A proper first date?'

'No chat-up lines?'

'Well not many, just me, like this. I mean, you do know I can't actually completely stop the lame chat-up lines.'

'And just me, like this.'

'Well almost, you could ditch the "bargain" sticker on your boob.'

Oh gawd, I have a cut-price sticker stuck to me! How could he not tell me? How many people have walked past us and got completely the wrong idea? It could be worse, I suppose, it could say '2 for 1' or 'slightly damaged'.

'And the white paint highlight in your hair if you like.'

'Haha.' I'd forgotten about that. My answer to sexual frustration – decorating the hell out of my home.

'No, forget it, just you, stay like that. What do you say?' He sounds nervous. 'Can we start again?'

'I don't think there's any going back after that kiss!'

'Maybe not.' He smiles. 'But I'd like to do this properly. I'd really like you to meet the real Noah, right from the start.'

'You are sure?' I need to know he's sure. At least for now. I'll forgive him if he changes his mind at some point in the future. Maybe.

'Positive, I've known the truth for ages, practically from the moment I met you. I just hadn't faced up to it until your mum's party.'

'That row at my mum's party really did this to you?' I giggle.

He chuckles. 'Well I was in shock; nobody has blown me out for years!'

'Oh God, I am so sorry about that. I was so wound up about Dad, then about you saying he was a shit, even though deep down I knew he was, but I didn't want to admit it out loud, and then—'

'Shh.' He puts a finger on my lips. 'It's fine. I got it. And I got that the last thing you wanted to do was date somebody who reminded you of him.'

'But I know you aren't—'

He grins. A disarming, cheeky grin that means the words die on my lips. 'Come on, Bea will be wondering where you are! I'll book a table somewhere for our date, if you're sure about it? Tomorrow?'

'Of course, I'm sure! But, Noah?'

'Yep?'

'No fancy table, I'm not sure that's me. Can we just meet at that bar? The one where we first met. Erase it, start again?'

'Well we can,' he looks doubtful, 'but it's a bit flash, obvious.'

'Meet there, have a drink, then move on?'

'It's a deal.'

'And Noah?'

'Yes?'

'What's wrong with tonight?'

'My God, you're a pushy woman! What am I getting myself in to?'

I smile, all sweet and innocent.

He grins. All naughty. 'But just this once, do you mind if we do it my way? I need to sort something?'

Chapter 28

Luckily when I got back to work after lunch yesterday, Bea was busy with a huge delivery of books, plus text-swapping with Jed so I could creep in unnoticed and wander round in a daze without her passing comment. She was also leaving work early for a dentist appointment, so I could try and get my head round the whole idea of a date with Noah in relative peace – apart from the odd annoying customer asking questions like 'do you know that book with an orange cover, and maybe a black bit, that's got a character whose name begins with an "s" or "d", who does something to the parrot halfway through? The funny one? It's great, I want to buy it for my sister'.

I hate these guessing games because they nearly always end up with them totally changing half the story and saying the parrot was in another book, and the name actually could have been Quentin, or saying, 'never mind I'll have that thriller instead' and leaving me trying to work out what they were talking about for the rest of the day.

But it didn't wipe the smile off my face. I just wandered around serenely and did my best to help.

I knew it wouldn't last though. It is Friday afternoon and Bea has been stalking me all morning.

'What's this?'

'It's a book recommendation, Bea. You told me to write some!'

'But it's nice! I can actually leave it on display!'

I shrug. 'It's a great book, even better than the hype.'

'What's happened? Something has happened, hasn't it?'

'It's past closing up time.' I point out, so we do the rest of the stuff we need to do and head for the door. She grabs hold of my handbag strap as I step outside.

'Hang on, you're not going anywhere! You're up to something. You've been weird.'

'I've got a date,' I say as casually as I can, because I know Bea. She won't give up. Just saying it makes my heart pound a tiny bit harder. I swallow hard, it's nothing, it's just a date!

'What? Why didn't you tell me straight away, this is ace! Fab!' She looks at me a bit more closely. 'You look like you're about to keel over! Are you okay, Rosie?'

'We're going to have a proper first date!' It's easier to say second time round. Shit, I wasn't going to tell anybody though, not a soul, not even Bea, until we'd actually done it and I knew that it wasn't all in my head. And I knew this could go beyond a few fake, and a few not so fake, kisses.

'Wow!' Bea giggles. 'You are being well weird!' She takes my hand. 'Oh my God, you're actually shaking! Who is it? Where did you meet? Was this on a dating thing, or did you just meet him? You met him! You met him when you were on your lunchbreak! Was it that sexy guy in the café? Or, I know, the one that walks his dog down—'

'Will you stop, just for a moment?'

'Tell me! This guy must really have something!'

'He has,' I say weakly. Putting off the moment when I have to tell her.

'Hang on a sec, just let me make sure the door is locked. Right, tell!'

'Noah.'

'What?' The keys hang limply in her hand. She stares at me, then laughs. 'For a moment there I thought you said . . .'

'Noah.'

'*The* Noah? Oh wow, I've got to tell Jed! You do mean a proper date, don't you?' She checks, finger poised over her phone. 'As in not a lesson, or fake stuff, or—'

'A date. I feel sick.'

'No you don't! You feel excited, nervous, stuff like that.'

'I do. Oh Bea, what the hell am I going to wear?'

'When is it?' I look at her blankly. 'Your date?'

'In approximately two and a half hours.'

'Bloody hell, come on, we're flagging a taxi back to your place. You are going to have the makeover to beat all makeovers, girl.'

'No. Bea, stop, please stop.' I put a hand on her arm, just as she flags a taxi down.

'Stop as in no taxi?'

'No, no get in the taxi,' we clamber in and I shout out my address, 'stop as in total makeover. I don't want to seduce him,

357

Bea.' The taxi driver winks at her in the mirror. 'I want to be me.' There's a fluttering in my stomach, but this isn't fear, or dread. This is excitement, anticipation. I'd go straight to meet him dressed as I am, if I could.

'Yeah, yeah, yeah, we'll do you, but the best you. Otherwise, you will regret this like hell when you're explaining how it started to your grandkids.'

'Hey, stop there . . .'

'Well Grandad was smart and sexy, but me?' She says in a funny voice. 'Well Granny had on her old big work knickers, and her sensible on her feet all day flat shoes, oh yeah, and her jeans. Cos when she's climbing up ladders all day she don't want them bookish geeks getting their thrills from her pantyhose, does she?'

'Shut up, Bea.'

She smirks. I grin back. 'Anyhow, it's only Noah so I don't know why you're in such a tizz. You've already dated! You don't need to seduce him from scratch, he knows the score, babe.'

'God, Bea, you're more excited than me!'

'Not poss.'

'But this is different! And I want it to be right. I want it to be special. I want him to feel special, it's all about him.'

She gives me a sideways odd look. 'I think you're not getting enough oxygen to your brain. Oh look, here we are, come on get a move on we've only got two hours and three minutes to get you defuzzed and looking completely au-naturel. And we all know that takes bloody ages! Can't you just go for tarty and high-maintenance? I can achieve that in half an hour flat.'

The First Date

I pay the taxi driver and follow her to my front door. I really shouldn't have told her.

'Hang on, Jed's texted me back! Jed says, oh no . . . I can't say that out loud. I'll show you later. Now come on woman!'

I really, really shouldn't have told her.

* * *

To be fair, Bea has been a brilliant help. Because for one my hand is trembling so much there is no way I could have applied eyeliner without poking my eye out. And for two she really does know her stuff when it comes to looking natural without actually being, er, natural. You know what I mean, right? Looking thrown together takes effort and years of practice.

And now I am standing outside the bar, ridiculously early, and feeling a bit like a kid on Christmas Eve. Excited, but prepared for disappointment. Yeah, I was one of those kids.

I stare at the door. This is where I met the wrong man, who might just be the right one. And if it turns out he's not, you know what? I'll cope with that. Because I have been taught that by the greatest person in the world, the one who has always had my back. Mum.

'Hi, Mum, it's me, everything okay?' I can't help myself. I have to speak to her before I take this step and move on.

'Oh fabulous, Rosie. I'm going to have so much to tell you about when I come home. And what are you up to?'

'I'm out on a date.' I pause and smile to myself. 'With Noah.'

'Ahh. Oh, I'm so pleased; it would have been such a waste to have just been friends!'

'Mum, do you ever regret marrying Dad?'

'Oh, good God, no! What on earth makes you even think that? For one I wouldn't have had you, and, well, it might have looked at times like I was letting him wreck my life, but he wasn't, love. I told you that! I've got my pride, and that's what stopped me admitting defeat earlier. A bit like you.'

'What do you mean, a bit like me?'

'Well you'd have realised you should be dating Noah ages ago if you hadn't been so stubborn and admitted you were wrong!'

'I didn't know I was wrong. I wasn't wrong at first!'

'Rosie?' It is a warning tone.

'Okay, okay. But you did love Dad?'

'I did. You know I did.'

I do. I just want to be sure. 'Even though he was totally selfish and only came back when it suited him?'

'Yes, Rosie, and not even passion made up for that in the end.' I think of all the times I watched them together, the way they looked at each other, the way the world seemed to shrink down to just the two of them and for a brief time not even I was important. Maybe Mum was right. She would never have wanted to miss out on that passion, even if at the end of the day it hadn't been right. She'd been brave. Far braver than I've ever been.

'I found a way to make it work for all of us; well I thought it worked, but it obviously didn't, or you wouldn't have grown up to think all gorgeous men would be just like your father!

The First Date

I'm so glad you came to your senses and moved on from Robbie. You'd have been bored senseless by the time you were forty. So anyway I did that bit of making it work wrong, but I've done something right now, I've left. I am allowed to change my mind, darling. You don't make one decision and it's a life sentence.'

'I know.'

'And if you find out your Noah is all good looks, charm and no substance you can move on, can't you? Not that I think he will be.'

'I can, Mum.'

'I'm sorry if we fucked up.' Her voice has a wistful edge to it, as though it's her one regret.

'Mum!' Honestly, I'm sure my mum didn't talk like this before she met Art. 'You didn't fuck up, you did what you thought was best!'

'True, and mother always knows best!' She laughs, a deep-throated laugh that makes me smile. 'I'll be back soon to sort things out. Maybe we could all go out together? I'd love to meet your man. Now hadn't you better get off?'

'Yes, Mum.'

'Have fun, love you, darling.'

'I love you too, Mum. And Mum? Can you stop swearing? It's weird, it's just too weird.'

She laughs. 'I'll try! No promises though!'

I click the phone off, drop it in my handbag and take a deep breath.

This is easy. I might still not be sure about normal first dates, but this one I can do. I know I can.

Chapter 29

I take a moment to pause at the doorway of the bar, and study Noah, before he sees me. I want to take in my date, because this is unreal.

I am about to have a first date with a gorgeous man who I feel I know better than I ever knew Robbie – the man I lived with for years.

I am about to have a first date with a man who is fun and flirty on the outside but has sad bits on the inside.

Who can make me laugh, and who can shock me into silence.

Who gives me confidence, but dares me to stray outside my comfort zone.

A man who is scared to love, but willing to give it a try.

He notices me watching, and smiles. Slides off his stool and stands up.

'You found it okay?' He grins and leans forward to kiss my cheek nervously as though he's not quite sure how to play this.

'Funnily enough I remembered!' I can't help it, I glance around, just to check Gabe isn't hiding away in a corner, out to trap another girl. 'It's not changed, has it?' I can't believe such a short time has passed since I first crept into this bar, wondering what Gabe would be like, nervous about a date with somebody who wasn't Robbie. It seems like a lifetime ago in some ways though. 'I got an Uber this time though, I didn't risk walking in these heels!'

'I ordered prosecco, is that okay?'

'Noah.' I need to break the ice, this is all too formal. Not us. 'Sorry about—'

We both speak at the same time. Both stop.

'That ki—'

It happens again. He leans forward, rests his finger lightly against my lips.

'Normally I'd say ladies first,' I raise an eyebrow, 'but I need to get this off my chest. I'm sorry about that kiss, at your mum's party.'

'It was fine, nice, I liked it.' I was going to say the same. Well, roughly.

'You liked it? Damning me with faint praise. It was sensational!'

'Okay, it was sensational.' I climb up on the stool, feeling more comfortable. 'Though not as good as the one on the bench, fuelled by Southern chicken wraps!'

'True.' His voice is gentle. 'But I'm sorry I launched at you like that, I'd just been waiting so long, and you looked as desperate as me, and I guess I misread . . .'

'Desperate? Moi? What are you suggesting?' His perplexed look makes me laugh. I take a sip of my drink, make him wait. 'Misread my arse. Noah, I was, as Bea would say rather

364

inelegantly, totally gagging for it. But, with Dad, and you, and Laurie and . . . well, sorry I had a meltdown.'

'I don't blame you. I got it wrong, I totally lost control.' He frowns. 'It caught me out. I don't do that!'

'Kiss?'

'Lose control. Ever. It was flaming scary if you must know, that's why I bolted the moment you gave me an excuse. I needed to work.'

'Work?'

'It helps me think, you know, designing stuff, tweaking, refining. It kind of releases the other part of my brain, or something.' He pulls a bit of an 'eek, what am I talking about' face. 'I sat in the office and made something. What did you do?'

I hope he's not expecting some kind of romantic equivalent. 'I talked to Mum about living a dirty life, and taking control, and then I shook my booty. Well, we all did, we cleared the dancefloor!'

'You?'

'Shake, shake, shake your booty, KC and the Sunshine Band. You'll have to get used to Mum's music taste if you're going to date her daughter! Though I think she's more into Bob Marley at the moment.'

'Was it better than Tina Turner?'

'Nowhere near,' I say, blushing.

He chuckles. 'She was right.'

'Who was?'

'Tina! You are simply the best.'

'My God, you are smooth.'

'I'm being sincere, can't you tell? Have I told you yet you look beautiful?'

'Not yet.'

He twirls a strand of my hair in his fingers. It sends a tingle to my scalp. A shiver down my spine.

'You look amazing, Rosie. You're gorgeous.' He smiles, breaking the moment that might have turned into a kiss. Damn.

'Even with the paint.' He grins. 'Good enough to kiss, but I'm trying not to lose control.'

'Selfish.'

'Not yet. I want this date to be a good one, you deserve a good one.' He leans in then, and drops the sweetest kiss on my lips, then draws back again. 'You have no idea how hard this is.' He groans. 'Pity me!'

I laugh. Put my hands on his knees, let my thumbs drift over his inner thigh. 'Were you really desperate at the party?'

'This far,' he gestures with thumb and finger, 'from dragging you off and stripping you naked.'

'Do you still want to do that?'

He nods.

Suddenly it hits me that I am not afraid of sleeping with another man. I am not worried about how I will cope with a penis I have not met before, or whether I will do things wrong. Noah will make sure it is right.

'Well maybe we should then?'

He chuckles. 'You're totally out to ruin my plan, aren't you?'

'Plans are made to be changed, or something like that.'

'True.'

366

'Needs must!'

'Oh my God you are such a turn on, stop teasing, I'm going to have to hold a cushion over my crotch!'

I snigger. I can't help it.

So we pay the bill, and call a taxi.

* * *

'Surprise!'

This is not how I expected our arrival at Noah's place to pan out. I had visions of clothes strewn up the stairs, of passionate kisses, of tripping up as we took our knickers off.

Not this.

A dog.

I stare at Noah. 'This was your plan all along, to come back here!'

'Well yeah, just not quite as quick. You kind of fast-forwarded things.' He holds his hands up. 'Not that I'm complaining.'

'But, but . . .'

Hugo is sitting in the hallway, on his favourite cushion. He has a bow tie around his neck, and a resigned look on his face.

'What on earth?'

He whines, so we both go over and sit down beside him, and he wags his whiplash tail and gazes at Noah adoringly.

'Was it safe to leave him here on his own?'

'Ophelia was here, left as we came up the driveway! I wanted to make sure he'd be okay. He's on his best behaviour!'

'But I don't get it.' I look at him, puzzled, over the top of the large dog.

Noah looks back at me shiftily, then strokes the dog's ears for a moment, avoiding my gaze. Then he looks back up.

'Rosie, I might have done something a bit crazy.'

'Even crazier than asking me out?'

'Even crazier than that.' He grins. 'And I wanted to know what you thought before I, er, committed.'

'This sounds dangerous.'

'Well the doghouse wasn't exactly a huge success.'

'And you call yourself an architect!'

'Hugo likes company, he doesn't like being home alone, and so I er, well I might have . . .' Hugo thumps his tail even harder. 'I might have told Ophelia that there was a chance I could take him, if you thought it was a good idea.'

I laugh. I can't help it. 'You want to know if *I* think it's a good idea? *Me?*'

'Yes, because, well I thought you might be here a bit . . . with me. And, am I rushing? Is this wrong? Yes, I'm mad, I know. Maybe I spend too long in my office, I just . . . I'm rushing, aren't I? You can say I'm bonkers.'

'You *are* bonkers,' I point out in a quavering voice; I'm feeling all funny inside. Noah means this; Noah is asking my opinion about something, as though he intends there to be a second date, maybe a third date.

'I don't expect you to be here much, well not more than you want, and I know Hugo's a bit of a handful, but we kind of clicked.' They did. I grin as I think back to that disastrous dog walk. Hugo fell in love, and I think I did as well. Just a bit. 'And it's not a huge commitment, because well, Great Danes aren't around forever but I was thinking he needed a good life now, as soon as he could, and if I put it off too many years Hugo might be,' he puts his hands over his ears and whispers, 'dead.'

'I think he'll be fine for a good few years yet.' I chuckle. I've never seen him this flustered.

He wipes his brow. 'Bloody hell, for a guy who doesn't want to get involved I think I've overdone it. A proper date *and* a dog.' I glow. He just called me a *proper* date. 'I might need a lie down. But you're both, well, irresistible?' He runs out of steam. 'Am I right?'

I chuckle. 'You're comparing me to a bloody dog again! You've really got to stop doing that.' I stroke Hugo's ears. 'How can I say no? It's a great idea. He's infatuated with you!' Hugo feels at home with Noah. Like I do. 'You've not said "am I right" for ages, you know!'

'I say it when I'm nervous!'

'I make you nervous?'

'Damned right you did, you do, you are. You scared the hell out of me then and I was right to be afraid!'

'Oh Noah.' I reach over Hugo and take his hand.

'But I didn't mean am I right like that, I meant am I right for you? Do you want to try a second date?'

I nod. Slowly. Then squirm so that I'm on my knees and can raise myself up and lean closer to him. Put my hands on his face. 'I think you might just be. You could be right, just this once, Noah Adams, you could be right.' And then I kiss him.

It's all a bit awkward, snogging over the top of a dog that

has collapsed onto its side and is snoring loudly. It also makes me giggle, which kind of kills the sexy vibe a bit.

'Did you ask me out again?'

He nods.

'Just so I'm sure.'

'And did you just say yes, or maybe, Rosie? Just so I'm sure.'

It is my turn to nod. To smile. To stare into his eyes and understand what Mum meant. 'We couldn't take this thing one step further, could we?'

He grins. The dirtiest grin ever, his eyes shining, his dimples so deep they make me want to touch them.

'You have no idea how desperate I've been to hear you say that since we went into that flaming lingerie shop. It's been torture!'

'That was your idea!'

'I know.' He groans. 'Worst one I've ever had! We couldn't go again some time though, could we?'

I shake my head. 'You're so rude.'

'Rude for you.' He's already on his feet, taking my hand, drawing me over the sleeping dog. Leading me towards the stairs. 'Are you sure?'

* * *

'Wow, that has to be the best first date ever!' I say and stop staring at the ceiling. I roll over onto my side so that I can look at Noah properly.

He smiles. 'Unrepeatable.'

'Were you being serious about keeping Hugo?'

'Definitely! Well, how can I not want to take care of him?'

'What do you mean?'

'He's played an important part in all this; he's my guardian angel.' He grins. 'I don't think you would have agreed to meet up if you hadn't had Hugo with you, would you?'

'Maybe not.' I smile. How did I ever think I didn't want to date Noah?

'And he persuaded me to get back in touch.'

'Persuaded you! He's a dog.'

'Shhh. Keep your voice down, he'll hear.' He rolls over onto his side. Strokes the hair away from my face. 'When I saw Hugo again all I could think about was you, how I'd walked away from the best woman I'd ever met. How I'd walked away from the one proper chance of falling in love with somebody who I was prepared to risk breaking my heart again for. He knew. He looked at me, looked at my phone. He wiggled his eyebrows.' He does a fair imitation of a Great Dane wiggling his eyebrows, and I laugh.

'You're mad!'

'I must be.'

'You are right though—'

'I'm right! Twice in one day! Result!'

'Shush.' I dig him in the ribs. 'You're right about him needing to be here. Hugo made me realise you weren't that bad.'

'Me, bad?'

'When you rescued me in the park and he liked you I thought you might be okay after all. Dogs know.'

'I know.' He pulls me in close, his words muffled against my hair.

'You do know Ophelia only wanted a house for him cos he's randy? Won't leave her visitors alone?'

'And I'm pretty randy too!' His hands stray down my back.

'And you said he reminded you of me!' I try and ignore the anticipation that is building in the base of my stomach, the tingle that is spreading through my thighs.

'Big,' he kisses my shoulder, 'lumbering,' I want to kick him, but his mouth is distracting, 'loving, sloppy, faithful, loyal.'

I don't hear any more words. I just let go of control, stop thinking and allow myself to feel.

THE END

Acknowledgements

With every book I've written, I've grown to appreciate more the fabulous team that beaver away making sure my books are the best they can be, have the loveliest covers, and are available to as many people as possible. You really are my heroes! Much as I'd love to, I can't thank everybody individually because 1. that would make this incredibly long, and 2. I'd be scared stiff of forgetting somebody and feel guilty forever, but please do know that if you've played any part at all in the making of this book, I think you are amazing. Thank you!

There are a few extra special people I'd like to thank individually though.

Amanda Preston, my agent, you are friend, confidante, scraper up off the floor (following mental exhaustion, desperation or exasperation – not inebriation, though I'm sure you'd be excellent at that too) and very funny lady. I can't imagine doing this without you.

Charlotte Ledger, my publisher, you are indeed a legend! It's been a tricky couple of years for both of us, and I couldn't have had a kinder, more thoughtful and considerate person to turn to. I can't thank you enough for your support, generosity, ideas and enthusiasm, and I'm so proud to count you as a friend. I'm already looking forward to working on the next book together.

Emily Ruston, my editor, you continue to amaze me with your ability to read beyond my words and understand what I am trying to convey – and then manage to tease it out of me in the nicest possible way.

Harry, my four-legged bundle of mischief who keeps me company, gives me kisses galore and helps to keep my waistline from spreading too much – I owe you some extra cuddles and long walks now this is done.

Thanks also to Deborah Carr and Louise Nicholson who suggested the name Hugo for the gorgeous Great Dane in the book – it suits him perfectly!

And last, but certainly not least, a massive thanks to you, for reading this story. Please do stay in touch – I love reading your messages, chatting to you on social media, and your lovely reviews make my day!